# Paths of Righteousness

# Paths of Righteousness

by

## Sharon K. Connell

*He restoreth my soul: he leadeth me in the paths of righteousness*
*for his name's sake.*
*Psalm 23:3*

Printed in the United States of America

Cover designed by author.
Photos from Pixabay & Shutterstock, used under license with Shutterstock by Ranta Images

Editor: Traci Sanders

Copyright © second edition
Sharon K. Connell
First published in 2014
10 9 8 7 6 5 4 3 2

ISBN: 978-1-7329237-0-6

Dedicated to:

My Lord Jesus Christ, who taught me the meaning of true love. Also, to Ann Lacy Ellison, my first reader, who has gone on to be with our Lord and Savior. See you on the other side, Ann.

Acknowledgements

Alan J. O'Reilly, author of Sound of Battle and Desired Haven, who added significantly to this story in its first draft.
Laura Harris, PAC, Michael Plunkett, M.D., many other friends and acquaintances in the medical field for advice. But especially my dear friend Faye Hamilton, Registered Nurse, with twenty years ER trauma experience, for her knowledge in medical treatment of head wounds and ER procedures.
Deputies Mr. and Mrs. Wilson with the local Pensacola Sheriff's Department, for legal advice regarding law enforcement.

Scripture quotations are taken from the King James Bible Authorized 1611 Version

Sharon K. Connell

# Paths of Righteousness

# Chapter One

## *Pensacola, Florida*

utterflies filled Kathryn Kendall's stomach. She sucked in a deep breath as she gazed up at the two-story stucco building. With a degree in business management and having finished at the top of her class, an administrative assistant position was nothing to worry about. But, her stomach continued to churn as she closed her eyes and reached for the bronze door handle. She could do this.

Kathryn smiled as the door closed softly behind her. She'd made quite a life for herself already. A mere two weeks after graduation, she had her own apartment and a job in a prestigious medical office, Kenner Family Medicine. Her adoptive family in Des Plaines, Illinois would finally realize she could take care of herself.

As she passed the lab area, a handsome man in forest green scrubs and sandy blond hair breezed by her with a cell phone glued to his ear. Her heart jumped as she caught a whiff of his woodsy cologne.

A few steps further, Kathryn glanced back. Mr. Gorgeous had spun around. He winked, raised his brows, and blew a soft whistle through his lips. She chuckled. Would the rest of the staff be as friendly?

The tall, bleached-blonde office manager named Grace met her in the hallway and led her to the front office. "Kathy, this will be your desk. I have new-employee paperwork for you to complete, and then we'll have you dive right into the medical records."

Kathryn took a seat at the desk. "Thank you."

After Grace placed a pile of papers on the desk, she gave a warm smile and retraced her steps to the hallway.

As Kathryn filled out the forms, the man she'd seen in the hall approached. She glanced up into pale blue eyes, which pierced her heart.

A crooked smile formed on his lips. "I think Grace neglected to introduce us. I'm Mathew Pierce, the PA. You must be the new hire. Love that long, wavy blonde hair of yours. Reminds me of the color of honey."

He held out his hand and Kathryn placed hers in it. As he squeezed, a twinge ran up her arm. Maybe this guy was too friendly. "I'm Kathryn Kendall."

Mathew stood upright and darted out of the front office when Grace reappeared.

Kathryn finished the paperwork and followed her supervisor to the medical records room.

When lunchtime came, she sat alone in the lunchroom, her head buried in a book. Mathew blew into the room and, without a word, swung his leg over the back of a chair next to her. He smirked. She smiled and continued eating her sandwich.

"Kate, right?" He bent his head to the right and again raised his eyebrows.

She swallowed and took a drink from her water bottle. "Kathryn Kendall. We met this morning—twice."

Mathew laughed. "Ahhh...a girl with a sense of humor. I like that. We'll have to get to know one another. I like spunky."

Had he really called her "spunky"?

"I'll call you Katy."

"I'd prefer Kathy, if you don't like Kathryn."

"No. Katy suits you better. Katy-bird."

Her Irish temper rose up the back of her neck. She took in a deep breath and narrowed her eyes. She'd heard that every office had its annoying character. Mathew must be the one assigned here. "No. I'm afraid it's not okay."

She stood and left the room.

Mathew followed her to her desk. "Oh, come on, Kathy. I didn't mean to offend you. You're definitely one of the prettiest girls I've ever seen. Can't blame a guy for trying to score some flirtatious points, can you?"

His lips pulled to one side as he raised his shoulders, palms up in front of him. Was this his way of apologizing? Then again, she'd probably been rude to him too.

She'd better make her disinterest clear right away, no matter what he did to her insides when he looked at her with those icy blue eyes and chiseled features. There were sure to be rules about employees getting involved. Why did she have to be attracted to a rogue like him anyway? "I didn't mean to be rude and the flattery is— Look, we have to work in the same building, and I don't want to cause any problems for either of us."

His tongue traced the inside edge of his lower lip as he gazed at her and smiled.

Kathryn lowered her brows. Nervous habit of his, maybe?

Then he grinned. "Okay, Katy-bird." He turned on his heels and swaggered off.

Kathryn shook her head as Mathew strode through the front office a few weeks later, making the rounds by each pretty girl's desk. He'd still not managed to talk her into a date. A scoundrel. A cute one, but a scoundrel nonetheless. She laughed to herself.

The other girls considered him nothing short of an Adonis with his muscular build, high cheekbones, and aquiline nose. They talked of little else.

As he approached her, Kathryn returned his smile.

He sat on the corner of her desk. "Katy...sorry...Kathy. At the risk of being turned down again, would you pa-lease join me for dinner tonight? I discovered a great steakhouse, and I hate to eat by myself."

"You? Eat alone? I can't imagine you having that problem. Every girl in the building vies for your attention."

He chuckled and leaned in. "Every girl?" He bounced his eyebrows up and down. "Maybe your eyes should be green instead of that beautiful shade of blue-violet."

As he leaned closer to her, she rolled her chair back.

He whispered, "Doesn't matter. I'm not interested in any of them. Not really." He straightened his posture.

Kathryn quirked her mouth.

He crossed his arms over his muscular chest. "I've taken a couple of these girls out. Once. So why won't you join me for dinner? It's not like I'm asking you to elope or anything." He grinned.

"Just dinner?" She twisted her lips to the side and considered the notion. "As co-workers?"

"Of course. I think we'd have fun. A few laughs, some good food. We'll get to know one another."

She bit her lower lip. He had proven himself to be a gentleman to her so far. Despite his flirting. "I guess we could have dinner. As co-workers."

"Wonderful." Mathew slid off her desk. "Write down your address, and I'll pick you up at six."

"I'll meet you at the restaurant."

"Oh, come now, Kathy. How do you expect a guy to be a gentleman if he doesn't pick up the lady? Especially on the first date."

Date? Yeah, guess it would be a date. She complied and wrote down her address on an index card, then handed it to him.

"You'd better give me your phone number too—in case I run late."

She added her cell number, and Mathew swaggered to the hall.

Did he just snicker? Her brows pinched together. He'd better get it into his head that this wouldn't become a relationship. They'd be two employees enjoying each other's company after work. That's all.

Kathryn brushed her hair and gathered a handful into the barrette at the back of her head, allowing the bottom tresses to hang loose. She and Mathew had gone out on a couple of dates, but he said this would be a special evening.

So far, he'd been a lot of fun. Not what she'd expected of a man so good-looking. Not once had he made demands of her or taken her somewhere she didn't enjoy. Yet, something about him made her uncomfortable at times. Maybe the way he looked at her.

Did men practice that hungry stare? She sighed. Where would he take her tonight? She'd been wanting to go to the new movie advertised on TV.

The doorbell rang. She opened the door to find Mathew in jeans and a tight red T-shirt, which showed his chest muscles as he unzipped the leather jacket. He was dressed for comfort.

She glanced down at her lace-trimmed white blouse and purple skirt, then into his crystal blue eyes. "Am I overdressed?" Maybe a rodeo was in town.

His eyes widened. "Not at all. You look good enough to eat." He snickered.

Why does he say such odd things? "I wondered, because you're dressed so casually."

"Yeah, well, I thought I'd take you for barbeque tonight. I'm such a sloppy eater with ribs. I chose to wear something that wouldn't show stains. You can change if you'd like." He shrugged.

"Okay. Be right back." She headed for her bedroom.

Before opening the bedroom door, she glanced back. He had followed right behind her.

"Have a seat while I change." She pointed to the couch.

Mathew smirked and turned. She entered the bedroom and locked the door. Strange. Wish he wouldn't smirk like that.

After changing into a pair of faded jeans and a sky blue, Pensacola Beach T-shirt, she checked her makeup and joined him in the living room.

"Hey. Wow, I don't think that helped," he said and then offered a low whistle.

Kathryn flinched and pinched her brows together in confusion. "What do you mean?"

He bit his lower lip. "You look just as desirable in that getup as you did in the clothes you took off." He grinned as his gaze travelled over her. "Let's get some food."

Kathryn gave a half smile and slipped into her jacket. She followed him out the door.

After their meal at the local Sonny's BBQ, which Mathew seemed to rush through, he drove his white Honda back toward her apartment.

Guess there'd be no movie tonight. What happened to the special evening? Well, she'd go to the movie by herself tomorrow. A Saturday matinée would be fun, and she could do her shopping on the way home.

Her head fell back on the headrest. She stretched out her legs and smiled. Not a bad date, even if it was hurried. He must be tired from work.

When Mathew pulled the car around the corner onto her street, he drove past her apartment and parked under a low-hanging Spanish Oak.

"Why did you park here? There was a space right in front of the building."

Mathew leered at her. "Privacy. It was nice of them to leave this undeveloped area at the end of your street." He turned off the ignition and slipped his arm behind her back, while he unclasped her barrette with the other hand. Her hair swept onto her shoulders. She stiffened. He pulled her toward him and slid his arm around her waist.

"Mathew, stop!" She wiggled away from him and reached for the car door handle.

He grabbed her wrist and pulled her tighter into his arms. "I think it's time for us to take this friendship to a new level, don't you?" He yanked her against his shoulder. His lips smothered hers.

She shoved him and turned her head away from his mouth. "I said stop it!"

Mathew raised himself over the center console, threw his leg over her knees, and pulled the lever to recline the back of her seat.

"Stop! Get off me." She tried to push him away.

He pulled at her T-shirt as she slapped him. He braced himself with his elbow on the console and tried to undo her jeans. "Quit being such a baby."

"No! Let go of me." Tears flooded her eyes.

"You shouldn't have changed tonight. The skirt would have made this a lot easier."

The sound of a siren filled the air, and flashing lights lit up the inside of the car.

Mathew dropped back into the driver's seat and glared at her. "It's your word against mine, and I'll tell them you've tried to seduce me since our first date."

Kathryn latched onto the handle and swung the passenger door open.

# Chapter Two

## St. Paul, Minnesota

r. Jacob McLeod walked through the doors of the St. Paul Family Practice and checked the schedule for the day. Admiring gazes from every woman in the building followed him. He was polite to all of them, but he had no desire for a relationship with any. They flaunted and flirted. It disgusted him. He'd rather focus his attention on the patients who needed the care he could provide.

As he put on his lab coat, a new face came into view. The auburn-haired beauty dipped her long dark lashes when she glided by. A smile spread across her face as she left the room.

Later that afternoon, Jacob poured a cup of coffee in the lunchroom. The girl he'd seen earlier approached the counter and lifted the carafe he'd replaced. As she filled the cup, the patient file she held in her other hand fell to the floor. Jacob bent, retrieved the file, and handed it to her.

She smiled. "Thank you. You must be Doctor McLeod. You're the only one I haven't met. I'm Patricia Campbell."

Her voice was low and sultry, but she looked embarrassed. Something about her seemed different from the other women. "Welcome to the practice, Miss Campbell."

Over the next few weeks, Jacob crossed paths with Patricia several more times around the building. She'd smile and he'd smile in return. Interesting woman, for sure. Not like the rest. So far, she'd only smiled at him. The only time she'd talked to him was when she had a question about a patient. Pretty much kept to herself as far as he could tell, except for laughing occasionally with the other girls.

Jacob finished his notes in a patient chart and dropped it into the lab outbox for the secretary. Patricia sauntered by, her arms loaded with paperwork. His gaze followed her down the hall to the front office. A figure like a model. Long shapely legs, becoming hairstyle, and beautiful, elfin-like features. Attractive. The deepest brown eyes and thickest lashes he'd ever seen— He clenched his jaw as a twinge ran up his neck. Red flag!

What was he thinking? Keep your mind on work. Almost every woman he'd ever met had messed up his life, except for his mother. Not that he'd been around many women. He'd made sure to stay far away from the pretty ones, and for good reason.

His counselor in medical school, Dr. Hartley, was the only man he'd ever met who seemed truly in love with his wife. And she with him. Keep to the decision you made back then. No females. They're trouble.

Jacob stopped by his boss's office with lab test results and listened to the weatherman's report on the TV in the corner. "Below normal for our last few days in October, starting tonight." That would be quite a change from a week ago.

After his final Friday patient, he headed toward his office. Patricia dashed out the back door. She'd better have a good heater in her car or she'd freeze with that light jacket. But that was her business, not his.

He entered his office, gathered up several patient charts, and carried them to the staff lounge. After he poured himself a cup of coffee, he sat down and took a sip before opening the first file. His favorite time of the day. Everyone else had left the building. Peace and quiet at last.

The back door slammed. Footsteps sounded in the hall. A moment later, Patricia rushed into the room. She drained the last drop of coffee from the carafe into a cup and wrapped both hands around it. "Brrr."

She shivered as she sat down at the table with Jacob. "Couldn't get my car started. Thought I'd come inside to figure out what to do next. But I don't know which bus to take." Tears welled in her eyes.

"How far do you live?"

"I'm not sure how many miles. I've never paid attention. Maybe I should call a cab."

She fumbled in her purse. "Oh, blast. Phone's dead too." She gave him a weak smile.

Was this woman really that helpless? Almost unbelievable. Jacob glanced at the dainty red heels she wore. She'd freeze if she stood outside for a bus. He could call a cab for her.

"I'll give you a lift home." What? Why did he say that? "You're not dressed for this weather."

"Thank you, Doctor McLeod. That's very sweet of you. I should have thought about the weather this morning, but since I drove— I never imagined my car wouldn't start."

"You know, it's always a good thing to have emergency supplies in your car. Blanket, flairs, a can of tire inflator. In case your car should break down on the road somewhere. You never know." What was he talking about? He sounded like a fool.

"You're right. I'm sure glad you were still here. I'd have really been in trouble if the building was locked. The other offices are closed."

Jacob nodded. You committed yourself McLeod. Couldn't back out now. "Let me put these records away and get my things."

Patricia followed him to his office.

He put the folders on his desk and snatched his coat. He was breaking his rule. But it would only be this once. They walked out the back door, and he punched in the code to secure the building.

Her eyes widened as they neared Jacob's car. "An Austin Healey 3000. Wow! Love the green."

Jacob opened the passenger door for her. She knew sports cars? After closing her door, he got in the driver's seat. "Thanks. Got a steal of a deal on her." He grinned.

Patricia unzipped her jacket. Her skirt slid up above her knees as she settled into the seat. Jacob glanced at her long, shapely legs. His pulse quickened. He'd better keep his eyes on the road. He put the car in gear and pulled out of the parking space.

"Doctor McLeod?"

"Yes."

"Why did you become a doctor?"

By the time he neared Patricia's apartment, he had steered the conversation away from his personal life. Not something he cared to talk about. Thankfully, she hadn't pressed the issue.

"Where did you go to school, Patricia?"

She seemed eager to tell him all about herself. Then she brought up the subject of cars.

Maybe driving her home wasn't such a bad idea. At least she spoke intelligently. And no flirting.

"Patricia, if you'd like, I'll pick you up for work Monday morning. It's not out of my way, and I don't live far from here."

"I'd like that. Thank you. Let me give you my number, and you can call when you leave your place. That way I'll be ready."

Patricia jotted down her cell number, handed it to him, and got out of the car before he could open the door for her. She sashayed to the red brick apartment building. Before stepping inside the front door, she turned and flashed a big smile, then waved.

Another red flag popped up in Jacob's mind. Tightness filled his chest. Why? He was only offering her a lift. What could it hurt?

Jacob stared at his reflection in the bathroom mirror in the doctors' lounge six months later. Had he really been dating Patricia for that long? He'd never been so interested in a woman before. Was she the one who finally caught his heart? But he'd vowed never to marry. Yet she was always on his mind. He shook his head. It must be love.

Patricia had pressed for a deeper relationship. Dropped hints that she wanted intimacy. When he explained it was something he wouldn't do outside of marriage, she seemed to accept it. Was he ready? He should talk to Patricia about their future. He'd take her somewhere quiet for lunch and they could...talk.

He washed his hands, left the lounge, and entered the next patient's exam room.

After seeing his patient, Jacob ducked into the front office. He glanced around the room. Patricia's desk was empty.

He strode to the front desk. "Do you know where Patricia is?"

The girl's eyebrows rose. She shook her head. "Sorry, Doctor McLeod. She didn't tell me where she was going, but she did say she'd be gone for at least a couple of hours. I guess she okayed it with the powers that be."

Jacob returned to the office he shared with the physician assistant. Strange. Patricia hadn't said anything to him on the way to work about needing a couple hours off this afternoon. He grabbed his jacket, scarf, and gloves from a hook on the wall and went out the back door to the parking lot. Her car was gone. He'd ask her to dinner later, and they could talk about their future then.

He unlocked his puddle jumper and opened the door but closed it again. It was a great day for a walk, and he needed the exercise. Besides, he could think better on his feet. He had a lot to mull over, and the cool, brisk air would help keep him alert while he considered the subject of marriage. Foreign territory to him. Should he? How should he ask Patricia, if he decided to go through with it?

He locked the car and hiked seven blocks to his favorite grill at the St. Paul Hotel.

The hotel's courtyard garden entrance, resplendent with newly planted spring flowers and foliage along the sidewalk, was a pleasant sight after the long winter Minneapolis had experienced. An aroma of seared meat drifted through the air. Jacob's stomach growled as he passed through the iron arch into the walkway that led to the front door. He took in a deep breath.

Several yards away, a couple meandered from the entrance of the hotel.

"Patricia?" Who was that with her? Jacob narrowed his eyes as the man slid his arm around her waist.

Patricia rested the back of her hand on the man's cheek, then tilted her head back and allowed him to kiss her. She turned into his full embrace and slipped her arm underneath his open jacket and downward onto his legs as passersby turned to gape.

Jacob's eyes widened. Heat rose in his face.

The stranger pulled Patricia tighter to him.

With a clenched jaw, Jacob turned and stormed out of the garden. His lunch forgotten.

He raged through the streets until he found himself in the parking lot at work. The return trip had been a blur.

Jacob burst through the back doors of the medical practice and entered his office, closing the door with a thud. Good, the PA wasn't there.

How long had Patricia been having an affair? Was that why the girl in the front office found his questions amusing?

He pictured Patricia's face, the way she gazed into the stranger's eyes, the way she touched him. How could he have fallen for such a—and here he thought he was in love with her. As devious as his stepmother.

The afternoon wore on, and Jacob spoke little to anyone but his patients. He'd never allow himself to be deceived again. Better to avoid women altogether as he'd vowed to do a long time ago.

For the rest of the day, Jacob focused on work. But every time he'd retrieve a chart from the front office, he'd glance at Patricia's empty desk. Did she ever return to work? Where was she now? With him?

After work, Jacob trudged home to his apartment. His phone rang, and Patricia's image appeared on the screen. He fumed. He had no desire to talk to her. But, maybe he should. He answered. "McLeod."

"Good evening, Jacob."

His teeth ground at her syrupy sweet voice.

"Will we be going to dinner tonight, handsome? Maybe you can tell me what you'd like me to wear?"

Jacob clenched and unclenched his hands. He should hang up. That would be too easy on her. He had a better idea.

"You can get dolled up as much as you like, Patricia. I'll be at your place in about an hour." He hung up before she could reply.

She had a good put-down coming, and he'd deliver it. His father's Scottish ire came to mind. Jacob had inherited it. The rage inside had annoyed him for as long as he could remember. Thought he'd gotten it under control, but this time he'd let it loose. He didn't care.

He threw on a clean shirt, grabbed his jacket, and hurried out the door. While his anger smoldered, he drove to Patricia's apartment. His neck muscles tightened, and his temple twitched as he ground his teeth.

Less than an hour later, Patricia opened her apartment door wearing an almost-see-through red blouse and skin-tight black slacks with a shiny silver zipper down the front. She smiled and slowly batted her lashes a couple of times. "Why don't you come in and we'll have a drink before we…go any further."

Her perfume overwhelmed his senses with its flower and musk combination. She'd planned to seduce him, right here, right now. His rage flared. He forced it down and stayed planted in the hallway. "Let's take a walk."

"But it's cold now that the sun's set. I thought we were going out to eat, honey."

Honey? She had the nerve to call him honey? He turned and started down the hall. A second later, he heard her apartment door close and footsteps behind him.

As they reached the sidewalk, Jacob spun to face her. "This afternoon I took a stroll through the Saint Paul Hotel garden entrance."

Patricia's eyes widened. "You were spying on me?"

He glared at her. "How many other men are you seeing, Patricia?"

"That's none of your concern. You had your chance, but you were too much of a prude to take it."

"Are you intimate with all of them, like you pushed to be with me?" He had a right to know.

Her hand swung at his face, but he caught her wrist before it reached its target. Patricia jerked her arm away and stalked back to the apartment building. Vulgar comments flew from her mouth.

Satisfaction filled Jacob but quickly left when he reached his car and slid into the driver's seat. He'd never been that close to slapping a woman in his life. Nor so close to making such a serious error…marriage. Were all women the same?

A month later, as Jacob reached for the entrance door of his apartment building, high heels clicked on the sidewalk behind him. He turned.

Patricia, hands on hips, glowered. Fire flashed in her eyes. "You may as well face it, Jacob McLeod. You're drawn to me by desire you can't control. Or understand. You'll come back. You won't be able to help yourself. But when you do…it'll be on my terms."

She spun on her red stilettos and tromped to her Chevy Cobalt, hopped in, and peeled down the street.

Jacob shook his head. How insufferable. How could he make her leave him alone? Calling her Pat, the nickname she hated, hadn't worked. She only ignored him. He was tired of picking up files he'd dropped as she accidently bumped into him. Not to mention the sight of her unbuttoned blouse when she'd come into his office and bend over his desk to lay a chart on it. She seemed to have radar, knowing when others weren't around.

That woman had turned his workplace into a silent battlefield. He'd have to find another job as soon as possible.

Jacob entered the apartment building, picked up the newspaper at his door, and went inside.

As he ate dinner, he scanned available apartments in the realty section. He checked off a few. He'd look at them after work tomorrow. Once he moved and found a new job, Patricia Campbell would be out of his life forever. Jacob slapped the paper on the table and exhaled.

Until then, he'd just have to endure the eight plus hours with her at work.

The following week, Jacob moved into a new apartment building and continued the search for a new position.

Monday afternoon, his cell rang as he stepped out of an examining room. "Hello?"

"Doctor Jacob McLeod?"

"Speaking."

"This is Doctor Bentley from the Marble Lake Pain Clinic, east of St. Paul. The agency sent us your credentials. You're looking for a position in a small practice, correct?"

Jacob released a long breath. "Yes, I am." He went into his office, closed the door, and sat at the desk. This was his chance.

"We need someone to start as soon as possible, but we're willing to wait until you've fulfilled your notice at your current job. Are you interested?"

"Yes, sir. Very interested."

"Good. Do you think you could come in this evening when you finish work so we can talk?"

"I can be there at five-thirty."

"Perfect. See you then." Dr. Bentley ended the call.

Jacob leaned back in the office chair. Finally. He'd get away from Patricia. And he'd make sure he stayed away from all women this time.

# Chapter Three

## Pensacola, Florida

Kathryn paced in her apartment. What should she do? Mathew wouldn't stop his harassment. Almost a year after he— The vision flashed in her mind. Would she never forget? She should have told the officer what he tried to do to her in the car that night.

Why couldn't Mathew just leave her alone? You'd think he'd be grateful that she hadn't caused him trouble and just stay away from her. He had left her alone for a couple of months, but now he was back at it.

Had she done something to bring it on? If only she could talk to her brother. She couldn't tell anyone else. It was too embarrassing. Maybe she had encouraged him in some way. Several times now, she'd made it clear to him she wasn't interested. Still he came on to her. Even more so this past week.

Kathryn picked up her purse to leave for work. At the door, she leaned her back against the wall. Her hands trembled. She needed another job. Never again would she be taken advantage of by a man.

Taking in a deep breath, she switched off the light in the foyer and opened the door.

She should say something to her supervisor. But Grace was his friend. To hear her talk, Mathew could do no wrong. He was careful with his actions and words in front of others. He had them all fooled.

As Kathryn walked out, her cell rang. She pulled it from her purse. Mathew. She dismissed the call and shoved the phone to the bottom of her purse. When she got to work, she'd find out how to block his number. She should have done it months ago.

Throughout the workday, she avoided the lab, and Mathew hadn't come into the front office. Perhaps he's off today.

A few minutes before five o'clock, Kathryn dropped her pencil on the floor and it rolled under the desk. She kneeled to recover it. What a mess she'd made with the hole punch. Tiny circles covered the floor. She'd better sweep it up before she left today.

After she hurried to the supply room to grab a broom and dustpan, Kathryn sprinted back to her desk. When she rose from picking up the stray dots, she glanced around the room. She checked the wall clock, then her watch. They sure vacate the place fast. A few minutes after five and not a sound in the building. The last person was sure to have set the alarm. They probably hadn't noticed her under the desk. She's have to put the code in and then reset it when she left.

Kathryn headed down the hall with the broom and entered the supply room. At the far end of the room, she tucked the broom and pan into the cabinet.

When she turned, Mathew stood in front of the closed door. She inhaled a sharp breath. The hair on her neck and arms rose as he stared like a hungry lion.

She gulped. "I have to leave."

He took a step toward her. She rushed for the door handle. Mathew grabbed her arm and pushed her back to the rear of the room.

Kathryn twisted her arm, but he held on. "Let go of me."

He pressed her to the wall with his lower body and flipped his scrub top off while she slapped at him. Then he kissed her neck and began to unbutton her blouse. She fought him as he pulled on the material. Several buttons popped off and flew onto the floor.

She pushed and pounded on him, but she couldn't get away. Tears flooded her eyes as his hands roved over her. "Stop, Mathew. Help! Somebody, help me!"

With a laugh, he hiked her skirt up to her hips. "Nobody here but you and me, baby. I have unfinished business to take care of."

With all the strength she had, Kathryn twisted her body and slipped out of his grasp. He snatched her skirt and pulled her back. His vise-like grip seized her wrists, slamming her back to the wall. His tongue licked her lips as he leaned into her again. "You still look good enough to eat."

Mathew let go of her right hand and lifted her skirt. She swung and slapped his face.

He pinned her to the wall with his upper body and let go of her hand to grip his scrub bottoms as he told her his intentions.

Kathryn screamed and shoved him backward as hard as she could. His heel caught on the edge of a storage box. He lost his balance and toppled over the box. As he fell, he snatched her arm and pulled her on top of him. His head hit the floor with a crack.

Mathew groaned and his grip loosened. She wrenched her arm free and jumped to her feet.

As she scrambled over him, his hand went around her ankle, but she pulled herself free. Kathryn made it to the door and yanked it open. She ran through the halls with Mathew's obscenities ringing in her ears. She had to get to the entrance. The alarm would go off once she opened the door.

She reached the front of the building and shoved on the plate glass, but no alarm sounded. He must have turned it off. She tore down the street and didn't stop until she turned the corner on the next block. The cleaning crew's van drove by. She peeked around the corner toward the practice. Mathew was nowhere in sight.

A quick glance around told her the other offices on the street were already closed. She had to get home. He'd catch her if she waited on the corner for the bus. Tears flowed onto her cheeks as she clutched her blouse closed over her camisole and continued the several-blocks run toward home.

Exhausted, she made it to the apartment building. "Oh no." She'd left her purse locked in the desk at work, with her keys. She bent over to catch her breath.

A woman came out of the entrance, and Kathryn caught the door before it closed and locked again. She rushed up the stairs, slid down onto the floor in the hallway outside her apartment, wrapped her arms around her legs, and sobbed.

Something cold touched her hand. She jerked away. A small white dog with black spots on her rump whined, and then wagged its tail. Kathryn sniffed back her tears and gazed at the dirty, scruffy canine. "Where did you come from? You must have slipped in when I did."

The dog sat on its haunches.

"I take it from the matted hair and ribs showing, no one's taken care of you for a while."

As she leaned against the wall between her front door and the neighbor's, the dog curled up next to her. Kathryn wiped her face with her skirt and then stroked the pooch's head. "We're both a sorry mess."

The man from next door stepped out of his apartment. "Kathy? Are you okay?

"Not really." She took a deep breath and clutched her blouse closer. "I left my purse at work, and now I can't get into my apartment."

"Is that your dog? How did he get out?"

"Not mine. Followed me in."

"Would you like a ride back to work? My girlfriend does this all the time. Leaves her purse at work, I mean."

"I—I can't go back."

The tall, dark-haired man stared at her with furrowed brows.

Kathryn glanced up at him. "Um. The doors...I don't have a key." Sort of the truth. They didn't have keys. "I'll get it tomorrow." A knot formed in her stomach. No way would she get into another man's car, ever.

"Why don't you and your little friend come into my apartment? I'll call the building super to let you in. You look beat. You're breathing as if you've run a race."

"No. It's okay. I'll wait here."

"Are you sure?" He gave her a fleeting smile.

"I'll be fine. But I'd appreciate your calling Mr. Haskins for me." She returned a forced smile.

The man nodded and entered his apartment. A few minutes later, he came out and squatted beside her in the hall. He didn't ask any questions. The dog walked over to him, and the neighbor scratched its ears. "I'll just keep you company until the super gets here."

Soon after, the balding, middle-aged building manager arrived. Kathryn's neighbor gave her a smile and left.

The white dog stood at Kathryn's side and watched as the older man unlocked the apartment door.

Kathryn shook her head. "I'm sorry you had to run over here on my account, Mr. Haskins. I don't know what I was thinking when I left the office." There was no time to think.

"It's okay, Miss Kendall. It happens. Are you okay? You look scared. Or sick. Or something."

Her skin prickled as the scene in the storeroom flashed through her mind. "I'm okay. Thanks for asking. Bad day at the office." More than an understatement. She must look horrible.

Mr. Haskins removed his key. "Well, if you need anything else, just call." He held the door open for her.

"Thank you. I'll be fine." The hairs on her neck bristled. The man stood in her doorway. Would he start something now? Don't be paranoid.

"You take care, Miss Kendall. You're a nice lady, but I think your dog needs a bath." He turned and headed for the stairs.

Kathryn slipped into the apartment and locked the door. She went into the bedroom and collapsed on the bed in tears.

A wet nose touched her cheek. Kathryn startled and sat upright. The dog wagged its tail, but its floppy ears drooped.

"Oh. You. What should I do with you?"

The dog whimpered.

"You want to stay, huh."

Its ears popped up.

"Well, we'll see about that. First, I have to call the office manager and tell her what happened."

She dialed Grace's number. The call went to voicemail, and Kathryn hung up. Dr. Kenner had told her she could get in touch with him, if she couldn't reach Grace. Should I? She dialed the number.

At the first ring, she disconnected the call. It would be her word against Mathew's. Her tears fell again. He'd worked there longer, and she'd never heard anyone complain about him. And he hadn't actually—

What would her brother have told her to do? Chris had always watched out for her in the past. Why did God have to take him away?

The only thing she could do was keep away from Mr. Pierce. Leave work when everyone else did, no matter what. She had to find a new job.

The following Friday, Mathew approached Kathryn in the lunchroom after everyone else had left the room.

"Kate, you may as well give up. I intend to have you. The other girls in this office would give their eye teeth for a chance to be with me."

"Then why don't you give your attention to them and leave me alone? She stood to leave, but he grabbed her arm.

"This hard-to-get routine of yours is getting old. Maybe you think you're too good for me." A sneer covered his face as he blocked her exit. "We could fix that with another trip to the storeroom. This time, I won't lose you."

His gaze roved down her body. A shiver ran through her. She turned from him. Mathew closed in behind her. He blew hot breath into her ear. She flinched. He slid his hands under her hair to the nape of her neck.

"Take your hands off me." She tried to move away, but he pinned her against the table edge with his body.

He gripped her shoulder while he slid his other hand around her waist to her midriff. Heat flushed into her face. With force, she elbowed him in the ribs.

Laughing voices in the hall drifted closer. Mathew let go and left the room. Kathryn took in a deep breath, smoothed her blouse, and trembled as the nurses flirted with him outside the door.

What was she going to do? Would he catch her in the storeroom again? So far, she'd been able to avoid going there or staying late. But for how long?

Two weeks of sending out résumés and still she'd heard nothing. Kathryn sighed. Why would anyone consider her when she'd only worked a year and already wanted another job? She couldn't tell anyone why she wanted to leave her current position. Who would want to hire someone who made unproven accusations like that against another employee? What could she do?

She placed a stack of stamped envelopes on the coffee table. She'd drop those off at the post office on her way to work tomorrow. She had to keep trying. The job market in Pensacola didn't make things easy.

If only God would do something. She wouldn't count on that. He'd failed her when He took away her family. And this wasn't half as important as keeping them alive.

Kathryn looked at her little dog snuggled beside her on the couch. "You haven't failed me once, have you, Sheila? You've even been ready to take on Mathew in those nightmares that keep me awake." She scratched the dog's rabbit-soft hair with both hands. "Now that you're all cleaned up, you're beautiful. I'm so glad you adopted me. I needed a good friend...someone to confide in and hug."

Sheila's tongue hung out as she sat on her haunches. Her tail swept the pillows behind her. "Yip."

"If only you could talk, girl. Maybe you'd have an answer for me."

Kathryn's stomach churned. Would Mathew catch her alone somewhere? She shook the thought away, picked up her purse, and left for church.

After the morning service, she pulled the pastor's wife aside. "I have a problem, Mrs. Marshall. I need someone to confide in. Do you think Pastor has time to talk to me?"

"Of course, dear. My husband has no one scheduled right now."

Mrs. Marshall led Kathryn into her husband's office and then went in search of him. A few minutes later, the pastor came in and sat at his desk. His wife took the leather chair next to Kathryn in front of the desk.

"Kathy, I understand you have a problem. What can we do to help?"

She wrung her hands. "I don't know where to start."

"Start anywhere and fill in the pieces as you go."

Kathryn explained the situation with Mathew.

An hour later, she leaned back in the chair and exhaled as if she'd been holding her breath the entire hour. She stared at her hands. "Thank you for listening. I don't know what to do. Mathew makes sure no one's around to hear him or see what he does. I don't know if it's only me he does these things to. Maybe the other girls like it. And I'm afraid he'll catch me at my apartment when no one else is around eventually."

Pastor Marshall pursed his lips. "I think you're doing the right thing, looking for a new job. In the meantime, we'll help you look for a new place to live. And we'll pray for you." He stood. "In the meantime, make sure you stay around other people."

Mrs. Marshall hugged Kathryn. "God knows what's happening, Kathy. He'll protect you. Right, dear?" She turned to her husband.

"He will. There's always a reason for the things that God allows to happen in our lives, even when we can't see one."

The pastor rounded his desk and patted Kathryn on the back. "We'll pray for Mathew. You should too."

She jerked her head to look at the pastor.

He gave her a gentle smile. "Praying for your enemies is the wise thing to do. Luke six, twenty-eight, 'Bless them that curse you, and pray for them which despitefully use you.'"

She loved her pastor and his wife, Nick's uncle and aunt, but she didn't need a sermon right now. She needed help. And praying for Mathew was the furthest thing from her mind. She bit her lower lip.

Kathryn rose and took a step toward the door. Mrs. Marshall followed and touched her shoulder. "Kathy, why don't you stay with us for a few days? If fear that Mathew might show up at your apartment has prompted your nightmares, it might give you a measure of relief."

"Thank you, but I have to work this out for myself. I have Sheila at home. She's proven herself a good watchdog. But I'd appreciate your help finding a place I can afford."

The last thing she needed was Nick, her brother's old college roommate, hanging around her. Once he found out she was staying with his aunt and uncle, he'd visit daily.

Pastor Marshall and his wife walked Kathryn out of the church office to the parking lot.

Mrs. Marshall touched her arm. "What did Nick say about this? I assume you've told him."

"No. I'd rather not involve Nick." How could she face him with something like this? She was so ashamed. "You won't tell him, will you?"

Pastor Marshall's brows knit. "Kathy, you know I'm not free to discuss the confidences of my flock." He turned to his wife. "Nor is my wife."

"I'm sorry. I wasn't thinking." She had to make sure.

Mrs. Marshall hugged her again. "Nick mentioned how tired you look. He's concerned. Maybe you'll tell him later."

The next Friday, the office held a pre-Independence Day celebration luncheon. Kathryn cleaned the tables in the employee lounge afterward. It had been nice of Dr. Kenner to allow this party. She'd never seen the employees so relaxed. Too bad he'd missed it.

Mathew came up behind her and wrapped his arm around her waist. "Hey, everyone." He held a twig of plastic mistletoe over her head. "Look what I found in one of the lab drawers. Katy-bird has to kiss me now." He put his head alongside hers. She tilted her head to the side. His lips slid across her cheek. She turned to avoid the kiss.

His grasp got tighter. "C'mon, a mistletoe demands a kiss." His breath reeked of alcohol, though they'd been told none was allowed at the party. "C'mon, Kate. Jus' for luck."

She struggled against him. If only Dr. Kenner hadn't been called to the hospital on an emergency. The rest of the staff laughed and egged Mathew on.

Kathryn whispered, "I will not kiss you."

She freed herself from his arm, rushed into the adjoining bathroom, and sobbed while laughter continued in the next room.

After washing her face with paper towels, Kathryn peeked out the door. Mathew was nowhere in sight. She slipped into the lounge, hurried past the other employees, grabbed her purse from the desk drawer, and headed home.

# Chapter Four

athryn had paced her apartment for the entire weekend after the luncheon, not setting foot out the door. Since living in Pensacola, it had been the first time she'd missed church on Sunday. The only time she went out was to walk Sheila in the courtyard.

She'd had a reprieve for two weeks while he'd been on vacation right after the party. But he'd be back today. She left for work.

Kathryn arrived at the practice and strolled toward the building. Mathew leaned against the employee entrance. Her heart slumped.

He snickered. "Miss me?"

She pushed past him. "No. Too bad you couldn't stay longer."

A nurse entered the building behind them, and Kathryn kept pace with her down the hall.

Mathew fell into step right behind. "Now is that any way to speak to your lover boy?"

Kathryn spun and glared at him. "You are nothing of the sort to me."

Another nurse came around the corner and slowed her steps as she passed. She smiled at Mathew. He left Kathryn and strode alongside the nurse to the lab.

Kathryn exhaled and, with shaky legs, resumed her journey to her desk. He was relentless. It was a game of hide-and-seek with the man every time she walked into the building. Would he ever tire of it? Would she ever find another job?

She'd had nothing but sleepless nights. This couldn't go on much longer.

The following Friday morning, Kathryn awoke with a start. "No." She'd forgotten to turn on the alarm. Her head throbbed and her stomach ached as if her entire insides were knotted and pulled tight.

She shuffled to the bathroom. The mirror over the sink reflected a sallow complexion and bags under her eyes. She needed more rest but was already late for work. She'd call in sick. Mostly sick of Mathew.

Kathryn dragged herself back to bed and grabbed her cell from the nightstand. She punched in Grace's number.

"Where are you, Kathy? Doctor Kenner's looking for you."

"I'm sorry. I'm sick. Can't come in today."

"I thought you've looked pale for the past few days. Have you seen your doctor?"

"No. I think I've come down with something."

"I'll tell Doctor Kenner. But if you're not better over the weekend, you need to see a doctor."

"Okay. Thanks Grace. I'm going back to bed."

Kathryn rolled over in bed. Sheila snuggled next to her and began to snore. If only she could sleep as well as this little dog. Tears began to fall.

It was the stress of waiting for Mathew to catch her. There had to be something she could do. She hugged the little dog and stroked her head. "Maybe I should tell Doctor Kenner. What do you think, Sheila?"

Sheila's eyes opened. She wagged her tail and sat up again. "Yip."

"If I get fired because of it, I could collect unemployment." Then she'd search full time for a new job. If worse came to worst...she'd have to move back to Des Plaines as her adopted family had been asking her to do for so long. Hopefully, it wouldn't come to that.

Unable to sleep, Kathryn rose and showered. She fixed herself dry toast and tea, and then set a full bowl of food on the floor for Sheila. "May as well go into work and get this over with, girl."

She dressed and headed to the office.

Instead of going through the employee entrance in the back, Kathryn walked through the front. No way was she going to pass the lab to get to her desk.

She punched in the door code outside the front office. Grace rose from Kathryn's desk. "I thought you were staying home."

"I'm a little better. But I need to talk to Doctor Kenner."

Her supervisor's brows furrowed. "Let me find him. Sit down. You look shaky." Grace hurried away.

Mathew strode into the front office and, like radar, zeroed in on Kathryn. She dropped her head into her hands, elbows resting on the desk. Go away, Mathew.

Before he could speak to her, Dr. Kenner came around the corner. "Pierce. Don't you have patients to attend to?"

"Yes, sir." Mathew made a beeline for the hallway.

"Kathy, I understand you want to talk to me. Let's go to my office. I've been meaning to speak to you too."

Kathryn sat in one of the hobnail armchairs in front of Dr. Kenner's desk. "I'm sorry I was late."

He took his seat on the other side and searched her face. "Don't worry about that. Kathy, I'm concerned about you. You've been pale off and on for weeks, and those dark circles under your eyes suggest you haven't been sleeping well."

She shifted in the seat. She had to tell him, but how? What if he didn't believe her? She dropped her head, and a tear fell into her lap.

The doctor handed her a box of tissues from the credenza behind him. He stood, walked to the door, and shut it.

She blew her nose and smiled at him. "Thank you. Forgive me. Lack of sleep does this to me."

"I'm inclined to think there's more to it than that. For some time, I've noticed that Pierce has taken an...interest in you. And I've seen the look on your face when he's near."

Tears ran down her cheeks.

"He's the reason you're upset, isn't he?"

Kathryn mopped her tears.

"Tell me what's going on, Kathy. I need to know if there's a problem here."

She'd let her pride get in the way of doing what she knew she should have done when all this started. Where would Mathew's aggression lead? Maybe to one of the other, younger girls? She couldn't allow that.

"I'm sorry I didn't come to you when it started, Doctor Kenner. Maybe things wouldn't have gone this far."

Kathryn told him about the attack in the storeroom. She choked. "He keeps promising to get me in there again." Her knees wouldn't stop twitching.

Dr. Kenner's brows were pinched. Did he think she was lying? It didn't matter anymore. "I'm having terrible nightmares. I never see a face. Only a dark figure. But I know it's him."

The doctor's temple flexed. "Kathy, you don't have to say any more. You go home and get a good rest. I'll handle Pierce. His behavior toward other girls in the practice has not gone unnoticed by me either. Even if they haven't said anything. Thank you for telling me."

He believed her. She stood and turned to the door. Dr. Kenner stepped around the desk and opened it for her. Mathew leaned against a counter in the nurses' computer area right outside. She sucked in a sharp breath. The doctor took Kathryn's arm and pulled her back into the office.

"Since you're ill, I'll follow you home to make sure you get there safely. It's almost quitting time anyway."

"Um...I don't drive, sir."

"Then I'll drive you home."

A chill ran through Kathryn's neck into her shoulders.

As Mathew stepped into his apartment after work Friday evening, his cell rang. With a snicker, he eagerly yanked it from his belt clip. Must be his redhead entertainment for the evening.

He gazed at the screen. Doctor Kenner? His boss had never called him at home after hours before. Great! Hope this wasn't going to mess up his date tonight, or his plans for the weekend.

"Hello, Doctor Kenner."

"Pierce, I'd like you to meet me at the hospital in about thirty minutes. I'm on rounds. I need to speak to you. It's important."

"Okay. Where should I meet you?"

"In the doctors' lounge on the fourth floor."

"Check. Be there in a bit."

Dr. Kenner hung up without another word.

That was odd. He'd better get overtime for this. His boss sounded stressed. Could be about one of their patients?

Hmmm. Kate had been in his office for quite some time. Would she have said something about the booze he brought to the office party? Not her style to be a tattletale. Probably just about a patient. Mathew left for the hospital.

A little while later, he stepped into the fourth-floor lounge. Dr. Kenner sat alone in the corner. Mathew crossed the room and took a seat opposite him. Whoa. Had his boss been sucking lemons?

The doctor's temple twitched. "I asked you here to talk about your harassment of Kathy Kendall."

The words hit Mathew in the gut like a boxer's glove. What had she told him? "What harassment?"

"You've made constant phone calls to her even though she's refused your inappropriate advances, Pierce. Then there's the incident in the storeroom."

Mathew hit the table with his fist. "That's a bunch of lies. She's been after me since she started working at the practice, and—"

"Stop. I'm not blind. I've seen the way you act with our other female employees. You will leave them and Miss Kendall alone. Understand? You're not to speak to her, in the office, or away from it. Any office business you have concerning her is to go through Grace. If you approach Miss Kendall again, you'll be dismissed."

Mathew's brows furrowed. Heat shot up his neck, and his jaw muscles tightened. No woman had ever made a complaint about him before. He stood. "She's the one pursuing me, and I'm the one getting the reprimand?" Would Kenner buy his indignation?

"Lying won't help your situation, Pierce. I've also observed Miss Kendall's conduct these past months. I've seen her reactions to you when you get near her."

Mathew opened his mouth but shut it again. He fisted his hands, opened them, and then closed them again. His boss's eyes had narrowed, and he glowered. He wasn't buying any of it.

Dr. Kenner rose from the chair. "Had you admitted your guilt and expressed a willingness to change your attitude, we could have put this behind us."

Mathew's eyes widened.

"Pierce, you'll receive two weeks' severance pay. Do not return to the practice for any reason. I'll have someone clean out your locker and see that any personal property is returned to you."

Without another word, Dr. Kenner strode from the room.

Heat fueled Mathew's neck and ran down to his stomach. Kate would regret this.

Kathryn poured water in Sheila's dish in the kitchen. Her phone rang and she grabbed it from the counter. "Good evening, Doctor Kenner."

"Kathy, I'm calling to let you know Mr. Pierce is no longer an employee of Kenner Family Medicine. I dismissed him this evening."

She took in a deep breath and let it out slowly as the doctor's words sunk in. Her boss was a good man. She'd been silly to fear having him drive her home.

"I told him he's to stay away from you, and I think the verbal warning and dismissal will stop the harassment."

"I don't know how to thank you, Doctor Kenner. I was afraid I'd have to find another job."

"It's okay, Kathy. I believe in taking care of my employees. Now you relax, get some rest, and have a good weekend."

Kathryn laid the cell back on the counter and squatted down to give Sheila a big hug. "Everything's okay now, girl."

Across town, Mathew Pierce entered his favorite watering hole. A large rock settled in his stomach. Who did Kenner think he was, telling him who he couldn't call, or see? Coming on to the girls didn't give that stuffed shirt any cause to dismiss his only PA. He'd get even with that spiteful vixen, Kate.

Mathew strode to the bar. "Give me a beer, and keep them coming."

Early the next afternoon, Mathew's head throbbed as he awoke. Had his redhead shown last night? He couldn't remember anything. How did he get home? No evidence of her having been in his apartment.

He showered and then ate scrambled eggs with toast and honey at the kitchen counter. As he chewed, Dr. Kenner's words replayed in his mind. Mathew slammed his fist down. Coffee splashed into the air as if he'd dropped a stone into the mug.

After downing the rest of the brew, he stormed out of his apartment. No woman had ever turned him down. Who did that Kate think she was? We'll see about this, sweetie.

Mathew sped down the street and pulled up in front of her apartment building. His blood boiled. He scanned the area. No one in sight. He charged the entrance but stopped at the glass door. If he rang the bell, she wouldn't let him in.

An elderly woman came out of the building. Mathew smiled and held the door for her. She thanked him, and he slipped in.

On the second floor, he checked the hallway and listened. No one around. He stepped up to Kate's door and ran his tongue over his lower lip. He'd push his way into her apartment when she answered, and then he'd have his revenge. That old woman at the entrance hadn't even looked at him. She'd never be able to identify him if asked.

Mathew pressed his ear to Kate's door. Nothing. If she was in there, she was alone. He'd finally have her. He snickered.

If she reported him to the police, who'd believe her? She hadn't reported him before when she ran from the car. He'd just say she invited him over and then came on to him. They'd started kissing, and one thing led to another. As he imagined her in his arms, he ached inside.

Mathew tapped at the door and covered the peephole with his finger.

A scuffling noise sounded at the bottom of the threshold. Kate's voice came from behind the door. "Who is it?" The scuffling sound stopped.

He didn't answer. Something metallic clanked against the door. Humph. A chain wouldn't stop him. The door opened a crack.

Kate's eyes widened. Her jaw lowered. She pushed at the door, but he slipped his foot between it and the frame.

"What are you doing here, Mathew?"

"You got me fired. Think you're too good for me, don't you?" He pressed on the door. It wouldn't open beyond the taut chain length. She must've planted her foot against the back side.

He grasped the open door's edge and leaned his body against the wood to give it a shove. A dog barked and snapped, just missing his fingers. He jerked his hand back, and his foot slid off the metal threshold. The door slammed shut. Curses flew from his lips.

As he ran down the stairs and stomped back to his car, Mathew fumed and muttered. "Where did she get that mutt?" It wouldn't stop him next time.

# Chapter Five

Peeking through the peephole, Kathryn watched as Mathew ran to the stairs. Her legs turned to rubber for a second. She lowered Sheila to the floor. "Thank you, girl. If I hadn't already decided to keep you, you'd have a home now for sure."

Sheila danced around in circles.

Kathryn led her to the kitchen. "You deserve a biscuit for that." She took a bone-shaped treat from a glass container and held it out to the dog. Sheila ate the treat while her tail swept the floor.

What would Mathew do next? If it hadn't been for this wonderful little dog, what would he have done tonight? She scrunched down to scratch Sheila's ears. Her stomach churned.

Should she call Dr. Kenner? She sat on a kitchen chair and stroked the dog's soft, floppy ears. If being fired and warned by his boss didn't stop Mathew, what else could Dr. Kenner do?

She should call the police. But who would believe her, other than her boss? No one else knew what Mathew had done. The things he'd threatened. All she could do was be careful. She had to avoid running into him. She'd take Sheila with her everywhere. Her heart sank. She couldn't take a dog to work.

Kathryn spent the rest of the weekend hiding in her apartment.

Monday evening, Kathryn came home from work and found a bouquet of red roses on her doorstep. She glanced up and down the hall, but no one was around. She hurried to unlock her door, kicked the wrapped flowers over the doorstep, and pushed the door shut behind her.

Kathryn slid the chain in place before she bent to pick up the flowers. A small envelope stuck out from the wrapping.

Sheila bounded out of the bedroom to greet her with a happy wag. "Just a minute, girl. Let me read this." She pulled a note from the envelope and read.

Kathy, I've been thinking and realized that none of this was your fault. Please call me this evening so we can talk. Sincerely, Mathew.

"No way." She tore the note into tiny pieces, marched to the kitchen with Sheila on her heels, and deposited the torn fragments in the trash. "Not in a million years."

Sheila followed her back into the living room. Kathryn attached a leash to the dog and left her apartment, flowers in hand. They climbed the stairs to the next floor and left the roses at the door of the apartment above her. After one knock on the door, they ran down the stairs. Her elderly neighbor could enjoy them.

"Let's go to the courtyard, Sheila. That way we won't run into any unpleasant company." They went out the back entrance of the building.

When Sheila finished her business, they returned to the apartment. A shiver snaked its way up Kathryn's neck. Something wasn't right. She peeked out her window.

Down the street, Mathew leaned against the side of his white Honda, his legs crossed and arms folded. He seemed to stare right at her.

She glanced at Sheila, who cocked her head. "He's out there. I'm trapped. Now what do I do? I'm a prisoner."

As Kathryn finished her work on Friday, her stomach knotted. Her nightmares had grown worse through the week, and she'd had little sleep. The lookout for Mathew each day had gotten old. She even had to stay on the bus past her corner on the way home one night to avoid him. Then she'd hidden in the bushes a block away until he left her street. How long could she keep this up? How long would he keep it up? Hadn't he found another job yet?

Her desk phone rang, and she jumped. She punched the speaker button. "Kathryn speaking."

"Kathy, come to my office, please?"

"Of course, Doctor Kenner."

Oh dear. He'd ask about Mathew for sure, and she couldn't lie to him. She made her way through the halls to Dr. Kenner's office and stepped in.

With pinched brows, he pinned her with his gaze as she approached his desk. "Kathy, have you heard from or seen Pierce since I fired him?"

Tears burned the inside of her eyes. She bit her lower lip.

Dr. Kenner took a deep breath and exhaled. "I thought so. Why didn't you say something? I've been watching the stress mount in your face all week."

"I'm sorry, Doctor Kenner, but what more can you do? Mathew came to my apartment the night you fired him. He was furious and tried to push his way in. Somehow, he got past the entrance. But my dog almost bit him, and he left." The tears fell.

Dr. Kenner handed her a tissue. "Has he been back?"

Kathryn blew her nose and took a deep breath. "He's shown up outside my apartment all week, staring at my windows from down the street. So far, I've avoided him."

The doctor motioned for her to sit down.

She dropped into the chair in front of his desk and dabbed at her eyes. "I—I know you're trying to help. But what can you do?"

"Have you called the police?"

She shook her head. "It's my word against his. Even my pastor agreed. He's been so careful not to let anyone see or hear anything."

Dr. Kenner slowly nodded. "Let me think." He took a sip of his coffee.

She could almost see the gears of his mind working. His brows met in a long line. The muscle in his jaw flexed as he propped his elbow on the arm of the chair. He raised his hand to his chin.

He finished the coffee and placed the cup on a coaster, pushing it to the side of his desk. "It's almost time to clock out. But don't leave, okay?"

"Yes, sir." She rose and returned to her desk.

Half an hour later, Dr. Kenner came through the hall and stopped next to her. He glanced around the front office. "They sure are quick enough to leave at night, aren't they?"

Kathryn laughed. "Yes, sir."

"Kathy, the first thing you need is a new place to live."

She nodded. "I've been looking for something I can afford, but there's not much available. At least, not in an area of town where I wouldn't be afraid to live alone, even with a dog. And I have Sheila to consider. Many places won't allow her. I won't give her up. She's already protected me from Mathew once."

Dr. Kenner smiled and crouched to eye level. "Well, we'll have to look harder. I'm joining the search, and my wife has offered to help. I told her about Pierce. She felt terrible that something like that happened to you...and here at my practice."

"That's very sweet of her." Kathryn's cheeks warmed. "I hate to be such a bother."

"Not at all. You come to our house tonight for dinner, and we'll start an online search for a place. Is that okay with you? We can stop by your apartment and pick up your little hairy friend too." He gave her a warm smile that reached his eyes. "My wife loves dogs."

Kathryn's neck prickled. She'd never met Mrs. Kenner. "You and your wife are too kind."

"Don't give me that look, Kathy. Noelle and I've never had children of our own. She's always telling me, 'Having young people over keeps me young.' Not that I'm that old, mind you." He grinned. "Noelle will enjoy the visit."

Kathryn followed Dr. Kenner to his car, and they drove to her apartment to pick up Sheila. As he parked in front of the building, she spotted Mathew lurking in the shadows of the apartment building across the street. She gasped. He backed deeper into the recessed doorway.

Dr. Kenner turned off the engine and touched her arm as she peered at the other building. "Was that him?"

"Yes. In that entrance."

The doctor followed her line of vision. "Kathy. Knowing my wife, she'll try to talk you into moving in with us...instead of just dinner."

He glanced at her. "Let's give her the enjoyment of your company for a few days while we figure out what to do."

Kathryn bit her lower lip.

"Let me escort you to your door so you can pack a bag and pick up that four-legged child of yours."

Mathew watched as his former boss followed Kate into the apartment building. Tonight's plans for the Katy-bird were ruined. What was Kenner doing here anyway? She must have squealed again. Or was he making his own play for her? Now what would Mrs. Kenner say? He'd have to find their address and tell her.

Twenty minutes later, the doctor carried an overnight bag and what looked like a dog bed out to his car. Kate followed with the small dog on a leash. She and the dog got into Dr. Kenner's vehicle, and he pulled away.

Could he be dropping her off somewhere? If she were leaving on vacation, she wouldn't be gone long with that little bag. He'd bide his time and save his special plans for when she returned. Or, he could follow them.

As the doctor's car turned the corner, Mathew ran down the street and jumped into his Honda. He brought the engine to life.

# Chapter Six

athryn squirmed in the passenger seat as Dr. Kenner drove his car up the long, curved driveway to a massive two-story colonial home set high above Scenic Hwy. A break in the trees alongside the house revealed Escambia Bay far below. She bit her lip. Had she made yet another mistake? She'd never heard anyone at work mention their boss being married, and he didn't wear a ring.

Sheila licked her hand. This little fluff-ball dog of mine had taken an instant liking to the man though. She let out an inward sigh. This paranoia had to stop. Not every man was a Mathew Pierce.

Her boss parked in front of the three-car garage and got out. She opened her door, and Sheila jumped to the driveway. Dr. Kenner waved at a trim woman with light brown hair who stepped out the front door of the house. Kathryn followed him up the half dozen steps of a wide staircase to the front porch.

He gave the pretty woman a kiss on the cheek and smiled at her in a way that made Kathryn's heart melt. "Noelle, this is Kathy." He turned to Kathryn. "Kathy, my wife, Noelle."

Noelle Kenner's hazel eyes sparkled with excitement as she greeted Kathryn with a smile and then a hug. "Welcome to our home. My husband has told me so much about you. I was excited when he called from your apartment and said you'd be staying with us for a few days. Come in."

"Thank you for having me, Mrs. Kenner."

As they walked into the great room, Kathryn gazed past her hostess. A curved wall of glass overlooked the bay and gave a panoramic view. Lights from boats twinkled in the deepening twilight.

A phone rang in the hallway, breaking the trance she'd fallen into while peering out over the water. She must have looked like a little girl staring at Christmas lights. Heat filled her cheeks as her eyes met Mrs. Kenner's.

Dr. Kenner set Kathryn's suitcase and the dog bed down and picked up the phone receiver. "Kenner residence."

Mrs. Kenner led Kathryn by the arm toward a curved stairway in the huge foyer. "Let's get you settled into the guest room while Steve takes care of business. That's what most calls to the house phone are about." She shrugged her shoulders. "Is your little dog a male or female?"

"Sheila's a she." Kathryn smiled, grabbed her suitcase, and followed her hostess, who carried the dog bed. As they climbed the stairs, Sheila ran to the top and waited for them.

Mrs. Kenner giggled. "Sheila? Never heard a canine named that before. Hello, Miss Sheila." When they reached the top of the stairs, the woman scratched the dog behind her ear. Sheila rewarded Mrs. Kenner with a lick on the hand.

As they entered the first room on the left, Mrs. Kenner pointed to folding doors taking up one entire wall. "You can hang your things in the closet." Then she pointed to an antique, dark wooden dresser with three drawers and a marble top. "You can put things in here too. Your little dog's bed can go anywhere you'd like."

Kathryn's mouth fell open as she viewed the huge room. She could put her entire living room inside the guest room and have space left over for a library.

Her hostess removed a dustcover from the four-poster queen-sized bed and folded it. Kathryn's eyes grew larger as she viewed the top of the canopy frame. It resembled an upside-down golden crown. This was where she'd sleep? Like royalty. Sheila jumped onto the bed. "No, Sheila. Get down."

Mrs. Kenner laughed as she stored the dustcover on the top shelf in the closet. "It's okay, Kathy. I don't mind her on the bed if that's where she usually sleeps. How long have you had her?"

"She just showed up the night I ran home from work and found myself locked out of my apartment. I have no idea where she came from. That day had been so stressful. But Sheila made me feel better. We kind of adopted each other."

"She sure is sweet, and beautiful." The lady sat on the bed and stroked Sheila's head.

"Now she is." Kathryn chuckled. "The day we met, she was a mess. It took two baths to get all the mud and dirt off her white coat. I even tried to scrub off those two black spots on her hind end, thinking they were dirt." She laughed. It felt so good to laugh again. She couldn't remember the last time she had.

"My neighbor said she looked like an Australian Cattle Dog, so I figured Sheila was a good name for her. That's what they call girls over there...in Australia. She seems to like it. Right, Sheila?"

"Yip, yip."

Mrs. Kenner giggled as Sheila spun around in a circle. "How cute."

Dr. Kenner walked into the bedroom. "Looks like you're getting settled." He turned to his wife. "I'm afraid I'll have to miss dinner at home tonight, sweetheart. That was Doctor Hartley on the phone. He's requested a consultation on one of our mutual patients, and he says it's important that we talk right away. He suggested over dinner near the hospital."

The doctor turned to Kathryn. "Sorry to abandon you right away, but I promise Noelle doesn't bite."

"Yip." Sheila shook her head, ears flapping.

Dr. Kenner eyed Sheila sitting on the bed as though she owned it. "Yes, I know you don't bite either." He laughed. "She's made herself at home too, I see."

Mrs. Kenner touched his arm. "I understand, honey. And I'm sure Kathy does too. This will give us girls a chance to get to know each other while you're busy."

He kissed his wife's cheek. "Okay, I guess I'd better be off then. Doctor Hartley is meeting me at the restaurant."

The Kenners left the room holding hands and began to descend the staircase. Kathryn glanced back at Sheila, who remained on the bed. The dog circled a couple of times and then plopped herself against the pillows. Kathryn followed her host and hostess downstairs.

When the doctor reached the front door, he turned and half closed his right eye as he gazed at his wife. His left brow rose. "I'm almost afraid to leave you two girls alone this evening." He winked at Kathryn. "I won't come back to find my home office adorned with pink walls and lace trim, will I?"

He kissed his wife and smiled at Kathryn. "Will you at least try to keep her from turning my office into a beauty parlor?"

Mrs. Kenner gave his upper arm a push. "I promise not to touch your masculine space." Then she stretched her arms up and around his neck. He lifted her by the waist and carried her out the door onto the front porch.

Kathryn stayed inside and watched through the open door. Warmth flowed into her cheeks at the sight of the couple kissing on the front stoop. She'd probably never have anyone to love her that way.

Mrs. Kenner stepped back into the foyer and closed the door. "My husband is such a kidder."

"I had no idea. I've barely seen him at work. He's pretty busy all day."

"Yes, Steve is a hard worker and a very good doctor. Do you prefer Kathryn or Kathy?"

"Kathy's fine. Most everyone calls me that."

"Kathy it is. Let's have dinner and then we can start on that apartment search. I made lasagna, salad, and Boston cream pie for dessert. I hope you like it."

"Sounds wonderful." Kathryn's stomach let out a loud growl. "Sorry. With all the stress lately, I haven't eaten very well."

"We'll take care of that tonight. Then…" Mrs. Kenner turned to Kathryn with an impish grin. "I really wanted to turn my husband's office into a beauty parlor. It's too bad he can read my mind."

Kathryn laughed. "I love the way you and your husband tease each other, Mrs. Kenner."

"Please, call me Noelle. I'm not that much older than you." Noelle led her to the kitchen and they set the table.

While they ate, Kathryn's mind and body began to relax. She'd be safe here.

Dr. David Hartley rose from his table in Skopelo's. He held out a hand to greet his friend and colleague, Dr. Kenner. "Glad you could join me, Steve. Hope Noelle will forgive me for stealing you away this evening. Didn't think we should wait until tomorrow to make a decision on our patient's change in her treatment."

Steve shook hands. "I'm glad you called. Nothing has worked so far for that poor lady. We need to figure out why." He seated himself at the white linen-covered square table. "Don't worry about Noelle. She never gets upset when it comes to the care of my patients. That's one of the reasons I love her so much."

"Good, good." David sat. "My Barbara's the same way."

Steve picked up the menu. "We did have a guest this evening, but I'm sure they'll have fun without me. Kathy is one of my employees. She's staying with us for a few days."

After the waiter took both their orders, David jumped right into the discussion of their mutual patient. They agreed on a new treatment for the elderly woman, and David called the hospital to make changes in her medications. As he hung up, their dinner arrived.

David held up a forkful of pink meat and pointed. "So. Why are you having an employee stay with you? What's that all about? Kind of odd, isn't it?"

"You might say." Steve frowned. "We had an incident at the practice. A male employee almost molested Kathy. Noelle and I felt horrible about it." He cut into his New York strip steak.

"Whoa...that's serious. Was he arrested?" David took another bite of his ribeye smothered in sautéed onions and mushrooms.

"No. Actually, he'd been very sneaky about everything, and it's only Kathy's word against his."

David chewed his meat. Steve was a good judge of character. He'd proved that in past years when the young doctor had worked for him. "What did she say to convince you?"

"That he trapped her in the supply room after hours one night. She thought she was the only one in the building. Unfortunately, he hadn't left."

David lifted a large helping of mashed potatoes to his mouth. "But she had no witness or proof. And still you believed her?"

Steve swallowed his food. "I did. I'd observed his behavior with her and with other young women in our office. I'd planned to talk to him about his flirting, bodily contact with some of them, and comments I've overheard."

After another forkful of food and a drink of water, Steve continued, "Kathy had shown a professional manner with all the employees, including him. I noticed her stress level rising when he hovered nearby. When her physical appearance changed, I knew something wasn't right." He finished his meal and pushed the plate to the edge of the table.

"So, what did you do?" David ate the rest of his meal and placed his fork on the plate.

"I called her into my office to talk to her, and she fell apart. Although reluctant to accuse him, she finally told me about the incident."

Their waitress removed the doctors' dishes and placed David's dessert in front of him.

As he ate, Steve told him about the male employee's attitude at the hospital when they met. "When the man became belligerent and blamed Kathy for everything, I told him he had two weeks' severance pay coming, and he wasn't to see or speak to her again."

"And that worked?"

"No. I'm sorry to say, it hasn't. He's harassed her at home instead."

Steve brought events up to his and Noelle's invitation to Kathy for dinner. "Then we spotted him lurking in the shadows outside her apartment when we went to pick up her dog. That's when I decided she needed to get away from there for a few days."

David shook his head and reclined in the wooden chair. He pushed his empty dessert plate away and placed his hands on his ample stomach.

"I felt horrible, David. I should have dealt with Pierce earlier. But like I said, he was very careful."

With elbows on the table, David rested his jaw on his folded hands and leaned forward. "Boy, that's one I'm glad I've never had to face. What's she going to do?"

"Well...Noelle and I had planned to help her find another apartment. But on the way here, it occurred to me he could find her again by following her home from the office."

"Right." David's lips pulled to one side.

"She can stay at our house indefinitely, but I don't think she will. Kathy seems very independent. Frankly, I don't know how to help her. Under the circumstances, I'm worried about her. She's a sweet girl."

David narrowed his eyes. He'd have a position open in his own practice when his office manager retired in a few weeks.

"Steve, what kind of work experience does Kathy have?"

"Our office manager told me she has a degree in business management and has helped her out quite a bit during the year she's worked for us, but this is her first job since graduation. Why? You know of something?"

"I'll need someone to replace my office manager when she retires in a few weeks. Haven't found anyone I want to hire yet, and the other girls in the office aren't experienced enough. I need someone who really knows what they're doing. We have a very busy office, as you know."

Steve's eyes lit up. "Like I said, Kathy has excellent credentials. She filled in while my office manager was on vacation last month and did a great job. Even put out a couple of fires between two of the girls in the front office. Is that what you mean?"

"Exactly. I don't suppose you've thought about her finding a new job too, have you?"

"Well, actually, Kathy did tell me she'd been job hunting, but the market for administrative skills is bad right now. Hundreds show up for one position. I hate to lose her, but even more, I hate to think of what might happen if Pierce gets his hands on her."

"Steve, if you don't mind losing your employee to me, I'd be happy to give her a chance, on your recommendation. Hiring Kathy would solve everyone's problem, except that you lose another employee."

"Ha! If it'll keep Kathy out of the clutches of that lowlife, I'll gladly give her up to you, even if it makes me shorthanded for a while. That's terrific, David. Now all we have to do is find her a new place to live."

David rubbed the stubble on his cheek. "I may even have an answer for that."

"Really?"

"Yes. Long-time friends of mine, Russ and Carole Weaver, have remodeled the second floor of their home into a studio apartment. It used to be their kids' bedrooms. They're all grown and on their own now."

"That'd be great, if she can afford it."

"I don't think that's a problem. Russ mentioned that a college student might like to live there. They don't need the money. Besides, she'll have a good salary as my office manager. Not only would she have a new place to live, but the Weavers are home most of the time, being retired. With what she's gone through, I imagine it would be a comfort to have someone around, and still live independently."

David chuckled as Steve's smile spread wider. "Plus, their house is a good distance from your office. It's close to the beach, which she'll probably love." He took his cell out and dialed the Weavers' number.

"Hi, Russ. It's David."

Steve sat back and sipped his coffee, while David's conversation played out on the speakerphone.

"Is your apartment still available?"

"Sure is. We haven't even advertised yet."

"Well, I think I have a possible renter for you. A nice young lady I plan to hire. Would she be able to move in right away?"

"That's great, David. She could move in tonight, if she wants to. Everything is ready and waiting."

David laughed. "That's wonderful news. I'll call you back when I find out how soon she wants to come over and see it."

He said his goodbye and hung up. "Okay, Steve. It's set. All Kathy has to do is give her thumbs-up. That goes for the job too. Should solve that harassment situation for good, don't you think?"

# Chapter Seven

### Eight Months Later
### Pensacola Beach, Florida

Seagulls dipped and soared against a clear turquoise sky as Kathryn took in a deep breath of salt air. She unfolded her legs, rose from the edge of the boardwalk bench, and stretched. "Oooo." After kicking the feeling back into her limbs, she did a couple of deep knee bends to get the blood flowing again.

A gust of wind blew in off the water. Strands of her long blonde hair tickled her face. She grasped the flyaway tresses in one hand, undid her ponytail with the other, and smoothed the wayward locks back into place.

Kathryn pulled a paper sack from her tote bag, reached in, and took out a handful of stale bread pieces. She threw them into the air, and the gulls swarmed in. She loved their acrobatics. Another handful flew upwards. She stretched out her arms, imagining herself as one of the birds that raced for the airborne chunks.

What a perfect day it had turned out to be. So comfortable, even with the cool breeze off the water. And not another person in sight. The entire deserted seashore to herself.

Preparations for Easter kept everyone else too busy to spend time relaxing on this warm, soft, sugar-white sand. They'd clean and cook, color Easter eggs and fix pretty Easter baskets for tomorrow. But not her. She had no preparations to make. She had no one for whom she'd cook a special meal.

Even the dress she'd wear to church tomorrow had hung in her closet for days, pressed and ready to slip on.

She glanced at the gulls. "You guys are so lucky. Lots of friends and family around all the time. What a life."

The gulls called back, as if to agree, "Kiiwa-ha."

As high as she could, Kathryn cast another handful of bread upward. None of them looked like they had a care in the world, except to beat each other to the food.

"Kiiwa-ha-ha-ha."

Now they snickered at her. "No wonder you guys are called laughing gulls." If only she could feel that lighthearted. Today, she felt old...and alone. Suddenly, the empty beach had lost its perfection.

At least she had her sweet little dog Sheila to come home to. Too bad they wouldn't allow dogs on the beach. She'd have loved chasing the gulls. Kathryn's heart pinched. Would she ever have a two-legged someone special in her life?

As she sat on the edge of the boardwalk, a warm tear dropped to her cheek. Would she ever feel whole again? Her heart ached as if it would split in two. Everyone was gone. Mom, Dad, even her brother Chris. Her adopted family, Uncle Eric, Aunt Sandy, and Beth lived so far away.

When she pictured their faces, the loving family who had taken her and her brother in after their parents' deaths, another tear fell.

A scene from her childhood played in her mind, and Kathryn's lips curled upward. She had teased Beth about her tightly curled chestnut hair falling in ringlets around her face and down to her shoulders. *"Beth, that kinky hair of yours will get caught in the branches of a tree someday, like pastor said Sampson's did. And there you'll be. Stuck."*

Beth's warm, honey-brown eyes had taken on a fiery sparkle. *"You're just jealous 'cuz you don't have any color in your hair. And I think you meant Absalom, not Sampson."*

A chuckle escaped Kathryn, while yet another tear fell. So long ago. Only five and six years old then. Little had they known they'd become sisters.

How she missed Beth.

"Kiiwa-ha. Kiiwa-ha-ha."

Kathryn jerked as she was brought back to the present by the gulls. "Quit scolding me. Not attentive enough with the bread, huh? Okay, here you go." She threw another handful into the air.

The bird-sounds faded as she pictured herself, her brother, and Beth. They'd become best friends. Even Chris thought of Beth that way.

Then that awful day in Mexico on the mission field. Why did her parents have to die? Why did their car have to slide off the treacherous mountain road during that rainstorm as they tried to bring medicine to a sick elderly church member? She and Chris had stayed behind to clean the church their parents had started. Why couldn't her parents have survived?

Her daddy's smile had been so warm. Why did it have to rain? "I still don't understand." Her whispered cry hung in the air, and she blinked back tears.

Kathryn shook her head to clear her mind. Would she never rid herself of the images? The nightmares? Now she suffered other dreams. Were they about the events that still haunted her from over a year ago? Nightmares about Mathew Pierce?

The flock of birds flew overhead for a moment, then landed and paced the boardwalk in front of her as she moved to another bench. She dropped the bag of tempting bread morsels next to her.

One of the gulls swooped down to the far end of the bench and crept closer to the bag. Kathryn smiled. "Friendly little guys, aren't you?" She returned to her thoughts.

A minute later, the flutter of wings next to her made her jump. Her arm swung out and the sack dropped to the boardwalk, its treasure scattered. She blew out the large gulp of air she'd taken as the feathered thief flew away with a large chunk of bread dangling from its beak.

"Now see what you've done?" She called after the gull and laughed. Then she picked up the bag and shook the rest of the pieces out. "Help yourselves."

Kathryn tossed the sack into a trash receptacle and headed toward the water. Before she had taken three steps onto the warm sand, dozens of gulls gathered on the boardwalk to partake of the feast. The squabbling-bird mêlée behind her made her chuckle. "Greedy little beggars, aren't you?"

She continued to the water's edge. As she strolled, her thoughts returned to Chris. If only he hadn't joined the Marines after college. The best brother any girl could have had.

The day they'd left Pensacola for Mexico, he'd wrapped his arms around her eight-year-old skinny frame. The corner of the almost empty orchid-colored room that had been hers for three years held her belongings, her world, compressed into three boxes. *Beautiful mountains will replace the beaches of Pensacola,* her mother had told her. She'd wanted sand, not mountains.

Ten-year-old Christian had tried to ease her fears. *"It's okay, Sissy. I'll be there with you, like always. We're going on a new adventure."*

She dragged her feet through the sun-warmed sand, while her mind flew past the next fifteen years. When her mom and dad died, Beth's parents had taken her and Chris to Des Plaines, Illinois to live with them because the Kendall's had no other family.

Her heart lurched as she relived the day the rest of her world fell apart. Was it two years ago already? A couple of Marine officers stood outside her college dorm room. Her legs buckled at their words, and she collapsed. Chris had been killed in action.

He'd always been her protector. Not any more. *Why did he have to die?*

Kathryn sucked in a deep breath of air. She'd lost so much in her almost twenty-five years. At least tomorrow she'd be with people who cared about her. People she had learned to trust.

She gazed out over the breakers. Once more, the gulls broke in on her thoughts. "So. You finished the bread at the boardwalk." They circled her at the edge of the water. Closer and closer, they swooped.

"What? You want dessert to go with the main course? Tough it up, my fine-feathered friends. The pantry's bare."

She cinched her mouth. She should take her own advice. *Tough it up, Miss Kendall.*

It had been her idea to stay in Florida after graduating from the University of West Florida, instead of returning to the Parkers' home in Des Plaines. Uncle Eric and Aunt Sandy had pleaded with her to come home. But she wanted independence.

That was before the ordeal with Mathew. Would she ever feel independent again?

Kathryn continued to walk along the wet strip of sand. She picked up a brown-and-pink-spotted scallop shell the water had left behind as it retreated to the gulf.

The gulls lost interest in her as she shuffled barefoot through the waves, shoes in her left hand. The water was so cool. Would it be cool in California too? *She didn't care.*

Easter was supposed to be with the Parkers as usual. Before Tom Rivers proposed to Beth, and his family invited the Parkers to spend the holiday in California to get acquainted.

Of course, everyone wanted to meet Mr. and Mrs. Rivers, especially since the soon-to-be-married couple planned to move to California.

Kathryn sighed. Here she was in Florida feeling sorry for herself, even though the invitation had included her. *Wonderful.* And why hadn't she agreed to go with them? Because she promised her bosses she'd *be available.*

Where had all this sarcasm come from? She bent and ran her hand through a wave of cool water. That was her, always accommodating and easy going. But today she had a different frame of mind. It was the first time she could remember ever having regret over a promise she'd made. Dear Drs. Hartley and Griffin would have understood if she backed out of the promise. However, that wasn't her way.

With her feet covered in the soft sugar-like sand, Kathryn walked back to the boardwalk and, from the beach bag she'd left there, retrieved the romance novel she'd been reading. She stretched a seashell print beach towel on the sand, brushed the sand off her feet, and unpacked her lunch. Then she settled her back against one of the boardwalk's wooden support posts.

The birds started to gather again, their beady eyes fixed on her sandwich. "Oh no. You guys find your own food. This is mine."

One paragraph into the book, loneliness overwhelmed her again. First time she'd spend a holiday without even her adopted family around. She tossed the book onto the towel and nibbled the sandwich. Her gaze traveled out over the Gulf of Mexico and the whitecaps speeding to shore across the emerald green water.

The diehard birds gathered on the sand around her. "Kiiwa-ha, kiiwa-ha, kiiwa-ha."

"Insistent things, aren't you? All right." She tore off the crusts and threw them onto the sand. Then she stuck the last morsel of egg salad sandwich into her mouth. "I'm leaving now, so you'd better look for another food vender."

All but one bird flew off as she rose. "I think I've spent enough time at this pity-party. Don't you?" She winked at the gull. He cocked his head as if he understood. The bird swallowed the piece of crust he held, and then flew away.

Kathryn sighed. She did have two wonderful bosses who each cared for her like a member of their own family. And their sweet wives. Then there was Nick. There was always Nick.

She strolled to her bike and unlocked the chain. A few gulls still hovered over her as she pushed the bike from the boardwalk to the road. She turned, waved goodbye to the birds, and headed back toward her apartment.

The sun had started to dip into the western sky, turning the cirrus clouds magenta, coral, and purple. The wind grew colder. She hurried her pace. How did it get so late?

Dusk turned into sunset quickly as Kathryn peddled her bike along the empty streets toward home. She frowned. Nick's face popped into her mind too often. Didn't she feel guilty enough that she couldn't return his affection? It wasn't his fault. She stayed away from men on purpose, after Mathew.

Kathryn redirected her thoughts to her present job. She enjoyed working at Scenic Bluffs Family Practice Clinic and loved the two middle-aged doctors she worked for. Who'd have thought she'd be an office manager at twenty-four?

Dear Dr. Hartley had hemmed and hawed last month before asking if she'd consider not taking time off work for the next couple of months while they searched for an additional doctor. He and his partner had been so overworked. She'd agreed without hesitation. That was before she knew of Beth's engagement.

She'd planned to fly to Des Plaines after work Friday for the Easter weekend and come back late Sunday. She would have been back at her desk on Monday. But a trip to California presented an entirely different story. It would be too rushed, and expensive. And she wouldn't allow the Parkers to pay her way. Nor would she go back on her word and take a longer weekend. Not when her doctors counted on her.

If only Tom hadn't proposed to Beth. Well, that wasn't a very nice thought.

She liked Tom. Had from the first time she'd met him at the Parkers' last year during Christmas. No way would she begrudge his taking her "sister" away. Or would she? No. He'd be a brother-in-law in her surrogate family. A very nice one at that.

Kathryn sighed. Would Beth be too tied up with her new husband to have time for an adopted sister?

As she steered the bike around a corner, her phone rang. Kathryn applied the brakes, hopped off the seat, and dug through the tote bag for her cell.

She grinned at the face that filled the screen, pressed a key, and raised the phone to her ear. "Hi, Curly Crop."

Beth Parker's exasperated breath sounded through the phone. Kathryn chuckled. Even after all these years, she could still get Beth's goat when she used her old nickname. It had always irritated her.

"Kathy. I've tried calling you all day. Why didn't you answer?"

"I was at the beach and had the phone turned off. Let me call back from the apartment before it dies. I'm almost there."

"You forgot to charge it again, didn't you? All right, but don't forget. This is important. Bye."

Kathryn stuck out her tongue at the screen. Then she laughed, plunged the phone back into her bag, and continued her ride home.

Her adopted family would have such a good time with Tom's parents. While she'd have dinner tomorrow with the Hartleys.

She sighed. How many single men would Mrs. Hartley have invited this time? She and Mrs. Griffin were determined to find *Miss Kendall* a husband. Surrounded by matchmakers. What could a girl do?

Kathryn parked her bike in the Weavers' garage and headed to the house. What a blessing it had been to move into their home last summer. Couldn't ask for better landlords.

When she opened the door of her second-floor apartment, an over-excited pooch pounced on her. "Okay, Sheila. I know. You need out." She tossed her beach paraphernalia on the dresser and plugged in her phone. "Let's go. It'll have to be a short trip though."

Upon their return to the apartment, she threw herself onto the bed, lay on her side, and propped her head in her hand. Sheila joined her, snuggling behind her knees. Kathryn tapped the speed-dial number while the phone was still charging.

Before it rang on Kathryn's end, Beth answered. "Took you long enough. At least you didn't make me wait an hour, like last time."

"Sorry, Beth. Sheila came first. What did you do, have the phone plastered to your ear? It didn't even ring. But go ahead. I'm plugged in now. What's your important news? You're in California, right?"

"Yes, landed a few hours ago and settled in. You really need to come out here and meet Tom's family. Please? You won't believe how nice they are." Her sentences picked up speed. "Or this beautiful house. You could fly out in the morning. They really want to meet you. We could have a ticket waiting for you at the Pensacola airport. All you have to do is say you'll come. Please?"

"Beth. Take a breath or you'll pass out." One of these days, she really would.

"Okay, okay."

A short pause for a large intake of air followed. Then Beth started in again. "Apparently, they have connections." Her voice lowered to a whisper. "And they're loaded. I knew Tom's family was well off, but I had no idea."

"I wish I could, Beth. But I told you. I can't take time off work right now. And arriving in California for dinner and then flying back to Pensacola the same evening doesn't sound practical to me, nor like much fun. Plus, I'd hate to spring dog sitting on the Weavers at the last minute. They've done so much for me already."

A deep sigh from Beth reached across the miles. Kathryn pulled her lips to the side. With her flair for the dramatic, Beth would've made a great actress.

"I'll get a chance to meet them soon. Give my sincere thanks to the Rivers. Try to make them understand the situation, okay?"

The girls talked for a few more minutes, and Kathryn hung up with a sigh of her own.

She fed Sheila and made a salad for herself. "Wish you could have been on the beach with me, Sheila. You'd have made those gulls leave my sandwich alone."

"Yip. Yip."

Kathryn laughed at her pet's enthusiastic agreement between bites of kibble.

After dinner, Kathryn grabbed Sheila's leash from the hook in the closet. "Come, girl. It's time for a real walk."

As they walked around the block, the evening air pressed against Kathryn's skin. Humid. Uncomfortable. Too bad tonight's air wasn't like the breeze from the beach earlier.

Sheila stretched her nose upward and then sneezed. The dog pulled on her leash, as if anxious to return to the air-conditioning.

"Guess the pollen has begun to fly. Okay. Slow down. We're almost home."

They reentered the apartment, and she prepared for bed. At least the day's fresh air on the beach would provide for a restful night's sleep. She slipped between the sheets and turned out the light. Sheila hopped up next to her, turned in a circle a couple of times, and settled into a fluffy mound at Kathryn's feet.

For the next hour, sad memories of her parents again rushed into her mind. She shifted her legs one way and then the other. "Sorry, Sheila. Guess I'm restless tonight. And the darkness magnifies every noise in the house. Can't get my eyes to stay shut for even a minute."

A soft snore came from Sheila. Kathryn sat up in bed. Why couldn't she sleep as soundly as that dog? She glanced at the clock. Midnight. *Great!*

After sliding into slippers, she shuffled to the kitchen in her nightgown and made a cup of cocoa. Mug and napkin in hand, she moved to the living room and eased into her favorite armchair, curling her legs under her. Sheila bounded out of the bedroom and leaped into her lap. Chocolate splashed onto Kathryn's arm. "Whoa. Easy girl."

With her napkin, Kathryn wiped cocoa from her arm and then placed the cup next to the novel she'd taken to the beach. She picked up the book and opened it to the bookmark.

Several chapters later, she tossed the book back on the table. "Drat." She had no idea what she'd just read. Now she'd have to reread those pages. Focus.

Her mind drifted instead. "Would there ever be someone to share her life with?" Someone gallant, like the knight in her novel. A man to love—

*Thunk*

"Woof!"

Kathryn jumped at the loud sound and Sheila's bark. Her book fell to the floor. And someone who could check those pesky noises in the night. She exhaled.

As she stroked Sheila's head, she retrieved her book. "It's okay, girl. Probably Mr. Weaver closing a door downstairs." She hoped.

She pulled an afghan over her lap. "A bit chilly with the air running." The dog whimpered and inched her way next to Kathryn's legs under the cover.

If only she could find someone special to love, like Beth had. She hugged her middle. He'd have to be as honest and trustworthy as Chris had been, and she hadn't met anyone yet who could equal her brother. If he'd lived, he'd have become some girl's knight in shining armor.

Her mouth pursed. Nick's image, light brown wavy hair, and gray eyes framed by curled lashes, crept into her mind. She loved the way his perpetual smile lit up his face. He certainly had expressed his interest in her. Why hadn't she ever thought of him that way? Close, but nothing more. He came nearer to being a duplicate of Chris than anyone she'd ever met. Yet—

Shouldn't dwell on him. If she got too close, she'd probably lose him too, like her family. Now she'd lose Beth. In a different way, of course, but still lost to her.

Was that why she kept Nick at a distance? She shook her head. No. She'd never fallen in love with him.

On her way to the kitchen, she polished off the dregs of cocoa. Sheila trailed behind as they entered the bedroom and hopped back onto the bed.

"Now, let's see if we can get to sleep. Mom was always so good at helping me relax."

The dog scooted under the sheet and licked her ankle before she curled into another circle.

Her mother's melodic voice, along with a verse she'd often quoted, floated into Kathryn's mind. *"Psalm four, eight. Remember, honey. 'I will both lay me down in peace, and sleep: for thou, LORD, only makest me dwell in safety.' That was written so you could know He watches over you, no matter where you are, or what's going on in your life. Trust The Watcher."*

Mom had always referred to the Lord as The Watcher. He was there, looking out for her.

Her eyelids grew heavy. It still worked. Maybe now she'd sleep.

# Chapter Eight

aster Sunday dinner came and went. Kathryn had juggled conversations between herself and three young doctors at the Hartley home all evening. The doctors were nice, but none had captured her interest. Kathryn laughed as she got ready for bed that night. Mrs. Hartley had done it again.

She fell asleep before the number one sheep cleared the fence in her mind, and before she knew it, it was Monday morning.

Haunted by the thought of love, she'd dreamed about each of the handsome doctors she'd met on Easter. If only dreams could come true. She'd been in love with all three, and they with her, but she woke before settling on one.

After she dressed and finished a light breakfast of toast and yogurt, she took Sheila out in the yard. When they returned to the apartment, Kathryn cleaned up her dishes from breakfast. "Could you imagine, girl? In love with three men at the same time. Ha!"

Sheila's head popped up from her water dish. She ran to Kathryn's side.

"It's okay, girl. I was only voicing—" What was she voicing? Her reluctance to believe in love, or that she'd ever be in love...or ever wanted to be?

"Oh well. Time for me to leave. You be a good girl. I'll be home right after work." She gave Sheila a scratch behind the ears and slipped out the door.

At the corner down the street, Kathryn caught the bus. After the short ride, she walked into the peach-colored stucco building of Scenic Bluffs Family Practice Clinic.

As she settled herself behind the desk, one of her bosses, Dr. Alex Griffin, strode into her office. "Kathy, as busy as our practice is with only two doctors and a PA, we don't have time to referee squabbles." He took a breath. "So David and I are very grateful that you took care of the situation in the front office last Friday." He grinned. "Not that you have time either, but you're better at it."

"Thank you, Doctor Griffin. We're all feeling pressure from our overloaded schedules. You'll make everyone's lives easier when you find a doctor to join the team, and I find another front office clerk."

"That's the second reason I stopped by." He grinned at her. "After last week's double bookings, we've decided to redouble our efforts to find that doctor. We hope to find a young man or woman before we leave for the medical conference in April."

Kathryn smiled at the middle-aged doctor as he ran a hand through his salt and pepper hair and over the somewhat thin spot on top. She'd grown very fond of both her employers. "I'll help in any way I can."

Dr. Griffin gave her a warm smile and moved his tall, lean frame in front of her desk. "It was a lot to ask of you over the Easter holiday."

"After Beth and the family decided to celebrate Easter in California, I had no special plans. Except for the Hartleys' beautiful dinner party with all of you yesterday."

Little did he know how relieved she'd been *not* to go to California.

"Still, it was a lot to ask, and now we have an even more challenging task for you." Dr. Griffin cinched his mouth. "But you'll do a great job, as always. First, David and I want you to delegate some of your other duties to whomever you feel can handle them while you're assisting us."

Kathryn cocked her head. As she did, Dr. Hartley entered her office and plunked his short, middle-aged, slightly rotund body into the chair next to her desk. He scratched his head through a thick shock of white hair, rumpled as usual.

A picture of the old comedy duo, Laurel and Hardy, came to mind every time she saw the two doctors together.

"So, Alex, has Kathy accepted the challenge?" Dr. Hartley twisted his body to view Dr. Griffin to his right.

With the usual you-interrupted-me look on his face, Dr. Griffin answered his partner. "I was about to explain it to her."

"Oops...jumped the gun again, didn't I?" He winked one of his deep blue eyes at her.

She couldn't prevent the laugh that burst out. Someday, she should write a book about the clichés Dr. Hartley used every chance he got. Did the man realize he couldn't get through a conversation without one? Probably not. But she loved them.

Then there were the looks Dr. Griffin would give his partner. Good thing they were best friends as well as partners. Their antics made them so endearing. Hopefully, the practice would find a nice, handsome, young doctor, who matched the wonderful personalities of these men. She might even find herself interested in a romance.

She blinked and shook the thought from her head.

Later that afternoon, Kathryn sat at her desk and stared at the list of qualifications Dr. Hartley had handed her. The process of acquiring the new doctor would occupy much of her day now since her bosses hadn't had time themselves to find one. Especially since she lacked experience in employee recruitment. But she'd promised to do her best.

After she'd contacted every top staffing agency in the phone book and emailed the qualifications and job applications, she sat back. Headhunters. What an expression. Made her feel like a cannibal looking for a meal.

Kathryn laid the list of agencies to the side. No telling how soon the applications would trickle in. She'd better get a few of her other duties out of the way before they did. Before she was tied up verifying credentials from each curriculum vitae, as the doctors called it.

She chuckled. Another strange name. No wonder they called them CVs instead.

Once she'd selected those best suited for the position from the résumés...or CVs, she'd schedule interviews with either Dr. Griffin or Dr. Hartley. Could she pick the right applicant? Kathryn rubbed one side of her neck. Wish she had as much confidence in her abilities as her employers. She glanced at the clock. Almost five. Still so much work to finish today.

There was an upside though. She'd be too tired to think of anything but taking care of herself and Sheila each night. Maybe she'd sleep better too.

"Ugh!" Kathryn tossed a CV in the corner basket on her desk. Another applicant who needed a new position because of a problem with his or her last place of employment. Was there no end to those who had just finished their residency and had no experience...or left the last job under a cloud?

She'd read and followed up on each submission. Dozens of them. She filled her cheeks with air and blew out a sigh. Then she picked up the stack of paperwork and trudged to the other side of the building.

As she entered Dr. Hartley's office, he grinned. "Are those the CVs? Looks like you've been doing a bang-up job, Kathy. Your search has been successful, I assume."

She attempted a smile. "Far from it." She handed him the stack and shook her head. "I'm sorry. None of these will meet your requirements. I've called the employment agencies again, but they have nothing new right now."

Dr. Hartley flipped through the pages and let out a long huff of air. He pitched the pile of papers into his to-be-filed tray.

"Alex and I didn't expect many well-suited candidates, but we didn't expect to strike out either. You're not holding out on me, are you? Got one more hidden behind your back, maybe?" He gave her a toothy grin.

One side of her lips rose in a half smile. "I wish I did. Perhaps if you double-check them. Maybe I missed someone."

He leaned over and patted the arm of the leather chair next to the left side of his desk. "Kathy, I trust your judgment. If you say nobody fills the bill, nobody fills the bill. We did give you an extensive list of qualifications to go by. Alex and I could go over them again with a fine-toothed comb, but why waste our time when you're so thorough?"

Kathryn bit her lip to keep from laughing at yet another series of his classic clichés. She pressed her lips between her teeth.

A glimmer of a smile brightened his face. He snapped his fingers. "I know. Alex and I can shake the bushes while we're at the conference in Atlanta next week. I'm sure we'll find a qualified applicant."

She stifled another laugh. *"Shake the bushes."* He was a riot.

Dr. Griffin stepped into the office. "Heard you mention the conference. Will we have a new doctor to cover for us while we're gone?"

Her impending giggles squelched, she pinched her brows together and slowly shook her head.

Dr. Hartley did likewise. "Afraid not, Alex. We'll continue our search at the conference."

"Hmmm." Dr. Griffin grimaced. "Don't look so sad, Kathy. I know you did your best. Looks like your job's done, and ours is just beginning."

Dr. Hartley picked up a peppermint-filled candy jar from his desk and held it out to her. "We'll put up a notice on the message board in the conference hall as soon as we get there. How large do you think we should write the letters *H-E-L-P*."

As she chuckled, Kathryn covered her mouth. "No thank you, Doctor. Never cared for peppermints."

He held the jar out to Dr. Griffin.

"That's worth a try. Good thinking, David." Dr. Griffin not only took a piece of candy, he removed the jar from his partner's hands. "What did I tell you about having this temptation sitting on your desk?"

His partner frowned and puckered his lips, then laughed. "Killjoy. You'll note that it's still full from last week. I was going to ask Kathy to put the jar in the front office for the girls. I've followed your orders to the 'T' ever since my last checkup."

With his hand placed on her shoulder, Dr. Griffin handed Kathryn the jar. "Here you go. Make sure it stays in the front office please, and if you catch this character sticking his paw in it, report to me."

Kathryn took the jar and glanced at Dr. Hartley, who gave her a wink. "Now don't fret, Kathy. I'll not put you in that position. Don't worry about finding that new doctor either. We'll find one. There's always a reason something doesn't turn out the way you want it to at first. You know, best played plans of mice and men, and all. I believe the right man or woman at the conference is just chomping at the bit for a new job."

Dr. Griffin erupted in a laugh.

Dr. Hartley peered at him over his reading glasses. "What."

"I think that line should be best-laid plans of mice and men, although I'm not sure how the rest goes. Still, we get the gist of your meaning." His mirth-filled brown eyes turned to Kathryn and back again to Dr. Hartley. "My fear is we'll find the doctors at the conference contented where they work. Most attendees who take time off for these events are well-established in their positions. At least, that's the way it seems."

"Yes, yes...but we might find someone who needs one last credit from a session before renewing their license and might be looking for a change." He pointed a pencil at Dr. Griffin. "Now don't get me depressed over this, Alex. If I go on a chocolate binge, it'll be your fault."

Kathryn shook with suppressed laughter. To keep it from escaping, she bit her lip. Who'd have guessed she'd have another job with a boss as nice as Dr. Kenner, or as much fun. Now she had two of them.

The new physician they'd pick would be just as nice. She hoped.

## Minnesota
## Marble Lake Pain Clinic

Dr. Jacob McLeod stood in the doorway of his boss's office. He took a deep breath as he waited for Dr. Michael Bentley to hang up the phone. Would the man listen to him? He hoped so. Jacob had worked for the practice for almost a year. That should give him credibility.

True, it was only the second group of doctors he'd worked for since his residency, but Dr. Bentley seemed levelheaded. He must have noticed the increased problems. Lax discipline in the staff, patients rushed in and out as if on an assembly line. No doubt, the patients had expressed their concerns to him.

His boss hung up and motioned for Jacob to take a seat next to the desk. "What can I do for you?"

"Thought I'd better bring this to your attention. Today, a patient caught me as she left the building and told me how irritated she was with some of our doctors and nurses. How they've spoken to her as if they didn't care what she had to say about her illness. They also made her feel foolish when she asked questions, and they rushed out of the room after her exam without giving any answers."

"Well, Jacob, there's only so much we can do for our patients. Most have no insurance. And they're uneducated about these things, so—"

"Excuse me, Doctor Bentley. I'm sorry to interrupt, but insurance is not the issue here. And how much education a patient has shouldn't have any bearing on getting an answer when they ask a question."

His boss grinned and stood from his chair. "I'll tell you what. Why don't you write down the patients' complaints? Give them to my secretary, and I'll go over them later."

He rounded his desk and held out his hand toward the office door for Jacob to leave. "I have hospital rounds to do now."

Jacob left the office.

As he entered the front office to get his next patient's chart, Jacob peered into the lobby. Needy patients filled the room. He *would* write everything down. Should he mention which complaint was against whom? What else could he do?

Had he known how things would wind up here, he'd have stayed at his former job. Jacob's jaw tightened. He trudged back toward the examining rooms. No, he wouldn't have. Not as long as Patricia worked there.

Jacob adjusted his stethoscope around his neck. Should he look for another job? Another change of employment so soon? He wished he'd never met Patricia Campbell.

From behind him, Dr. Bentley's voice broke into Jacob's thoughts. "Jacob, you're still going to that conference this weekend, right?"

He turned to face his boss. "Yes, sir. Is that a problem? I need the credits. Time is getting close for renewal of my license."

"No problem. We have you covered here. Just get that list we spoke of to my secretary before you go, and we'll talk it over when you get back." Dr. Bentley turned and then spun back around. "But you'll be here Friday all day? You don't leave until after work, right?"

"Yes, sir." Jacob sighed. He had hoped to leave early for the trip to Georgia, but with one of their physicians on his honeymoon and a nurse on vacation, he'd already given up the idea of catching an early flight.

*Pensacola*

After work, Kathryn took heavy steps up the worn wooden stairs to her apartment. She hadn't been this tired in a long time. Mental fatigue. But it was worth it to know her bosses understood she'd given it her best to find a new doctor, even if her efforts had failed. She'd have to remember to pray that they'd find the right person at the conference this weekend. If God even listened to her prayers.

Her little white dog met her at the door. "Yip, yip."

"Yes, I know you have to go out. Just a sec."

She shoved a frozen macaroni and cheese dinner into the microwave and took Sheila down to the enclosed yard. "I'll be right back for you, girl."

Kathryn returned to the kitchen and set the table.

*Ding*

After removing the container from the microwave, she stirred the contents. Then she returned to Sheila and let her in. "Slow down, girl. I know you're hungry." Sheila sat at the top step before Kathryn could climb halfway up the stairs.

As Sheila ate her dinner, Kathryn took a couple of bites of the mac and cheese. She dropped the fork, which seemed to weigh thirty pounds. Too tired to eat, and the food had no appeal. She pushed herself to her feet, covered the plate with plastic wrap, and placed it in the refrigerator. Maybe later.

She should go to bed early and try for a good night's sleep. Tomorrow would be catch-up day. She had piles of work to do.

Kathryn cleaned the kitchen and then settled into the overstuffed armchair in the living room. Sheila jumped into her lap.

"Girl, try as I might, I couldn't bring myself to delegate many of my duties to the other girls during the past week." The dog whimpered and stared at her. "Everyone has such a load on their plate with the increased patients. How could I give them even more work just because I had a new responsibility? Hope the new girl I hired works out."

She got to her feet and plodded toward the bedroom but stopped short. "Drat." Sheila needed to go outside again before bedtime.

While Sheila ran down the stairs, Kathryn held the railing and followed with weary steps. She sat on the porch swing while her four-legged friend ran to the back fence and returned. "Okay, girl. Let's call it a night."

The little fluffy dog scampered up the stairs, Kathryn trailing behind.

After locking the door, she slogged to the bedroom once more and laid out her clothes for the next day. "Sheila, the doctors told me to have the employment agencies send over more résumés to find extra office staff while they're gone. A new doctor, new medical records clerk, and an extra front office person sure will ease the pressure on everyone."

Sheila yipped.

Kathryn changed into her nightclothes, washed her face, and brushed her teeth. She pursed her lips at her reflection in the mirror. Dark shadows beneath her eyes matched her purple PJs. Droopy eyelids. Even her hair looked tired. "You'd better get more sleep."

The dog yawned and smacked her tongue noisily. Kathryn laughed and then turned back to the mirror. A smile spread across her face. "One of those new hires for the office might just be a handsome gentleman. *Ha!*" Dreamer.

She shuffled into the kitchen, leaving Sheila on the bed in the process of her circle routine before dropping into a fluffy ball to settle for the night.

Hot chocolate. That's what she needed. Kathryn mixed cocoa, sugar, and water in a saucepan over low heat until everything was blended and smooth. She pulled the milk from the refrigerator and poured a cupful into the hot, dark brown mixture.

A few minutes later, steaming mug in hand, she curled up in the cushy armchair in her living room and opened her Bible. She needed to do this more often.

As she read and sipped the hot chocolate, the aching muscles in her neck eased. After trying to read the same chapter several times with no understanding of what she read, she carried the mug to the sink. Maybe she should have prayed for understanding first. Would it have helped?

Kathryn yawned as she entered the bedroom. Sheila lay curled at the end of the bed, making her usual soft snoring sounds. How could such a small animal fill her heart with so much joy? Yet, something was still missing from her life.

She slipped into bed and switched off the lamp. The cool fresh sheets soothed her tired body. Hopefully she wouldn't have another horrible dream like those that had returned lately. Why had they? Shouldn't dwell on it right before sleep. *Think good thoughts. Think good thoughts.*

She rolled over and her eyelids drifted shut.

*"Where do you think you're going? You can't get away from me."*

Kathryn jolted to a sitting position. She trembled and her heartbeat raced. Sheila sprang into her lap and whimpered. Faint light filtered in around the window shade. What woke her? "It's okay, girl. Just a dream. I think."

She turned on the nightstand lamp and checked the alarm clock. Half an hour before the alarm was set to go off. Must have been a nightmare, but she couldn't remember the details. Was it the same dream she'd had before?

Why was this happening again?

# Chapter Nine

## *Medical Conference*
## *Atlanta, Georgia*

Dr. David Hartley sat at the speakers' table and waited for the second half of the morning session to begin. His stomach knotted. He had to stop worrying. They'd find someone to join their practice. The weekend had just begun.

He took a sip of coffee and sighed. So far, not one person had responded to the notice they posted on the message board when they first arrived. Discussions with their colleagues during the break after Alex's lecture had proved unfruitful. They had to find someone.

Alex came into view and took the chair next to David without a word. When the room filled, David rose from the table. He gave his partner a half grin and started toward the stage to give his lecture.

Alex cleared his throat and chuckled. "David, don't forget your notes and handouts."

Again, David sighed. He turned and grasped the flapping pages from his partner's hand. "Thanks." Then he strode to the platform.

Once behind the podium, he scanned the room. He'd given this talk on ethics so many times the words flowed from his lips like a recording. Good thing too. He couldn't get his mind off the fruitless search. Could one of those sets of eyes staring at him belong to the physician they needed?

As he ended his talk and descended the stage stairs to rejoin Alex, enthusiastic applause broke out and continued until he retook his seat at the table. He turned to his partner. "Let's get our lunch while everyone finishes their notes."

They snaked their way through the crowd to the buffet table at the rear of the room.

At the end of the line of food, Alex touched David's shoulder. "Easy on that fried chicken, red beans, and rice. You've got enough on your plate for supper too."

"Oh?" David glanced at his plate and shook his head. "I didn't realize I'd taken such big helpings." His stomach churned. He couldn't eat any of this. "Do you really think we'll find our new doctor here? We can't keep working at the pace we have, but we can't turn patients away either."

A confident grin spread across Alex's face. "Relax, David. Something will come up. You said so yourself before we left. Think positive. With all these men and women, there has to be someone who'd be interested in the opportunity. And remember where we live. The Emerald Coast. Who could resist that?"

That was one of the reasons he'd chosen this man to be his partner. "You always have something uplifting to say." The hollow sensation in David's stomach remained. So depressing.

They returned to the speakers' table and took their seats.

Alex laid his napkin across his lap. "That was only the first half of the first day." He leaned forward and stared at David with his eyebrows furrowed. "Quit looking at that dessert table. It won't combat discouragement."

David frowned. "Who's discouraged?"

"Since when have you turned up your nose at fried chicken?" Alex's brows rose and he pointed to David's plate. "You've lost your appetite. Eat something and let the problem go for now. No sense getting sick over it. The right person will show up at the right time. Have a little confidence."

He grinned, but the mirth didn't quite reach Alex's eyes.

Three hours later, the partners stood at the elevator in their hotel. Neither had spoken since they left the conference room. David glanced at Alex's stony expression. *He's as depressed as I am.* Just wouldn't admit it.

Alex extended his hand. "I'll take our briefcases up to my room. Why don't you find us a good table for dinner? We can eat early and then mill around latecomers to the conference as they arrive and check in this evening."

"Sounds good."

As Alex stepped into the elevator, David turned and headed for the far side of the hotel. When he pulled open the gilt-edged plate glass door of the restaurant, the tantalizing smell of steak and onions greeted him. *Mmm.* He should have no trouble eating now.

A maître d' led him to a table halfway across the room. David breathed in the heavenly aroma and lowered himself into a high-backed, tapestry-covered chair. To his right, he had a full view of the lobby through wide, beveled-glass windows on either side of the restaurant's entrance. On the opposite side of the room, a wall of windows looked out on an outside artificial tidal pool and waterfall, surrounded by lush foliage. Beautiful. What a tranquil scene. His neck muscles relaxed.

He continued to scan the elegant dining room. Crystal chandeliers, pristine white tablecloths, sparkling vases filled with fresh red carnations in the center of each table. Large parlor palms in giant pots gave a tropical atmosphere to the room.

David glanced across the lobby at the registration desk, busy with several men and women in line to get their rooms. Could one of them be their new doctor?

His gaze turned back to the pool where a guest dove into the water. Hope more attendees show up. He pulled his mouth to one side.

A young woman in a pink bikini emerged from the far end of the pool and mounted the diving board. Her perfectly executed jackknife dive parted the water with scarcely a splash. She swam with long, graceful strokes in front of the falls and into a wide channel that appeared to flow around the lifelike rock formation at the other end of the pool.

*Wow!* David closed his mouth, and then searched the room. Had anyone seen him gaping? He could imagine his wife's comment, had she been there. A snicker escaped him. It had been like watching a movie with that famous female swimmer from long ago. What was her name? Esther...something. Dad loved to watch her. Until Mom thumped him on the head. David snickered again.

From behind him a deep voice said, "Boy, do I remember that look."

David's head snapped back to the lobby side of the restaurant. A well-built young man with wavy, dark brown hair and bright green eyes stood next to his table. He wore an exaggerated frown, muscular arms folded across his chest. The frown morphed into a big grin.

As David leaped to his feet, his chair teetered. He caught it before it fell backward. "Jacob. Jacob McLeod. You are a sight for sore eyes." David extended his hand to the newcomer. "Where did you come from?" He stepped back. "What, thirty-one years old now and still looking as young as you did in school? It's not fair, I tell you."

Jacob laughed and shook the outstretched hand. "Good evening, Doctor Hartley."

David motioned for him to sit at the table. "Are you here for the conference? I didn't see you at my lecture. Sit down. Sit down. My partner will be here in the blink of an eye, and you can meet him. So, tell me—" David pursed his lips. "I haven't let you get a word in, have I?"

Jacob chuckled. "It's great to see you too. I just arrived for the conference. Sorry I missed your lecture. I couldn't get away from work."

He took a seat to David's right. "While I stood in line to register, I peeked in here and saw you watching the scantily dressed diver out by the pool." Jacob grinned and waggled his brows. "What would Mrs. Hartley say?"

"Never mind what she'd say. You know what she'd have done. My head still hurts from the last time she smacked me." He chuckled. "But don't worry about the lecture. You've heard it before. Shame you didn't catch Alex's talk on preventing diabetes though. Here for credits or just bumming?"

"Credits. If I didn't need them, my boss might not have freed up my weekend from rounds at the hospital."

"Glad you came." How he'd missed Jacob's pleasant, deep voice. It had been far too long since they'd spoken on the phone.

"Jacob, my boy, we haven't seen each other since you graduated from medical school. You sure have filled out."

"Exercise and weightlifting helps me stay fit, and it keeps my mind off things." Jacob grimaced. "It's been way too long since we last talked. Time slips away."

David nodded. "Time sure does fly." He'd been Jacob's teacher and counselor through medical school, knew all about Jacob's past, and his desire to forget. They'd been close through the years. He'd always thought of Jacob like a son. Something troubled the boy.

A blond curly-headed waiter drew near the table. David pulled his eyes away from Jacob and glanced up. "Someone else will join us. We'll order then."

The server nodded and left.

Jacob picked up the menu and perused it. "You haven't changed a bit either, sir. How are you?"

"Oh, I've been doing fine. Fair to middlin'. Overworked and underpaid." He guffawed and picked up his own menu. "And my partner has me on a diet because of my heart and high cholesterol. Other than that, I'm hunky-dory."

A flicker of concern crossed Jacob's face. He laid the menu on the table. "Nothing serious, I hope."

David shook his head and smiled. "Not really."

"Good. While I'm here, will you spare some time for me, like you did back in school? I plan to...ahem...pick your brain, as you phrased it so often in class."

David's heart warmed. Couldn't be fonder of this boy if he tried. "You can have as much of my time, and brain, as I can spare. So, how's that new job you wrote about? No longer new, is it? Fill me in while we wait for Alex."

Jacob gave a quick history of the last few months in his career. "This clinic looked to be the perfect place to work when I took the job. But lately, it's become a disappointment."

David placed an elbow on the table and rested his chin on his hand. "Really? And what happened with the practice before this one? I don't recall what made you want to find another position."

"I don't think I ever explained it to you, sir. But I'll save that story for another time, if you don't mind. My problem now is...well, the management runs the place like an assembly line. Overbooking is encouraged. My boss says it makes up for cancelled appointments, but I find it downright scary. It leaves no time to spend with the patient."

David pinched his lips together. Jacob's first concern had always been for the patient.

Jacob continued, "Most of our patients are poor and can't afford to go elsewhere. On top of everything else, yesterday I overheard a rumor of an investigation. It didn't sound good."

While he listened, a light-heartedness filled David's chest. Could Jacob be the man they'd been looking for?

Heat rose in Jacob's neck as he spoke of his concern for the patients at the Minnesota clinic. "Sorry, Doc. I didn't mean to dump on you."

"Glad to hear you call me 'Doc'. I've missed that. We've become too formal when we address each other on the phone."

Jacob chuckled. "Well, I'm not a student anymore. I've learned some manners."

"But I always liked it. As if you were calling me Dad. Don't go all politically correct on me, okay? And your manners are fine."

It warmed Jacob's heart to know this dear man had such fond thoughts of him. More than his own father ever had. He raised his hands in surrender. "Okay, Doc it is."

"Good. Now continue. I don't see it as dumping at all. Seems like you need to get this off your chest, son."

Jacob smiled. Dr. Hartley still thought of him as son. He *did* need to get this off his mind. "It's frustrating. I need to move on, but I've been there for just under a year and wasn't at the other practice long before I found this position. Wish I'd never taken this job now...but I was in a hurry for a change because—" Doc didn't need to know that part. "Anyway, I'll have to tough it out for a while, or prospective employers will think of me as a risk. Who knows, things might change."

Dr. Hartley's face was unreadable. He said nothing after that last statement. Maybe Doc thought he'd grown into a complainer.

A tall, wiry, middle-aged man with salt-and-pepper hair stepped up to the table.

Dr. Hartley stood and slapped the man on the bicep. "Alex, meet Jacob McLeod, my former student. You remember me telling you about him, don't you? Top of the class. Best student I ever had." He turned to Jacob. "This is my partner, Doctor Alex Griffin."

As Jacob stood, the man held out his hand. "Of course. David mentions you often. It's good to finally meet you." He glanced at Dr. Hartley and winked.

Jacob furrowed his brows. What was that about? "Doctor Hartley's mentioned your name to me a few times too."

"So, has David given you the details?"

"Details?" Jacob's head tipped to the side, and his gaze traveled from Dr. Griffin to Dr. Hartley.

His mentor laughed. "No, I haven't asked yet. Jacob has been bringing me up to date on his current job while we waited for you to come downstairs."

"Oh. Sorry. I assumed." The smile dissipated.

The men sat, and Jacob turned to Dr. Hartley. "Details of what? Asked about what?"

Dr. Griffin's eyes rounded. Then he held out his hand toward his partner as if introducing an act on stage.

One side of Jacob's mouth rose. "What's going on? Is this a private joke? Doc?"

"No joke at all, son. We need a third doctor at our clinic."

The smile returned to Dr. Griffin's face. "Would you be interested?"

Prickles danced across the back of Jacob's neck in his excitement. Had the man been kidding? He'd get a chance to work with Dr. Hartley, his mentor, whom he had idolized for years. *YES!* And Dr. Griffin. Doc wouldn't have a partner any less his equal.

Before Jacob could answer aloud, Dr. Hartley spoke. "We have a good practice in Pensacola, and it's growing fast. Alex and I need help. Patients are coming out of the woodwork. More than the two of us and one PA can handle. You're exactly the man we need."

Jacob's pulse throbbed. He opened his mouth but couldn't get a word out.

Dr. Griffin tilted his head. "I know it's a big step. Don't answer right now. We'll tell you more about the position and our practice while we eat dinner."

Jacob looked from one side of the table to the other. Would he really be the right man for the job? "I'm a small-town doctor and nowhere near as knowledgeable as either of you. Are you sure you don't want someone more experienced?" He turned to focus on his mentor. "You don't think I'm a troublemaker and complainer after the comments I made about my current position?"

A smile spread across Dr. Griffin's face. "I like your humble attitude."

Dr. Hartley's hand slapped the table. "What do you mean? You were the smartest student in school. And surely you wouldn't be hinting that we're snobs who wouldn't give a young lad a break because he got hooked up with a bunch of money-hungry Yankees, would you?"

There it was. Doc's strange sense of humor that had cheered him during the hardest days in med school. "No, sir." Jacob struggled to keep from shouting for joy.

The curly-haired waiter returned to the table as the three doctors laughed.

Dr. Hartley handed his menu to the young man. "I'll have the steak and onions and an order of fries." Doc glanced at his partner, who stared wide-eyed. "Ahhh...make that a serving of green beans instead of the fries."

The waiter turned to Dr. Griffin, who chuckled. "Give me his fries with my steak and onions. David, you can have a couple of them, if you're nice." He snickered under his breath.

With a grin, the waiter relieved Dr. Griffin of his menu and then stepped over to Jacob, who peered up with a forced straight face. "Make it three on the steak and onions, but I'll have a baked potato."

A groan sounded to Jacob's left, and he stifled a laugh.

While they waited for their food, Dr. Hartley told Jacob the history of the practice. After their food arrived, Dr. Griffin added a few anecdotes to the conversation.

Dr. Hartley leaned back in his chair and put his hands on his stomach. "Wow, that was good. How about dessert?"

His partner gave him a narrow-eyed stare. "David, you're pushing it. But okay. A small dish of ice cream, and I'll look the other way." He grimaced.

During dessert, Dr. Griffin explained the benefits package.

Between bites of blueberry pie, Jacob asked questions. He savored the last morsel and set down his fork. "Everything sounds great."

As Dr. Griffin laid his napkin on the dessert plate, still half-full of chocolate cake, he disclosed the salary and then faced Jacob with upturned brows. "So, what do you think? Would you be interested in the position?"

"You're kidding, right?" Jacob glanced at Dr. Hartley. "This man taught me almost everything I know about medicine. And I'm sure I'll learn more from both of you." Jacob laughed. "When do I start?"

Both doctors thumped Jacob on the back.

Dr. Hartley slapped his hand on the table again. "Jacob, you start as soon as you can get yourself to Pensacola."

Jacob gestured thumbs-up. He couldn't wait to get back to Minnesota. "I'll have to give proper notice to my present employer."

"Of course you will, my boy. I'd be disappointed in you if you didn't."

"In the meantime—" Dr. Griffin looked around his chair as if trying to find something he lost. "Oh yeah. I took the briefcases upstairs. I guess I'm more tired than I thought. The applications are in my case."

Lifting his coffee cup in a toast, Dr. Hartley grinned at him. "I believe we'll be getting more rest shortly, my friend."

Dr. Griffin lifted his own cup and tapped his partner's. "Jacob, if you'll follow us upstairs to my room, I'll give you the paperwork to fill out. You can work on it this weekend at your leisure. Just a formality, but we need it before we leave on Sunday night. Do you have your CV with you?"

"I'll download it from my laptop and get it printed before the conference is over this weekend."

Dr. Hartley waved the notion away. "Don't print it. Just email it to my office. I'll have our office manager make a file for you."

"Great! Can't wait to pack." He'd start the minute he got back to Minnesota. That part of his life was almost over...for good.

Dr. Hartley peered at Jacob as if he were wearing his reading glasses. "I feel like I've rushed you into this. Are you sure you don't want to think it over for a while? You know from our past I can be a taskmaster." He stuck his tongue in his cheek. "Don't be hasty."

"Doc, you sounded just like that talking tree from The Lord of the Rings movie." He chuckled.

Shaking his head, Dr. Griffin joined the laughter. "He did, didn't he? Besides his clichés, you'll get a steady barrage of quotes from those movies...all day...every day." He turned to Jacob. "This will be a big change from your life in Minnesota."

He could handle any change that allowed him to leave the horrible conditions at his current job and Patricia. "I've learned to live with many changes in my life, sir."

"Welcome aboard, son." Dr. Hartley's grin couldn't have gotten any bigger. He rose from the table and held out his hand. "I think you'll love Pensacola. And you'll be pleased with our staff, too."

As Jacob grasped his mentor's hand, Patricia's sneering face entered his mind. When he got his first job after residency, his supervisor had told him the same thing. He shuddered. *Things will be different this time.*

## Minnesota

On Monday morning, Jacob strode into the Marble Lake Pain Clinic. He couldn't wait to give his two-week notice and escape to Pensacola.

As he stepped into his boss's office, resignation in hand, a pang of guilt hit him. What about the needy patients he cared for? What would happen to them now? He'd have to convince Dr. Bentley of the drastic need for change.

"Welcome back, Jacob. Did you get those credits you went after at the conference?"

"I did, sir." He handed his letter of resignation to his boss. "This is sudden, but I hope I've explained everything."

Dr. Bentley accepted the letter and read as Jacob took the seat in front of his desk.

His boss peered up at him from the page. "It's a rare thing to have the opportunity to work with a man who taught you medicine. I envy you. We hate to see you go. You've been an asset here."

"Thank you, but there's something else I'd like to talk about." Jacob looked straight into his boss's eyes.

"What's that?"

Jacob folded his hands and took a deep breath. "Before I leave, I need to emphasize the seriousness of the lack of patient care I've seen. Did your secretary give you the list I handed her before I left for the weekend?"

Dr. Bentley nodded. "I read the report you submitted. And I agree."

Relief filled Jacob's body.

His boss continued, "I appreciate you taking this initiative. I plan to hold a meeting with the staff this afternoon to discuss patient complaints. I'd already noticed the problems. My only excuse is procrastination. It was wrong of me. Things have to change. Things *will* change."

Jacob smiled.

"I wish you had come to me earlier. If you had, I might not be losing one of my best doctors. The frustration I saw in your eyes before you left for the conference made me take a hard look at things." He frowned.

When his boss rose, Jacob stood.

Dr. Bentley thrust his hand out to Jacob. "I wish you the best in your new position and home." But if things don't work out there, we'll always have a place for you here.

At the end of the following Monday, a new doctor right out of residency followed Jacob into an examining room. Jeff seemed like a fast learner. He might be ready to take over the schedule by Wednesday, under observation.

When Wednesday came, Jacob felt excitement growing as he thought about leaving Minnesota that coming Friday. Jeff had handled everything by himself, instructing the nurses what he wanted done, not needing any assistance. The young doctor would be doing his own physical exams the next day. What a relief.

That night, with a smile plastered on his lips, Jacob left the clinic and pulled his Austin Healey roadster into a parking place at his apartment. He locked the car and strode to the front door. He'd already given his landlord notice. Come Saturday morning, he'd fly to Pensacola.

That night he had the best sleep he'd had in months. The alarm went off in the morning, and he dressed for his next-to-last-day at the clinic.

When he entered the building and walked into the lab, a nurse approached him. "Doctor Bentley wants to see you in his office."

Jacob dropped his jacket off on his desk chair, headed down the hall, and entered his boss's office. One look at the man's clenched jaw sent a dark cloud over Jacob's thoughts. "You wanted to see me, sir?"

"Our new doctor will be out for at least the rest of this week. Got a call from the ER early this morning. He started vomiting late last night and couldn't stop. He has an infection and was ordered to bed. I'm hoping no one else here comes down with it, much less one of our patients."

The bottom fell out of Jacob's stomach. "I'm sorry to hear that. But if it's any consolation, Jeff hadn't touched any patients. The nurses did everything as he instructed. Today would have been his first physical exam. Plus, he used the hand sanitizer before we entered each room."

His boss nodded and offered a faint smile that morphed into a grimace. "Jacob, I know you planned to leave this weekend. Under the circumstances, is there any way you can hang on until we're better staffed?"

# *Chapter Ten*

*J*acob's muscles tightened like a drum as he explained the situation at his current job to Dr. Hartley on the phone. "I know this doesn't help your situation at all, but I'm afraid I can't leave them shorthanded. Besides the sick trainee, one of the doctors is still on his honeymoon. A nurse on vacation last week had a personal emergency come up and won't be back for another week, and another nurse wound up in the hospital last weekend with pneumonia. It's been nothing short of pandemonium here." Jacob gulped in a breath. "I can't leave this weekend."

"Of course, you can't. I understand. Just tells me even more you're the right man for our practice."

Jacob sighed.

"Don't worry about a thing, my boy. I wouldn't expect you to run out on them. Just call me as soon as you have a date when you can leave. I'll let Doctor Griffin know and advise the rest of the staff."

"Thank you, sir. I anticipate an extra week. Hopefully, I'll leave Minnesota by then, but I'll know more by next Monday." He hoped it wouldn't be longer than that. He was ready for a new life.

It'd be a welcome change of pace to work in a place where clinical and clerical got along so well, as Dr. Hartley had described his practice.

As David laid the phone on his desk, he rose and then strode into his partner's office. "Have to admire the boy for his loyalty. That clinic will miss Jacob when he leaves. He'll be an asset to this practice, Alex. I feel it in my bones. Someone we can count on. He has a real heart for patients."

Alex nodded. "Couldn't help but overhear the conversation with both our doors open. He'll work out fine."

"Well, I'd better tell Kathy about Jacob's delay in plans. What a joy it'll be to have two such dedicated young people working here."

David left his partner's office and meandered through the hall to Kathy's office. He stepped inside and leaned against the open door behind her as she worked on the computer. "Ahem."

She jumped and spun in the chair to face him. "Doctor Hartley. You startled me."

"Not surprised, the way you were focused on that screen. Maybe you should turn your desk so it faces the hall instead of the side wall."

Kathy gave him a sweet smile. "I had the desk temporarily moved this way to avoid the distraction of traffic past my door to the file room. Better for concentration."

"Oh, okay, I can understand that." David rounded the desk and lowered himself into a chair in front of her. "Just thought I'd let you know Jacob's been delayed due to staffing problems at the Minnesota clinic. He thinks it'll be another week before he gets here. Will that be a problem with the accommodations you've made for him, or the car?"

"There shouldn't be any problem with the car. And I haven't found a place for him to stay yet. A decent apartment with a short-term lease is proving hard to find. This weekend I'll find something, for sure. I still have several ideas. If worse comes to worst, I'll set him up in a nice hotel."

"Splendid. My wife and I planned to have him stay with us until we remembered how much he likes his privacy." David shifted in the chair, rested one elbow on the arm and leaned his cheek against his fist. "Since he's flying in, Jacob will need that rental car until he can arrange for his own to be transported here."

Kathy nodded and grinned. "That should make the car rental agency happy."

"Right." He chuckled. "Then there's all that...oh, you know...those practical things you do for visiting doctors. Maps and what-have-you. Are we asking too much? Don't want any straws breaking our camel's back."

"Thanks for the analogy, but this camel will be fine." Kathy laughed.

As he leaned back and relaxed, he stretched out his legs. He could count on her. She'd handle everything from hotel room and rental car, to local maps and restaurant suggestions. Most efficient office manager he'd ever had.

Kathy folded her hands on the desk. "The only difference in these arrangements will be that they're longer-term."

He sat upright. "Kathy, I should tell you a little more about Jacob." He got up and closed the door to her office, then sat again and leaned back.

"I've known him for a long time. When he attended medical school, I made it my business to find out what troubled him. He's had a hard life thanks to a hard father, whom he rarely speaks of."

Kathy placed her elbows on the desk and crossed her arms. A look of concern filled her violet eyes.

"After I learned of his history, my wife and I sort of adopted Jacob as part of our family. I became more than just his advisor and teacher. Almost a surrogate father." He tugged one side of his mouth upward along with his shoulders. "Jacob was an outstanding student. Smart as a whip. But sad, like he had a broken heart."

Kathy bit the right side of her lower lip.

David leaned forward. "This is between you and me. In confidence."

"Of course, Doctor Hartley."

He sat back again. "One day, Jacob disclosed the entire story to me. You see, when he was only sixteen, his mother died. Her letters to him at boarding school had stopped, and he had no idea why. When he tried to reach his father to ask what was wrong, the man wouldn't take Jacob's calls. He got in touch with the housekeeper, who told him his mother had been ill for weeks and passed away. The housekeeper assumed Jacob knew."

As she gasped, Kathryn's mouth dropped open. "That's terrible. How could he not tell his son that his mother was ill, much less that she died? That's cruel."

"He was a cruel man. A selfish one at that. Although, I only heard Jacob's side, I trust it was the truth. He kept everything bottled up inside all those years, but he finally needed to tell someone."

As Kathy shook her head, her eyes glistened with tears. "Did his father have something to do with her death?"

David leaned forward. "When I spoke with a colleague in Minneapolis, who treated her back then, there was nothing suspicious about her death. Later, he told me he believed Jacob's mother died of a broken heart. He attributed to her decline in health to that. Jacob said she tried to please his father all their married life, but never could."

How he hated to tell Kathy such a horrible story. But it would help her understand Jacob better. "Jacob's father physically and mentally abused both his wife and son but took care that no one found out. McLeod no doubt made threats to keep his wife from reporting the abuse.

"Jacob tried to stand up to him, but his father sent him away to military school. At thirteen. All the man ever wanted was an heir to his fortune.

"Holidays and summer breaks were the only times Jacob was allowed home. He wasn't sure what his mother went through while he was away. Mrs. McLeod always assured her son everything was fine. When Jacob did come home, his father would stay out until late at night, then come home drunk and smelling of perfume."

David fisted his hands in front of his chest. "Some of the things Jacob told me, things he and his mother had endured, made me want to beat the daylights out of the man. It broke my heart." David ground his teeth. How much should he say? This was so hard.

Kathy put her hand to her heart. Tears edged her eyes.

"Jacob said it was because of his mother's death he became a doctor. He hoped he could someday save the life of someone else's mother, since he hadn't been able to help his own."

A tear slid onto Kathy's cheek. She grabbed a tissue from the corner of the desk.

"Kathy, I'm telling you all this because Jacob has had a problem with women in authority ever since his father remarried, which he did much too soon after his wife's passing. He married a domineering woman only nine years older than the boy.

"When I offered Jacob this job, I didn't think about you being the female in charge of the office." He pursed his lips.

"But I wouldn't be in charge of Doctor McLeod."

"No, but you'll have to work together on the daily paperwork until he's acclimated to our office procedures. So, you need to be aware of his background in case he has a problem with your telling him what to do."

"Okay." She sucked in her lower lip.

This was a lot for a young woman to take in. David rubbed his temple. Had Jacob gotten past those issues?

"But you said Doctor McLeod is a caring person."

"Yes, he is. Still, the wounds go deep. Jacob's stepmother was critical and found delight in ordering him around. His father let her. When I met Jacob, he had a hard time relating to any woman. Never even talked about dating a girl." He smiled at Kathy. "But I know you can handle any abruptness he might show."

Kathy's brows wrinkled, and she bit her lip again.

"Despite everything, Jacob is a gentleman and very charming—once you get to know him."

David stood and grabbed the doorknob. He glanced at Kathy. She'd manage. He had every confidence in her. "Jacob is...different."

Kathy gazed up at him. "What do you mean? His likes and dislikes? What?"

"Well...Jacob doesn't smile a lot. But when he does, it lights up the room." He gave her his best toothy, Cheshire cat grin.

She laughed. "Well, that smile would light up a closet maybe."

"Okay, smarty." He chuckled. "Jacob is secretive. Doesn't appreciate people knowing his business."

"That's no different from me."

"That's why I trust you with this information. I wanted to make sure you understand where the man is coming from."

He stepped through the doorframe, and then turned. "And, for heaven's sake, don't let the cat out of the bag that I've told you any of this."

With a frown, Kathy cocked her head. She stood and placed her hands on her hips.

David drew in a deep breath and then let it out. "Okay. I'm telling tales out of school. Makes me uncomfortable."

"Don't worry, Doctor Hartley. I'll be discreet. And I appreciate you telling me."

"Good girl. You'll see. He is the best there is, and we're very fortunate to get him. I'd even say he's a Godsend."

As he strode back down the hall to his own office, David let out another huge breath of air. She'd handle Jacob just fine.

"Doctor Hartley, you never answered—" Gone. Kathryn sat down and reclined in the chair. The rascal never really answered her question. What could he have meant by different? What would the new doctor look like?

She had slipped the emailed copy of his CV into an envelope with the application Dr. Griffin had brought from the conference, and left them on his desk without reading either. Dr. McLeod was her boss's friend. She hadn't felt the need to read them. Was there a picture with the application? She'd check when the envelope came back to her desk to file. Although, she could get them now.

No. Snooping had never been a part of her nature. She'd keep it that way. When Dr. McLeod arrived, she'd meet him in person.

Aside from the fact that he was a bachelor, he'd been her boss's student in medical school, and had a terrible family history— according to what she'd just heard—she knew little. Probably late thirties, maybe even forties. It had to be a long time since he was a student.

Kathryn rested an elbow on her desk and cradled her chin in her hand. Was he tall, short, dark-haired, blond, husky or skinny? Curiosity killed the cat. She chuckled. Now she sounded like Dr. Hartley. Any friend of her boss had to be a great guy.

She resumed searching online for the information Dr. Griffin had asked for. *Wait a minute.* She laughed. What did Dr. Hartley mean by "He's different"? Nope. She would not hound her boss for an answer.

It's only another week or so.

# Chapter Eleven

*J*ust before midnight, Kathryn woke with a start and trembled. Sheila whimpered.

"It's okay, girl. I'm awake now."

The dog snuggled its head against her arm.

"That was a horrible nightmare. The worst ever. I need a cup of herbal tea to relax before I try to sleep again."

Kathryn swung her legs over the edge of the bed and slipped into her robe. Sheila jumped down to the floor and followed her into the kitchen.

As Kathryn took her steaming mug from the microwave and put a teabag in the hot water, the dog gazed up at her with a cocked head. "Yip?"

"You want to know what happened, don't you?"

Sheila's tail wagged.

"Wish I knew, girl. It was a weird dream. I had no idea where I was, but I kept calling out for someone. Everything was dark. I was lying on something cold and hard. A haze surrounded me." Kathryn shuddered.

She retrieved the milk from the refrigerator. "A dark figure came toward me. I tried to run but couldn't move. Then I screamed, but no sound came out. I think I was in pain."

Kathryn slumped into the kitchen chair and dipped her teabag until the water turned dark. She added milk. "The figure had no features. I kept praying for someone to help me."

Tears dropped from her eyes to the table. She rose and tore off a paper towel to wipe her face. Her heart raced as she sat back down.

Sheila put a paw on Kathryn's knee and whined.

She scratched the dog's ear. "Whoever it was crept closer. A man's voice said, 'I've got you now. You won't get away.' His laugh...sinister."

When Kathryn finished her tea, she placed the mug in the sink and returned to the bedroom. Sheila hopped onto the bed.

After slipping under the sheet, she turned off the light. "I sure hope I can get back to sleep...with no more dreams." She lowered her head to the pillow. Her eyes fluttered shut.

"No! Stop!"

*Beep, beep, beep.*

Kathryn lurched to one side of the bed. "Oh no." Another nightmare. She'd almost knocked poor Sheila off the bed...again.

*Beep, beep, beep.*

She reached over and turned off the alarm.

The little dog scrambled into her arms and licked her cheek.

"Sorry, girl. I have no control over these dreams. You're not hurt, are you?"

With her tail wagging, Sheila bounced to the edge of the bed.

"I understand. You're okay, but you need to go out."

Kathryn wiped the tears from her face with her sleep shirt, slipped her feet into scuffs, and rose from the bed. "I'm still not sure what that dream was about, but I'm glad it's over. What a way to start the day."

In her closet, she slipped on a pair of jeans and tucked her nightshirt inside. Sheila bounded off the bed.

They headed downstairs. If these nightmares didn't stop, she'd be too tired by the weekend to get everything done. She had such a long list.

Wish she could figure out what was happening. Why the nightmares had started again?

Saturday morning, Sheila pranced into the bedroom, leash hanging from her mouth and trailing behind. Kathryn flipped a T-shirt over her head and pulled on a pair of jeans. "Thank you, girl. Such a smart cookie." She attached the leash, slipped into a pair of gym shoes, and followed as the dog led the way downstairs for their morning walk.

"Well, Sheila, I got to sleep through last night with no nightmare. Bet you're happy, aren't you?"

"Yip."

After rounding the corner of the first block, Kathryn broke into an easy jog. Sheila kept pace.

An hour later, they returned to the apartment. "This morning, I'm ready to tackle the day."

As Kathryn ate breakfast, she wrote a list of tasks. So many things to do. The cleaning would have to wait. She sighed and picked up her cell. "But this message from Beth can't."

Sheila looked up from her dish of kibble next to the table. She cocked her head to one side.

Kathryn laid the phone on the table then bent and stroked the dog's back. "You haven't met Beth yet, but when you do, you'll understand. She's my adopted sister and has fancied herself in charge of me from the moment Chris and I went to live with her and her parents." As she straightened in her chair, her eyes moistened. "The Parkers were my parents' best friends." A tightness gripped her heart.

She blinked away the tears. "Beth must have called while we were out jogging."

Sheila went back to crunching her food.

After placing her dishes in the sink, Kathryn sat back in the chair and leaned toward Sheila. "Don't suppose you'd call Beth for me." The dog sneezed.

"That's what I thought." She laughed. "The message said they've extended their stay in California." She could imagine Beth and her honey of a fiancé stretched out on the sand behind his parents' cliff-side home.

A pang of loneliness pierced Kathryn and she swallowed the lump in her throat. No pity party today. Too much to take care of. Besides, how could she be lonely? She had Sheila.

The dog hopped up on her hind legs and rested her front paws on Kathryn's knees.

"We're a team, aren't we?" She bent forward and received a lick on her nose. She chuckled. Where had this emptiness come from? Get busy. The moodiness would pass.

She picked up her cell and pressed the speed dial number.

"Kathy. It's about time you called me back."

"We were out for a jog, and then I had breakfast. What's the urgency?"

"No urgency. Just wanted to make sure you got my message. That's all."

"Really? Okay. I have a ton of things to do today, so I can't talk long. Let me call you back tonight after dinner. Then you can tell me everything about your trip. Do you mind?"

"No. Go on. Don't forget to call me though."

As she disconnected the call, Kathryn shook her head. She'd better take care of Dr. McLeod's accommodations first. She wanted to have everything arranged for the new doctor before Monday morning. Her bosses counted on her.

The car rental agency already had a vehicle reserved. But she needed to find a suitable place for him to live until he could make his own arrangements. Kathryn rested her elbows on the table and dropped her chin into cupped hands.

Several nice hotels and motels were in the area. That wouldn't do. Too impersonal. Dr. Hartley said his friend liked privacy. There wouldn't be much of that in a hotel. Plus, she had to consider the practice's budget.

"There must be an apartment somewhere that will take short-term occupants."

An idea flashed in her mind. Maybe Pastor or Mrs. Marshall would have some ideas. The pastor's wife arranged for visiting preachers and missionaries who came home on furlough.

Kathryn phoned the parsonage.

"Roman's Road Baptist Church. Mrs. Marshall speaking."

"Good morning, Mrs. Marshall. It's Kathryn."

"Good morning. What makes you call this early on your day off?"

"I need to find short-term housing for the new doctor my office hired. Would you or Pastor have any ideas?"

"Hold on while I tell him you're on the phone, dear. We'll both get on so we can discuss it."

After a couple of minutes, shuffling and clicking sounds came through the receiver. Pastor Marshall's baritone voice came on the line. "Good morning, Kathy. My wife said you needed advice. But before I could ask her what it was about, she had a brainstorm."

A spike of adrenaline flowed through Kathryn.

"For a few months now, the two homes that the church owns and uses for visiting missionaries and evangelists have been sitting unoccupied. I'm looking at our calendar, and we have no missionaries coming off the field, nor meetings scheduled for several months."

Mrs. Marshall added, "It would work out well for both your new doctor and our church budget to rent out one house. We've talked about renovations in both. Work could start on one house while the doctor stays in the other."

Kathryn let her head fall back and blew out her relief. "Praise God. That's perfect."

Pastor Marshall chuckled. "So, when will he need the house, and for how long?"

"We think he'll arrive a week from this Monday, but we're not positive yet. And I'm not sure how long he'd need a place until he finds his own."

A scratching noise came through the phone. Then the pastor mumbled, "Making a note here. We won't worry about the length of time. I'm sure everything will work out."

Mrs. Marshall broke in again. "Do you have time to go with me to look at the houses this morning? You can decide which would suit your doctor's needs better. I'll call the couple who takes care of them and make sure everything is ready for a visitor. Then I can pick you up."

"That'll be great. The new hire is a friend of Doctor Hartley, and I'm sure he's just as easy to please, but I should check the houses, so I can tell my boss about them."

"Okay, I'll leave in a few minutes."

"I'll be ready when you get here. Bye." Kathryn ended the connection.

What a relief. They always had an answer for her when she had a problem. Unless it involved their nephew, Nick.

After she slipped into the passenger seat of Mrs. Marshall's car, Kathryn pulled out a pad of paper from her purse. She jotted notes as the older woman described each missionary home.

As they drove through the quaint area, Kathryn smiled. "Visiting this part of Pensacola is like travelling back in time. I can't believe the church owns two houses here."

"It's been a blessing, dear. Former members, who had no children to pass them on to when they died, left both to the church. The houses are within a few blocks of each other."

Mrs. Marshall parked the car outside a two-story Victorian home on a corner. They got out and walked up to the front yard.

"How many bedrooms does this one have? It looks awfully big."

The pastor's wife opened the gate. "It is large. I take it your new doctor is single."

"He is." Kathryn walked through.

Mrs. Marshall led her up the front porch steps. "The house has four bedrooms. It used to have five, but the former owner remodeled and made two into a master bedroom. It's one of the older houses in town. Built when people had bigger families."

Kathryn smiled. "And the second house, is it the same size?"

"Oh no, much smaller. Besides the missionaries, we sometimes use this house for weddings and receptions. The girls love the Victorian style with its steeple-like roof."

"I can imagine." She wouldn't mind having her wedding reception in a beauty like this. If she ever got married.

While Mrs. Marshall tried to find the correct key for the door, Kathryn surveyed the landscaped front yard. "Is the other house as old and the yard as beautiful as this?"

"Yes, both are old, but solidly built, and each house has modern conveniences. Ah, here it is. You'll have to decide for yourself about the landscaping at the other house, but I love it." She grinned and unlocked the door.

Kathryn stepped through the entrance. What a gorgeous house. Homey touches everywhere. Overstuffed chairs and a couch in warm colors of browns and burgundy cradled forest green throw pillows.

A car roared down the street, screeching as it rounded the corner. Right on a busy corner, and too big. Maybe the other house would be quieter.

She could only dream of living in a house like this someday. "I think this will be too big for Doctor McLeod."

The two women sauntered back to the car.

A few minutes later, Mrs. Marshall pulled up in front of a white-frame, two-story bungalow.

Now this was more like it. Kathryn followed the pastor's wife into a small foyer with silver-gray walls and a dark wooden floor. From there, she could see the living room where the color scheme continued. Royal blue drapes framed sheers over double windows, which looked out onto the front porch. A square, wooden coffee table sitting on a dark blue rug separated a couch and two Queen Anne chairs in a slightly lighter shade of blue. Tucked away in opposite corners sat two recliners in light blue. The colors had a calming effect. This would suit her taste more than the grand Victorian.

"As you can see, Kathy, the rooms are smaller than those of the first house. Two bedrooms are upstairs."

"What a charming little house." Dr. McLeod didn't need four bedrooms, anyway. Two would suffice. A bedroom and an office.

As they climbed the stairs to the second floor, Mrs. Marshall turned. "Unlike the first home, this house has only one bathroom."

"I'm sure that won't be a problem, and the house is located on a dead-end street. Nice and quiet."

After viewing the bedrooms, decorated in earth tones of beige and greens, the ladies headed back downstairs. Kathryn strolled through the living room, which opened to a dining room with pale green walls. At the other end, she entered an all-white kitchen, complete with white appliances and countertops. "From the inside, you'd never know the house was so old."

Mrs. Marshall grinned. "Now check out the backyard." She opened the sliding glass door.

As Kathryn stepped onto the cedar planks of a covered deck that stretched from one end of the house to the other, her mouth dropped open. Wide wooden-railed stairs led into the yard and met a stepping-stone path, which meandered around either side of a floral island filled with yellow snapdragons. Variegated ivy lined the stones on the outside of the walk. "Oh. I love the stone birdbath in the middle."

She followed the stones across a plush lawn to a small building resembling a miniature antebellum mansion. White pillars and an eye-level balcony overflowing with dark ivy adorned the front. "Wow. What's that?"

Mrs. Marshall giggled. "It must have been a little girl's playhouse at one time. It's now the toolshed."

Kathryn chuckled. "Some toolshed."

Her gaze followed privet hedges that stretched six feet into the air and surrounded the entire yard. "The house and yard are incredible. Forget Doctor McLeod. I want to stay here."

Her pastor's wife burst into laughter.

Kathryn grinned. Complete privacy and a backyard to relax in after a long day. Dr. McLeod would no doubt grace her with one of his light-up-the-room smiles when he saw this.

"I think this one is perfect for our new doctor."

That night, Kathryn called Dr. Hartley to share her excitement over finding a place for Dr. McLeod to live when he arrived. "Do you think you should call him and check before I make the final arrangements? Just in case?"

"That's not necessary. I've always found Jacob to be easygoing. I'm sure he'll be pleased with what you've found. And it's only temporary."

"Okay, if you say so. Now all we need is the doctor."

After they hung up, Kathryn curled up in the armchair to read. Now she could get lost in the novel she'd been trying to finish. Sheila jumped into the chair and snuggled next to her.

"What a great sense of accomplishment. Every task done, girl."

A few chapters later, Kathryn's eyelids drooped. "Time for bed." She rose, tucked the bookmark firmly in place, and placed the book on the end table.

When she entered the closet to change into her nightclothes, her phone rang. "Great! I forgot to call Beth, again." She snatched the cell as it rang a third time. "Hi, Beth. Sorry I didn't call you. It's been a packed day, and I'm exhausted. I was about to get into bed."

"You do sound tired, Kath. Okay. I forgive you. I guess we can have a nice long talk when I get back to Des Plaines. We're leaving tomorrow. I'll call you before bedtime."

The girls said their goodbyes and Kathryn slipped into bed. As she lay listening to the soft sounds of the night, images of her nightmare intruded. "It was just a bad dream."

She forced her eyes closed and fell asleep.

# Chapter Twelve

athryn turned on her computer the following Monday morning as Dr. Hartley hurried into her office. She peered up at him. "You look like a man on a mission."

"You guessed it. I have fantastic news for you."

After placing her purse in the bottom drawer of her desk, she leaned back in the chair and folded her hands. "Must be good news from our new physician to cause such a smile on your face."

"No." He sank into the chair in front of her. "Haven't heard from Jacob. But this will make you happy. Alex and I brainstormed last night about how to bring things up-to-date around here and make life easier for everyone concerned. What do you say to that new electronic records program you mentioned a few months ago?"

She leaned forward. It had been several months since she'd mentioned it. At the time, they decided it wasn't in the budget. "It sounds wonderful. What's changed?"

"I know we didn't sound very gung-ho when you first brought it up, but with the explosion of patients, we discussed it again. We knew the idea had merit."

"That's wonderful."

Her boss chuckled. "Thought you'd say that. However, this will probably increase your workload for a while. You'll have to set up schedules to make sure everyone receives the necessary training. But in the long run, it should cut down on how long you'll have to hold Jacob's hand."

She suppressed a giggle. Odd choice of words. Surely, he didn't plan to match her with the new doctor when they'd never even met. Besides, he'd be too old for her.

Dr. Hartley gave her a cheesy grin. "It'll enable him to take care of his own paperwork, what little remains. And we can pull ourselves into the twenty-first century. We're counting on you to keep both Alex and me in line, like ducks in a row, with this training. And out of trouble."

Kathryn laughed aloud. She never knew what funny phrase would come out of his mouth next. "I'm sorry, Doctor."

He turned his head to the side and looked at her out of the corners of his eyes. "Love to see you smile and laugh." Then he frowned and puckered his lips. "Even if it is at my expense."

She grabbed a tissue from the box on her desk and covered her mouth as she drew in a deep breath. "But you say those things on purpose, don't you?"

He smiled again. "Of course, I do. How else can I get attention? Now, where was I? Oh yes...I'm sure you're much better at learning this electronics stuff, so you can guide us through everything once you're trained."

"I'd be happy to. When do you think we'll have it?"

"Alex and I have just started our research, so it won't happen for a while yet. But I wanted to give you the heads-up."

"Thank you. As far as keeping you and Doctor Griffin in line, you give me far too much credit. With your antics, how could I possibly keep you two out of trouble?"

"Well, if anyone can, you can." He rose, took a stance with hand on hip, and swaggered out of her office like John Wayne. As he cleared the doorway, he glanced at her with a sheepish grin.

Kathryn shook her head. What a character. Soon there'd be three of them.

## Minnesota

As Jacob walked into the lab Monday morning, he said a short prayer of thanksgiving. His schedule for the day was light. Every missing staff member had returned, except for Jeff, the new hire. And Dr. Bentley had decided to take over the new man's final training when he returned from sick leave. What a relief. Now he could finish out the week and make his way to Florida. The good news should please Dr. Hartley.

Despite each patient's genuine expression of sadness at his leaving, Jacob was anxious to get the day over. Only one patient to go and he'd have a good break for lunch.

He entered the examining room where a patient, who had expressed her disappointment in the rest of the staff weeks ago, waited. "Doctor McLeod, I'm so sorry you're leaving. It isn't because of the complaint I made, is it?"

"Not at all. I had an offer to work in Florida that I couldn't refuse. But don't worry about problems in this clinic. Doctor Bentley appreciated that you spoke up. Things have already started to change."

He finished the exam and wrote out a prescription. "Now, you follow those instructions and take care of yourself."

As Jacob left the room, he grinned. Only two more physicals after his lunch break, and he was finished for the day.

He turned the corner and stepped into the lab.

"*Surprise!*"

Dr. Bentley stepped forward and handed an envelope to Jacob. "We wanted you to know how much we'll miss you around here."

He hadn't expected a sendoff. "Thank you, everyone. And cake, too?" A nurse handed him his coffee cup.

For the next several minutes, Jacob stayed busy with handshakes. One by one, the staff members took their pieces of cake back to their workstations.

"Doctor Bentley, I appreciate the gift card." Jacob turned to his co-workers. "And all of you. I've learned a lot here at Marble Lake Pain Clinic." Both good and bad. Still, they were very useful lessons for the future. "Now, if you'll excuse me, I have some calls to make."

He strolled off while the rest of the staff continued to dig into the cake. One senior staff member called after him. "Great speech, McLeod. Short and to the point." Then he chuckled.

Jacob waved him off and strode to the back door.

Outside, he slid into his roadster, put his cake and napkin on the passenger seat, and leaned back to relax for a minute. He needed to call for his ticket. No time like the present. He had everything packed and was ready to leave on the first available flight.

Several minutes later, Jacob sighed with relief. He hadn't expected to get a seat for early Monday morning. Yes. Things were really looking up.

He punched in Dr. Hartley's number on the cell. After a few rings, the call connected.

"Hello, Jacob."

"I have good news, Doc. I'll be arriving next Monday."

"I'm sorry. I didn't catch what you said. Seems we have triplets in the examining room next to my office. Those kids have the loudest sets of lungs I've ever heard."

"I said I'll be able to leave Minnesota after this week. Wow, you aren't kidding about those lungs. I hear them over the phone."

"Those toddlers will bring the roof down on us one of these days. They're in for shots today." Dr. Hartley yelled through the phone as if Jacob were the one having trouble hearing. "But I'm glad you have good news. Got that part."

Jacob spoke distinctly louder. "I made my reservation, and I'll arrive at the Pensacola airport a week from today, Monday morning. Glad I don't have to stay for another week as I feared."

"Got it. That's fine, Jacob. Don't worry about a thing. You can call me when you land. I'll pick you up. Your accommodations are on hold."

"Great. I'll talk to you next Monday morning."

"I'm sorry, Jacob. I have to see if I can help with those toddlers. You take care, and we'll see you when you get here."

The connection ended with a click.

Jacob slipped the cell into its holder on his belt and drove off to find a burger for lunch. Gathering storm clouds overhead threatened rain. They couldn't depress him today. Everything was settled.

After helping the nurse and physician's assistant with the screaming triplets, David headed down the hall to Kathy's office to tell her Jacob's new plans and give his ears a rest. He rubbed his right ear as he entered the room. "Kathy, Jacob won't arrive for another week. He called a few minutes ago. Couldn't understand much of what he said with the kids in the other room yelling at the top of their lungs, but I got the gist of it. It seems he'll have to stay an extra week in Minnesota and arrive here two weeks from today. I told him you had everything on hold."

"That's too bad he has to stay an additional week. Are you sure that's what he said? Those children were so loud, their screams carried all the way down here. Must be the Anderson kids in for their shots. Do you think we could consider one *soundproof* room for the practice?"

David laughed. "You got it. Those kids could be a secret weapon. Just threaten to give the darlings an inoculation and send them into the interrogation room. The enemy would spill the beans." He laughed again. "But yes, I heard him well enough to make out 'leave Minnesota,' umm...the phrases, 'made a reservation, arrive at the airport Monday morning, and stay for another week.' He'll call again next Monday, and I'll make sure of the details then. Jacob will be here when he gets here."

Kathy nodded. "I picked up the extra set of keys for the house. The pastor's wife said they were having it cleaned this week. I'll call Hertz and reschedule the car."

David smiled. "What would we do without you?"

"I don't know, Doctor. I just don't know." Her teasing grin burst into laughter.

As he retraced his steps through the hall to his office, David chuckled. These two young people would get along great. They both had such a desire to help others. Jacob just needed to give Kathy a chance. He'd realize she wasn't the bossy type. If he even had that hang-up about women in authority anymore.

# Chapter Thirteen

Kathryn finished washing out her dinner dishes and stacked them in the drainer on the kitchen sink. With Sheila at her heels, she entered the living room and settled into the armchair. The pooch curled up next to her.

"Ahhh...now to relax and read."

Not more than two pages later, her cell rang. Kathryn jumped up and retrieved it from her purse. "Hey, Beth. I take it you're home."

"Hi. Yep. Home at last."

"I was tempted to call last night when you didn't phone me, but I figured you were tired and went to bed early after that long trip back from California." Kathryn returned to the armchair.

Beth's laughter came through the speaker. "You've got it. I think I need a vacation from the vacation. But the work on my desk was piled to the ceiling this morning when I got in. Sorry I didn't call. I guess I pulled a Kathy on you."

"Well, it's a good thing you love your job." Kathryn chuckled.

"Right. And here's some interesting news about that. The moment I stepped through the door this morning, my boss called me into his office. He's sending me to Florida to set up a new satellite office. Guess where?"

"Florida's a big state. How would I know?"

"I couldn't believe my ears when he said, 'Pensacola.'"

"Seriously? Of all the places to choose, he picked Pensacola?"

"Yeah. Our services are in demand, and Mr. McCarthy decided it was more cost effective to set up a crew in the area than to fly them back and forth."

"That's wonderful, Beth." Kathryn scooched forward in the chair. "When will you get here, and how long will you stay? I'm afraid I've been feeling pretty lonely, even with my little Sheila around. It'll be nice to have you here for a while."

"It'll probably be a couple of weeks before he needs me there, and I'll stay for maybe a week, or until I get a crew hired. One of our secretaries here will be transferred to the new office to be the manager, and she'll set up everything else. He offered it to me but, well, we'll be moving to California after the wedding. I'm not sure exactly when I'll get to Pensacola, but I'll tell you as soon as I know."

Kathryn rose to her feet and meandered to the window overlooking the side yard of the house. Mrs. Weaver came into view with a bouquet of pink azaleas and white roses from her garden. "Can't wait to see you again, Beth."

"Sa-a-ay, how can you be lonely with all those doctors running around? Didn't you tell me there were three or four hospitals in town and at least a couple of colleges? Not to mention the military bases. You need to get out more, sis."

"Really, Beth." She turned, strolled to the bedroom, and fell backward on the bed.

"Then there's Nick. I'll bet you still spend most of your time reading and dreaming of Prince Charming, don't you? You should spend more time dreaming of Nick."

"I do not dream of Prince Charming. I'm not a child." Heat rose in Kathryn's neck. "I don't care to be with strangers, and I find I don't have much in common with the girls I do know. And don't push Nick on me."

"I'm not pushing anyone on you. But you know how he cares for you. He's not the same as most men these days."

Kathryn pressed her lips together for a second and sat up. "No, he isn't. I'm aware of how he feels. But he's like a brother to me. I'd rather he found someone who loves him...the right way."

In her mind, Kathryn could see Beth shake her head as she always did when they disagreed, the ringlets around her pixie face swinging back and forth.

"Everyone expected you to fall in love with Nick from the first day Chris brought him home for Christmas. Mom thought he was perfect for you."

At least Chris had understood how she felt about his college roommate. Kathryn sighed. Wish Chris was here now. He'd make Beth understand.

"Kath, he's such a sweet guy, and he's been in love with you for a long time."

And she'd tried to discourage him since day one. Kathryn bit her lip. Maybe if she refused to respond, Beth would get the hint. Subject closed.

Friday night, Kathryn called Beth. "Any more news on your trip to Pensacola? I'm so excited that you'll be here. It'll be like old times, sharing a bedroom and staying up giggling the night away."

"My itinerary is set. I'll arrive at the airport a week from this Monday. Can't wait to see your new place. Now, do you suppose we could discuss my wedding? I need help with ideas."

"Sure, but what help could I be? I've never planned a wedding. Don't you think Aunt Sandy would be more helpful in this department?"

"I think she'd be great at planning, but Mom has this thing about not taking over. She says she's seen one too many mother who makes her daughter's wedding into her own dream. She'll do whatever I ask of her, but she's not going to tell me *what* to do."

"Sounds like Aunt Sandy." Kathryn laughed. "Okay, I'll try. What are you having trouble with?"

Her adopted sister listed everything already finalized for the big day, which wasn't much. She then rattled off a string of new ideas almost in one breath and then paused to suck in air.

"Those are good ideas, Beth. I love the colors you've chosen. Emerald green and royal purple would be my choice to go with the white too."

"Great! We sure do think alike. Kath...Nick's invited. It'd be nice if the two of you flew into Chicago together."

Kathryn's jaw clamped shut. Beth wouldn't let the topic die. "We can talk more about this when you get here. We'll start a notebook and put our thoughts on paper. Have you picked up a wedding planner yet? Some magazines on weddings? I've seen plenty of them at the bookstore."

"Well. No. I haven't. I'll look into that."

*Good.* Distraction successful. "We've contributed enough ideas to the topic for one night. There'll be plenty of time to work on plans while you're here."

"We have been talking for a long time, haven't we?" Beth giggled. "I sure miss the good ole' days when you and I weren't so busy, and we spent hours chitchatting."

"Hours?" Kathryn chuckled.

"Oh, you know what I mean." Beth giggled again. "Good night, sis. Sweet dreams."

"Good night. Same to you."

Kathryn tucked her phone back into her purse. She hoped Beth's wishes would be prophetic. It'd be nice to get through the night without that horrible nightmare.

*"Now I've got you."*

Kathryn awoke with a start. "Not again. Horrible way to start off Monday."

Sheila bounded to Kathryn's side and licked the tears from her cheek.

"Thank you, girl. Sorry I scared you." She glanced at the clock. Five a.m. She might as well get ready for work. A soak in the tub should ease her nerves.

Maybe she could talk to one of the doctors at work about her nightmares. She'd be so embarrassed to admit her fears. Fears of what, though?

Then again, she could talk to Pastor Marshall. He'd know what to do.

Kathryn blew out an exasperated breath. Sheila cocked her head. "But if I talk to the pastor, he'll ask me if I've been reading my Bible or praying. And I haven't, girl." First thing after work, she'd spend time in the Scriptures and in prayer.

She turned on the water for her bath and let it run while she made the bed. Pastor would be right. She needed to take this problem to the Lord. She hadn't talked to God at all about those stupid nightmares. Would He listen?

As she eased into the tub, she peered out the bathroom's open door. Sheila made a beeline from the bathroom to the bedroom, bounced up on the end of the bed, made her circle routine, and plopped down. Guess the fur baby hadn't gotten enough sleep last night. The nightmares must have caused a lot of tossing and turning. Were they from fatigue and lack of sleep? She had been staying up late.

She rested her head back in the old clawfoot tub. Tension flowed through her limbs and out into the warm water. Her eyelids drooped, and her mind went blank. She jerked upright. "Oops. Better not fall asleep here."

Kathryn finished her bath and slipped into a pair of jeans and T-shirt to take Sheila out.

Back in the apartment, she entered her closet. She gazed at the light green Easter dress she'd worn to the Hartleys'. The dress swayed on the hanger from her finger. "What do you think, Sheila? Too dressy for the office? I sure could use something cheery to wear today. It's the only bright thing I have clean."

From the direction of the bed came the answer, "Yip, yip."

Kathryn lifted a crocheted, white cotton bolero jacket from another hanger. *Perfect.* Just the right touch. She left the closet and rested the outfit on the edge of the bed.

After she dressed, she studied herself in the full-length mirror on the back of her closet door. Her nose wrinkled. White shoes? "Yes."

In the closet, she spotted her sandals with the two-inch heels and multiple white straps. "These will do. Better hurry. A ton of work waits for me at the office."

While Sheila finished her morning kibble, Kathryn ate a quick bowl of cereal and then led her four-legged child out to the yard once more.

Back in the apartment, she gave one final glance at herself in the mirror and dashed out the door.

The late spring sun warmed the skin on her arms. She looked up at the cloudless sky, a deep azure blue, and smiled. Despite her lack of sleep and jangled nerves from the nightmare, this promised to be a great day. No telling what wonderful surprises God might have in store for her.

# Chapter Fourteen

athryn strolled into her office and laid her purse in the bottom desk drawer. She grabbed her mug and took off for the breakroom. The echo of her heels made a hollow sound as she walked on the tiled floor between the tables in the center of the room.

The recurring nightmare flooded her mind. What a horrible, sinister figure she'd conjured. Perhaps after she brewed a pot of coffee and enjoyed a cup in this quiet atmosphere, her nerves would relax. It'd be another half hour before the rest of the staff arrived.

How she loved her early morning solitude. Her quiet time. All alone. No one to bother her. The beginning of the workday always set her mood for the rest of the day.

Early that morning, carrying his duffle bag and briefcase, Jacob approached the cab he'd called from the Pensacola motel. The driver got out and glanced around. "Any luggage?"

Jacob patted his duffle bag. "This is it for now."

The cabbie opened the passenger door, and Jacob got in. It was great the way things had worked out, even if his flight for Monday morning had been canceled. He'd gotten a seat on an earlier flight for late Sunday night.

The driver got in behind the wheel and turned. "Where to, buddy?"

"Scenic Bluffs Family Practice Clinic." He handed the man a sticky note with the address.

As the cab pulled away from the curb, a loud grumble came from Jacob's stomach. "Oooh." Still upset from his snack during the layover in Chicago. Maybe a greasy burger, potato chips, and sugar-laden snack cake hadn't been such a good idea.

If only he could avoid large airports for the rest of his life. Too hard to maneuver through. But he had caught his flight in plenty of time, unlike the connection at Bush International in Houston.

Another gigantic hub. What a place to get lost. If he hadn't rushed through that concourse, he would've missed boarding. Got there just before they closed the doors. Air travel should not be in his future. Too much stress.

The cabbie turned a corner. "First time in Pensacola?"

"Yes. It is."

"Great little town. Born and raised here ma 'self. You'll love the beaches. Be sure you wear sunglasses if you're not used to white sand. Sun blindness, ya know?"

"Thanks for the info." No telling when his luggage would make it to Pensacola. Jacob's jaw clamped tight at the thought of his missing suitcases. Where had they sent them?

He took a deep breath and exhaled. His stomach growled again. He'd eat breakfast later, if his gut felt better.

At least he'd gotten a room at a good motel, and he'd managed a couple hours of sleep. Doc would give him a lecture for not calling, but by the time he reported his missing luggage, it was one in the morning. *Why wake up the doctor at that hour?* Better to surprise him. Jacob stared out the window and smiled. Couldn't wait to see his face when he walked in this early.

The cab pulled into the clinic's front parking lot.

Huh. No cars. Jacob checked his watch. Still early. "Can you drive to the back of the building? I doubt the front doors are open."

The cabbie lowered his brows in a doubtful look.

"It's okay. I'm the new doctor here. My boss is expecting me."

"Okay, buddy." He pulled to the rear lot.

No cars here either. A black Ford Focus pulled in behind the cab and parked. The driver, a tall, slender woman with curly, shoulder-length light brown hair, stepped onto the blacktop. Must be a nurse. Jacob grasped his wallet.

She opened the back-seat door and bent into the vehicle. Sharp creases marked the legs of her immaculate purple scrubs.

Jacob handed the fare and tip to the driver, snatched his duffle bag and briefcase, and got out of the cab. At the entrance to the building, he pulled on the latch, but it didn't open. Of course. Locked. He turned to wait for the nurse.

As she strolled across the lot, she tucked a thermos into a huge shoulder bag. When she reached the portico, she glanced up at Jacob. Her pale pink lips curved into a smile that lit her deep brown eyes. "Good morning. This isn't the patient's door. Are you new?"

Jacob chuckled to himself. Did he look sick? Possibly, as bad as he felt from the trip. "I'm not a patient. Doctor McLeod, the new physician. Would Doctor Hartley be in?"

"Doctor McLeod, yes. Welcome to Pensacola. Everyone has been looking forward to your arrival. We thought it'd be another week. That's what Doctor Hartley told us a few days ago. Did he misunderstand?" She held out her hand to him. "I'm Haley Smith, the PA."

He shook her hand. Oh, joy. A female assistant. "Yes. Guess he didn't hear me. When we spoke on the phone last week, there was a lot of noise in his office. I should have called him this weekend, but I was busy with the move. Is he inside?"

Haley punched in the alarm code and opened the entrance door. She stepped back and allowed Jacob to enter first. Halfway through the hall, she motioned for him to turn into a second corridor, which opened to the lab. At a counter along the rear wall, a picture of a teenage girl, who resembled Haley, sat in the corner. "You can leave your bag and briefcase at my station for now."

"Thanks." He plopped his bag on the desk chair and placed his briefcase next to the picture. Then he turned to face her. "You still haven't told me if Doctor Hartley is here."

"Oh, I'm sorry. As a rule, he comes in just in time for his first patient. He likes his quiet mornings at home. He'll arrive around nine-thirty today. Doctor Griffin's first patient isn't scheduled until ten, so you'll want to see the office manager. There's bound to be paperwork to complete. Come on. I'll head you in the right direction."

He followed Haley into the first hall. "I didn't see any car besides yours in either lot."

"No. You wouldn't have. The manager takes the bus."

"Oh?" Strange. At least this female PA seems pleasant.

She stopped and pointed to the other end of the hall from where they came into the building. "You'll find the office manager in the breakroom. That last door. You can get a cup of coffee there too. It's nice to have you here, Doctor."

He nodded, and Haley returned to the lab. Jacob glanced at the floor. No wonder he didn't hear a sound. Multi-colored carpeted floors, except in the lab area. Nice, quiet work environment.

He turned and headed in the direction Haley had pointed. Why hadn't Doc told him the PA was a woman? No matter, she'd be someone he could work with. No flirty attitude and she had a wedding band on her finger.

Okay, time to see the manager about the paperwork. Hope he wouldn't expect him to fill out too many documents today. He'd fall asleep for sure with a boring task like that.

Jacob's stomach grumbled once more. If they didn't have any food in the lunchroom, he'd need to eat first. There must be a place to get a bagel near here. The manager should know.

He pushed open the door and scanned the room. The only occupant was a girl who stood at the far side next to a watercooler. She hummed in a velvety tone. Long blonde hair fell over one shoulder as she bent her trim frame and watched a coffee pot fill with water from the cooler. Must be the receptionist.

Following the carpet that circled the tables, Jacob approached the girl. Her reflection came into view in a large mirror on the wall behind the cooler. Beautiful face. *Red flag!* Don't even think about it.

He paused inches behind her, mesmerized by the sound of her humming. Something stirred inside him. His jaw tightened, but he couldn't stop his eyes from roaming over her wheat-colored hair, down her figure, to the white, toeless heels on her tiny feet. Then back up again. Heat flowed into his face.

She looked deep in thought. Probably about some guy on her hook and how she could manipulate him into whatever. Stop it. He couldn't know that. Nix on the prejudgment, just because she was pretty. Jetlag and sleep deprivation must have set him on edge.

Once she'd filled the glass decanter, the girl swung around. The pot hit Jacob in the stomach, splashing water onto his suit coat.

"Oh! I beg your pardon. I didn't know anyone was in the building." She smiled at him.

He blew a frustrated breath from between his lips. "Obviously."

Her heart fluttered and chest pounded as Kathryn gazed into sea green eyes with hints of silver reflecting the fluorescent lighting. Had he stepped off the cover of Men's Vogue magazine? His physique...terrific. Her breathing quickened.

Get a grip. She couldn't let herself become attracted to a medical student assigned to the clinic. How unprofessional. His eyes twinkled. He stood so close to her.

As he took a step backward and peered at the droplets of water on his coat, a stray lock of hair fell over his left eyebrow. He finger-combed it away, but the curl slipped back down.

He gazed into her eyes and a tingle ran up her neck and down her arms. She tried to speak. The words wouldn't come. Someone was in the hallway. Pull yourself together. Warmth filled her cheeks and she looked down at the coffee pot. "Um, my apologies. I didn't know anyone was here." Perfect. She'd already said that.

"Obviously." he repeated.

His hand wiped away the drops of water from his jacket and then pushed the persistent curl away.

Kathryn stifled a chuckle. Staunch and proper, except for that lock of hair. Good thing he'd only be working with them for a short while. Dr. Hartley mentioned they had a student for a week, although she was sure it wasn't until next month. Her heart kept up its rapid beat.

"I suppose you had your shower for the day and didn't need another." She smiled. "Again, forgive me for my clumsiness, and let me show you where to put your things." She placed the pot of water on the counter.

The man's well-shaped, dark brown brows furrowed. "Excuse me? Who are you?"

Whoa. Why *that* tone? It was a slight sprinkle of water. No way had it harmed his jacket. Haley said their next med student was a budding young doctor with a chip on his shoulder. Someone she knew in college. "Arrogant and thinks way too highly of himself." No surprise. No doubt he knew just how gorgeous he was, too.

The curl fell again. With his fingers, he pushed it into his thick, wavy mop of dark brown hair. Kathryn restrained another laugh. Why did they get all the self-centered ones? She held out her hand. "I'm Kath—"

Before she could finish, her boss walked in. "Ah, there you are, Jacob."

Her head whipped around to the breakroom entrance.

"One of the staff told me you were here, my boy. Thought you weren't arriving until next week. Things must have turned for the better after your phone call."

Jacob? Doctor McLeod? She drew in a deep breath and dropped her hand as her jaw lowered.

Her boss strode between the tables toward Dr. McLeod.

As a smile formed on the new doctor's face, he met the older doctor in the middle. "Well...they did, sir. It's good to be in Florida."

"I see you've met Kathy, our office manager." Dr. Hartley shook his friend's hand as he held out the other toward her.

She closed her mouth.

The handsome new doctor glanced at her, his brows pinched together even more. "Manager." He focused his attention on Dr. Hartley. "No. Actually, I haven't. Just her coffee pot." He turned to face her.

She pressed her lips together and fumed. Was that supposed to be funny?

The older doctor snickered and dragged the younger man toward her. "Jacob, this is Kathy Kendall. She'll get you oriented to our modus operandi in no time." When they reached her, her boss smiled. "Kathy, meet Doctor Jacob McLeod."

Her eyes locked onto Dr. McLeod's. Marvelous. Wasn't here for a week, but...forever. She groaned inside as she offered her hand once more.

He smirked as they shook. "Kendall, that's an English name, isn't it?"

"It is." She pulled to free herself from his firm grip. Why wouldn't he let go?

"You hummed a melody as I came into the room. Irish, right? It'd fit a Kennedy more than a Kendall. But an English name is better than Irish." The smirk morphed into a half grin, and his brows puckered.

She inhaled sharply. "My mother was Irish, and I'm pleased to be both." Did this guy know how absurd he was? Or how rude? Her heartbeat raced as she glared. Why didn't Dr. Hartley say something?

Well, handsome or not—her boss's friend or not, Dr. Jacob McLeod was a—oooo, he got her temper up after what? Five minutes? Did he dislike women in general, or had he singled her out?

Kathryn recalled her boss's comment, *"He's different."*

Not the word she'd use.

# Chapter Fifteen

hat were you thinking, McLeod? Nice play. Insulted Dr. Hartley's top staff member in nothing flat. He'd better do something to repair this.

Heat rose in his neck as he peeked at his boss. Doc looked none too pleased with him either. What should he do?

Jacob faced the office manager. He'd always hated forward, loud, obnoxious females. But this girl...correction...woman was different. Despite her youthful appearance, she reacted with dignity and reserve, even when he made such a fool of himself and insulted her. She answered with pride to correct him in his failed attempt at humor.

"Excuse me. I meant no offense. I don't find much in common with the Irish...or the English, for that matter. I'm a Scotsman myself." Oh, yeah. That was much better, McLeod. Could he have sounded more foolish? His jaw clenched. What was wrong with him?

Sharon K. Connell

Her crystal blue eyes held a touch of violet. His heart skipped a beat, and he clamped his teeth tighter.

Jacob dragged his eyes away from her to Dr. Hartley, who seemed dumbfounded, mouth opened, his eyes blinking. Couldn't blame his boss for being in a state of uncharacteristic speechlessness. Not good.

Doc's hand wrapped around Jacob's upper arm and tugged him toward the door. "Let's go to my office." His expression spoke volumes as his voice lowered to a whisper, "No doubt you have jet lag and aren't the shiniest apple in the barrel this morning."

The little energy Jacob had left, along with his self-confidence, seeped out through his feet. At least the office manager hadn't heard what Doc said. Yep, McLeod, you've really blown it.

What had gotten into him? Doc probably couldn't believe his ears. What could he say to his mentor?

Still whispering, Dr. Hartley led him across the tiled floor between the tables. "Don't worry, Jacob. Kathy will be fine. She'll take it all in stride, as she does everything. And you'll come to realize what a wonderful person she is."

As they reached the door, his boss's hand still fastened like a vise to his bicep, Doc's voice returned to its normal volume. "Now, tell me how you wound up here earlier than expected and why you didn't call me from the airport."

"Well, I—"

Doc pushed the door open. "You'll stay at our house tonight. Tomorrow, we'll get you set up in the house Kathy rented for you. Barb's been waiting with bated breath to see you again." He chuckled. "And she'll have my head if I let you stay anywhere else on your first night in Pensacola."

Doc turned and winked at the office manager, who still stood at the counter. "She's in shock. I'll have a talk with her. Later."

Jacob's glance went from her to Dr. Hartley. "I—" No. It'd be best to let this incident with her slide for now. Doc would work it out. Everything would work out. He hoped.

The breakroom door swung shut behind them.

As her boss and Dr. McLeod left the breakroom, the sinister figure from Kathryn's nightmare came to mind. The fiend had enjoyed her torment in the dream last night. Now that she thought about it, that figure could have been Dr. McLeod. A premonition?

She made her way to her office and shuddered when a chill ran up her back. What kind of man was he? How could her boss have a friend like him? There must have been a drastic change in his personality from the man Dr. Hartley knew from medical school. How would she work with a rude, unthoughtful person like Jacob McLeod?

Throughout the morning, she tried to keep herself busy enough not to think of him. How could she get him off her mind with employees stopping by her office every few minutes to ask questions about the new doctor?

She picked up a stack of letters for Dr. Hartley to sign and headed for his office. As she entered the room, her eyes focused first on her boss and then the clutter on top of his desk. As usual, piled high with charts and notes from one edge to the other. She coughed to cover a laugh. When he left for lunch, she'd come in and straighten the mess. It would give her a chance to hide from the staff and their curiosity about Dr. McLeod. A subject she'd prefer to avoid.

Dr. Hartley glanced up from the note he penned. "Kathy, would you make a reservation for lunch at that quiet restaurant where the drug reps usually take us? We'll need to discuss what changes to make since Jacob has joined the staff. Too many interruptions here." He handed her the note. "And would you get these charts for me?"

Kathryn took the paper from him and laid the letters on his desk. "Yes, sir. A reservation at Jackson's for two."

"Make it for four. I want both you and Jacob to join Alex and me."

She sucked in a quick breath. Now she had to endure lunch with Mr. Arrogance. "Yes, sir."

Jacob relaxed in a burgundy wingback chair tucked in the shadow of the far corner of Dr. Hartley's office. He rested his left elbow on the chair's arm, his head braced between the thumb and first two fingers of his hand. His gaze roamed Kathy's fine flaxen hair falling down her back in soft waves as she listened to Dr. Hartley behind the massive oak desk. She had a flawless figure, right down to her feet, each ankle encircled by the top strap of white, two-inch heeled sandals.

When she turned to leave, Jacob snapped his eyes from her legs to her face. She froze in place, her eyes scrutinizing his. *Uh oh.* She'd caught him admiring her figure. He bolted out of the seat. What was he doing? He had to view her only as a staff member, not a woman. He smiled sheepishly.

With narrowed eyes, she stormed out the door.

Just great. Now she'd think he was a creep.

Dr. Hartley leaned back in his desk chair. "Okay, Jacob. We'll have a working lunch, and Kathy will get you situated as far as the new-employee paperwork she needs to process. Then we can get down to the business of patients."

"Are you sure you need me at this meeting, Doc? I could fill out the paperwork while you're gone. It would give you and Doctor

Griffin time to talk about things with Kathy, without me around. Your office manager is not too happy about my presence after that fiasco in the breakroom. She needs time to get over it." After he apologized.

"Forget what happened this morning, Jacob. Kathy probably has. You two got off on the wrong foot. That's all." Doc chuckled. "She'll be fine. She's very professional."

Kathryn seethed inside all the way to her office. Who did Dr. McLeod think he was, ogling her from one end to the other?

She pinched her brows. Why had it bothered her so much this time? Men had stared at her before. She'd always ignored the ritual, regardless of her discomfort. But, he...he—

Her lips pulled to one side. His expression had differed from most men who eyed her. He hadn't smirked, only smiled. Why had she gotten so angry? She wasn't uncomfortable...exactly. Her jaw relaxed. And his smile. Dr. Hartley had it right. It lit up the room. Somehow, she'd noticed that, even with her anger.

"Focus, Kathryn, focus."

She sat down behind her desk, picked up the handset on the phone, and flipped through the cards in her Rolodex. "Jackson's. There you are." She dialed the number and made a reservation.

By the end of the call, her anger had fled. Why had she been so angry? He only acted the same as most men...except for Nick. He'd never ogle a woman. Would he? She'd never seen him do it. Nick was a gentleman.

She'd overreacted, especially this morning. From what she'd heard, Dr. McLeod had a long, difficult flight from Minneapolis to Pensacola.

An hour later, Kathryn slid her laptop into its carrying case. She'd better remind Dr. Hartley of the time. They only had an hour to make their lunch reservation. Dr. McLeod would probably act more like a human being instead of a pompous medical student when more rested and relaxed. Maybe...just maybe, if she tried hard, she'd find some good points about him. She'd give him another chance.

She gathered the pile of charts she'd finished working on and left her office.

What was wrong with her? She'd never been so uptight about a new employee before, not even with the most snobbish. However, if the new doctor had taken the attitude of superiority over her because of her Irish...or English— *Oooo*. The fire in her neck surged again.

That must be what Dr. Hartley meant when he said Dr. McLeod was different. He was prejudiced.

What did she care if he didn't like her? They could still work in the same office. They were adults. He obviously had as many personal issues with people as their patients had with the insurance companies.

She hurried down the hall to Dr. Hartley's office, juggling the patient charts. Good, he left the door open. She'd just stick her head in. "Doctor Hartley, we should leave for our lunch reservation in no more than thirty minutes."

"Thank you." He gave her a heartwarming smile that reached his deep blue eyes. "We'll be ready in about fifteen."

Kathryn stepped into the room to pick up a chart from the corner of her boss's desk. She turned and glanced at Dr. Griffin and Dr. McLeod, who sat in front of the desk.

Jacob stood. "Do you need a hand carrying those, Miss Kendall?"

Her heart raced. "No. I can manage quite well myself." She bit her lip. Rather icy. No, downright rude. First time he'd acted nice, and she bit his head off. She picked up another chart from the table next to him and left the room. She'd apologize later.

Kathryn dropped the charts off in the billing room and returned to her office. She'd had such a strange sensation when Dr. McLeod spoke to her. Like feathers in her lungs. As if she weren't confused enough about the man.

She grabbed her laptop and joined the doctors at the back door.

As Dr. Hartley drove the four of them to Jackson's for their lunch meeting, the three men talked about the young doctor's skill with pediatric patients.

Dr. Griffin turned to face Dr. McLeod, who sat next to her in the back seat. "We definitely need to make full use of that talent, Jacob. We've never had anyone in the practice able to pacify the kids."

"Well, I wouldn't go that far." Dr. McLeod laughed. "But I do love to work with children."

Kathryn kept her eyes fixed out the side window as the men continued their discussion. He loved working with them? Couldn't be civil to someone of a different nationality, but children he coped with? If only he were here for only a few days as a visiting doctor. She pinched her lips together. What happened to giving the man another chance?

His booming baritone voice interrupted her thoughts. "Miss Kendall, aren't you going to take notes about the equipment we were discussing?" He grinned and pointed to the laptop she cradled in her arms.

"Oh, I'm sorry, Doctor McLeod. I didn't know you had started our meeting already." Heat flooded her face. She was letting her ire get out of control. But why?

"Sorry to have disturbed you." He gazed out the window in the opposite direction.

The widened eyes of both her bosses caught her attention as they glanced at each other.

Kathryn turned once again to face the side window. Acute silence filled the car for the rest of the drive.

When Dr. Hartley pulled the car into a parking place at the restaurant, she opened the door and jumped out before he took the key out of the ignition. She dashed into the restaurant without waiting for the others.

When the men joined her, the hostess showed them to their table. The partners sat across from each other. At least Mr. Arrogance wouldn't sit next to her. She only had to face him. Stop it. Get a grip.

As they ordered their food, Kathryn's mood lightened. During the wait for their club sandwiches and fries, Dr. Hartley told tales about the days at med school when he was the teacher and Jacob a student. What a prankster. What had happened to turn the fun-loving young Jacob McLeod into such an ill-mannered grump? She covered her mouth with her hand to suppress a laugh.

Jacob chuckled as he told his side of the stories. He hadn't looked at her once since they sat down. She bit her lip and sighed. She deserved the cold shoulder after her rudeness in the car.

During a lull in the conversation, he turned to her. "Miss Kendall, may I apologize for my remarks about your name this morning and anything else I've said or done since to upset you. It truly was unintentional. I'm sure my lack of sleep over the weekend had something to do with it, although that's no excuse. I'm very sorry. Can we try again?"

He rose and walked around their boss's chair, stopping next to her. "Doctor Hartley, would you mind reintroducing us?"

Her jaw lowered. Dr. Hartley and Dr. Griffin both beamed.

"Why of course, my boy. Jacob, please meet our lovely office manager, Kathy Kendall. Kathy, this is the newest member of the team, Doctor Jacob McLeod."

He held his hand out to her. She placed her fingers onto his soft palm. He slid his hand completely under hers and closed his fingers, enveloping her hand.

Her pulse quickened as they shook. He was even more handsome than this morning. Bad enough that dratted smile of his made her heart skip a beat. Now his eyes sparkled at her in the daylight flowing through the windows all around the room. Drat. Her face was on fire again. She just knew it.

Jacob let go of her hand and returned to his chair.

She pursed her lips.

As his light-up-the-room smile spread further across his face, her pulse danced a jig. Not again.

Their food arrived and she bowed her head to give thanks. When she finished, her bosses were already digging into their lunch, but Jacob's head was bowed. Well, that was something positive about him.

His head rose, and their eyes met. Kathryn quickly picked up her fork.

Dr. Hartley stabbed a bite of lettuce and tomato with his fork and pointed it toward Jacob. "We'll run over and take a look at the house Kathy leased for you before returning to the office."

Her brows lowered. "But, Doctor, what about your patients?"

After wiping his mouth on the napkin, Dr. Griffin touched her arm. "The only patients scheduled for the next couple of hours are nurse visits. We'll have plenty of time."

She glanced at the new doctor. "I hope the accommodations I've arranged will be satisfactory." She dropped her gaze to her plate.

While they finished their food, Jacob kept glancing at her. Each time, her cheeks grew hotter. She wished they would get this part of the afternoon over with already. What if he hated the house she'd rented for him?

# Chapter Sixteen

fter lunch, Kathryn and the three doctors proceeded to the rental house. She smiled as Dr. Hartley's car pulled up in front of the charming two-story home with white siding, forest-green shutters, and an old country-style porch spanning the front. Mounds of flowers along the edges of the front yard peeked at her through the white picket fence.

She glanced at Jacob.

He smiled. "Looks nice."

So far, so good. She bit her lip. The men got out of the vehicle. Should she join them? Just hand over the keys and then wait here?

Her bosses approached the gate, but Jacob hurried to the passenger side and opened the door for her.

"Thank you, Doctor McLeod."

He offered his hand, but she stood and slipped by him without accepting the assistance. Jacob followed her through the gate and across the front yard while the older doctors climbed the stairs to the porch.

Kathryn retrieved the keys from her purse and unlocked the front door. When Jacob smiled at her again, her heart did a flip. She tightened her jaw.

Once in the house, the young doctor meandered from room to room and then raced up the stairs three at a time to the second floor. She glanced at her bosses, who shook their heads.

"Alex, do you remember when you could run up the stairs?"

Dr. Griffin chuckled. "Oh, for the good old days when we were agile."

A few minutes later, Jacob bounded back down the staircase and joined them. "Great job finding this house, Miss Kendall. Love the second bedroom where I can work out."

She lowered her brows. "Work out?"

"Yes, I have my own equipment. It saves time not having to go to a public gym, and I don't have to worry about their hours of business matching my schedule."

She nodded. That explained his well-built frame. No doubt, he loves the privacy so he can admire his muscles in front of a mirror when he's done, too. No call for the sarcasm. She had to get it together

"The garage is a bonus. At least my little puddle jumper won't have to sit out in the elements." He chortled. "Oh yeah. I guess there's not much in the way of elements here, is there...besides the sun."

"Oh, but there are." Dr. Griffin grimaced. "The coastal salt water on the breeze wreaks havoc on the paint job. Then there are storms that knock down tree limbs and blow debris everywhere, bird droppings, annoying lovebugs, and sap from the trees. Talk about elements. We've got 'em here. Guess we neglected to add that in our promotion of Pensacola to get you here."

As the men laughed, Kathryn let out a sigh of relief. What a change. Dr. McLeod acted so different now.

"You'll be grateful for the little garage, son. You'll see." Dr. Hartley grasped Jacob's arm and led him toward the front door. She followed.

In the foyer, her boss turned. Dr. Griffin had settled himself into a recliner in the corner next to the doorway. Dr. Hartley reentered the room and plopped himself into the other recliner opposite his partner. "Good idea."

Jacob leaned close to her ear and whispered, "Must be the heavy lunch." She stifled a giggle.

He turned to face her. "This house will do nicely until I decide where to settle. Thank you for finding it." He smiled again as she handed him the keys.

Her hand brushed across his palm, and a surge of warmth rushed through her. She gasped and stepped away. "You're welcome." Dratted unsteady voice. When would the next anti-Irish slur come out of his mouth? He tried so hard to make his apology at the restaurant sound convincing, but he didn't fool her. His actions that morning had not pleased Dr. Hartley.

A twinge of guilt made her wince. *Stop that.* Why did she go on the defensive every time he did something nice? "I can show you the deck and backyard while our bosses relax, if you like."

"Okay."

She led him through the sliding glass door onto the deck. Now if she could just get rid of this mounting attraction to him. It didn't mean she hadn't given him a second chance. She just didn't want to get involved with another employee, that's all. Besides, he wouldn't be interested in someone like her anyway. He'd be more interested in a beautiful model.

Jacob glanced back at the older doctors half-asleep in the recliners, and then followed Kathy onto the deck. He took in a deep breath. Whatever that fragrance was, he liked it. Was it her perfume? He hadn't noticed it in the house. Must be the flowers.

A breeze tousled his hair. He ran the fingers of his right hand through his thick mane to push the pesky locks from his forehead. Her tresses glowed like golden honey in the sunlight. Strands whipped about her face. She's beautiful.

He turned to the yard and scanned the landscaping. Wow. Midafternoon and all he could hear was the soft hum of a spring day. No traffic at all. Only birds and the distant bark from a dog. "This is great." He gazed into her violet eyes. "Quite a change from where I lived in Minneapolis."

Kathy stepped to the far corner of the deck. "The dead-end street and tall hedges provide the quiet."

He drank in her loveliness as he had when he first saw her. Oh no. *Red flag.* He had to stop going there, as lovely as she might be. The looks she sent his way now and then all but turned him into an iceberg. She must still be upset over this morning.

He was the one who should tear the wall down since he'd laid the first stone. She was young, pretty, and in a position of authority, but that didn't excuse his actions. Nor did his being tired and out of sorts. She *was* very nice. Even apologized for the splashed water on his coat this morning. Not what he'd expected. Every inch a lady.

"I do enjoy beauty." His eyes popped open. Had he said that out loud?

She turned to him. "That's good because it's a beautiful backyard. If you entertain...the perfect backyard." She stared at the small structure at the back.

Good, she thought he was talking about the yard. His gaze went to the heavens.

She turned back again. "I've never seen this yard at night, but I can imagine."

As her eyes moved from him to one side of the yard and then the other, it seemed as though her attitude warmed. Jacob smiled. He leaned back on the deck rail, his hands gripping the rough wood. Her face lit with imagination as her eyes sparkled in the afternoon sun.

When Kathy faced him, she smiled back at him. A rosy hue filled her cheeks. Her long lashes dropped. He had the power to make her blush. He liked that.

Warmth rose in his neck. He pushed off the rail and stood upright. "Why don't you show me the garden? But don't expect me to know anything about plants. The only ones I can discuss with any amount of intelligence are those used for medicinal purposes, and I wouldn't recognize them either in their natural state."

They laughed together. The red flag in his mind waved frantically. He'd have to ignore that blasted warning for the time being. At least until he was sure he'd made things right between the office manager and himself.

Something rubbed against Jacob's leg. He jumped back and looked down. A small white cat gazed up at him and mewed as he backed away and frowned. "Don't tell me the place comes complete with resident animals. I don't like cats. This one looks like a powder puff, or it stuck its claw in a light socket."

Kathy chuckled, stooped down, and coaxed the cat to her. She stroked its thick white coat while it brushed up against her legs. Then she stood and glanced around the deck. "Well, there isn't as much as a water dish around, so I think you're safe. It probably belongs to one of the neighbors. I hope it wasn't just dumped off by someone."

She crouched to pet the cat again. "She's beautiful. Look how thick her fur is." Her hand disappeared into the cat's coat. "I'd love to take you home with me, but I doubt Sheila would understand."

"Who's Sheila? Your roommate?"

"Sort of." Kathy grinned. "She's my dog."

"Dogs are much better." Jacob crossed his arms over his chest. "I could handle a dog."

Her eyebrows rose. She crouched again and scratched the cat's ears. "If you were mine, I'd name you Muffy. You look like the rabbit-fur muff I once had when I was a little girl in cold, cold Illinois."

"That hairball won't make a habit of visiting me, will it?"

Kathy pursed her lips and rose. "Just don't feed it and it won't spend any time around here."

"Don't worry. Feeding a cat is the last thing I want to do. Now go home." He waved his hand at the cat. It ran off the porch and scampered to the small building in the back of the yard.

Jacob held out his hand to help Kathy down the steps of the deck into the yard, but she ignored it.

As they visited each section of the yard, the white cat peeked its head out from a plant or bush. Kathy pointed out the different trees and plants, the antique birdbath, and the unusual settee off in one corner.

Jacob kept an eye on her facial expressions. Such enthusiasm over a little backyard. Maybe it wouldn't be so hard to make things up to her. She seemed easy enough to please. He blew out a long breath. He'd never seen anyone as graceful as his mother...until now.

When they returned to the deck, Jacob held out his hand to guide her up the steep steps. This time she accepted. His heart swelled at her touch. More color flowed into her cheeks.

At the top of the stairs, he released her velvety soft fingers. *Red flag.* He really had to stop thinking about her that way.

Kathryn glanced at Jacob on the other side of the back seat as Dr. Hartley drove them back to the office. How could a mere smile make her pulse race like that?

Her bosses were engrossed in a discussion about the patient Dr. Griffin would see next, and Jacob was quiet, staring out the window.

What was behind that strange flicker, almost pain, he often had on his face when he looked at her? She turned to stare out her own window.

Once they reached the office, she opened the car door and got out. She hurried to her office, placed her laptop on the desk, and stuffed her purse in the bottom drawer.

The twinkle in his eye had sent her heartbeat into overdrive. Stupid blush of hers. *Oooo.* She had to be on her guard. He'd revert to true form soon. When he was comfortable and won over the bosses. She just knew he would. There she went again. Thinking the worst.

Each day during the week, Kathryn waited for another rude remark from Dr. McLeod, but none came. Here it was Friday, four days later, and he'd been a perfect gentleman. His apology must have been genuine.

She glanced at the clock in her office. Four-twenty. Would five o'clock never come? She'd never watched the clock before Dr. McLeod came to work with them. Never longed for the workday to end. But why? If only he wouldn't pop into her mind all day long. The way he looked at her...with those magnetic green eyes. The way her neck tingled each time he glanced her way.

Bible verses. She needed to quote Bible verses. It had helped in the past when emotions plagued her. Why not now?

*Finally, brethren, whatsoever things are true, whatsoever things are honest, whatsoever things are just, whatsoever things are pure, whatsoever things are lovely, whatsoever things are of good report; if there be any virtue, and if there be any praise, think on these things. Philippians four, eight.*

She seriously doubted that Dr. McLeod fit that verse. Something other than his green eyes and actions disturbed her inner peace. What was it?

True. He'd shown himself to be true in the way he helped his former employer.

Honest? *Hmmm.*

Just? Doubtful. At least, he hadn't been in his attitude toward her the day they met. She lifted her chin but then lowered it and cinched the left side of her mouth. He had apologized.

Pure? She wouldn't know. Dr. Hartley would probably say yes.

Lovely? Her mind drifted to his smile. Oh yes. Lovely smile and eyes that— She shook her head in a vain attempt to rid it of his image. *Stop it!*

Good report? He certainly had a good report with Dr. Hartley.

Virtue? Too soon to tell.

Praise— She interrupted her own thoughts. Her mind had completely wandered off to Jacob again. Drat.

She had to stop this. But how? Between the new doctor and nightmares, she'd go crazy.

Kathryn shut down the computer and turned out the lights in her office. Good thing Beth would arrive soon. It'd be wonderful to have someone to anchor her, get her thoughts back where they should be, on Beth's wedding. She'll take my mind off Doctor Jacob McLeod.

# Chapter Seventeen

The next Monday, Kathryn sat with Jacob in the breakroom at the clinic. "I know you've seen similar forms in the clinic where you worked before, but Doctor Hartley said to show you everything that goes into the patient's chart."

"No harm in being thorough." He took the paper from her and perused it as if he'd be tested later. The concentration with which he examined each sheet fascinated her.

As he studied, her mind wandered. He had such strikingly handsome masculine features, just like the hero in her latest historical romance novel. *Quit!* She did it again.

Now that they actually had to work together, she'd almost prefer he ignore her, as he had at the beginning of their business lunch the other day. But nooo, he gave her his undivided attention when she spoke to him...and at other times, too. It was unnerving.

Jacob laid the paper down and gazed into her eyes.

Those eyes...so green. She mentally whacked herself in the side of the head. Those romance stories gave her ideas she shouldn't have. That's it, no more romantic novels. She handed him the next form. "We use this one for the billing department."

After the short session with forms, she returned to her office to catch up on postponed work. Backlogged patient-visit charges glared at her. Not her best decision to take over this function while the checkout clerk took her vacation. She'd be happy when Lisa returned. Even happier when Jacob...Dr. McLeod...could handle his paperwork on his own.

She eased herself behind the computer and began to type. As she entered the charges, his adorable curl, which dropped over his left eyebrow while they worked together, wormed its way into her thoughts. She giggled. What was she, a teenager? She needed to get control of herself.

Kathryn glanced at the clock. Oh, no. Ten minutes before the last mail pickup. She snatched a stack of envelopes that had accumulated in her corner tray, stepped out of her office, and dashed down the hall. As she turned the corner into the next corridor, she slammed into a solid object. Envelopes scattered in all directions. Strong arms wrapped around her shoulders and then quickly pulled away. At the loss of support, she teetered backward. The powerful arms grasped hers in time to keep her from falling and pulled her close.

She gazed into brilliant green eyes. "Jacob." She sucked in a deep breath.

"Whoa, little lady."

Her heart raced. He'd used that same silly impersonation of a movie cowboy as Dr. Hartley always had. She squirmed out of his hold. "I'm fine."

He let go of her and bent to collect the envelopes from the floor. Jacob handed them to her. "Guess we're both in too much of a hurry."

Her cheeks warmed. "Guess so." She flashed a quick smile, sidestepped him, and resumed her previous mission at a fast pace to the front office.

Jacob followed close behind. "I was on my way to your office to clear up something, but I'll wait until you're not so busy. Have to meet Doctor Griffin at the hospital for rounds anyway. Nice to hear you use my first name, by the way."

As heat flooded her face, she placed the mail in the receptionist's outgoing tray. She watched Jacob leave the building and get into his rental car, which was parked in one of the doctor's spaces in front of the office. She'd been rude again. Not very cordial of her when he'd kept her from falling. And she'd called him Jacob.

This attraction to him had to stop. She bit her lip. It would once her adopted sister arrived tonight. Beth would keep Doctor McLeod off her mind. Kathryn returned to her office.

As she finished her work for the day, she peered up at the doorway where Dr. Hartley leaned on the frame. He wore a big grin.

She pulled her mouth to one side and raised one brow. Her head nodded toward the wall clock. "That clock has crawled all day. On purpose."

He laughed and pushed away from the doorframe. "I imagine it does seem so. Will Beth's flight be on time?"

"When I checked five minutes ago, it was."

Her boss eased into the chair in front of her desk. "So, what are your plans for this evening, since you and Beth won't join us for dinner? There's still time to change your mind. Jacob will be there."

Kathryn's jaw tightened. She shook her head. "We have so much catching up to do. For Beth's first night here, I want her all to myself. I made reservations at—"

Jazzy music played from Dr. Hartley's cell phone. He stood and pulled it from its holder. "Excuse me. I think this is the call I've been waiting for."

He stepped into the hallway. "Yes, I was afraid of that, Jacob. I'll be there in a few minutes, and we can decide on our next step." Her boss returned to the doorway.

"Sorry, Kathy. I won't be able to give you a lift to the airport. Mr. Chaney has regressed again. I have to meet Jacob and Alex at the hospital right away."

"I'm sorry to hear about Mr. Chaney, but don't worry. I'll call a cab."

He rushed out the door, and Kathryn looked up the number for the taxi company. At least her boss wouldn't have another chance to invite them to his house tonight. With Dr. McLeod.

Kathryn waited in the airport terminal. She spotted Beth's head with its curly chestnut hair pass the security portal and rushed to give her a hug. "I'm glad you're here. I've missed you." Then she grabbed the handle of her adopted sister's carryon.

"Missed you more." Beth's honey-colored eyes lit with a smile. She hung on Kathryn's free arm.

After collecting the luggage, the girls left the terminal and approached a cab. The cabbie loaded the bags into the trunk.

Kathryn glanced at Beth. "How long did you say you were staying? Looks like you brought enough for a month."

Beth giggled. "Mom insisted on helping me pack, and she sent goodies for you, too. She also bought every bridal magazine she could find to help us with our planning. I told her I'd buy them here, but you know Mom."

"That's Aunt Sandy all right. Can't wait to get started on the plans. The more I thought about it, the more excited I got." And the more nervous, anxious, and miserable as her thoughts constantly drifted to Jacob.

Beth leaned back in the seat of the taxi and gazed at Kathryn. "Okay, little sister. Tell me. How's your love life?"

Kathryn's mouth dropped open.

After conferring with Dr. Griffin about Mr. Chaney's next line of treatment, Jacob held the glass door open for Dr. Hartley, and they headed to the hospital's back parking lot. "Good plan, Doc. I'm sure the patient will exhibit signs of improvement soon."

"I sure hope so, son. He's been through a lot, and nothing else has made a difference. But you're right. This treatment should be successful. It was a relief when Alex suggested it."

Dr. Hartley reached for the keys to his car. "Now, let's get to the house and see what Barb has planned for our dinner."

Jacob grinned. The Hartleys had always been generous to him back in his med school days. They'd picked up right where they left off when he arrived in Pensacola. What a blessing to have run into Doc at that conference. Working with him was everything Jacob had always hoped for. Everything had turned around for him.

They wound their way between the cars in the lot until they arrived at Doc's silver Mercedes. He turned to Jacob. "Where did you park?"

"Closer to the street."

"Do you remember the way to my house?"

Jacob chuckled. "I should, I've been there every night for the past week."

Dr. Hartley guffawed. "Okay. I'm being a mother hen." He slid into the driver's seat. "See you at the house."

Jacob strode to his old Austin Healey, which had finally arrived in Pensacola, and brought the engine to life.

On the way to the Hartleys' home, his mind wandered to Kathy. If only he could do something to make her realize he wanted to be friends. He needed a good friend besides the Hartleys and Griffins. Someone more his age. She seemed to be a good choice. It didn't mean they had to get involved romantically. Didn't need more entanglements like— He needed to stop thinking of that female disaster, Patricia.

What could he do to convince Kathy to be his friend?

He pulled into his boss's driveway, jogged up the sidewalk and steps, and joined Dr. Hartley on the porch.

Mrs. Hartley, wearing green scrubs, opened the front door before his boss touched the handle. "Honey, I'm so sorry. I planned on Chicken Cordon Bleu for dinner tonight, until I got a phone call."

Doc nodded and gave her a hug. "You're on your way to work. It's okay. Jacob and I can go out to dinner tonight. It's not his first dinner here, nor will it be his last."

She pursed her lips. "The hospital tried to get someone else since I requested a short leave, but they couldn't find anyone available. You remember my friend, Lynne Temple. She had a family emergency and left at the start of her shift. What could I say?"

He kissed her cheek. "You had to say, 'Yes.'"

When his boss stepped through the door, she hugged Jacob. "Don't stand on the porch. Come in." She turned to her husband, and her eyes narrowed. "Out to eat, huh?"

"Yes. Jacob wouldn't want to eat my cooking, and I'm not in the mood to heat up leftovers." He displayed his toothy Cheshire cat smile.

"Remember your diet. No fast food, which is why you're on the diet in the first place. What did Alex tell you?"

Jacob pinched his lips together to stifle a laugh.

After closing the door behind Jacob, she placed her hands on her hips. "David, I know what you do when I'm not home to cook for you. You take every advantage to cheat. And, I'll bet Jacob eats his share of junk food as well."

"I promise I'll be good, dear. We'll run over to that nice restaurant downtown you enjoy so much and have a good time rehashing med-school days while we eat."

She stared into her husband's eyes. "Not your choice of hangouts down the street?"

He planted a kiss on her forehead. "I'll even pick up your favorite ice cream, and we'll come back here for dessert. Now stop fussin' at me."

"You mean your favorite ice cream, don't you?" Her mouth pulled to one side.

Jacob clamped his lips together again to keep from chuckling.

Doc rolled his eyes. "Okay, I'll get Jamoca fudge for the two of you, and that non-fat yogurt stuff you're always pushing on me. Now stop worrying."

"You promise. No fast food?"

"You have my solemn word on it." Jacob's boss held his right hand in the air and laid his left over his heart. "What hospital is in need of your capable hands tonight?"

"Baptist. I should be home a little before nine. The shift was supposed to end at eleven, but one of the girls on the next shift will come in early to relieve me."

Doc rested his forearm on Jacob's shoulder. "Well. Are you hungry, boy?"

"Starved."

Mrs. Hartley turned to Jacob. "I'll make the chicken for you tomorrow night. Is it still your favorite?"

"Yes, Ma'am. Can't wait. You spoil me."

"You're like the second son we never had. I'm entitled to." She giggled, pulled his head down, and kissed his cheek.

Standing on her tiptoes, she wrapped her arms around her husband's neck. He lifted her off the floor in his embrace and kissed her.

"David! Put me down before you get a hernia."

She giggled again, and he placed her back on her feet. She picked up her purse from the table in the foyer and turned toward the door. Doc gave her a gentle slap on the posterior as she passed him. Her eyes and mouth opened wide. Color rose in her cheeks.

Doc grinned and raised his brows.

Jacob couldn't stop the chuckle from escaping. One of the reasons he loved being around them. Their relationship seemed so much fun and their affection for each other so deep. He longed to one day have what they had. So opposite the relationship between his own parents. A sad ache traveled through Jacob's heart.

As he watched Mrs. Hartley walk out the door, Kathy's face appeared in his thoughts.

Dr. Hartley's resonant voice caused the image to fade. "Okay, Jacob. Off to Barb's favorite restaurant. It's a nice place, and the food is fantastic. As good as my wife's. But don't you dare tell her I said so." He winked. "I'll deny it to my death." He wagged his right forefinger in the air.

"That good, huh?" Jacob laughed and followed his boss out to the car.

As Dr. Hartley drove, he glanced at Jacob. "So, are things falling in place for you at the office? Has Kathy managed to get you up to snuff on everything?"

"Yes. She has. She's quiet, isn't she? Can't tell what she's thinking. But she gives precise answers to my questions." The problem was he couldn't get her to talk about anything other than work.

His boss turned onto a side street. "Well, she has a lot on her mind with her sister's visit, I suppose."

He pulled the Mercedes into a parking space in front of an old home with pink siding. A sign out front displayed Dharma Blue. Next to a white railing on the covered wooden wraparound porch, blue tablecloths draped a few small tables set for diners. Blue umbrellas shaded a few more tables in the front of the home where a brick patio took the place of a lawn.

"Here we are, son. Hope you'll enjoy the place."

As they approached the entrance, the appetizing aromas of steak, garlic, onions, and spices drifted out the door.

Down the street, Jacob glimpsed similar shingles hung outside other businesses in converted older homes. "There's such a great atmosphere in this old section of town." He followed his boss into the entry and up to the hostess podium.

Doc leaned on the stand. "Good evening, young lady. Might you have a table for a couple of famished doctors who have been left to fend for themselves tonight?"

"Good evening, Doctor Hartley." The young woman with jet-black hair tittered and tilted her head to peer behind him. Her shoulder-length tresses with their blackberry-colored streaks fell to one side. "Where's your wife?"

"The hospital called her to work at the last minute. That's why we're on our own."

The young lady gazed at Jacob, then lowered her lashes revealing glittery eyeshadow that matched the color of the streaks in her hair. "You and your friend are fortunate. I just had a cancellation. I'll have you seated in a moment."

She walked across the room and removed the "Reserved" sign from a center table. As she returned, her attention riveted on Jacob.

He let out an exasperated breath. He'd seen the look all too often, and he did not appreciate it. He was not on the menu.

The glare Kathy had given him two weeks ago shot into his memory. Had he eyed her the same way when she turned to leave Dr. Hartley's office? Couldn't blame her one bit for her response toward him, if he had.

His boss latched onto Jacob's arm. "Look. The table at the wall. It's Kathy. And the girl next to her must be her sister, Beth."

Kathryn ordered crab cakes and Beth took her suggestion of the ribeye. Once the waitress left the table, Beth rattled on nonstop through ideas she and Tom had come up with for their wedding and reception.

"Slow down, Beth. We have a whole week for you to fill me in on everything. How much coffee did you drink on your flight here, anyway?"

Beth joined in Kathryn's laughter. "I get so excited when I realize I'll spend the rest of my life with Tom. He's the best guy in the world." She gave a dreamy sigh and then shook her head for a moment. "But enough about my love life."

Kathryn fought to keep from groaning aloud.

"You never answered my question in the cab before we dropped off my luggage at your place. You rushed me in and out as if the apartment was on fire. And you talked about this restaurant all the way here. Now fess up, girl."

Jacob's face loomed in Kathryn's mind.

"Oh, but before we delve into your current love life, I have a question." Beth grabbed her arm. "Will you be my maid of honor? I know it's not a surprise I asked, and you probably wondered why I hadn't already, but—"

Kathryn placed her hand on her sister's. "It's okay. I assumed you wanted one of your girlfriends back home to be your maid of honor since I live nine hundred miles away. But if it's what you want, I'd be honored." Good. Sidestepped the subject of my love life again.

"Kathy, do you remember when we were kids and used to make wedding plans together? I wouldn't choose anyone else. Sure wish you were engaged too, though. We'd plan a double wedding."

"I won't be getting married any time soon." Kathryn tried to smile. Not when she couldn't trust men her own age. The only trustworthy younger man she knew was Nick, but he was like her brother. "So, unless you want to postpone the date for several years, you'd better plan on a solo performance."

"I know someone you might consider." Her sister glanced out of the corners of her eyes as she played with the flatware on the table.

"Oh no, you don't. Stop that thought right there. I do not want to discuss Nick tonight."

Beth tilted her head. Her brows furrowed as she stared into Kathryn's eyes. "You look positively worn out. Are you okay?"

"Yes, I'm all right. I've had a hard week at work, and I haven't slept well lately."

"You said the clinic hired another physician. Did it add a lot to your workload?"

"No. But I find working with the new doctor stressful. We had a rocky start from the first day. He claimed he was fatigued from the trip and not feeling well. But now—" She shouldn't have told Beth anything. She was sure to meet Jacob before she leaves. Knowing Beth, she'd say something to him. *Something I'll regret.*

"'But now...' what? Come on, Kath. Tell me."

"I had to acquaint him with the practice procedures, and it made me tense."

"Why? Has he said or done anything to upset you?"

"Well…it's more the way he looks at me…and how he says things." Her muscles tightened as the memory of his words the first day at the clinic replayed in her mind. "The first words out of his mouth, on his very first day in the office, insulted me." *Great!* Now she'd want to know what he said. Besides, he'd apologized, and she'd accepted his apology. Hadn't she?

"What did he say that was so rude?"

Kathryn sighed.

Beth's eyebrows rose. "Did he do something awful?"

Kathryn gritted her teeth. She had counted on Beth to take her mind off Jacob, not give her a third degree about him.

"I suppose nothing all that bad." Kathryn explained about the coffee pot incident in the breakroom. "Now he's patronizing, and he glares at me."

"I see." Her sister grinned.

"What do you mean, 'I see?'"

"I just see. That's all." Beth covered her lips with her hand to hide an obvious giggle. "Has it occurred to you that perhaps the doctor likes you? How old is he?"

"Likes me?" Kathryn's muscles knotted from her neck down to her hands. "A gentleman does not offend a lady if he likes her. On the contrary, he would show courtesy toward her." She clenched her jaw. But Jacob *had* conducted himself as a gentleman after their walk in the garden. Even before. "Let's drop the topic. You're so exasperating at times."

Beth leaned forward, one elbow on the table, chin resting on her hand, and pushed back the curly hair from her face. Her eyes sparkled. "Is he good looking?" A distinct smirk showed on her face.

From the entrance to the restaurant, Kathryn spotted Dr. Hartley heading their way, followed by Jacob. She grabbed her sister's hand. "Stop."

Beth pushed her hand away. "I'm just asking."

"Kathy, what a pleasant surprise." Her boss beamed at her.

Jacob broke into his heartwarming smile.

Kathryn quivered and turned her gaze to Dr. Hartley. "What brings you here, sir? I thought you had invited Doctor McLeod to have dinner at your home tonight. Is Mrs. Hartley okay?"

Heat filled every millimeter of her neck and face. She glanced at her sister, who eyed Jacob with her brows raised higher.

Beth leaned over the table and whispered in Kathryn's ear, "The perfect age."

# Chapter Eighteen

*J*acob tried to suppress a grin as color rose in Kathy's face. What had the other girl said to make her blush?

Dr. Hartley glanced at him. "Isn't this a pleasant surprise?"

"Yes, it is. Good evening, Miss Kendall."

His boss turned back to the girls. "And to answer your question, Kathy, my wife is fine. The hospital called her in to work. I promised her I wouldn't let this young man starve, so...here we are. This must be the sister you've spoken of?"

"Oh. Yes. My adopted sister, Beth Parker. Beth, this is my boss, Doctor Hartley."

He held out his hand. "It's nice to meet you, Beth."

"Likewise." She shook his hand. "Kathy's always telling me how much she loves her job."

"I'm glad to hear it. Meet the newest member of my staff, Doctor Jacob McLeod."

Jacob extended his hand to Beth.

Her lips pressed together as she smiled, revealing deep dimples. Her eyes appeared to hold a secret as they twinkled at him. "I'm happy to make your acquaintance, Doctor McLeod. I've heard all kinds of things about you." She placed her hand in his.

Kathy's body jerked, and her sister's eyes got larger as she sucked in a breath and squeezed his hand at the same time.

If his guess was right, Miss Parker had received a swift kick under the table from her sister. Wonder what that was all about. Jacob shook her hand and released it. "Oh? And what has she said?"

When he looked at Kathy, his pulse quickened.

"I told Beth about the shower I subjected you to the first morning you arrived in our office." She gave him a piercing stare. "When you came up and startled me from behind in the breakroom. And how *gracious* you were."

His boss burst into laughter.

Jacob quirked his mouth. "Uh huh." He pictured her leaning over the coffee pot, silky blonde hair hanging over one shoulder, while she hummed the lilting Irish melody.

The hostess stepped up next to him and motioned for them to follow her.

Dr. Hartley nodded. "We'll not detain you two ladies any longer." He faced Jacob. "Barbara and I will have to bring you along from now on. We've never gotten a table this fast before. Must be those pearly-whites you flashed her." He nodded toward the hostess.

Doc turned to the girls. "Hope we meet again soon, Beth."

Jacob glanced back. "Nice meeting you, Beth. Miss Kendall."

Before they'd gotten two feet from the table, his boss did a turn-about. "Say, Kathy. Can I talk you two young ladies into having dinner with me and my wife Friday evening?"

"Sounds wonderful. Thank you." Kathy touched her sister's shoulder. "You'll really like Mrs. Hartley."

"I look forward to meeting her. Will you be joining us, Doctor McLeod?"

Kathy jerked again, and Beth winced.

His boss thumped him on the back. "Well, of course he will, won't you Jacob?"

"Wouldn't miss it." He grinned at Kathy. Her cheeks turned crimson. Her sister giggled.

The hostess flounced as she led the two physicians to a table in the center of the room. She batted her eyelashes at Jacob. Kathryn bit her lip. Could the woman's flirtations be more blatant? Or Jacob's amusement with her more apparent? Might have known. Nothing but a skirt–chaser, just like all the rest.

Kathryn's teeth clenched and her jaw tightened as she dragged her gaze from the scene to her sister. "Beth, what were you doing inviting him to the Hartleys' for dinner? It was rude. How could you do that to me? I told you how much he annoys me. And what would Tom think of your flirting with Jacob?"

"Hmmm...Jacob?"

Kathryn sighed.

Beth flipped her napkin open and placed it across her lap. "As an astute observer of human nature, I believe you're only annoyed by the young doctor's attention to the girl at their table."

"Huh?" Kathryn's mouth opened.

"And...the sole source of your current irritation with me is your own attraction to Doctor McLeod. Plus the fact that you're in denial." She smirked. "Boy, the way you two looked at each other."

Kathryn blew air through pinched lips as she laid her napkin across her legs. "You're delusional."

"Calm yourself, Kath. As far as Tom goes, he wouldn't have thought my conversation with your doctor the least bit flirtatious. I merely wondered if he'd be there. Secondly, I didn't invite him, your boss did."

"He's not my doctor."

"Well, anyway. He passed."

"Passed what?"

"My test. I wanted to see his reaction."

"Reaction?"

"Kath, for such a smart girl, you sure are dumb to the ways of men."

"Enlighten me." She leaned back in the chair, peered at Jacob for a second, and then snapped her eyes to her sister.

Before Beth could say more, their meals arrived. Kathryn gave thanks for their food.

After the blessing, she cut a piece of crab cake, smothered in rich mustard sauce, and took a bite. She sighed with half-closed eyes. "I love this place."

Her sister tasted the savory ribeye. "Hey. This is good."

"I knew you'd love it."

After Beth chewed and swallowed, she stared across the room at the physicians. "Would a man jump at the chance to spend time with a woman he was not attracted to?"

Kathryn held her fork over the plate. "Please drop this. Doctor McLeod is not attracted to me and that's that." She frowned as she glanced his way. The hostess still lingered at the doctor's side. "I'm obviously not his type."

"Oh? And who is?" Beth's brows arched.

"Over there." Kathryn pointed her fork toward the hostess and then stared at her sister. "Don't look at me that way. He's not my type either."

"Your eyes may be blue, Kath, but they're leaning toward green at the moment." Beth snickered.

"I'll not dignify that with a response." Kathryn studied her plate. She speared a stalk of broccoli. "Why should I be jealous? Of whom?"

"Thought you weren't going to respond."

"Drop it, Beth. Don't say another word about Doctor McLeod. Don't make me sorry you're here."

"Not *Jacob*? Nick will never have a chance with you now that Jacob is on the scene. Poor Nick."

As she stole a peek at Jacob, Kathryn bit her lip. The hostess continued to talk to him. He looked over at Kathryn.

Her heart leaped into her throat.

Jacob drew his gaze away from the other side of the room where Kathy ate her dinner. He had embarrassed her tonight. He should have bowed out of dinner with the Hartleys for Friday, but he wanted the chance to talk to her away from work. Prove to her that he wasn't the jerk she probably had chalked him up to be.

The hostess stepped closer to Jacob while a waitress took Dr. Hartley's order. "I'm so glad you came in with Doctor Hartley tonight. My name is Erica. I'll make sure you're well taken care of." With the corners of her mouth pulled upward, she winked.

Jacob rolled his eyes. Really? He buried his nose in the menu, ignoring her as she continued to speak. A second later, the waitress rounded Erica and wedged herself between the hostess and Jacob.

He flipped the menu closed and looked up. "What's the catch of the day?"

"Snapper, sir. And it's good."

"Okay. I'll have the snapper, grilled, with basmati rice and asparagus. Also, a salad with ranch dressing on the side, and a large glass of milk." He handed her the menu.

"Very good." She left the table with a side-glance at the hostess, who glared and followed hot on her heels to the rear of the restaurant.

Dr. Hartley seemed amused. "Hmmm...a heated discussion between those two is about to explode, and I'll bet it has something to do with you."

Jacob glanced at the two employees as they entered a hallway. Before he returned his attention to his boss, his line of vision drifted again to Kathy as she conversed with her sister.

His boss chuckled. "The hostess tried her best to gain your notice. A futile effort, because I believe our lovely office manager holds your thoughts captive."

"Just curious about her. That's all." Jacob unwrapped his flatware.

Dr. Hartley leaned back in the chair. "I have something I need to say, Jacob."

Jacob's gaze wandered to Kathy's side of the room once more. "Go ahead, Doc."

"After that nonsense in the breakroom on your first day, I halfheartedly wondered if I had made a mistake bringing you here."

The comment hit Jacob like a punch to his gut. He faced his boss. "Have I done anything else to upset you?"

"No. But I'm worried about you. And Kathy. What's going on? You've had it rough through the years with your family problems, but what have you got against her?"

"Against her?" He'd treated her with the respect she deserved ever since he apologized.

"Since you've been with us, Kathy has seemed under a lot of strain. On the verge of tears, at times. I've never seen her act this way. The only change around here, that I can tell, has been you."

Jacob blinked. Could his anger toward himself over his growing attraction to her have made him seem hostile?

An incident came to mind. He'd stood in the front office viewing a patient's chart on the previous day. Kathy had walked across the lobby and bent over to pick up a magazine from the floor. Because she had on a straight skirt reaching just below her knees, he'd caught a glimpse of her long, shapely legs from behind. When she straightened and turned, their eyes met. He abruptly turned away in embarrassment over his unguarded behavior. How often *had* he upset her like that this past week?

"Doc, I haven't meant to be disrespectful to her, but I could be overreacting." He grimaced. "When I look at her, old feelings that I've repressed are stirred. Feelings I don't want to have."

A grin flickered across his boss's face. "Feelings, huh? I didn't think you were still suffering from jetlag."

"No jetlag." Jacob sought understanding in the face of his longtime friend. It was there. He should have confided in Doc a long time ago.

Dr. Hartley straightened in the chair. "Well? Are you going to tell me what's troubling you? You're not the same Jacob lately."

"I should have told you months ago. Pride and embarrassment kept me from saying anything. I've become more and more frustrated with women since Pa—"

The waitress arrived with their salads. He took another glimpse at Kathy.

As they ate, Jacob told his boss about the disastrous relationship he had with Patricia in Minnesota, her deceitfulness, and how he didn't trust pretty women in general because of it. "After it was over between us, she stalked me. When I ran into you at the conference, I thought my troubles were over. But sometimes, when I look at Kathy, I see Pat."

The waitress returned and set their meals in front of them. Jacob bowed his head and said a quick, silent prayer to thank God for the food and for his friend.

When he looked up, Dr. Hartley swallowed a mouthful of food and smiled. "I don't think you could find anyone more different from this Pat if you searched for a million years."

Jacob glanced at Kathy. "I'm sure that's true. But when it comes to pretty women, I'm afraid I've developed an automatic defense system. Red flags go up, and it's hard to get past them." He stared across the other diners at her.

"Can you stop fixating on her for a minute and focus on what I'm saying to you?" Dr. Hartley snickered. "You sure don't look at her as if she's the enemy. Are you sure there's not something you're not telling me?"

Jacob breathed in deeply. "Okay, I'll admit it. I'm attracted to her." Very attracted. He sighed. "She's beautiful. Sweet, too. But, I don't want to get involved. No woman will ever humiliate me again."

As he sliced off a big chunk of steak, Dr. Hartley nodded. "Let me tell you a story, my boy. Before Kathy started working in our office, she had her own bad experience involving a man she worked with. That's the reason she wound up as my office manager."

"You're saying she doesn't trust men any more than I trust women?"

"Let's just say it may make her a bit leery of you. You see, a PA at her old job made advances, and, well he almost succeeded in his attack on her. Her boss decided she needed to get outta town, so to speak. He and I had dinner after work one night to discuss a mutual patient, but he was so upset about what the PA had almost done to Kathy, he wound up confiding in me. No way to prove what happened, so the police never got involved. Turned out, our practice needed her, and she needed us. Understand what I'm saying?"

"Yes. Thank you for telling me. I'll be careful to treat her with more reserve." Jacob pondered what he'd been told, while they ate. He wanted to be her friend. Nothing more. How would he make her understand that?

When they finished eating, Dr. Hartley picked up the black folder the waitress had left on the table, opened it, and perused the check. He placed money inside and handed the folder to the waitress when she passed by again. "No change."

"Thank you, sir." She sashayed off.

After rising from the table, Jacob's boss touched his shoulder. "Let's say goodnight to the girls before we leave. And for Pete's sake, try not to step on Kathy's toes, okay?"

"I'll be on my best behavior." Jacob laughed. He'd be more respectful to lessen her fears. Now if he could only do something to rein in his emotions.

As they strolled toward Kathy's table, he examined her soft features and silky hair. What would it be like to hold her in his arms? He smiled. His eyes met Beth's. She glanced at her sister and back at him.

*Nuts.* Not good. He'd let his guard down again, after he promised Dr. Hartley he'd be cautious. He could only hope Beth wouldn't say anything to Kathy about his eyes being glued to her. His jaw clenched.

Dr. Hartley bid the girls good night and slapped Jacob on the back. "Well, my boy. Say your adieus, and let's be on our way. The ice cream shop isn't open all night. It won't be a pretty sight if I don't bring home that dessert I promised Barbara."

Jacob nodded. "Good night, Miss Kendall. Miss...Parker, was it?"

Beth produced a mischievous grin. "Good night, Doctor McLeod. I guess we'll see you Friday night."

He turned to his boss. Might be a good time to excuse himself from Friday's dinner invitation. Doc would understand.

Kathryn's insides tingled as she watched Jacob walk to the front of the restaurant.

Beth stared at her. "Kath, there's something else going on I don't understand. Your reactions to Doctor Handsome tell me you're interested in him. And I'd say it's obvious he's attracted to you. So, why the attitude?"

"Not talking about this, Beth."

As Jacob passed the hostess, the minx handed him a piece of paper. He stuffed it in his pocket without a look. Then he rushed to catch up with Dr. Hartley at the door.

The remark her boss had made earlier about Jacob smiling at the flirtatious girl replayed in Kathryn's mind. She sighed as the men left the restaurant. Was the flirt's phone number on the paper?

# Chapter Nineteen

Sheila bounced up and down as Kathryn and Beth entered the apartment. "Okay, girl, okay. We were gone a long time. Beth, can you grab her leash from the hook while I put Sheila's doggy bag in the fridge?"

"Sure. Come on, you sweet little thing. I'm going to ask Tom if we can find a doggie just like you."

Kathryn smiled as she reentered the room. She took the leash from Beth and peered at the dog. "Try not to make this a forever-circle-the-yard-until-you-find-the-right-spot night. Okay, girl? It's getting late and we have to get up early tomorrow morning."

"Yip." Sheila panted.

When Sheila and Kathryn came back upstairs, the girls laid out their clothes for the next day and prepared for bed.

As she slipped under the covers of the full-sized, four-poster bed, Beth took in a sharp breath. "You're kidding me. A canopy of beaded cord lace? It's almost the same as the lace on my wedding gown. Where did you get all these antiques?"

"Mrs. Weaver told me her mother had the canopy made for her as a wedding gift, but they have a king-sized bed now. And all this furniture had been in storage until I moved in."

Beth leaned over to Kathryn's side of the bed to admire the lamp on the nightstand. "A genuine Tiffany lamp?"

"I told Mrs. Weaver they should have it displayed in their foyer, but she insisted it went with the bedroom furniture."

"The whole place is darling, Kath. Until we're able to afford our own home, I hope Tom and I can find something as nice in California."

A hollowness filled Kathryn's stomach. California was so far away. She set the alarm while Beth scooted back to her side of the bed.

"Goodnight, Beth. I'm so glad you're here."

Sheila hopped up on the bed and did her circle thing, then plopped down at the foot. She cocked her head at Beth, and then whined.

"Sheila's glad you're here, too." Kathryn chuckled.

"Night, baby sister."

"Yip."

"Goodnight to you too, little Sheila." Beth patted the dog on the head and then plopped her own head onto the pillow.

Kathryn turned off the light.

A few minutes later, Beth sat upright. Her footsteps rounded the end of the bed, and she switched on the light. "Kath, we're not going to sleep until you tell me what's wrong." She stood at the side of the bed with her arms folded in front of her. Sheila's head popped up.

As she squinted against the light, Kathryn sat up. "What are you talking about?"

"This attitude you have toward Doctor What-A-Hunk. Where did it come from? And don't tell me you don't want to talk about it."

"Oh, Beth. I told you everything at the restaurant. Let's not go over it a second time." She turned off the light and rolled over.

Her sister flipped the switch on again. "That wasn't the whole story. It can't be." She grabbed Kathryn's shoulder and pulled her onto her back. "I've never seen you act this way. What's going on?"

"He started it. He's the one who's been so hateful to me right from day one." Stretching the truth, but she had to make Beth stop. Yeah, right. She wouldn't let it go until she had her answer.

"After startling me, he made such a big fuss over my sprinkling his jacket with water from the coffee pot. He's found fault with everything I say or do ever since. What about how he's treated me?" Now she'd really stretched the truth out of proportion.

Kathryn took a deep breath and searched Beth's face to see if there was a hint of satisfaction. None.

Beth folded her arms in front of her chest again. "'The lady doth protest too much, methinks.'"

Great. Now she's quoting Shakespeare to me.

With hands on her hips, Beth pinned Kathryn with a stare. "Tell me why you're so touchy."

"Maybe I'm tired of being a rug for people to walk on." Kathryn jutted out her chin.

"No. Not you." Beth shook her head. "I know you better. Something has really upset you. I'll find out what it is if it takes all night. So, if you want any sleep, you'd better tell me what happened."

Tears welled in Kathryn's eyes.

Beth's brows furrowed.

Kathryn sat up. She should tell Beth about the nightmares. The dark figure she'd been telling herself was Jacob, wasn't. It was Mathew.

Kathryn wiggled into the pillow between her back and the headboard to brace herself after she'd told Beth her experience with Mathew. "Except for these horrible nightmares, things have been going well for me. And I've seen no sign of him since I left my old job."

Judging by her expression, Beth was in shock. A lecture would follow for sure. "I think the Mathew Pierce chapter of my life is closed. But I don't understand why I'm having these dreams."

"Oh, Kath. I wish you had told us when it first happened. What an ordeal. And now your mind is revisiting it." Beth reached over and hugged Kathryn.

The hug was a sweet relief to her tight nerves. Maybe she'd escaped Beth's lecture after all. "It's okay. Aside from those nightmares, I've been content with my life. At least, I was, until Doctor McLeod showed up and had his little hissy fit."

Beth stretched to hold her at arm's length. "Such emotion. It isn't the doctor you're angry with, sis. Can't you see that? It's that horrible Mathew. You assumed you were guilty, as though there was something you could have done...or shouldn't have done. And now you're taking it out on poor unsuspecting, handsome, slightly arrogant...but oh so handsome...Doctor McLeod. Did I mention he's handsome?" Beth let go of her and leaned on the other half of the headboard.

With a frown, Kathryn glanced at her. "All right, all right, I get the idea. You sure can go on." She folded her hands in her lap. "Still, you might be right. Maybe I have transferred my anger to Jacob somehow." The egotistical smirk on his face at the restaurant flashed into her mind. "He deserved some of it though."

"Stop, Kath. Almost being molested by this other man has obviously affected you. Don't you see? When Jacob looks at you...and boy does he look at you...it must trigger the memory of Mathew. Did I mention that Jacob is extremely handsome?"

"If you say he's handsome one more time, I'm gonna clobber you." Kathryn grasped her pillow with one hand and held it ready to strike. "And I'll tell Tom how infatuated you are with Jacob." She tilted her chin upward and pulled her lips into a tight smile.

Beth quirked her mouth, then giggled. "Do other men make you tense?"

"No. The only men I'm typically around are the doctors I work for, Pastor Marshall, and the other men at church. I trust all of them. There are no other men at the clinic, except for the male patients. All of them have been very nice so far, even when they do flirt with me. I don't see many of them, since I spend most of the day in the back offices." She adjusted the pillow behind her.

"You didn't mention Nick." Beth's brows rose.

"Don't start. Nick is one of the men at church. Enough psychoanalysis already." Kathryn eyed her pillow again. "You should have gone into the field of psychology. I pity your kids someday. And the friends they bring home."

Beth wrapped her arms around Kathryn in another hug. "Okay. I'll back off. But, despite his numerous transgressions, you will give the handsome doctor a fair chance to redeem himself, won't you?" Beth released her, returned to her own side of the bed, and reclined against the headboard. "After all, he was very cordial tonight." She giggled softly. "Although he scowled at me when he caught me, catching him, eyeing you with his handsome face and green eyes." She pulled the cover up in front of her face.

Kathryn whipped the pillow out from behind her back and smacked her sister in the arm with it. Muffled giggles came from under the covers.

"I suppose I could give the doctor a second chance."

Beth lowered the bedding. "Good."

As Kathryn repositioned her pillow, she glanced at the clock. "Oh, dear. It's after one."

"Wow! We'll be two zombies tomorrow. This morning. Today." Beth fluffed her pillow.

"Right." Kathryn slid under the covers and stared at the ceiling.

Her sister straightened the sheet and cotton blanket. "Did I mention to you how often he looked at you tonight in the restaurant? Not to mention the adoring smile on his face when he approached our table before they left? And have I mentioned how handsome he is?" She fell into a fit of giggles.

After Kathryn had lightly smacked Beth on the back of the head with her open hand, she rolled over and turned out the light.

Beth settled back in bed.

Kathryn closed her eyes. No one needed to tell her how handsome Jacob was. The thought of the way he'd gazed at her that night with those amazing green eyes sent a tingle through her arms.

It would be even harder to work with him now.

# Chapter Twenty

The following morning, Kathryn stepped out of a cab at the clinic. "Okay, Beth. I'll be off work at five if you really want to pick me up. Are you sure you won't get lost?"

Her sister waved the local map Kathryn had given her that morning. "I'll be fine once I rent a car. Don't worry. If I do get lost, you can send your handsome doctor out for me." She laughed and yanked the cab door closed.

Kathryn glared at her. "Stop calling him that."

The cab pulled away, and she entered the building. Working in the same office with Jacob was hard enough without her sister's needling.

When Kathryn walked into her office, she found the man himself in the chair next to her desk. Wonderful. Her heart fluttered. Just great.

He stood. "Good morning, Miss Kendall."

She rounded the desk and put her purse in the bottom drawer. "Good morning, Doctor McLeod." She straightened up and folded her arms. "May I ask why you're sitting in my office?" Drat. Forgot her promise to give him a second chance already. But they were the only two in the building. A slight shudder ran through her. She rubbed her hands along her arms.

His brows rose, and Beth's comments played in her mind. *"Have I mentioned how handsome he is?"* She tried to avoid looking at him and pretended to search for something on her desk.

He spoke with a soft tone. "I hoped you'd be here early as usual so I could talk to you. Will you honor my white flag?" From behind his back, he brought out a single long-stemmed white rose wrapped in green florist paper and tied with a pale pink ribbon. "Truce?"

When she looked up, a charge of electricity sprinted up her arms. A smile erupted on his face, and she collapsed into her desk chair. "I thought white meant surrender. What's this all about?" Drat her unsteady voice.

Her mother had once told her each color of a rose had a meaning. She'd said that a white rose meant young love and sent the receiver a message. It meant the receiver was worthy to be loved.

"Okay. Surrender then." Jacob shrugged his shoulders. "But what I really want is to apologize to you again, in all sincerity. Last night Doctor Hartley pointed out how unfair I've been to you."

She thought so. Only another attempt to please the boss.

"Don't stare at me that way. I agreed with him one hundred percent. He made me see how insufferable I've been toward you and how you've had—"

"I had...what?" She narrowed her eyes.

His smile died. "Well, you've endured my rudeness, even though you didn't deserve it. Truce? Or, surrender? Whichever will end the hostility between us." He gazed into her eyes and held out the rose.

He pushed the flower closer, and she took it from his hand.

Jacob smiled again. "I'm not up on flowers, but the lady at the store told me a white rose also stood for purity. That sounded like cleaning the slate and starting over."

The unruly curl fell to his left eyebrow. The way he pushed it back reminded her of her brother. Except Jacob's mane was thick, dark, and wavy. Chris's had been fair. Like hers. His features less rugged than Jacob's. But her brother used to run his fingers across his hair the same way, before the Marines all but scalped him when he enlisted.

Her heart pinched. She took in a sharp breath. "Okay. We'll forget the past week."

"Good."

Kathryn laid the rose on her desk. "I have to admit that my own actions were far from above reproach. It seemed the more you offended me, the more I wanted to insult you. So, if we're going to call a truce, I owe you an apology as well."

"No, you don't. I'm sure your responses were more self-defense than insult. However...I will accept your apology as part of the truce, *if* you insist. Now, may I take you out to lunch to make amends for my rude behavior?"

Her jaw clenched. *Remember Mathew.* Still, she was so tempted to say yes. "Thank you, but no. I brought my lunch." And just like that, she'd put the wall back up between them. *Sorry, Beth.*

"Right." Jacob's smile faded.

What was he thinking? After the disaster with Patricia. If Kathy had taken that lunch invitation wrong, he'd have started something. Something he'd regret later.

"Okay. If not lunch—" He stood and held out his hand to her. "Hello, I'm Doctor Jacob McLeod from Minnesota." Perhaps a little levity would relax the tension. "Here to wow the patients with my charismatic bedside manner and obvious charm." He cocked his head to the side and gave her a cheesy grin.

She rose and shook his hand. "How do you do, Doctor McLeod? Kathryn Kendall, office manager. Daughter of an Englishman and of Irish heritage on my mother's side. Welcome to the practice."

Her lips pressed together, and she seemed to brace herself against the edge of the desk. Her line of vision traveled to their hands and her face flushed, but she kept smiling. Had a hint of mischievousness flitted over her face?

As he enveloped her hand, warmth flowed through his body. She looked into his eyes, and they held each other's gaze for a second.

"You have a strange way of accepting an apology, Miss Kendall." He laughed. "You're not going to let me forget that Irish/English thing, are you?"

"Never." Her smile grew into a big grin. She slowly pulled her hand out of his and sat down at her desk.

"Okay. I guess I deserve that. Now, I'd better check my schedule for today." He stepped toward the door.

"Doctor McLeod?" Her voice held that melodious quality he'd heard when she hummed the first day he came to the clinic.

He turned back. She'd risen from her desk. "Yes?" Maybe she'd changed her mind about lunch. But her smile was gone.

"We will keep this rose a secret between us, won't we? You won't say anything to anyone? To avoid gossip."

He nodded. Dr. Hartley had mentioned her desire for privacy. He'd like to keep it that way himself. "So be it."

Jacob executed a courtly bow and left her office.

Kathryn stared at the white rose. She glanced at the empty doorway. Then at her hand, which Jacob had held so gently, still warm from his touch. She sighed.

Would he keep this between them or make a big deal of how gracious he'd been to mollify her? He had sounded sincere.

From the bottom of the filing cabinet, she pulled out a bud vase, unwrapped the flower, and dropped it in. She entered the ladies' room, filled the vase with water, and returned to her office. She placed the rose on the corner of her desk.

The muscles in her neck tightened as her thoughts went from Jacob to Mathew. She had to get that bad experience out of her head. Jacob wasn't Mathew.

Should she have accepted the invitation to lunch from Jacob? *Oh, Lord. I'm so confused.* He was only trying to be nice. She was sure of it.

One thing she wouldn't do, she wouldn't mention the rose to Beth. She might know what the colors of roses meant and wouldn't hesitate to tell Jacob if she had the chance.

*Oh no.* The Hartleys' dinner on Friday...with Jacob. And Beth. Would he tell her about the rose?

# Chapter Twenty-One

After church Sunday morning, Kathryn tucked the bridal magazines and stack of notes they'd worked on for the wedding into her sister's carryon. "I've got the last of them. Sure hate to see you leave so soon. You just got here."

Beth's voice traveled from the bathroom. "I know. Can't believe hiring the techs for the new office went so fast, much less the approval from my boss. I'd hoped for more than a week's visit. But, he needs me back in Des Plaines." Sadness filled her voice. "At least we had fun through the week. Mrs. Hartley matched your description exactly. Dinner was so much fun Friday night. What a gracious lady. Plus, seeing you and your doctor in a more relaxed setting was precisely what I'd hoped for."

Kathryn rolled her eyes. *My doctor.* She wouldn't quit.

"Icing on the cake, as Doctor Hartley might put it." Beth giggled and entered the bedroom. She spun. "Well, what do you think? Is this a classic Florida outfit or what?"

She had changed from the white business suit she wore to church into a cream ankle-length sundress with green vines and burnt orange flowers that complimented the color of her hair. The pattern ran along both sides of the dress from shoulder to hem.

"Very becoming, and suits your coloring. When did you get it?"

"Friday. After I completed the business at the new office, I took a long lunch and went shopping. I wanted something to take home that shouted *Florida*. Check out the sandals."

She pulled the bottom of the skirt up to her knees. Tan flat-soled sandals with a strap of heavy strings of beads running across the top adorned her feet. Beth dropped the hem and swung a dark straw purse that completed the ensemble. "Got this too." She did another pirouette, and then dropped the purse on the bed. "Oh, wait."

Beth dashed into the living room, calling back over her shoulder, "I got something for you too."

When she returned to the bedroom, she handed Kathryn a large plastic bag sporting the name Mermaid Island. "Go ahead. Open it. You just have to go to this ladies' wear shop on Pensacola Beach. It's nearly right on the water."

Kathryn pulled the tissue paper out. The bag crinkled as she lifted up a white gauze sundress with a long, royal purple scarf tied around the waist.

"I knew you wouldn't go for this flashy design." Beth twirled again. "And I thought solid white with a touch of purple was more your style. Do you like it?"

"It's gorgeous, Beth. But you didn't have to buy me anything."

Beth squeezed her in a tight hug. "What's a big sister for but to spoil the baby of the family?" She let go of her and bent to gather the bag and tissue from the floor.

"Speaking of spoiling, Jacob sure wants to spoil you, doesn't he? I'm glad you two have worked out your problems."

As Kathryn hung her new sundress in the closet, she thought back to last Wednesday. Things had gone well between her and Jacob. He'd kept their secret about the rose, even when he teased her about it as they ate lunch with a couple of the staff nurses in the breakroom.

*"That sure is a pretty rose you have on your desk, Miss Kendall. What does a white rose stand for?"*

He seemed to relish teasing her. And oh how tempted she'd been to kick him under the table as she had Beth at the restaurant. But she'd given him a glare instead. She chuckled to herself.

The nurses seemed to have their own opinions about what the rose stood for and fortunately hadn't asked where she got it.

Jacob had returned an apologetic nod with his heart-clenching smile. Then he stifled a laugh with his hand over his mouth, but still moved his feet out of her reach. He must've known she'd kicked Beth that night at Blue Dharma. What a character he was turning out to be.

"Kath? Everything is okay between you and the handsome—"

Kathryn came out of the closet and glared at her.

"I mean Jacob. Isn't it?"

"Yes." She closed the closet door. "And you'd better stop calling him handsome, or I promise I will tell Tom. You know, I may never forgive you for embarrassing me Friday night at the Hartleys' dinner. Asking him to take care of me as we left. What were you thinking? Jacob was right when he said you're as bad as one of his pint-sized patients. I never know what will come out of your mouth next."

"Oh, Kath. How could I resist after he was so attentive? Pulled your chair out at the table. Refilled your punch glass how many times?"

Kathryn's brows flinched. He was attentive, wasn't he?

"And when he said he'd consider taking care of you his personal charge, I observed a distinct glimmer in his eye." Beth's features held a self-satisfied grin. Her chestnut ringlets jiggled as she tried to hold back her laughter.

"But Beth, I was so embarrassed. My face must have turned the deepest shade of red ever. I almost strangled you, especially when I saw his amused expression." What magnetic eyes he had. She couldn't turn away.

"Surely you suspect he has a thing for you by now. He wasn't about to let those other guests, the young doctors Mrs. Hartley invited from the hospital, get near you." Beth tossed the shopping bag and tissue onto the dresser.

Kathryn picked up the items and stuffed them in the top drawer. "Jacob's used to being the center of attention, and my boss's wife is the one who placed him at the table next to me."

"Nope. He's smitten."

As she moved to the bed and pretended to smooth the bedspread, Kathryn shook her head. "No. You're wrong if you think it means anything but friendly gestures. That's all he wants. He told me so. He wants a friend. That's all."

"Sure he does. You keep telling yourself that, sis."

Kathryn bit her lip. It had been wonderful though, to have a real gentleman, so good looking and polite, pay attention to her that way. But she had to stop thinking of him. Nothing would come of it. It couldn't. Not again. Any man that handsome couldn't be looking for a permanent relationship when he could have any girl he wanted. Like the hostess at Dharma Blue.

That note the flirt had given Jacob no doubt had her phone number on it.

A vehicle door slammed outside. Kathryn ran to the dormer window. Nick's white Ford truck took up half the driveway. "It's

Nick, and he's coming inside. We've lost track of time. Better get down there."

Beth snickered. "There's plenty of time, but that's our Nick. He'd never expect his *lady* to load luggage."

"Quit. I am not his lady. I'm his friend, just like you. You beat all, you know that?"

Beth picked up her carryon and purse from the bed and headed out of the bedroom. "What will Kathryn Kendall do? Two men in love with her."

Kathryn pushed her through the living room. "I'm going to beat you if you don't stop."

Beth giggled. "It was sweet of Nick to pick me up after I dropped off the rental car yesterday. I could've driven it to the airport and dropped it off there, but he said he wouldn't hear of my leaving Pensacola without a sendoff. What could I say? Nick's always there for ya."

Kathryn followed Beth. Yes. Nick had always been there. "We've been so busy he's hardly had a chance to talk to you." Which may actually have been a blessing. She'd have brought up Jacob for sure.

The left side of Beth's mouth curled. "Nah uh. He wanted to come for an entirely different reason." She smirked. "Now that I think of it, Nick never mentioned Jacob. He does know about him, doesn't he?"

"Why should he? I've had no reason to tell Nick about our new doctor. You're not going to quit, are you? As for his *reasons*...Nick's as much your friend as he is mine."

"Yes, we're friends. But he's in love with you. And why haven't you told Nick about Jacob?"

After she opened the door, Kathryn started down the stairs leading to the Weaver's foyer. "There's nothing to tell." Beth closed the door behind her and followed her sister down the staircase.

The stairwell filled with the sound of Beth's giggles. "Well, you may be spoken for now."

"Don't make me thump you on the head again, Miss Smarty Pants."

As they reached the bottom step, Kathryn turned the knob. The door cracked open an inch.

"Kath...I am happy your nightmares subsided, and you and Doctor McLeod are getting along so well. You never know what might happen."

"Hush, Beth. Someone might hear you."

When they entered the foyer, Nick smiled at Kathryn, then at Beth.

Mrs. Weaver radiated affection as she handed Beth a bag of homemade cookies for the trip home. "Something to nibble on during the flight, dear." She fingered one of Beth's curls, and then turned to Nick. "I was just telling Nick how I'll miss all those nice waves in his light brown hair now that he's gone and cut it short."

"Believe me, Mrs. Weaver. It'll be wavy again, soon enough." He ran his hand over his buzz cut. "It grows like crazy."

She turned to Beth. "Kathy will keep us up-to-date on your wedding plans, but I'll expect a letter from you once in a while too."

"I promise to write. Take care of my baby sister."

Nick hoisted the two swollen suitcases that Mr. Weaver had brought down to the foyer earlier. The muscles in Nick's arms bulged. "We'd better go so you don't have to rush." He headed for the truck.

Kathryn let out a breath she'd been holding. Hopefully, there would be enough of a rush at the airport to keep Beth from saying anything awkward in front of Nick.

Kathryn sat in the back seat of the truck as Nick kept the conversation going between himself and Beth with questions about her company's new office. He wouldn't ask anything about the clinic, she hoped.

After what seemed like the longest fifteen minutes she'd ever lived through, they arrived at the airport. "Nick, maybe you should drop us off at the departure entrance and park the truck. Beth can check her bags, and we'll meet you at security."

"Sure thing." He pulled up in front of the plate glass entry, got out, and then unloaded Beth's bags. He hopped back into the truck and pulled away.

Beth breezed through the check-in process, and they waited for Nick outside the security check. She glanced at Kathryn. "I'll bet before long it'll be 'honey this' and 'honey that' between you and Jacob."

"That's it, Beth. No more visits to Florida for you if you don't stop pushing Jacob on me. First, it was Nick, now it's the doctor. You're worse than Mrs. Hartley."

"Okay, okay. I don't want you mad at me when I'm leaving." She patted Kathryn's shoulder and giggled. "Speaking of Nick, though, what's happened to him?"

Both girls craned their necks to peer over the crush of travelers.

"I hope he gets here before you have to leave, Beth. There isn't much time left. He'll be disappointed to miss saying goodbye."

"Aw, you know Nick. He'll write an apology. Actually, I'd better get to the gate now. I don't want to be the last one to board. I'll call you when I land."

The girls hugged each other, and tears moistened their cheeks. Beth moved to the screening gate. She stepped through the body scanner and picked up her carryon and purse at the end of the conveyor belt. Then she glanced back over her shoulder, and an impish grin spread across her face. "Take good care of your sparkling green-eyed doctor, Kath. I'll expect good reports."

Kathryn's jaw lowered. She whipped her head around to see if Nick was around to hear the comment. Nowhere in sight. She let out a sigh of relief as she watched her sister disappear into the mob of people. The imp just couldn't resist, could she?

Shaking her head, she walked to the terminal entrance and waited. A few minutes later, she glimpsed Nick running toward the plate glass doors.

He burst in. "I missed her, didn't I?"

"Yes, and she'll expect a full written apology from you." Kathryn chuckled.

They headed out of the building toward the parking garage as he joined her laughter. "Took forever to find a place to park. Guess the tourist season has already begun." He gave her a sidelong glance. "So...I take it your office finally got a new doctor. I overheard Beth mention the name Doctor McLeod as you entered the foyer before we left. What's he like?"

Great. "Oh, he's nice enough. He's a friend of Doctor Hartley's." Change the subject fast. "Could we stop for coffee on the way back to your aunt and uncle's for dinner? I need the caffeine."

She had to avoid the subject of Dr. McLeod. The last thing she wanted was to hurt Nick. They'd been such close friend. He might sense her growing feelings for Jacob.

# Chapter Twenty-Two

hen Kathryn arrived at work Monday, a couple of weeks later, a new fresh white rose sat in the bud vase on her desk. She dropped her purse into the bottom drawer, stepped across the hall to the storeroom her bosses had cleared out to make a temporary office for Jacob, and shut the door behind her.

His head popped up from the chart he read. "How can I help you, Miss Kendall?"

A knot formed in her stomach the moment he smiled. She hated those dratted butterflies. She turned her eyes away and fingered the charts on the edge of his desk. "About those white roses." Heat flooded her cheeks.

"Don't tell me you want to break our truce." His eyebrows pinched together. He folded his arms over his broad chest as he leaned back in his chair. "I thought we had this settled. Or, did I do something else for which I need to apologize? I was only teasing you that day in front of the nurses in the lunchroom about the rose, after they mentioned it. Thought I'd throw them off. I didn't tell anyone where it came from. And when you riveted me with that warning glare—" He smirked.

She laughed. "No. You've done nothing wrong. But I should have been upset with you for those remarks." Maybe had gone ahead and kicked him in the shin.

When she returned his smile, he flinched. There was that odd response again. Could he actually feel her imagined kick? "Anyway, you need to stop giving me roses. The girls are teasing me. They say I have a secret boyfriend." Her face had to be beet-red by now.

Jacob's eyebrows rose.

Kathryn cleared her throat. "Well?"

"You don't like them?" His forehead wrinkled, and his lower lip stuck out.

Was he pouting? Could he look more adorable? With those big puppy eyes, and yet so—so masculine.

She shook her head. "No. They're beautiful. I've always preferred white roses. I've never told anyone they're my favorite, and it surprised me that you picked white." Why had she told him that? "But, you've already given me four. I'd say it's enough to call a permanent truce, wouldn't you?"

She dropped her gaze to the charts on the desk again.

"No, I don't." Jacob unfolded his arms, sat up straight, and grinned. "You still haven't allowed me to take you to lunch, and until you do, there's a wall between us. I told you, I want to be your friend."

He picked up the chart and resumed his reading. Without looking up, he said, "You have no obligation over an occasional rose. Tell the girls it's my peace offering after being such a blockhead the first day. I'm sure they'll buy it."

Jacob dropped the chart and locked eyes with her. He quirked his mouth. "Or, does everyone still view me that way?"

She chuckled. "No one thinks of you as a blockhead, Doctor." She pointed at him. "And you remember your promise. Do not tell them where the roses come from."

"Yes, I'll remember. Look. I really do want us to be friends. As far as the roses go, I don't intend to stop giving them to you. It's worth it to see the smile on your face when you walk into your office and find a new one. Don't begrudge me such a pleasure." His brows lifted. "Okay?"

What a stubborn man. She bit her lip and turned to leave.

"Miss Kendall. Is there something wrong with going out to lunch with a co-worker or friend? Or do you refuse to be my friend?"

She spun and took a deep breath. "Of course not."

"Then please join me for lunch today. Simply as my friend and co-worker."

Her eyes narrowed. A tingle went up both arms. He was every bit the gentleman. But she'd thought Mathew was, too. Still, Jacob never said things to make her feel uncomfortable like Mathew had. She'd felt nervous maybe, but not fearful. It was only lunch, after all.

"All right. On one condition."

"What's that?" Jacob quirked his mouth again and lowered his brows.

"We go somewhere where our staff will not see us, you don't tell anyone, and you never tell a soul that the roses are from you. I have no desire to feed the clinic's grapevine. Deal?"

He grinned. "Deal. But that's three conditions." He chuckled. "Where shall we go?"

"I'm not sure. We'll discuss it later." She turned and hurried into her office. The rest of the staff would arrive any minute. Why did Dr. Hartley have to give him the room right across from her? And why, or why, had she had her desk moved to face the hall again?

She sat at her desk and logged in on the computer. The phone rang. Without looking at the lit display to identify the caller, she hit the speaker button. "Hello. Kathryn speaking."

"There's a place—"

Her jaw dropped. She snatched the receiver from its cradle and glowered at Jacob through the perfectly lined up doors. He grinned at her from his temporary sanctum.

She whispered, "You're calling me on the phone...from across the hall?"

"Yes. Now, there's a small restaurant several blocks from here. It's called the Country Cottage Café. On the corner of Main Street and Berry Drive. I've eaten there a couple of times now. Good food. Quiet. Have you been there?"

"No. I don't eat out much. Okay, that's fine." She hung up.

Why so nervous? Nothing bad would happen this time. Not with Jacob.

One patient left to see and then they'd go to lunch. Jacob strolled into his office. He glanced in at Kathy, who stared at the computer screen. Such concentration. Wish she'd concentrate on him that way. He clenched his teeth. He had to stop thinking like that. But, would it be so bad having her in his life? As more than a friend. A big chance. Was he willing to take it? He'd never met anyone like her.

Jacob flipped the chart he carried onto his desk and stuck his head out the door to check the corridor. Coast was clear. He crossed the hall, leaned on her doorframe and whispered, "Don't forget our date."

She glanced up with a grimace but didn't respond.

He winked and then sauntered down the hallway toward check-in. Stupid idea. *What were you thinking, winking at her, calling it a date? What about his conviction not to get involved again?*

After his last morning patient, Jacob returned to his office, arms full of charts to review later. He deposited them on his desk and stepped into Kathy's doorway. "I'm leaving for the café now. Don't forget."

Her eyes rounded. "How can I? You've reminded me all morning. Go! I'll follow along in a few minutes."

"You said you'd never been there before. I did pick somewhere easy to find, right?"

"Will you stop before someone hears you? Another word and I'm not going anywhere."

Jacob laughed and headed out to the back parking lot. His driving there and her walking still hadn't set right with him. But it was the only way she agreed to go. In spite of her annoyance at his teasing, she smiled at him. Beautiful smile.

He jumped into the sports car and headed to the restaurant. He'd convince her to let him drive her back after lunch.

A few minutes later, he pulled onto Berry Drive, parked at the curb, and turned off the engine. Sure was a quiet street during the workweek. No cars to speak of.

As he climbed out, he spotted a young man with long blond hair standing on the opposite corner from the café. One solitary soul. Jacob entered the café and approached a girl with menus in her hand. "Table for two, please."

"Sure. Follow me." She led him to a window-side table overlooking Main Street, left two menus, and walked away.

He peeked at his watch. Kathy should be here in a few minutes.

The waitress returned with napkin-wrapped utensils. "Can I get you a drink while you wait?" She smiled, showing a dimple. Her thick black lashes fluttered.

"A glass of water." When he picked up the menu and focused on it, she left.

The only woman's attention he wanted was Kathryn Kendall's. There had to be a way to develop their relationship without scaring her away. Could they ever be anything more than friends? *And...do you really want to be?*

Mathew Pierce ran his fingers through his shoulder-length sandy blond hair and waited at the corner of Main and Berry for his contact to show. Why had the guy chosen this part of town? More insisted than chosen.

Pierce leaned against the brick wall of an abandoned building across the street from a little eatery. Man, this part of town was a dump. Historical neighborhood. Ha. Almost deserted, too. Only one guy in an old sports car in the past hour that he'd been standing there. Hurricane Ivan sure did a number on it a few years ago, and some buildings still haven't been rebuilt. Like most of his own neighborhood.

If Kenner hadn't dismissed him from the practice, he'd still be in his luxury apartment. But selling this stuff had gotten him by for the moment, along with his current job at the nursing home for cover. He'd be able to afford a better place soon.

At least at that run-down nursing home, he hadn't had to report to another schmuck like Kenner. A string of obscenities flew out of Mathew's mouth.

His new friends had made a good choice letting him in on the action. Drugs and residential break-ins. So many ways he could make the big bucks. Who would've known it'd be so easy? Life owed him, and he'd collect.

"What's keeping this guy?" he muttered. He didn't have all day to hang around. Five more minutes.

A stocky, middle-aged man with dark brown hair strode up the street from the end of Berry Drive. Pierce's eyes narrowed. Thought he'd be meeting someone younger.

Before the man reached him, Pierce caught a glimpse of a young woman as she stopped outside the florist shop a few doors away on Main Street. *Kate?* That little priss had him fired. Thought she was too good for him. He muttered another round of expletives.

The heavy-set man stopped in front of Pierce. "Hey. You the guy I'm supposed to meet?"

Pierce glared and brushed past the man. "I have more important business to take care of."

Kathryn fingered a petal on a bouquet of violets in a flower cart outside the florist shop. What was she doing? Hadn't she had enough trouble keeping Jacob out of her thoughts without having lunch with the man? But she couldn't refuse to be his friend.

She glanced at the shop window. Her eye caught the shadowy reflection of a man behind her. *Mathew!* Before she could turn, his strong arms circled her waist. His lips pressed on her neck.

"Stop!" She spun and shoved against his chest, but he grabbed her arm and held her with his vise-like hands.

An instant, terrifying flashback of the day he trapped her in the storeroom at the old practice filled her mind. Bile rose in her throat. She shuddered.

Kathryn glanced around. No one else on the street.

Mathew pulled her to his chest. "So, here you are, my beautiful Katy-bird. I've been hoping to run into you."

A clammy chill ran through her body. "Take your hands off me." She twisted to escape his grasp, but he wouldn't let go.

Mathew snickered. "I like my hands on you."

"If you don't let go, I'll scream."

He grinned. "Go ahead. I'll kiss you. Anyone who'd hear would assume we're having a lovers' spat. But, oh my, look. There's no one around."

"Leave me alone." As hard as she could, she stomped his foot, jerked her arm free, and ran across the street. The restaurant was only two doors away on the corner. She had to get there.

# Chapter Twenty-Three

*J*acob looked down at the drink straw he held. How could this have happened so fast? It wasn't the same as with Pat. He'd never felt like this about a woman. He was sure he wanted more than simple friendship from Kathy.

He gazed back out the window. The blond-haired man from the corner had slid his arm around Kathy's waist and then lowered his head to her neck. He'd been waiting for her, and they were gone now. Jacob jerked his eyes away. She had a man in her life.

While his heart continued to thump, Jacob focused on the indoor waterfall encircled by a mix of bright-colored flowers and surrounded by a raised stone wall in the middle of the dining area. His heart squeezed. Not her fault. He'd let his emotions get the better of him.

Jacob hailed the waitress, and she rushed to his table. "Would it be okay if I moved to one of those tables over there?" He pointed to the other side of the room next to Tudor-style windows.

"No problem." She picked up his water glass and utensils, and Jacob followed her.

He sat down and peered out windowpanes of tiny crisscross patterned glass, held together with lead.

"Are you ready to order, or is someone still joining you?"

"I—I think I am."

The waitress flicked her ponytail away from her shoulder and smiled. "O-kaaay. Still expecting someone or ready to order?"

What should he do? He rubbed the edge of the menu with his thumb. Tell Kathy how he felt...or forget about her.

"Shall I give you a few more minutes?"

Jacob nodded at the waitress. When she left, he turned to the window and stared outside. A hollowness filled him. What a fool he was.

Kathryn rushed through the entrance of the Country Cottage Café. Her eyes blurred from bridled tears. As she stood breathless in the entry, she blinked to clear her vision and surveyed the quaint round tables covered with white cloth. A bud vase with a red carnation and sprig of fern sat on each. When she spotted the fountain in the center of the room, she took in a breath and let it out slowly. She listened to the splashing water as her pulse calmed.

Movement halfway across the room to her right drew her attention. Jacob rose from a table. She let out a second deep breath and hurried toward him. "I'm sorry I took so long, Doctor McLeod."

He pulled out a chair next to the window.

She sat down and smiled. "Doctor Griffin stopped me as I was leaving."

"Not a problem. I was people-watching while I waited." He sat in the chair across from her and looked out the window at the garden surrounding a patio.

She glanced at him. Was this the same man who was so cheerful earlier today?

After a long moment of silence while they read the menus, Jacob tilted his head and gazed at her. "I was sitting at one of those tables." He glanced to his right. "You stopped at the shop across the street. A man...approached you."

She stared at him for a second, then turned her gaze toward the windows across the room and pictured the sneer on Mathew's face. She snapped her eyes back to Jacob. He saw Mathew.

"Are you all right, Miss Kendall? You sound out of breath, and you're pale. Did something happen to upset you?"

"Hungry I guess. I'm sorry. What did you ask?" He was a man of character. Why not trust him with the truth? She had nothing to fear from him.

"I asked if you're okay. Did something upset you?"

"Yes, actually. Someone—someone I'd hoped never to see again."

Jacob's brows furrowed.

Would he understand her fear? He couldn't. He didn't know what had happened to her. "But why spoil our lunch? He's gone, and I'm hungry." She managed a slight smile.

His iridescent green eyes sparkled from the lighting as he nodded. He returned her smile. Her heart melted, and her pulse thumped even harder than it had from the shock of Mathew's appearance. She'd fallen for Jacob. The most handsome man she'd ever known. Beth was so right.

"Okay, milady. What would you like to eat?"

A waitress sauntered up to their table and faced him as though he were alone. Kathryn laughed to herself. Did every woman look at him that way? Like he was dessert.

He lowered the menu. "I'll have a hamburger, fries, and pop. Ah, whatever cola you have."

The girl wrote his choices down and spun. "And you, Miss?"

Kathryn clapped a hand over her mouth to hold back a laugh. What happened to Miss Flirty's charming smile? "A chicken salad sandwich on wheat, no fries, and a glass of water, please."

Was it possible her own face had that fixed stare the day she and Jacob first met? She turned to the window next to her.

The waitress picked up the menus and sashayed away.

"What a charming restaurant, Doctor. How did you find it? Reminds me of a garden party with that patio and all the potted plants out there."

"I stumbled onto it when I took a walk one evening after work. It's close to the house."

"Really? I didn't realize we were that close. We're not far from where I live either."

He folded his hands, propped his elbows on the table, and rested his chin on his clasped fingers. "And speaking of garden parties. I have a favor to ask of my new friend."

She was right. He only wanted to be her friend. Just as she told Beth. "And what would this favor be?"

"Before I ask the favor, I need an answer to a question that's driving me nuts. Whenever I walk in this neighborhood, I get a whiff of a flowery fragrance. I noticed it again when I stepped out of the car a while ago. Can you tell me what it is?"

She peered through the window to the outside garden dining area. Vines covered the fence surrounding the tables. "I'll bet it's honeysuckle. See those little white and yellow flowers on the vines growing over the fence? Honeysuckle grows abundantly here and it flowered a bit late this year. I noticed a bunch of them climbing on the fence at the house I found for you."

"No kidding." He sat up straight and gazed through the diamond-shaped panels of glass. "No wonder it was familiar. I haven't been outside much since you led me on that tour of the garden." He grinned as his gaze drifted to her.

Butterflies took wing in her stomach.

"Honeysuckle. Odd name." He chuckled. "But, now, to my favor."

She wrung her hands under the table. Lord, let it be something simple.

"That day at the house, when you showed me around the backyard, you made a comment about it being a perfect place to entertain. I want to invite the Hartleys and the Griffins for dinner. The garden at the house would provide a nice backdrop, would it not? I'd like a late dinner party after the heat of the day."

Her cheeks burned with the memory of their walk along the stone path and through the flowers. The strength in his hand as he held hers when they climbed the steps to the deck. She took in a deep breath.

He leaned back in the chair. "When you showed me the garden, you said you could imagine how it might look at night. I assume you meant lit up with torches or strings of lights. Right?"

Her eyes misted. She'd so love to see it like that. "Yes, I remember."

"If I have this dinner party, would you help me? I've never given one, and I'm not sure where to start."

She smiled as her heartbeat raced. "I suppose I could help. As your friend." But no more than a friend.

Friend. Jacob repeated the word in his mind. It'd be too much to hope she remembered their stroll in the garden the way he did. But she had agreed to help him with his plans.

He'd finished orientation, and he'd exhausted his excuses for running into her each day. Thank goodness Doc had set up his temporary office across the hall from hers instead of in the other storeroom at the back of the building. Planning this dinner party, they'd have to get together a lot. "So, what's the first step, milady?"

"First, will the doctors and their wives be the only guests?"

"Well, that's what I thought at first, but if you're going to help, I'd like to invite a few others."

"How many others?"

"Hmmm...can I make the list and give it to you later? The house is small, so it won't accommodate everyone at work. Why don't you make up a list for me?"

"Me? No. It's your party. You make up the list. When do you want this dinner?"

The waitress placed their plates in front of them, flashed Jacob a big grin, and left. He rolled his eyes and clenched his jaw.

Kathy bowed her head.

He touched her arm. "Would you like me to ask the blessing on the food?"

She smiled and lowered her head again.

He spoke little above a whisper. "Lord, please bless this food you've provided, and watch over us as we go about our day. Help us to please You in all we do. In Jesus' name, Amen."

When they raised their heads, she seemed pleased.

As she lifted the first triangle of her quartered sandwich to her mouth, she asked again, "So, how soon do you want this party?"

"End of the month? Gives us more than three weeks to plan, and puts the event before the Fourth of July weekend. Is it enough time to get everything done?"

"That would depend on what you had in mind and how formal?"

"Formal? Ha! It's a yard party." Happiness bubbled up inside him. She was good at making him laugh. He definitely wanted more joy in his life.

While they lingered over the remains of their lunch, Kathy began to fidget. Had she grown tired of him already?

"Doctor McLeod. Look at the time. We've been here for over an hour. You don't want to keep your first afternoon patient waiting. And what will everyone say when we both come in late?"

"It's okay. My first afternoon patient isn't until three. Doc told the girls up front to give me an extra couple of hours on my schedule at lunch so I have time to review patient charts. I'll catch up with the reviews tomorrow."

The muscles in her jaw flexed. "This may sound silly to you, but I don't care to answer a bunch of questions at the office if we walk in late together. If you leave now, I can head back in a few minutes. With me walking, there should be a long enough interval between our arrivals."

He shook his head. "Kathy, it was bad enough that you walked here. I insist on driving you back."

Her eyes widened. "No. I'll walk."

"Even if I promise to drop you off a block from the clinic?"

"Someone might be returning from their lunch and see me with you."

He pursed his lips. "Okay. But only to avoid embarrassment for you. Thank you for finally going to lunch with me. I hope you enjoyed the company as much as I did."

"I did." She smiled. "I'm glad you talked me into it, Doctor McLeod. Or should I say shamed me?"

He chuckled and picked up the check. As he stood and pulled his wallet from his back pocket. A piece of paper fluttered to the floor and landed at Kathryn's feet. She picked it up and handed it to him.

He glanced at the paper and frowned. Nuts. That note from the hostess at the restaurant he'd gone to with Dr. Hartley. Thought she'd handed him a credit card receipt to give to Doc. Never checked it and then forgot about it.

Jacob stuffed it back into his pocket. "Before I leave, could we dispense with the formality of last names? I'd like you to call me Jacob. And I feel odd calling you Miss Kendall all the time."

"You don't need to call me Miss Kendall. You're one of the doctors. Everyone at work calls me Kathy. No one even calls me Kathryn."

"Kathryn. I prefer Kathryn, if you don't mind. It's a pretty name."

She shrugged, and her cheeks colored. "I've always preferred it myself. I'll agree to use your first name, but not at work. I'll show you the same respect I do Doctors Hartley and Griffin in the office."

"Okay. I can live with that. Am I safe to assume you'll go out with me again...as friends?"

"Perhaps."

He took a step, and then turned. "You'll be okay on the walk alone? What about the man who upset you?"

"I'll be fine. I'm sure he's long gone."

Kathryn sat at the table and watched Jacob pay the bill at the register near the entry. Her insides tingled. He left the building, strode past the front windows, got into his car, and drove off.

Her gaze drifted to the florist shop down the street and a chill ran through her. Why hadn't she left with him? She could have checked to make sure no one from the office was around a block away. It would have been fine.

She didn't have to wait. Mathew was probably gone, as she said. He wouldn't stick around. Besides, there were plenty of courtyards along the way to the office. She'd duck in and out of them and zigzag her way back to work. If he did try to follow her, she'd easily lose him. She rubbed her forehead. Oh, why hadn't she left with Jacob?

She could call a cab. But she hated cabs, never knowing who the driver was. And she'd be even later getting back to work.

At the restaurant entrance, she peered out the door to survey the streets. No sign of Mathew. She left the building at a quick pace and hurried down Main Street to the first courtyard. After she turned the corner and entered the passageway between the two buildings, she sprinted to the next street. Good thing she had decided to wear sandals instead of heels today.

What was that? Sounded like someone walking on gravel. She spun, but no one was in the courtyard. Must be her overactive imagination. She took a deep breath and continued to snake her way toward the clinic.

Why, oh why, hadn't she left with Jacob?

# Chapter Twenty-Four

*J*acob paced his tiny office. Behind the desk, out into the hall, and back again. Where was she? Kathryn should have been here by now. Something nagged at him. What if that guy she mentioned hadn't left? He'd better go out and find her. But he had a patient at three. It was almost time now. What should he do?

He sat on the corner of his desk and pulled his cell out of the holder to dial Dr. Hartley's phone. He'd better tell Doc what happened at lunch. The phone rang once, and he hung up. She'd kill him if he told Doc about lunch. But what if that guy was the one Doc told him about? He'd ask his boss to see the three o'clock patient. Make up some excuse why he had to leave.

Jacob hit redial and hung up again. Doc would already be at the hospital with Dr. Griffin by now, and the PA was off today. There wasn't anyone to cover for him so he could go look for her. Jacob resumed pacing. What should he do?

Footsteps echoed in the corridor.

As Kathryn rushed into her office, Jacob bolted in right behind her and shut the door. "It's about time you showed up. What happened?"

Her eyes grew wide, and her jaw dropped. She was breathless.

"Kathryn. What happened to you?"

She collapsed onto the chair behind her desk and threw her purse in the drawer. "I'm okay. Winded. Walked too fast. Winding in and out of courtyards."

"Did you see that man again? Did he come after you?"

"No. Let me...catch my breath."

"I'll be right back." Jacob dashed out the door and zipped down the hall to the lunchroom. He put change in the pop machine and punched the button for a bottle of water. The drink clunked into the tray. He raced back to Kathryn's office and handed her the ice-cold bottle.

"Here. Drink this."

"Thank you, Ja—Doctor McLeod." She still gasped for air.

He pushed the door closed and sat down next to her desk. "Now tell me what happened. Do you realize I left the café an hour ago? You said you'd get here fifteen minutes after me."

She bit her lip and blinked her eyes. "It's okay. I had to make sure M—he wasn't around. But after you left..." She gulped. "...it occurred to me...he might not have...and...I didn't want to talk to him. I almost jogged through the streets. Zigzagged my way back to the office. Cut through every courtyard I found. It took longer."

Jacob laid his hand on top of hers on the desk. "I know who he is."

Her brows pinched. "How? Who told you?" She pulled her hand away.

"Look. Don't blame Doctor Hartley. He thought it was best for me to be aware of your experience in your former job. He decided to tell me because of how I'd treated you, and your reaction."

Her face turned red, and she buried it in her hands.

"Kathryn. The same thing has happened to others. It's best that Doc told me. It's why I worried when you failed to show up. I blame myself for not insisting you ride with me."

She said something, but the words came out garbled.

"What? I didn't understand you." He touched her hand.

She dropped both hands into her lap. "I'm sorry I didn't tell you. And made you worry. Please go away now."

He slid the tissue box from the edge of the desk closer to her, rose, and left, closing the door behind him.

Tears fell as she watched Jacob walk out. The tenderness in his eyes had pulled at her heart. If only he wanted more than a friend. He'd shown the same concern any gentleman would. Concerned. That's all.

Dr. Hartley should not have told him. But she'd forgive him under the circumstances.

Should she tell her boss what happened this afternoon? She couldn't. The doctors had helped her enough already, and she didn't want to worry them too. She'd ask Jacob not to say anything either.

The café's neighborhood would be off limits to her forever. Fortunately, Mathew never showed up on her trek back to the clinic. Probably left after he'd accomplished what he wanted to do. Scare her to death. He hadn't hurt her, at least not physically.

She opened her computer and started her afternoon tasks. It'd be a shame not to visit the café again. Such a cozy, romantic place. At least she'd have the memory of her lunch with Jacob. And they'd work together on plans for his dinner party.

She slapped her hands on the keyboard. *Oh, dear.* Had she upset him when she asked him to go away?

Kathryn bolted out of the chair and swung open the door. He must have gone to see his patient. She sighed and returned to her desk. How would she concentrate on these figures after the way she treated him? Not knowing if she'd insulted him. He'd had such a worried expression on his face.

By four o'clock, her wrist was red from twisting her watch around to view the time after checking the wall clock. Had he decided to stay away from her after her rude remark? She had to find him. Kathryn dashed into the corridor and slammed into Jacob. "Oof!"

His hands grasped her shoulders. The chart he carried flew to the floor. "Milady...we've got to stop meeting like this." A heart-stopping grin spread across his face.

Nervous giggles burst out of her. She picked up the chart and handed it to him. "I was on my way to find you."

"Tell me I'm not in trouble again." His brows furrowed.

Kathryn pressed her lips together, trying to keep from laughing. "Um." She cleared her throat. "I apologize."

"For what?"

"For telling you to leave. I was embarrassed."

"Let's go in your office." He shut the door behind them and they sat down. "Doc left out the specific details. He told me you were attacked. Actually, that it was an attempted attack. I knew what he meant. Many patients who had been *attacked* came into the hospital during my residency.

"I understand your embarrassment, but these guys are scum. Pure and simple. That's why I became so concerned when you didn't arrive within a reasonable amount of time this afternoon. I saw him put his arm around your waist and bend over you. I assumed he was kissing you. At first, I thought he might be a boyfriend. That was before you said you hoped not to see him again. Then I remembered what Doc had said and the distress on your face when you came into the café. Wasn't hard to put two and two together."

"Jacob, I'm sorry I didn't trust you enough to tell you about him."

"It's okay. We haven't known each other long, so I can understand."

She smiled. Had it only been that morning when they'd decided to become friends? It seemed as though they'd been friends for months. Strange.

"Are you sure you're okay? The guy didn't pop up again?"

"He must have left. Just wanted to scare me. Had his big laugh at my shock and continued about his business."

"Good. That's a relief." Jacob rose and turned toward the door. As he opened it, he glanced over his shoulder. "Still game to help me plan the dinner?"

"Of course."

"Excellent. While I waited for you, I wrote up a tentative guest list. Do you want it now?"

"Sure."

He left her office and returned seconds later. In his hand was a sheet of yellow paper from a legal pad. He laid it on her desk. Three sets of names in physicians' scrawl were written on the sheet.

She wrinkled her nose as she peered up at him. "You expect me to read this? Do you doctors practice this penmanship?"

He laughed and checked his watch. "I have ten minutes before my next patient. Let me see if I can read it." He took the sheet. With a silly smirk, he held it at arm's length and brought it back. He sighed, dropped into her visitors' chair, took a pen from her desk, and printed the names next to the writing. Then he handed her the paper and stood.

While he leaned on the doorframe, one leg over the other and arms crossed in front of his chest, Kathryn perused the list. "Doctor and Mrs. Hartley, Doctor and Mrs. Griffin, Haley Smith and her husband. It's a good group. Not too large. Nice that you included the PA and her spouse. You have everyone paired off but you. Don't you want a dinner guest to round out the number?" She peered up at him from under her lashes. "Perhaps the waitress at Dharma Blue, for instance?"

His eyes narrowed. He pushed himself off the doorway and took a step closer to her.

Oops. He sure wasn't pleased with that remark. She shouldn't have said anything.

"Kathryn. I'd appreciate it very much if you'd forget the flirt at that restaurant."

She laughed under her breath. Guess the temptress wasn't his type after all. She was so sure the girl had handed him her phone number that night. And he'd kept it.

He grinned at her. "I assumed you'd come. I guess I should have put your name on the list. See how inept I am at this? Would you consider being my hostess for the evening?"

Her heart thumped so loud she was sure he'd hear it. "Me?"

"Yes, you. Who else? You don't think I'd ask you to help plan the party and then leave you out, do you? I do need a hostess, seeing I'm so ignorant about this. Please?"

The green pools deepened as his eyes pled while he gazed at her.

She swallowed. "Yes. I will. Thank you, Doctor McLeod." She'd have a heart attack if her pulse continued to race like this.

"Thank you for not making me beg." He let out a slight snicker. "Time for my last patient of the day. However, before I go...may I drive you home from work? You've had a rough day, and you're exhausted."

She shook her head. "It's okay. I'll catch the bus as always. It stops on the corner one building from here, and I get off one block from where I live. No need to worry. Mathew has no idea where I work, much less where I live."

"Still, I'd feel better. Humor me? We can stall around until everyone leaves so no one sees. The other doctors are already on rounds at the hospital and will be with Mr. Chaney for a while, who, by the way, has finally started to show signs of improvement. No one will know I've driven you home. I promise. Please?"

How could she say no? "Okay. I'll wait here until you're done. And that's wonderful news about Mr. Chaney."

Jacob nodded and headed to the front office.

Oh, brother. No doubt, Jacob had always managed to get his way with those sad, green, puppy-eyes. Not to mention his charm. This better not be another mistake.

From the doorway across the street, Mathew glared at the man who left the building with Kate. What good had it done him to follow her here? She had a boyfriend taking her home.

He watched as the musclebound man opened the door of an older green Austin-Healey. Kate smiled up at him and slipped into the seat.

*He-e-ey.* He was the one who parked outside the restaurant this afternoon. She must have been meeting him there. Same car, and he sure looked the same as the guy who got out of it. But why did he drive there, and she walked? Maybe he was her boss. Odd.

The vehicle turned out of the parking lot. Mathew ducked into the shadow of the doorway as it rolled by.

If they weren't a couple, she'd probably leave work on her own tomorrow. With his early shift at the nursing home, he'd make it here before her quitting time in the evening. Then he'd follow her home.

Hope she got rid of that mutt. No matter. The mongrel wouldn't stop him next time. He'd make sure of it.

The Katy-bird thought she'd been clever with all those twists and turns this afternoon. But not enough to lose him. Although she almost caught him in the first passageway when he stepped into the rock garden. Lucky he found an alcove to duck into.

She had a surprise date coming tomorrow. And it'd be fun. At least for him. *You're mine, Kate.* He ran his tongue over his bottom lip and sneered.

# Chapter Twenty-Five

*A* couple of weeks later on Friday, Jacob pulled up in front of the Weavers' house. Before he could get out of the car, Kathryn ran down the porch steps. He rushed around to the passenger door.

"We have plenty of time, milady. I don't mind coming to the door to get you."

"Don't be silly. I can at least be ready to leave when you get here. It's enough that you're giving me a ride each day."

"A lift to and from work is not a big deal. You live between the clinic and me. It makes sense. Why should you take a bus every day?"

"Well, I do appreciate your kindness. And will even more so, when the cold weather starts. If you're not tired of me months from now, that is."

Fat chance of that happening. His feelings for her grew stronger each day.

After she slipped into the seat, Jacob closed the passenger door and returned to the driver's side. He eased behind the wheel and pulled out into an almost deserted street. It was great that they both wanted to get to work before anyone else. "Out of curiosity, why don't you drive?"

"Guess I've never been able to justify the expense of a car with the gas, insurance, and monthly payments. It seemed too extravagant with my apartment so close to work. I might change my mind if I could summon enough confidence to take the driving test." She chuckled.

He shook his head and smiled.

When he pulled to a stop at a red light a block from the office, he glanced at her. "These past two weeks have flown by. The dinner party will be here before you know it."

"Yes, and the Pediatric Conference next week, too. That'll make the time fly by even faster."

The light turned green, and he drove through the intersection.

"Jacob, do you have your program for the conference lined up yet?"

"How did you find out about my lecture?"

Kathryn laughed. "Haven't you learned yet? Any request for my doctors' participation in a program is scheduled by me."

Her doctor? Freudian slip? His brows rose. "Back to the subject of the garden party. We can discuss my program later. Is everything worked out for the dinner yet? Is there anything I need to do?"

"About what?"

"About the party, of course." He shot her a narrow-eyed stare. "You're messing with me, aren't you?"

She bit her lip and giggled. "It'll be fun to order you around. I have carte blanche on the decorations, right?" She grinned.

"Within reason." He pulled into his parking place at the clinic. "Why don't you come over tomorrow? We can talk about everything still to be done. Give me a list of what I need to pick up. If you trust my judgement."

"I'll have to check my busy social calendar."

"Good, what time should I pick you up? How's a casual dinner on the deck sound?"

"Doctor McLeod. You're taking for granted that I'll come."

He grinned and got out of the car.

Mathew stopped a block from where Kate worked and hid his motorcycle behind a clump of bushes. He scurried to the doorway across the street from the clinic just as she walked out to the front parking lot.

Every night he'd managed to get there in time for a chance to follow her home, she'd left with that same guy. They must be a thing. Tailing his sports car with a red motorcycle would be too obvious. Couldn't take the chance.

*Don't think I want to mess with him.* The guy looked like he could take care of himself. But he couldn't let Hercules keep her all to himself. There had to be a way to find out where she lived.

When the green sports car passed out of sight, Mathew swung his leg over the bike and started it. The tires screeched as he took off in the direction of his own apartment. He'd get together with the guys at Cage's Lounge tonight and see if they had any ideas. They'd know what to do. Been at this kind of stuff a lot longer than he had. Two weeks of waiting for his chance to trail her home was long enough. He wanted payback.

Saturday afternoon, Kathryn's pulse raced at the thought of having dinner with Jacob in his cozy rental house. She'd never had dinner all alone with a man before. Not outside of her father and brother. But she was an adult now, twenty-five years old. At least, she would be next month. And Jacob had proven himself a gentleman.

Out her second floor window, she spotted his green sports car as it rounded the corner a few houses down from the Weavers' home. "He's here, Sheila. Let's head downstairs."

With Sheila on her leash, Kathryn skipped down the staircase. "Be on your best behavior, girl. After all, it was nice of Jacob to include you."

"Yip."

At the bottom of the stairway, Mrs. Weaver's voice came through the door. "It's very nice to meet you, Doctor McLeod. Kathy told us a little about your arrival at the clinic weeks ago."

As Kathryn came into the foyer, Jacob's gaze took a sharp turn in her direction. His brows rose.

Mrs. Weaver continued, "But we haven't heard much since then. Except that you've been kind enough to pick her up for work each day." The silver-haired woman placed her hand on Kathryn's shoulder. "It worries us so when she has to take the bus early in the morning with hardly a soul on the streets."

Kathryn's face grew warm. She looked up at Jacob. "When you started at the clinic, I explained to Mr. and Mrs. Weaver how you and Doctor Hartley knew each other, and what a drastic change it was for you to move from Minnesota to Florida." She glanced at her landlady, who smiled, winked, and nodded. When she got home from Jacob's tonight, she'd give Mrs. Weaver a big hug for not mentioning what else she'd told them.

Jacob bent down to pat Sheila's head. "So, this is the little roommate you mentioned. Hello, Sheila. I hope we can be friends, too."

At the word "friends," Kathryn's heart twinged.

Sheila's tail wagged her approval as she tugged on the leash. "Yip, yip."

He chuckled. "Your little girl here is in a hurry for a car ride."

Kathryn reeled in the leash and picked Sheila up in her arms. "The minute she sees me pick up the leash now, she anticipates an adventure beyond the backyard."

Mrs. Weaver joined in their laughter. "You two young people have a nice evening." She turned toward Jacob. "I understand you've planned a garden party. How delightful."

"Well, Kathryn's been in charge of the planning. I've just taken notes. And orders."

Mr. Weaver stepped into the hallway from the kitchen with a small piece of donut in hand and hurried to the foyer. "You must be the Doctor McLeod we've heard of." He extended his hand to Jacob and swallowed. "Sorry. Had a little pre-dinner snack. Didn't realize someone came in until your voices drifted down the hall."

"Jacob McLeod, sir." He shook Mr. Weaver's hand.

Mrs. Weaver winked at Kathryn again and then took her husband by the arm. "Dear, let's let these young people get on with their evening. And now that you've had your first dinner for tonight, we can finish our game of Scrabble before I make supper for both of us."

"Don't know why I bother playing board games with you, Sugar. You always win."

As the older couple left arm in arm, Kathryn and Jacob smiled.

She sighed. What a blessing a marriage as sweet as theirs would be. Like her own parents had.

Jacob opened the front door. "Sweet couple."

"They are." She stepped out the door onto the front porch and put Sheila down on the wooden planks. "They've been very good to me."

He closed the door behind them. "I can tell they're very fond of you."

Jacob led her to the car and opened the passenger door. "You'll have to hold Sheila in your lap. Not much room in this little puddle-jumper."

"That's fine." Kathryn slipped into the seat, and Sheila leaped into her arms.

Once Jacob pulled onto the street, he glanced toward Kathryn. "How did you end up living in the Weavers' home?"

"Actually, I live upstairs. When they finished remodeling their children's old bedrooms into a studio apartment about a year ago, they had the Hartleys over for dinner and showed them around. Turned out to be perfect timing. Doctor Hartley told my former boss about the apartment when he and Doctor Kenner had dinner together. Just at the time when things looked bleakest for me, and I needed to move."

Jacob turned the last corner onto his dead-end street and parked the sports car in the narrow driveway. "It always amazes me how things work out."

He hopped out of the car and ran around to the passenger side to open the door for her.

As she put one foot out, Sheila jumped to the ground and tugged on the leash. "Whoa, girl. Wait for me. Good thing I didn't unleash her. She's ready to explore."

"Why don't you let her into the backyard while I unload the things I picked up today for the party?"

Jacob led them into the foyer, and Kathryn took Sheila through the house to the kitchen. She unlocked the sliding glass door leading to the backyard.

Jacob rushed up behind her. *"Wait!"*

She spun as he grabbed the handle. "What?"

"Um…" He opened the door and stuck his head out, searching the deck.

Kathryn followed him. Sheila sniffed the boards as if a steak had dropped onto them. A couple of bowls sat in the corner of the deck. "I see you've already anticipated Sheila's need for something to eat and drink out here. She usually eats in the kitchen at the apartment, but I'm sure she won't mind the deck."

"Well, um…those bowls are—"

Something touched the back of Kathryn's leg and she bolted forward. The leash dropped to the deck as she grabbed Jacob's forearms with both hands. Sheila ran behind her and whined.

"Meooow."

As she sagged against Jacob's chest, Kathryn let out a breath of relief. She straightened up and heat rose from her neck into her cheeks. "It's a cat. It's only the neighbor's cat." She peered down at both animals circling her feet. "And it would appear that she doesn't mind Sheila one bit."

Jacob chuckled. "Your little friend doesn't mind the cat either. Her tail's going to wag right off."

Kathryn eyed the bowls in the corner, and then Jacob. "I thought you didn't like cats. It seems to me the powder puff has found a new home."

He grinned. "I like them now." His gaze went to her hands, which still clung to his arms.

She let go and backed up to the railing, then squatted to unhook Sheila's leash. "There you go, girl. Have fun with your new-found friend."

The cat padded her way to Sheila. It rubbed up against the dog's white fur and received a lick on the nose.

Kathryn laughed and peered up at Jacob, who towered over her. "You've adopted her?"

"It's more like she adopted me." He reached down to scratch the cat's head and then took Kathryn's arm to help her stand. "She returned every day, meowing all the time like she was hungry. I gave her some food. Figured it was either feed her or watch her starve to death."

He glanced at Kathryn with his brows lowered. "Something told me you'd never forgive me if I let her waste away."

Kathryn laughed so hard she doubled over and tears came to her eyes. Jacob handed her his handkerchief.

When she had regained her composure, she said, "You know, if you really don't like cats, there are such things as animal shelters."

He shrugged. "I've gotten used to her now."

"What did you name her?"

"Muffy."

Her heart fluttered as she recalled the day they first visited the deck when she stroked the cat's coat and told him she'd call her Muffy if the cat were hers. Was it only weeks ago?

A chime rang inside. Jacob turned to head for the front door. "That's probably our dinner. Hope you like Chinese. I ordered sweet and sour chicken, egg rolls, and chicken fried rice."

"Love it." She followed him into the house.

They returned to the back porch and set the food on the patio table to begin their meal.

An hour later, Jacob swallowed the last of his egg roll, leaned back, and gazed at Kathryn as she finished hers. "Would two more guests overcrowd the party?"

"I don't think so. Who did you have in mind?"

He smiled. "Since the Weavers are the Hartleys' friends, and you're so fond of them, they should be included."

"Aww. That's thoughtful of you, Jacob." How she wished she could share a life with him. Wouldn't ever happen, though, would it?

She gathered the empty white containers from their dinner and headed to the kitchen. They'd never get any closer to sharing their lives than this.

Jacob hung white patio lights across the covered deck and switched them on. He backed up to the end of the porch and sat next to Kathryn on the glider swing he'd purchased earlier in the week. Dusk had fallen. Her eyes sparkled with reflected light. Soft classical music drifted out through the slightly open sliding glass door from the CD player in the living room.

He stretched his arm behind her and rested it on the back of the swing. After a moment, he pushed his legs to set the swing into motion. With a sigh, she leaned back against his arm. She bit her lip and suddenly straightened.

Tonight had been great, and he'd made progress in their relationship. She had laughed easily and seemed so relaxed. Now she was nervous. Not what he wanted. You blockhead. Moved too fast.

He withdrew his arm. "We should go inside. The yard fogger will wear off soon, and we don't want to be on the mosquitoes' menu." He chuckled.

They stood and strolled to the sliding glass door. As he opened it, Sheila and Muffy scooted past them into the kitchen. In their rush, Sheila bumped Kathryn, who lost her balance and fell against Jacob's chest.

His arms circled Kathryn to keep her from falling. She gazed up at him. Her lips parted. He bent his head closer. His heart drummed and his pulse surged. Her eyes began to close, but then popped open.

She turned away. "I think...I should go home now."

# Chapter Twenty-Six

On the evening of the garden party, as Kathryn stood under the decorated canopy on one side of Jacob's backyard, she thought back to the night she had dinner with him. What would have happened if she hadn't asked Jacob to take her home right away that night? He almost kissed her. And she'd wanted him to, so much. But why would he? He kept telling her they were friends. What was he thinking? He didn't seem the kind of man...not like Mathew.

A movement at the back of the yard caught her attention and brought her back to the present. A puffy white tail flicked and disappeared behind the shed. Had to be Muffy, the co-instigator.

She resumed her pondering. Over the last two weeks, she'd spoken to Jacob only in passing. Granted, the practice had been unusually busy lately, and he'd spent little time in his office. When he did sit at his desk, he'd kept his head buried in charts. Even to and from work, they'd hardly spoken, except about the preparations for tonight's dinner.

When he picked her up tonight, he'd kept his eyes on the road all the way here. He'd been quite talkative with the Weavers before they left the house. Things were so strange between them.

The doorbell chimed. Kathryn ran up the steps to the deck and gazed out over her handiwork. Jacob had said, *"I want this night to be something everyone would remember."* A night for everyone to remember. She didn't know about anyone else, but she certainly would.

Candles and tea-lights flickered atop square folding tables set on the covered deck. Beneath the canopy in the yard, a row of tapers twinkled in the soft breeze down the middle of a long table. From one end of the large canvas-covered metal frame to the other, tiny white Christmas lights hung overhead in a crisscrossed pattern resembling stars. The snowy tablecloth glowed in contrast to the deep green ivy woven between cut-glass candleholders.

She grinned. Tulle pulled through the intricate, curved black uprights and crossbars of the gazebo fluttered as the ends of the fabric trailed onto the grass. "Absolutely beautiful," she whispered.

Classical music filled the air from the outside speakers Jacob had mounted on the deck. He must have switched the CD player on.

When she faced the sliding glass door, heat filled her cheeks. *Right here.* He'd almost kissed her in this very spot.

Dr. Hartley's booming laughter interrupted the thought. With one last look at her handiwork, she entered the house.

Jacob grinned as he opened the door for his guests. "Come in. Make yourselves at home."

After everyone roamed from the foyer, through the living room, and into the dining room, Mrs. Hartley stepped up behind him. "What an enchanting way to decorate for the evening, Jacob. Tea lights and ivy everywhere. I'll have to remember this the next time I have a dinner party. Which reminds me, I need to speak to you about something." His boss's wife glanced toward the kitchen doorway.

Kathryn leaned against the counter. His heart pounded as she smiled at him. He dragged his gaze back to Mrs. Hartley. "Thank you. What did you want to talk to me about?"

"It'll wait until later."

Doc came up behind them. "Well, I'd say you've learned a few domestic skills, my boy." He slapped Jacob on the back.

Jacob chuckled.

Mrs. Weaver sat down in a recliner in the living room. She raised her brows at her husband across from her in the other recliner. "These chairs are nice."

The Griffins and Smiths returned from the dining area to the living room with cups of punch in their hands.

"Make yourselves comfortable, everyone. Dinner will be ready in a few minutes. I'll give Kathryn a hand and then come back for you."

Doc settled back into a Queen Anne chair across from the couch. Mrs. Hartley sat in the other next to him and leaned forward, taking in a deep whiff of the multi-colored roses in a basket on the coffee table.

Jacob entered the kitchen and beamed at Kathryn. "So far, so good. Everyone seems pleased to be here."

"I'm so glad you decided to have this party." She wrapped her arm around a huge bowl of spinach-strawberry-walnut salad and picked up a fancy pitcher of raspberry balsamic vinaigrette with her free hand. "I wanted so much to see the yard all fixed up like this." She headed for the sliding glass door.

Jacob hurried to open it for her and then followed her out with a platter of glazed chicken drumettes and a dish of sweet and sour meatballs.

They descended the stairs and placed the food on the long table under the gazebo. She covered the food with mesh domes.

He frowned. "Won't the fogger I used half an hour ago, plus the citronella torches all around the yard, keep the bugs at bay?"

She laughed. "I'm sure they will, but I don't want Muffy thinking she can sample the food. I should have agreed to bring Sheila tonight to keep your little furball busy."

"Ooh. Okay. I'll get the potato salad and that fruity thing, whatever you called it."

She nodded. "Fresh Fruit Arrangement. Thought it made more sense to have a centerpiece we could eat."

He watched as Kathryn repositioned the lit tapers to accommodate the fruit arrangement. She made a perfect lady of the house. His heart swelled.

When he returned with the salad and fruit, he found her with her head bowed over the end of the table. "What's wrong?"

She peered up at him with glistening eyes. "Nothing. Everything is perfect. Just thanking God for helping us get it all done in time."

Jacob deposited the food on the table and took her hands in his. "Kathryn, there's something I need to say."

Her brows lowered. "What?"

*Not now, dumbbell.* He had to wait for the right time. Not with a house full of guests. He'd made her nervous again. "I really appreciate all the work you did for this evening."

She grinned. "It was my pleasure. I knew it would be like an enchanted garden."

That was why he'd wanted it. For her. He'd have to wait for just that special moment to tell her how his feelings had grown for her.

After dinner, Jacob sat in the glider on the porch following Kathryn's every move as she meandered through the garden with his guests. Was there anyone as lovely or sweet? And what a gracious hostess. She'd make the perfect wife.

Mrs. Hartley stepped out of the house and took a seat next to him, while her husband went to join the others. "Finally caught you alone."

He turned to her.

"I've been trying to talk to you without Kathy around."

"Is there a problem?"

"No problem. Kathy's twenty-fifth birthday is on July twenty-fifth." She giggled. "Coincidence, huh? Anyway, Bonnie Griffin and I want to throw her a big formal party since her family isn't here to do it. Our husbands have promised not to say anything to her at the office so we can surprise her. But we need your help."

"Great idea. What can I do?"

"First, we need you to keep David from letting it slip. Secrets are not his forte. If you hear him say anything close to tipping her off, derail him. Okay?"

Jacob laughed. "I'll do my best, Mrs. Hartley. What else can I do?"

"This is the most important task. We need you to get her to the party. After watching the two of you this evening, it shouldn't be hard."

He shifted on the glider to face her better. Had everyone noticed how he felt about her...except Kathryn? He'd better be more careful. "I'll be happy to bring her to the party, but how? We're not exactly dating. She only agreed to help me plan this garden party as a friend."

"Tell her that I told you about her birthday, and you'd like to take her out to dinner. David said he only knows of one close friend of hers here in town. A young man named Nick, I believe it was. But Kathy introduced him as her late brother's former college roommate. So, I don't think they're dating. Could you at least try? If you run into a problem, call me. I'll figure out something."

Jacob leaned back in the swing. This might provide the opportunity he'd been looking for. "Sure. I'll find a way to convince her to go to dinner with me."

"Wonderful. I'll give you the details when we get everything planned."

As Pachelbel's Canon in D Major drifted out from the house, Jacob kept his eyes focused on Kathryn. How beautiful she looked in her long, flowing white summer dress, which shimmered in the moonlight. Rhinestone-studded barrettes sparkled in her hair to create a crown-like effect around the fine spun-gold curls piled on top of her head.

*Yes, that will be the evening I tell her.*

Kathryn glanced at Mrs. Hartley, who came down the steps and joined her husband under the gazebo. He slid his arm around his wife's waist, and she grinned at him.

How wonderful it would be to have someone to love, and return that love. A man like Jacob. A twinge swept through her. But he had the same feelings for her that she had for Nick. Regardless of what had almost happened the other night. It sure was odd that no woman had yet captured Jacob's heart.

Out of the corner of her eye, she saw him leave the deck. He strolled over to her. "Well, milady. You made my first dinner party a colossal success. You deserve a reward."

"I don't need a reward for having the best time of my life." She smiled. "Just to see the doctors, their wives, the Weavers, Haley, and her husband enjoy themselves like this is reward enough."

He glanced around the yard. "Everyone has moved into the house. Shall we join them?"

She nodded, and they went inside.

In the living room, Dr. Griffin held out his hand to Jacob. "This has been a great evening. Thank you for inviting us. We'll have you over to our house again soon." He winked. His wife jabbed him in the arm with her elbow.

Mrs. Griffin gave Jacob a hug and then embraced Kathryn. "I know you had something to do with all the arrangements for tonight, my dear. They were fantastic." She glanced at the jeweled watch on her wrist. "It's getting late for us. Almost midnight."

From the foyer, Dr. Hartley called, "Jacob, we have to go, too. We're not as young as you whippersnappers." He guffawed.

"Don't mind him." Mrs. Hartley shook her head. "He's hopeless." Then she laughed. "But I do feel the lateness of the hour. Thank you for a lovely time."

Jacob saw the doctors, their wives, and the Smiths to the front porch. He then returned to Kathryn's side.

She sighed. "The Weavers must be ready to leave too. Good night, Jacob."

With his hands on her shoulders, he turned her around to where Mr. and Mrs. Weaver napped in the recliners.

"Oh dear." She covered her mouth with her hand to stifle a giggle. "They must have dozed off after dinner."

Jacob led her away toward the deck. "Why not let them snooze for a few minutes longer? We never got to stroll through the garden this evening together."

A tingle ran up Kathryn's arms.

"You did want to view every corner of the fantasyland you created, didn't you?"

"Yes." Her heart skipped a beat.

After a tour of each section of the backyard without a word between them, he led her to the gazebo and placed a couple of folding chairs facing each other. She sat, and he took the other seat. Their knees touched.

She scooted her chair back. "Jacob?"

He gazed into her eyes.

Her heart had done things tonight she'd never experienced before.

"Yes?" He smiled.

"Why do you keep calling me milady?"

"It fits you. You remind me of someone from long ago when women were different than most are today. More genteel." He looked down at her hands in her lap and reached for one. As he held it gently in his, her face grew hot.

"You're not like a lot of the modern women I've met with their loud mouths, crude talk, and unladylike manners. Do you mind my calling you milady?"

She pulled her hand away and pushed a stray tress of hair behind her ear. "I like it."

Her thoughts ran to the hostess at the restaurant the night he dined with Dr. Hartley. As the girl flirted with Jacob that night, he seemed to pay particular attention to her. Had he seen her again? He seemed annoyed when the subject was brought up last time. Regardless of what he just said about modern women, was he drawn to that type?

He reached for her hand again and said something about porcupines as she tried to imagine him on a date with the young woman.

He chuckled.

She snapped her eyes up to his. "Huh?"

"Okay, milady." He chuckled. "You drifted off to your never-never land again. You didn't hear a thing I said, did you?"

She sighed. "I'm sorry, Jacob. What did you say?"

He chuckled again. "I asked if you knew that porcupine quills are a delicacy. Especially when served on clamshells smothered in cod liver oil."

She knitted her eyebrows together.

"Only a bit of nonsense to see if you were paying attention."

"You missed your calling, Jacob." She raised her nose in the air. "You should have been a comedian, not a doctor."

"Okay. But may I have your attention?"

"I'm all yours, Doctor." At least she'd like to be.

His brows rose, and his eyes grew wide. "Oh really?"

She giggled. "You know what I meant."

He threw his head back and laughed.

"Shh. You'll wake up the Weavers." And she wasn't ready to leave yet. "What were you saying before I so rudely zoned out?"

Muffy ran across the yard and jumped into Kathryn's lap. "I wondered where you disappeared to. You obviously don't like people invading your new home." While she scratched the cat's neck, she tilted her head and stared at Jacob.

Jacob ran a hand through his thick head of hair. Then he scooted his chair closer to hers. "A little birdie told me you have a birthday coming up."

"Who told you? Our bosses are the only ones in town who know."

"Well...Doctor Hartley isn't one to keep secrets." He grinned. "I'd like to take my friend out to dinner for her special birthday."

She blinked at him.

"After all, it is your twenty-fifth birthday. There'll be no buts about this, Kathryn. Understand?"

She bit her lip. The pout again. How could she say no? If she stayed home, she'd only dwell on the past.

Jacob reached over and touched her arm. A charge of electricity surged through her. There was nothing she'd rather do than spend her birthday with him. She'd have one more sweet memory.

If only he loved her.

# Chapter Twenty-Seven

O n Friday morning, the twenty-fifth of July, Jacob left early to pick up Kathryn for work. He hurried to the front porch and waited on the swing until the front door began to open. He sprang to his feet.

As she stepped onto the porch, he held a bouquet of twelve white roses tied with a royal purple lace bow out to her. "Happy birthday, Kathryn." The smile on her face as she accepted the bouquet made his heart overflow with love. He handed her a card.

As she held the roses in the crook of her arm, she stared at the envelope and read, "To My Special Friend." She bit on her lip and her brows furrowed for a moment. "This is sweet of you, Jacob." She sniffed the flowers and glanced up at him with misty blue-violet eyes. "The roses are beautiful. You are such a good friend."

Jacob clenched his teeth. That word was beginning to irritate him. He should never have addressed the card that way. However, he had signed it affectionately. That should say something. Should he tell her right now how he really felt about her, and what he'd like to happen between them? Better to wait until later, when he gave her the special present he had for her. She'd have no doubt about his feelings for her then.

He tilted his head to gain her attention. "It's always a pleasure to see the glow on your face when you receive flowers, milady. I figured you'd rather get the roses here than be given them at the office. Can't have those grapevine tongues wagging." He laughed.

"Thank you...again." She rolled her eyes as she opened the card and read the inside and smiled. "I'll run these upstairs. Be right back."

*Yes.* He'd make sure their relationship took a different path. Tonight's affair would be unforgettable. His pulse raced.

At the clinic, Jacob followed Kathryn down the hallway to their offices. Halfway there, he asked, "What's on your door?"

She rushed ahead, Jacob right behind her. Crime scene streamers covered the entry. Her jaw dropped open. She grabbed the knob and slowly opened the door. Jacob reached inside, slid his hand up the wall, and switched on the light. Colored balloons on the desk, floor, chairs, filing cabinet, and credenza behind her desk greeted them.

He stifled a laugh as she broke through the yellow streamers and shuffled her way into the room. Helium balloons filled every inch of the ceiling. Their colorful ribbons hung down like skinny tails. Taped to the side wall was a huge birthday card.

She spun on her heel. A frown on her face. "Who did you tell about my birthday?"

Jacob's hands went up in defense. "I promise. I didn't say a word to anyone." He clamped down on his lips to keep the laughter from coming out.

As Kathryn pushed the ribbons out of her way to get to her desk, Haley Smith peeked around the corner at the far end of the hallway. He grimaced and shook his head at her. She shrugged and came down the hall.

Standing in the doorway, Haley put her one hand on her hip. "Well, Miss Kathy. I finally got the truth out of Doctor Hartley about your birthday. The staff and I decided we needed to catch up from last year, so, voila. You received two years' worth of inflated mess."

"Seriously?" Kathryn burst into laughter. She brushed the balloons off her desk. "Okay. Now, if you will, help me get all of them out of my office and into the breakroom so I can work."

"Happy to. Did you like the crime scene tape?" A serious expression formed on Haley's face. "That was for the crime of keeping us in the dark about your birthday all this time."

Kathryn shook her head and laughed again. "I'll get even."

Haley turned to Jacob with a smirk. "Come on, Doctor McLeod. No slackers allowed. You help too." She giggled.

With a fistful of ribbons from the helium balloons, Kathryn headed to the breakroom. She fought her way through the doorway with the reluctant orbs. One escaped her grasp and rose to the ceiling in the hallway as she passed the door and it automatically closed behind her.

Haley came into the hall with the rest of the balloons' ribbons wrapped around her hand, dragging them behind. She slipped past Jacob.

"Nice save, Haley."

"Thanks. I thought she'd enjoy this. She's been working pretty hard around here. And she seems to be stressed."

"You're right." He grinned. "Judging from her face, she did enjoy this."

He snatched the plastic liner from his office trash basket and picked up all the balloons he could fit in it from the floor. Then he followed Haley into the lunchroom. Kathryn stood in front of the table next to the coffee pot. The helium balloons she'd carried in had drifted away from her and settled onto the ceiling.

A huge Happy Birthday poster, covered with wishes from everyone on the staff, hung on the wall. Tears filled her eyes.

Haley let go of her collection of balloons and came up behind Kathryn. "Hey, Kathy. Didn't mean to make you cry. The staff wanted you to know how much we appreciate all the work you do for us." The PA wrapped her arms around Kathryn. "Now let's get the rest of those colored rubber sacks of air out of your office."

The girls left the room.

As the door closed, Jacob took a deep breath and examined the white liner filled with balloons still in his arms. By tonight, his arms would be around Kathryn. He dumped the orbs on the floor and turned to the door.

Kathryn laughed as the girls reentered the breakroom with more colorful spheres. "So far, it's been a beautiful day." She glanced at Jacob.

He winked at her and left for another load.

After Kathryn was seated, Jacob closed the passenger door on his sports car. He'd thought the workday would never end.

As he rounded the back end of the car, he noticed the same red motorcycle he'd seen parked near the bank almost every day for the past week. Surely, it didn't belong to an employee. They'd park in the lot. Who would have so much banking business that they'd be here this often? It had shown up in other places near the clinic, too. Peculiar.

He slid in behind the wheel and started the engine. When he looked in the rearview mirror, a man emerged from the far corner of the bank and flipped a helmet over his light hair. Then he straddled the seat of the bike.

Jacob's eyes narrowed. It couldn't be.

Kathryn's head rested against the back of the seat with her eyes closed. He'd better not tell her. If he told her his suspicion, she'd be filled with tension tonight and not enjoy the party. He'd tell her afterward.

Kathryn showered and changed into a regal-looking pale orchid, ankle-length gown she'd bought months ago. She was beginning to think she'd never have a place to wear it. But Jacob said he planned to take her to an exclusive restaurant.

In the closet's full-length mirror, she studied the curved neckline with an embroidered satin band. She turned to Sheila, who had stretched out on the bed. "What do you think, girl?"

The dog picked up her head and tilted it to the side. She wagged her tail.

"I agree. This dropped waist does flatter my figure." She laughed. "Pretty vain of me, huh?"

Sheila shook her head and returned to her nap.

Kathryn fingered the lace sleeves that reached to an inch below her elbows. She twirled. The skirt flared out in soft waves.

When she came to a stop, her white two-inch toeless heels peeked out from below the hem. If only she could wear this dress for Beth's wedding instead of getting yet another she'd probably never wear again. Oh well. She closed the closet door.

Speaking of Beth, why hadn't she heard from the Parkers today? It was unusual for them not to have called first thing in the morning with their happy birthday chorus over the phone. They hadn't even sent a card, much less a present. Not that they needed to. They'd always remembered her birthday, though. Probably too swamped in wedding plans and expenses to have thought about her.

As she brushed her pale wheat-colored hair, twisted each side, and pulled it to the back of her head, tears welled in her eyes. She missed hearing her brother's off-key version of Happy Birthday. All this time, and she still expected him to call. Would she ever get over the grief? She sniffed.

Sheila hopped up from the bed and gave her a distressed yip.

"It's okay, girl. I'm all right."

Kathryn turned to the mirror and fastened her wound-up locks of hair with a small sparkling pony tie. She loosely interwove the tresses with the remainder of her hair into a French braid down the back of her head and secured it at her neck with another decorative elastic tie. The rest of the hair she brushed out and let fall down her back in soft waves.

The bouquet of roses from Jacob sitting on her nightstand reflected in the mirror. She laid the brush on the dresser. A tingle ran up her neck as she thought about the way he signed the card, Affectionately, Jacob.

She waltzed over to her four-legged friend. "I have an actual date with Jacob this evening. He's taking me to a fancy restaurant for dinner."

Sheila whined.

"I'll make sure we bring leftovers home for you and Muffy. Okay?"

"Yip, yip." Sheila spun around.

"Jacob should be here any minute."

She tucked glittering hair combs into her twisted locks and gazed into the mirror. Strung together like that, the combs gave the appearance of a crown. At least the back of one. Perfect.

A motorcycle roared down the street. "Well. I sure hope that isn't him. I'm not dressed for a ride on a motorcycle." She laughed.

Jacob's jaw lowered when Kathryn opened the door and stepped into the Weavers' foyer. "Wow."

"I'll take that as a compliment, Doctor McLeod."

"I should have expressed myself better, but—Wow. You're gorgeous. And your hair. You look like you belong in a throne room, or you just stepped off an historical movie set. Very royal."

"Thank you." Her cheeks grew pink.

He picked up her hand and fastened the band of a white rosebud corsage on her wrist. At the touch of her warm, soft skin, goosebumps skittered up his arms. Had it done the same to her?

She stepped back and peered into his eyes. "And may I say you are striking in your white evening attire?"

Maybe her interest in him had grown. Encouraging.

Mr. and Mrs. Weaver waved from the living room as Jacob followed Kathryn out the door.

Once he'd settled her in the car and drove out of the neighborhood, she turned in her seat to face him. "So, where are we going? You never told me the name of the restaurant."

"It's a surprise."

He turned onto the Interstate at the sign to Mobile and drove for fifteen minutes. "Oh no. The papers for Doctor Griffin." He pulled off the highway and entered the ramp to get back on in the opposite direction. "I was supposed to drop them off."

"What papers?"

"Well, it's— Something he wanted me to look over and make notes on. It's very important that I drop them off before we go to dinner. Do you mind? It won't take long."

"No. Of course not."

Ten minutes later, Jacob drove into the Griffins' long winding driveway. "Glad they live out this way." He parked in front of the three-car garage.

She peered out the window. "The house seems dark."

"They're probably in the back." Jacob smiled. "Why don't you come inside with me and say hello? Mrs. Griffin will want to see your dress. She'll never forgive me if you don't, and I can't afford to let the doctors' wives get mad at me. They might stop their care packages." He patted his stomach.

Her head fell back on the headrest as she laughed.

Jacob got out of the car, grabbed a folder from behind the seat, and hurried to open her door. When he did, she peered up at him. "Are you serious? You know we'll get into a discussion about something. Aren't you afraid we'll be late for our reservation?"

"I promise I won't let them detain us. And we'll be right on time." He held out his hand.

As she got out, a breeze lifted a strand of hair from Kathryn's hairdo. The tip of the curl brushed his neck. He groaned inside.

She gazed at the sky. Wispy clouds of turquoise blue, purple, and coral stretched from one horizon to the other like layered strokes from a paintbrush. "How beautiful."

A soft glow lingered under the coral layer where the sun had vanished behind a line of ponderosa pines. He took her hand and slipped it through the crook of his arm. "We couldn't have asked for a more perfect evening. Look up there." He pointed to the east. A sprinkling of glittering stars had begun to appear.

They made their way to the grand stone entry of the Griffins' Mediterranean style home. Jacob held her elbow as they ascended the wide staircase to the front door. He rang the doorbell.

# Chapter Twenty-Eight

athryn stood with Jacob at the oak door of the Griffins' home. No one answered. "They must have gone out for the evening."

Suddenly the door swung open. "Jacob. Kathy." Bonnie Griffin smiled at them. "How nice of you to stop by. Come in."

She ushered them across the tan marble foyer and into a darkened room. "Let me get the switch."

A loud, *"Surprise!"* greeted them as light flooded the room.

Kathryn's heart pounded as she whirled and buried her face in Jacob's shoulder. His arms circled her. She took in a deep breath and peered into his eyes.

He grinned. "Surprise."

Heat filled her face as she realized she was in his arms. She stepped back from his embrace, then turned and faced the room. Laughter and birthday greetings filled her ears.

As she glanced around the room, she spotted Nick at the rear of the group, an injured expression on his face. He smiled at her, and her heart pinched. The last person in the world she wanted to hurt. She'd led him to believe Jacob was an older man. What could she say now?

Beth ran up to Kathryn and wrapped her arms around her. "Surprised to see us? Look. Even Tom's here." She pointed toward her fiancé at the punchbowl and then turned to face Kathryn again. "What a knockout you are tonight, sis. And you thought you'd have the handsome doctor all to yourself." She giggled.

Kathryn whispered, "Beth. Ni—someone will hear you."

Behind her, Jacob cleared his throat.

"And, what was that little interlude you two had when you walked into the room? Hmmm?" Beth stepped back and winked at Jacob. She looked back at Kathryn. "Sorry. Just had to needle you after all the denials you gave me a few weeks ago. Were you really startled? Or, did you use that for an excuse to—"

Aunt Sandy swooped in and gave Kathryn a kiss while Uncle Eric embraced them both in a hug. With his curled index finger, he lifted her chin. "Well, Princess. I'm happy you have so many friends who care about you here in Pensacola."

"Thank you. They are good friends. But I'm happy to see all three of you here. This birthday wouldn't be the same without you."

She saw Nick heading to the punch bowl table. She had to explain. "Will you excuse me? I need to speak to someone."

Aunt Sandy gave her another kiss on the cheek. "Of course, honey. We'll talk later."

Kathryn hurried to Nick's side.

He turned and smiled. "Can I interest you in a glass of punch?"

"Thanks." She bit her lip.

"Beth told me Doctor McLeod was bringing you to the party tonight. Thought he'd be older." Nick handed her a cup of golden yellow liquid.

"I don't recall saying he was old."

"You said he was a friend of your boss's. Guess I shouldn't have jumped to a conclusion." He peered over the rim of the cup with raised eyebrows as he took a sip.

"I'm sorry, Nick."

He chuckled. "It's okay. You two seem to have gotten very close."

How could she explain? "We're friends. That's all. Jacob and I became friends...recently." She scanned the room.

"You call him Jacob? Not by his title as you do your bosses?"

*Oh no.* Had anyone else heard her? She twisted around and then faced Nick. "Normally I do, but when...we aren't at work...I mean when...in situations like...Nick, Jacob and I are co-workers, and we go out to lunch together sometimes. As friends. We agreed it would be awkward to call each other by our last names then, being friends and close in age." She pursed her lips.

"I understand." The smile left his lips.

She shook her head. "I'd like you to meet—"

From behind, hands grabbed her around the waist. "Kath, lover boy's looking for you."

Heat flushed through Kathryn's neck and face. She turned to her sister. "Beth. Will you stop?" She glanced at Nick. "Excuse us while I bring Beth back from her fantasies."

She latched onto Beth's arm and pulled her away from Nick. "I could strangle you." She lowered her voice. "What possessed you to say such a thing in front of Nick? He's hurt enough after my silly display at the door. Now get control of yourself."

Her sister pulled her lips tight. "Sorry, again. I was only joking." She walked away.

With a sigh, Kathryn returned to Nick. "Ignore her. She's been teasing me about Doctor McLeod almost since the day he joined our staff."

Nick nodded.

If she introduced them, Nick would see that Jacob wasn't interested in her. "I'd like you to meet him. You two will get along great."

Jacob eyed the man across the room as Kathryn spoke to him. Who could he be? Obviously not that Mathew. This man had short, darker blond hair. An old boyfriend from Illinois? His eyes narrowed. The man seemed at ease with her.

She turned from the man, and he followed her straight toward Jacob.

"Doctor McLeod, meet my friend Nick. Nick, this is Doctor Jacob McLeod." Her face glowed a rosy pink.

He loved to see her blush, but why now? Had this guy made some remark to embarrass her? He took Nick's hand in a firm grasp. "It's nice to meet you."

Their hands gripped one another as if in a contest of strength. Nick's eyes bored into him. "Likewise. Kathy told me there was a new doctor at the practice." He glanced at her.

Jacob let go of the man's hand, still feeling a tingle from the grasp. "I'm sure Kathryn didn't have much to say about me when I first arrived." He grinned at her. "How long have you two known each other?"

Before Nick could respond, she answered for him. "Nick was my brother's roommate in college, and his best friend. He's been a dear friend to me ever since." She smiled up at Nick.

"Yes. Very dear friends." He confirmed with a slight smile.

Just how dear of a friend was this man to her? Jacob's heart squeezed. This evening had not taken the turn he'd planned. Never expected to meet a rival. Judging by the scowl Nick gave him, the man was in love with her, too. But she'd only called him a friend.

Kathryn turned to Jacob. "I'll leave you two to get acquainted. You can exchange horror stories about me." As she strolled away toward Beth, her soft snicker faded.

Jacob turned to Nick. "Did you travel with the Parkers from Illinois?"

"No. I live here in Pensacola. I'm the youth pastor at my uncle's church. Kathy's church."

Great. The situation had not gotten any better. How could he compete with someone like Nick?

The men watched as Kathryn took Beth's arm and led her out the French doors to the balcony. Jacob glanced at Nick. Oh, yeah. That was a definite gleam of love in his eye.

*So, where do we go from here, Nick?*

"Happy Birthday to you, Happy Birthday to you, Happy Birthday, dear Kathy...Happy Birthday to you."

Cheers erupted as Kathryn blew out the candles on her two-tiered birthday cake. "Drat! I missed one." She snuffed it out with a quick puff. "Thanks, everyone. I never expected anything like this."

Mrs. Griffin rushed over and gave her a tight hug. Mrs. Hartley followed right behind. Dr. Hartley led her to a forest green wingback chair and sat her down. "Now, young lady. It's time for you to open presents."

Her eyes misted. Here she thought even the Parkers had forgotten her birthday. Speechless, she gulped in a breath and let it out slowly.

As the guests gathered around, Mrs. Griffin handed her a large flat box wrapped in shiny purple paper, tied with a huge white bow. "Mine first."

After reading the Griffins' card, Kathryn untied the bow, removed the paper, and opened the box lid. She lifted out a white lace shawl with a delicate fringe. "It's beautiful. Thank you, Mrs. Griffin, Doctor Griffin."

The Weavers handed her their gift, followed by one from the Parkers. Then one by one, each of the staff members from the clinic presented theirs. Several gifts later, Jacob handed her a slender box wrapped in pale pink paper with multi-colored ribbon spirals. "Here you go, Miss Kendall."

Her heart skipped as she accepted it. Too narrow to be a book, and too small to be roses. She giggled to herself and unwrapped the present. "A frosted-crystal bud vase." She peered up at him. "It's lovely. Looks antique."

He smiled. "It is. For that mysterious rose that pops up on your desk now and then." He winked with a mischievous smirk.

Warmth filled her neck as she gave him a sharp glance. "Thanks, Doctor McLeod."

When she'd finished opening her gifts, she stood. "I can't thank you all enough."

Nick sat in a corner by himself, a look of pain on his face. Kathryn pursed her lips. The collection of classic books he gave her was so thoughtful. She started to make her way over to tell him how much she appreciated it, but Jacob stepped in front of her.

"Having fun? Better than an old stuffy dinner at a fancy restaurant?"

"This is wonderful. I can't think of a better way to spend my twenty-fifth birthday." She peeked around him to see if Nick still sat across the room. "Would you mind if we joined Nick?"

She headed for the corner and Jacob followed. Nick stood as they approached.

"Jacob, I thought you might introduce Nick to the other clinic employees while I find my sister. He's never met them. I have to talk to Beth."

She left them without an answer and joined her sister at the cake table. A few seconds later, Kathryn slipped through the French doors alone onto the stone balcony, which overlooked the Griffins' backyard.

Hearing Nick's laughter, she smiled. They'd get along fine. They both had good hearts.

Jacob's smile and green eyes filled her thoughts. If only he loved her. She leaned against the stone rail of the balcony and let her gaze drift upward to the midnight blue sky. *Father, is there a man somewhere who will love me? Truly love me?*

"Penny for your thoughts." Jacob drew close to her side.

Her heart fluttered. "I thought you were in a deep philosophical discussion with Nick."

He laughed. "Pastor Parker walked up after you left. He was curious about Nick's work with the youth group. I told Nick we'd get together later and excused myself to find you." His eyes twinkled in the moonlight. "Now, milady. About those thoughts?"

She gazed over the backyard. "I was counting my blessings." She glanced back at him. "The vase truly is lovely, Jacob."

He smiled, sending a tingle through her. "Have you seen Mrs. Griffin's rose garden?"

"Yes, she took me for a walk in it the first time she invited me for lunch."

"But, have you seen it at night, all lit up?"

Kathryn stared across the lawn to what resembled an army of giant fireflies gathering for a siege. "Oh. So many lights."

"May I take you on a guided tour?" He offered his arm. "You need to hold on. The stone path may be slick with mist rolling in."

As she placed her hand on his arm, he laid his hand over hers. Butterflies filled her stomach.

Jacob led her down the stone balcony steps to a flagstone pathway that led through the rose garden. At the end, they came to another set of stone steps and descended them. A lower path led to a gazebo at the edge of a pond.

The fragrance of roses wafted in the night air as a mist rose from the water. Shreds of vapor pulled by unseen fingers drifted to the edge of the pond. Spanish moss hung from the surrounding trees, adding to the ethereal setting, while soft lapping waves and a choir of frogs and insects serenaded them in the background.

Kathryn turned to Jacob. "You haven't known the Griffins for long. Have you been here before?"

"I've had dinner here a couple of times while getting settled. The Hartleys and Griffins figure I'll starve if one of them doesn't feed me once a week." He chuckled. "One evening, I wandered down here after dinner."

They entered the gazebo and stood at the cedar rail overlooking the water. Her jaw lowered. "How beautiful with all the neighbors' backyards lit. It's as if we've wandered into a fairy tale."

From his pocket, he brought out a small silver box tied with a white ribbon and held it out to her. "Happy birthday, milady."

"You've already given me a gift."

"Not this one."

She sat on the wooden bench that circled the inside of the gazebo and stared at the box in his hand. He laid it in her lap.

After she removed the ribbon and opened the lid, she gasped. "A Claddagh necklace." The silver chain extending from a section of

Celtic weave on either side of a crowned cut-emerald colored heart sparkled as moonlight caught it.

"I can't accept this." She looked up at him.

"Why not?" He sat next to her.

"Because, it's too—it wouldn't be right." He didn't understand what this symbol meant. Mother said it stood for love and loyalty...far beyond friendship.

"It's perfect for you. I waited until now to say this, so we could be alone."

"But, Jacob. It's a Claddagh."

"I know. The jeweler told me. She said it's an Irish design—"

"But a Claddagh." How could she explain to him its true meaning? Undying love.

His lips pressed tight and he winced. He loosened the necklace from its box, and then opened the clasp.

She didn't want to ruin the evening for herself or for him. She'd accept it tonight and return it later. "All right. On one condition. You don't tell anyone."

Jacob pulled her up and turned her around toward the entrance of the gazebo. "Allow me to put it on you. Then we'll talk."

She removed her locket, and he lifted the Claddagh over her head. As he fastened the clasp under her hair, his warm fingers brushed her neck, sending a rush of adrenaline through her.

From behind, he rested his hands on her shoulders and whispered in her ear, "Kathryn, I want—"

Movement at the stone stairway caught her attention, and a footfall sounded on the path at the bottom. "Tom. Beth."

"Oh, sorry." Tom pulled Beth back toward the steps.

"No. Please." Kathryn rushed past them. "We were about to leave, anyway. You two lovebirds enjoy the view."

# Chapter Twenty-Nine

acob stood dumbfounded as Kathryn lifted the long skirt of her gown and ran up the stone steps away from the pond. He'd missed his chance to tell her he was in love with her.

Leaving Tom and Beth with their mouths open at the pond, he sprinted up the stairs. "Kathryn, wait."

Before she reached the backyard lawn, he caught her hand in his. When he turned her to face him, she bowed her head. He lifted her chin with his free hand. Tears streamed from her closed eyes.

"What's wrong? Why are you crying?"

She opened her eyes. "I thought I could accept it, but I can't." Her hand went to the necklace around her neck. "It would be wrong. Dishonest." She wiggled free of his hand and slipped both of hers under her hair.

He should have waited. She was going to give the necklace back. If he took it now— "Stop." Jacob reached his hands up to hers and pulled them away from her neck. "You have to listen. I will say this no matter who or what tries to interrupt me next."

Her glistening eyes widened.

The moon made her hair and face glow. He smiled at her. She was the most beautiful woman he'd ever met. "Why would it be dishonest of you to keep the necklace? Unless it means you have no feelings for me whatsoever. But you do, don't you? I saw it in your eyes the night I almost kissed you."

She turned away, but he touched her chin, and she faced him again.

"Kathryn, I know what the Claddagh means. Back at the gazebo, I tried to tell you. It means love."

Across the yard, two staff members came down the balcony steps to the path leading toward the rose garden. Jacob put his arm around her shoulders. "Let's take the circular path around the garden."

They strolled away as the others changed direction and meandered down another path around the house.

At a cement bench in front of a tall hedge, Jacob stopped Kathryn. "Please, sit down." She lowered herself to the seat.

He sat and took her hands. "I said I want to be your friend."

Her head bowed again.

"Please, don't look away. Let me finish."

She lifted her violet-blue eyes to him.

"The truth is...I want more than your friendship. You've come to mean much more to me than that. By giving you the Claddagh, I was trying to let you know how I feel. As I said, the jeweler told me its meaning. When I visited the shop to find your birthday present, I wanted something special that showed how I felt. I asked if they had anything to express my affection to a beautiful Irish lady. She told me she had the perfect gift. Turns out, she's Irish too."

Kathryn gaped.

"What I'm trying to say is...I've fallen in love with you, Kathryn Kendall."

Her bottom lip trembled. Her eyes shimmered.

He touched her cheek. "Yes, it's too soon, less than three months since we met, but try to explain that to my heart. And it's way too soon to ask you—well, ask more of you than to accept the Claddagh, and my love."

"Oh, Jacob." The tears spilled over and down her face.

He handed her his handkerchief. "I'd better keep an extra in my pocket from now on."

A soft chuckle escaped her.

"That's better. Now the only question is...will you accept me along with the Claddagh? I won't push. I promise. All I ask is acceptance as more than a friend right now. Someone whose love for you grows each day."

She took in a deep breath and wiped away the tears. "I'd be a fool not to. But you shouldn't love me."

"Why not? You're lovely, sweet, kind, and even funny, although mostly at my expense." Instead of a smile at his joke, her face took on a sober expression.

"Everyone I've loved has died. It's not safe to love me. I've tried not to care about you as more than a friend. It's not a good idea."

"You've tried?"

Voices drifted in from the direction of the pond steps. Beth and Tom came into view. Jacob held a finger in front of his lips. "Shh." The couple passed without a glance in their direction. He whispered, "They're so in love they've blocked out the world." He grinned.

Jacob turned back to Kathryn. "I want what they have. Maybe it's too soon right now, but somewhere down the road."

She tried to stand, but he held her hands and wouldn't let go. She faced him. "You're not listening. Everyone I've loved, who loved me, is gone. They died. I don't want you to die too."

He grabbed her shoulders and kissed her lips. Then he stared into her violet, tear-filled eyes. "If you've tried not to care, it means you already do."

She closed her eyes.

"Look at me, Kathryn."

Her lashes fluttered open. Tears welled again.

"No one died because they loved you or you loved them. I don't know why God took them, but He had a purpose."

The pain in her eyes broke his heart. "And your brother died in the service of his country, not because you loved him. Yes, he loved you. And probably because he did, he joined the service to defend this country. But he died because of the people who attacked us, and then attacked him."

Her shoulders shook, and her head fell forward.

He wrapped her in his arms. "You're not superstitious and neither am I. Nothing will happen to me. And I'll make sure nothing happens to you either."

Kathryn squeezed her brows together. How could he guarantee nothing would happen? He couldn't. But if he already loved her, it was too late anyway. She slipped her arms around his waist and melted into his embrace. Her muscles relaxed.

Jacob backed away and held her chin in his hand. When he smiled, she quivered. "Can we give this a chance?" He kissed her forehead."

"I want to. I've never felt this way before. But it scares me."

"Nothing will happen unless God allows it. And He never does anything without a purpose." He let go of her chin and held her hands in his against his chest.

She gazed at their intertwined hands. Through his shirt, his heart pounded against her hands as wildly as the beat of her own. "You're right. Thank you for reminding me. It's exactly what my parents and brother would have said." She smiled and peered into his loving eyes. "Let's not tell—I mean—"

He chuckled. "Anyone in the office?"

She winced. "It's just...I'm a little uncomfortable with this change in our relationship right now. Can we give it a few days? Is it horrible of me to ask?"

"Not at all. I'm as guarded with my privacy as you. I promise, not a soul, our secret. We're getting pretty good at secrets, aren't we?"

They both laughed.

Kathryn pulled one hand away from his and fingered the necklace.

He glanced at it. "You will wear it, won't you?" His gaze traveled to her eyes.

If she slipped the Claddagh inside the neck of her dress, who'd be the wiser? She bit her lip. "I'll wear it tonight, but out of sight." She slipped it under the embroidered satin neckline.

He nodded his agreement, and they stood.

Jacob took in a deep breath and smiled. "What is that wonderful perfume you're wearing?"

"Jasmine. One of my favorites."

"It's not your usual rose fragrance."

She smiled. "No. I chose this one for our date." She narrowed her eyes. "And I'm glad I did. Even my favorite rose perfume can't compete with the fragrance of natural roses." Her hand swung out as if introducing the garden to him.

Out of the corner of her eye, she saw Beth rushing across the lawn toward them. Kathryn spun back to him. "Jacob, we can't tell Beth. The secret will be out in a flash if we do."

He pulled her into the shadow of the hedge behind the bench and covered her mouth with his lips. His fingers ran through a few loosened locks of her hair sending a current of electricity through her.

Jacob released her and brought her back into the lantern light. "Okay. Mum's the word. As long as I can get one of those once in a while. Whew."

Her knees buckled, and she gasped. A wave of dizziness struck. She reached out and grabbed his arm. He caught her, and they sat on the bench.

"Are you all right?" Worry covered his face.

Beth rushed up. "I've been looking all over for you, Kath. What's going on? Why did you run away when Tom and I came down to the pond? And why are you two hiding out here in the shadows?"

Kathryn peered up at her sister. "I wanted you and Tom to enjoy the pond...the two of you...alone." She glanced at Jacob.

"Then why did Jacob run after you? Did he do something to upset you?" She turned to him and glared.

He chuckled. "I figured I'd be in trouble if I didn't follow her lead. She's in charge of scheduling my seminars. I'd hate to think where she'd send me if I upset her."

*Nice cover, Jacob. Thank you.* "Why are you so worked up, Beth? What do you need?"

Beth's eyes wagged back and forth, as she swept her gaze from Kathryn to Jacob and back again. "You two are up to something. What is it?"

"We're not up to anything." Kathryn's face flushed with heat. Good thing it was dark out here.

When she glanced his way, Jacob's green eyes held a glint of mischief. *Lord, don't let him tell her. And please don't let me get dizzy again thinking about that kiss.* "We'd better get back to the house. We're missing a good party." She hurried from the bench, past the rose garden, and onto the stone path across the lawn.

Beth caught up to her. "You may as well tell me. You know I'll find out what you're up to, anyway."

Jacob's hurried footfalls raced up behind them.

# Chapter Thirty

athryn sat at her desk fingering her Claddagh necklace. She glanced up from where she'd been doodling while reading office equipment brochures. Two weeks had gone by since her birthday, and Jacob had been faithful not to tell anyone of the change in their relationship.

She reached over her keyboard and touched the soft petals of the white rose he'd given her when he picked her up for work. Monday mornings had become such a joy with its fresh token each week, now displayed in the gorgeous budvase he'd given her.

Her phone rang. "Good morning. Kathryn Kendall speaking."

Beth's frantic voice came through the receiver. "Kath! I can't do this without you. It's the maid of honor's duty to help me with these decisions. You've got to come."

"Calm down, Beth. What's wrong?" The wedding plans must be getting to her.

"There's just too much to do. I'll never get everything done before the wedding in October. I need you here."

"It'll be okay." Kathryn rolled her eyes. "Your mother is there to give you a hand."

"The bridesmaids cornered me at church last night. They wanted details on the dresses. I can't make up my mind."

"Breathe, Beth. Breathe." Kathryn took in a deep breath herself.

"It doesn't help. I need you. You're the expert on fashions. Please."

Kathryn sighed and let her head fall back on the chair.

"Please come next weekend. I have to decide." Beth sniffled.

"I'll be there two weeks before your wedding as it is. Can't someone else help you pick out the dresses? Everything else is almost done. Your bridal shower, the rehears—"

"But I need you now."

"Try to understand. An extra trip is out of the question. There are four other girls to help, and I'll go with the majority rule."

"But Mom said they'd buy your ticket."

"No, Beth. They have enough bills right now with the wedding."

Her sister started crying.

"Calm down. Let me take another peek at my budget. I'll call you tonight, okay?"

"All right. You'll find a way. I know you will."

"I'll try." Kathryn hung up the phone. What was she going to do? She'd never known Beth to be rattled by anything. But then, she'd never had to plan a wedding either.

A twinge of guilt hit Kathryn. After her parents' deaths, Beth became a sister to her. Then Chris left for college in Florida, but Beth was there. Through the long nights after Chris died in Iraq, Beth had come to Florida to comfort her. *Now she needs me.*

Kathryn folded her arms on the desk and rested her forehead on them.

*Oh Lord, what should I do?*

Jacob rose from his desk and stood in Kathryn's doorway as she laid her head on her arms. When she didn't notice him, he cleared his throat. "A penny for your thoughts, milady."

Her head popped up. Tears welled in her eyes. Why was she upset?

He walked into her office, shut the door behind him, and leaned on the back corner of her desk. "What's wrong? You're about to water those papers in front of you."

She grabbed a tissue and wiped her eyes. "I don't know what to do." Her voice quivered. "Beth wants me to fly to Des Plaines to pick out bridesmaids' dresses. It's not the only reason she wants me there. She needs me. She'll leave her parents soon." Taking a gulp of air, she continued, "She'll start a new life with a man, and a family of her own. How can I make it happen?"

Jacob stifled a laugh. "Make what happen? Fly to Des Plaines, pick out dresses, or start a new life and family?"

She didn't respond. "The money isn't in my budget, and I won't let my adopted parents pay for the trip. There's so much expense on them now as it is. She's always been there for me. How will I tell her?"

Tears trickled down her cheeks.

He handed her his handkerchief. Then he skirted the desk and pulled her up from the chair. His arms circled her shoulders.

"Have a good cry," he whispered. "Let it out."

She sobbed against his shoulder as he rested his cheek against her silky hair.

When her sobbing calmed, she jerked back from him. "Jacob, what if someone walked in?" She sat behind her desk. "I'm all right now. Thank you for the shoulder. I shouldn't let things get to me."

"Why not? You and your sister are very close. So what if someone came in and saw you crying on my shoulder? You were upset. It's what friends do." He grinned.

She glanced up at him. "I didn't mean to seem ungracious. I can't stand the idea of all this pressure on Beth. Not after all the support she's given me over the years. Forgive me. I'm more emotional than I should be. Can't get a good night's sleep with the nightmares I've had."

"Is there anything I can do to help?" Her distressed face tugged at his heart. He dropped into the chair at the side of her desk. "I'd be happy to. You name it."

Her brows furrowed. "I know you would, and I appreciate the offer, but I doubt you can do anything about my bad dreams."

"Actually, I meant with a trip to Illinois. What if I give you the money? Of course, I'd miss you...but I understand you need to be there for Beth."

She shook her head. "It wouldn't be appropriate to accept money from you. But thank you for the offer."

"I suppose you're right." He pinched his lips together. "If it leaked out." He grinned.

She turned away. "Quit teasing. This is serious."

"I was only trying to cheer you up. Guess I'm not doing such a great job. Maybe if you talked about your nightmares, it would help you feel better."

"Maybe."

Jacob rested his elbow on her desk. "Now, tell the doctor about these troubling dreams."

She gazed into his eyes and fidgeted with a pen. "There's a dark figure with no face. When I call out to ask who's there, he laughs. He says things like, 'I've got you.' It's all I remember. But I wake up with my heart pounding as if I've run a marathon."

"Not a nice dream. Have you talked to Pastor Marshall? Or your dad?"

"I'll talk to Uncle Eric, if I can figure out how to get there."

"Speaking of Illinois, why don't you explain your problem to Doctor Hartley? He tells everyone you're like his daughter. There'd be nothing inappropriate if he helped you out."

"I have plenty of vacation time coming. But I couldn't ask on such short notice. He and Doctor Griffin have done so much for me already. Besides, with budgeting for updated medical and office equipment, things are tight." Kathryn pointed at the brochures scattered from one side of her desk to the other.

She glanced back at him. "Promise me you won't say anything to him about this."

Jacob fingered his early-emerging five o'clock shadow and frowned. "I promise. However, I think you're wrong not to talk to him. He'd be hurt if he found out you needed help and didn't ask."

Elbow resting on the desk, he propped his chin on his fist. His gaze landed on the brochures. He picked up the top flyer, jumped to his feet, swung the door open, and shot into the hall. "Wait here."

He strode through the halls, brochure in hand, until he reached his boss's office. The door was open, and Doc had his lunch spread out in front of him.

As Jacob stepped through the doorway, Doc looked up from his sandwich. "What can I do for you, my boy?"

"I've a question."

"Don't tell me you're wondering why we're not paying you what you're worth." He winked. "You'll have to hold your horses and wait 'til your six-month review."

Jacob chuckled. "I was reading these brochures Kathryn has been agonizing over." Hope this works. "You said it's important for you to go to Chicago to check the new clinical equipment before spending the money, correct?"

"Yes. We need to make sure we're getting exactly what the clinic needs. And I have questions."

"So, wouldn't you want your office manager's opinion on the equipment for the front office...for the same reason?" He placed the brochure on the desk. "You'll be paying a small fortune for it. And both are at the same company."

Dr. Hartley looked up from the brochure. "You're right." He picked up the phone receiver and punched in three numbers. "Kathy, I need to talk to you and Jacob. Please come to my office."

Jacob rushed out of the room and met her halfway to Doc's office. She glared at him.

"I didn't say a word about your problem. I promise. Don't let that Irish temper of yours get the better of you. I knew you'd jump to a conclusion when he mentioned my name."

As she tried to sidestep him, he caught her arm. She yanked it from him and turned away.

He touched her shoulder. "Just listen to him."

Daggers flew from her eyes. He turned, and she followed him into Dr. Hartley's office, taking the chair in front of his desk. Jacob sat next to her.

Doc eyed him. "Where'd you disappear to? One minute you were here, and then you were off like a shot...vanished into thin air...like a puff of smoke." He chuckled.

"Sorry. I had something to take care of." He glanced at Kathryn.

"Kathy, Jacob has brought something to my attention."

The muscle in her jaw flexed.

"Our astute young physician here asked me a very good question." Dr. Hartley rattled on about the new equipment. "I agree with him. Not sure why we didn't think of it before. I guess Alex and I have spent all our time focusing on the clinical side."

He waved his hand back and forth in front of his face. "Anyway, I wanted to ask you what you thought about going with us to Chicago. I'd like you to check over the new office equipment we're considering."

Jacob said a quick prayer.

The doctor peered at her over his reading glasses. "We'll have to leave here Wednesday and won't get back before the following Tuesday night. I'm sure I can get you a seat on the flight for a midweek trip."

Her eyes stopped pinning Jacob with darts, and she drew her attention to their boss. "You want me to go with you to Chicago?"

"Yes. You'd be able to spend the weekend with your family while you're there. I'm sure they'd like to see you." The doctor grinned. "They'll probably welcome a diversion from wedding plans right about now. Especially your dad."

She glanced at Jacob. Color flooded into her cheeks.

Dr. Hartley's brows wrinkled. "Did I say something wrong?"

Jacob glanced at Doc. "Don't think she's digested it yet, sir."

Her gaze shifted to their boss.

"Kathy, is there anything to keep you from leaving with us this coming Wednesday? It's short notice, but last-minute changes have never bothered you. How about it?"

She bit her lip. "Of course, I can go."

With a pleased smile on his face, Doc leaned back in his chair. "Now for you, my boy. I haven't had a chance to ask, but I'd like you to go as well. Alex said he doesn't want to be away right now. He has a critically ill patient to keep an eye on. And I'd like a second opinion on the equipment. Can you go?"

Jacob stifled an outburst of joy. This couldn't have worked out better. "Sure. I have no ties here to stop me." His one tie would go with him.

"It's settled then. Now, outta here, you two. Let me finish my lunch in peace." He picked up his sandwich. "You are the worst pests I've ever seen." Doc laughed. "And close the door behind you."

They stood, and Jacob followed Kathryn out of the office. "You thought I snitched on you."

She peeked at him out of the corner of her eye. "You have no idea how ridiculous I feel right now. Please forgive me."

"Not a problem.

"Wait until I tell Beth...about everything."

"Everything?" Jacob grinned. *That'll be interesting.*

When Mathew arrived outside Scenic Bluffs Family Practice Clinic Monday evening, he shoved his motorcycle between the buildings across the street. His sudden family business trip to Louisiana two weeks ago had lasted longer than he'd expected. Really messed up his plans. But he was back now, and patience would get him his prize. He waited for Kate to appear.

Now that he'd found out where Katy-Bird lived, he'd just bide his time. If lover boy was still dropping her off, he'd lag far enough behind not to be noticed, and then after dark, he'd find a way into the house. At least he'd know she was home that way.

"I don't care how long it takes. I will have you, Kate." A string of obscenities followed. "Hopefully, tonight will be the night."

He scowled when she got in the Austen-Healey with the dark-haired Herculean. As the car drove past the doorway, Mathew backed up and let fly another stream of vulgarities.

After the sports car sailed through the green light on the corner, Mathew noticed a black Ford with the driver's window down across the street. He'd seen that Crown Victoria before, more than once.

Mathew inched his way toward the vehicle. The engine started and the car pulled away. As it passed, the window closed but not before Mathew caught a glimpse of the driver's face.

Back at his bike, Mathew straddled the seat, put on his helmet, and kick-started the motor.

Where had he seen him before?

When Jacob dropped Kathryn off at her apartment, she rushed inside and pulled out her cell. The minute Beth answered her call, Kathryn said, "I'll be in Chicago by Wednesday."

She pulled her ear away from the squeal that sounded through the receiver. A grin spread across her face. "And I've got more news for you."

"Really? What?"

"That...I'll tell you when we get there."

"We?"

"Yes. Doctor Hartley asked me to go with them to look over the new office equipment we're getting." The rest of *the we* could wait until they got there.

"That's not fair. Tell me now. Or should I guess?"

"Beth, no assumptions, please. I promise I'll tell you soon."

Could be a good time to talk to Uncle Eric, too. *I'll find out what he thinks of these nightmares...and Jacob.*

# Chapter Thirty-One

ate Wednesday morning, Kathryn followed Jacob as he carried her suitcase down from her apartment to the Weavers' foyer. Sheila scampered behind and ran into the living room.

While he took her luggage out to Dr. Hartley's car, Kathryn stepped through the foyer into the living room and bent to scratch her dog's ears. "Now be a good girl while I'm gone, okay?"

Sheila bounced up and licked her cheek. The dog gave an excited, "Yip." and then snuggled next to Mrs. Weaver on the couch.

Kathryn smiled. This would be the first time since Sheila showed up in her life that they'd be apart, except for when she went to work each day. "She sure loves you and your husband."

"We love her too. She's such a dear thing." Mrs. Weaver laid her hand on Sheila's soft white hair.

Mr. Weaver ambled through the hallway. He slipped his arm around Kathryn. "You be careful in that big city, young lady."

"I will. And thank you for taking care of Sheila." Kathryn crouched down and took the dog's head in her hands. "I'll miss you."

Sheila whined and slowly wagged her tail. Then she gave Kathryn another lick.

Jacob reentered the foyer. "Doc said it's time to leave." Sheila bounded over to him. "Bye, little lady." He bent and scratched both ears. "I suppose you'll be spoiled rotten by your adopted grandparents before Kathryn gets back." He glanced over to the Weavers sitting beside each other, and then at the dog. "You take care of them, girl. Okay?"

"Yip. Yip." Sheila ran and jumped on the sofa between the older couple.

Mr. Weaver rose and held out his hand. "And you, young man, watch over our Kathy."

They shook, and Jacob grinned. "I will, sir."

A short blast of a horn sounded from the street. He relieved Kathryn of the carryon bag she'd slung over her shoulder. "Better get out there before he leaves without us."

Mrs. Weaver stood. She gave Kathryn a hug, and then grabbed Jacob's waist and squeezed. "You both have a good time. See you when you get home." He wrapped his arms around the sweet woman in a gentle embrace.

Kathryn followed Jacob out to the curb. He opened the rear passenger door of Dr. Hartley's silver Mercedes, and she slid in.

Her boss turned to her. "That's all you're taking? I thought for sure you'd have a whole set of luggage." He chuckled and faced forward. "And we're off."

Twenty minutes later, bags checked, Kathryn hurried to keep up with Jacob and her boss as they left the security area and headed for the departure gate. Her dress heels had gone from click-click on the floor as they entered the concourse of the airport, to a clickety-clack. She should have worn track shoes to keep up with these men. What was she thinking?

After the plane took off and the seatbelt light went out, Dr. Hartley strode down the aisle to her seat a few rows back from where he and Jacob were sitting. "Way too much activity this morning for me. Do you mind sitting with Jacob? The businessmen in your row, absorbed in their laptops, should give me the quiet I need to nap inflight."

She laughed. "Not at all, Doctor." She rose and maneuvered her way up the aisle to join Jacob. She wouldn't mind at all.

As she lowered herself into the seat, he grinned. "I think Doc has an inkling about us."

"You didn't tell him anything, did you?"

"Not a word. But he's good at reading people. He didn't say anything. Just winked at me as he headed your way."

Her pulse quickened. "Beth and her parents are good at it, too. Good thing I decided to tell them when we get there. Beth would be so angry if our boss knew about us before she did." Kathryn tittered. "I didn't tell them you were coming."

As he gazed into her eyes, a wave of tingles rolled through her.

He took her hand and glanced in the direction of Dr. Hartley. "I think Doc had the right idea. Why don't we get a little rest before we arrive in Chicago?"

"Good idea. I was up late last night trying to decide what to take." She pushed the seat to recline, closed her eyes, and drifted off to sleep, her fingers laced with Jacob's.

A voice echoed in her mind. *"Now I've got you."* Kathryn's eyelids flew open and her heart pounded. Jacob was sound asleep. She glanced around her. No one looked her way.

She let go of his hand and dropped her head to her knees. Not again. Why when everything was going so right?

Mathew pulled his motorcycle up on the grass beside the bank. He dismounted and took his position in the shadow of the doorway to watch for his Katy-Bird.

"No green Austen-Healey tonight." This might be his chance. About time. So far, he'd not been able to find a way to get into the house where she lived. That stupid yappy mutt made such a ruckus every time he got close to the place. Like it knew.

Mathew waited until everyone left the clinic and the cleaning crew entered the building. Must not have come to work today. His fury found vent in a string of obscenities. Now she was taking days off with her new fling.

Time he got rid of that guy. He stormed to his bike, kicked the starter, and sped off with a squeal of tires.

His cronies at the lounge would tell him what he should do.

After dropping their things off in their rooms at the hotel in Des Plaines, Jacob returned to the lobby with Dr. Hartley. Kathryn stood between Beth and her father.

As Jacob approached, Beth smirked and stepped in front of him. She whispered, "I figured it out."

He furrowed his brows. "What?"

Kathryn grabbed her sister's arm. "Don't start." She moved Beth behind her.

The pastor shook Dr. Hartley's hand. "So, how was the flight?"

"Haven't had a good rest like that in a long time. Slept the entire way. What do you and Mrs. Parker say to going out for dinner tonight?"

"That would be nice, Doctor Hartley, but my wife already has supper planned for tonight and is expecting you. Did you pick up a car yet?"

"Yes. They had the Mercedes I reserved ready and waiting. Couldn't get a silver like mine, but black's okay. Please, call me David."

"If you'll call me Eric."

"Deal." Doc slapped the pastor on the shoulder.

The pastor offered his hand to Jacob. "Kathy told us you're adapting well to Pensacola, young man. That was quite the change from Minnesota to Florida."

"Yes, sir. But I'm finding the change a good one." He gave Kathryn a quick glance. She was busy talking to her sister.

The pastor let go and turned to Doc. "Shall we head to the house? You can follow me."

Kathryn took her sister's arm. "I have something to tell you."

"And I'll bet I already know what it is," she sang.

"I doubt it."

Beth giggled and glanced back at Jacob right behind them.

He pursed his lips as he eyed the curly-haired imp. It would be just like Beth to assume...and be right. As soon as Kathryn let her know about his declaration of love, a tease like Beth wouldn't let that fodder go to waste.

The group left the hotel, loaded themselves into the cars, and headed for the Parkers' home.

Jacob rested his head on the back of the passenger seat. Kathryn needed to relax on this trip, not wind up stressed by her sister's teasing. She needed to talk to her dad about those dreams, too. Maybe she'd be free of them while she was at home. Although, she hadn't mentioned any since telling me about them.

Pastor Parker pulled his blue mini-van onto the driveway of a two-story, white-framed Cape Cod style home. Doc pulled to the curb and parked on the street in front.

Jacob gazed out the car window. Charcoal gray shutters on the house matched the roof. He stepped out of the vehicle and grinned. No wonder she liked the little cottage she'd chosen for him. It reminded her of home, even if this one dwarfed his house.

The group climbed the stairs to a porch that wrapped around the left side of the front door. A trellis, sporting a red climbing rose, sheltered the right side of the entry.

The door opened, and Mrs. Parker swept out. She rushed to Kathryn and held her in an embrace for several seconds. Jacob's pulse quickened as his arms ached to hold his lady again himself.

Mrs. Parker then turned to Dr. Hartley. "I'm so happy to see you again. And you, Doctor McLeod. Come in and make yourselves at home."

As they entered the foyer, from the corner of his eye Jacob caught a flurry of movement. Beth hustled her sister up the stairway.

*Would Kathryn tell Beth about us while they're alone?* He glanced at Pastor Parker. What would her adopted father say when he was told? Seemed like the protective type.

Kathryn grabbed the railing at the top of the stairs as Beth pulled her other arm. "Slow down. You want me to fall and break my neck?"

"I'm just so excited to have you home again."

They entered the bedroom they used to share, and Kathryn lowered her carryon and purse to the floor. She dropped onto the edge of her old bed. "Wow. This brings back good memories. You've kept the orchid walls and frilly white lace curtains on the windows. Even the same deep purple comforters on the beds."

"Yeah. Didn't want to change anything. I missed you, and you don't get home that often. Besides, I love it." She plopped on the bed next to Kathryn. "Now, spill the beans. What did you have to tell me?"

Beth popped to her feet again and spun to face Kathryn. "But first, what exactly was going on down at the gazebo with you and Jacob at your birthday party? When Tom and I reached the bottom of the stone stairs, you rushed out of there so fast, with Jacob right on your heels. Tom whisked me into the gazebo before I had a chance to find out what was happening."

Kathryn fingered the Claddagh necklace and smiled. *Lord, thank you for Tom.*

"Does it have something to do with what you want to tell me? I'll bet I can guess. I saw you two coming out from behind the bushes in the rose garden that night. You had that familiar glow on your face you always get when you're embarrassed. He proposed, didn't he?" She giggled. "I couldn't get any information out of either of you all weekend."

"Beth, you really are the limit. I've a mind not to tell you anything. Proposed? Really? We only met a few months ago."

"It happens. Okay, then what? I've been waiting for two days. Spill it." She sat down again.

"I will, if you'll let me get a word in. Now hush." Kathryn raised her hand to cover Beth's mouth and laughed. "You're impossible."

More giggles spilled out of her sister, who pulled away. "Yes, but you love me."

"I do, and I want to share my good news with you. If you'll let me."

Beth pressed her lips together with a thumb and index finger.

"That's better." Kathryn sighed. "Jacob and I have decided to try a closer relationship."

"Is that all?" Her brows wrinkled. "Did he kiss you?"

Kathryn's face heated. "Yes, he did. And in the gazebo, before you and Tom arrived, he gave me this." She slipped her hand under the Claddagh, letting it rest on the tops of her fingers.

Her sister jumped up from the bed and twirled around the room. "The Claddagh. I knew it, I knew it, I knew it. I told you so." She stopped spinning. "Now we can have that double wedding we've always wanted."

Kathryn's mouth dropped open.

After dinner, Jacob sat beside Kathryn on the swing at the corner of the front porch. He reached for her hand and interwove their fingers. "Your adopted parents sure are nice. Even your dad." He chuckled. "More than I expected after you told him about us."

She tittered. "He's always been happy if I'm happy. And he trusts my judgement."

"You mean your judgement of me now, don't you? I'm glad you didn't tell them what you thought of me when we first met."

She shook her head.

He let go of her hand and stretched his arm behind her on the back of the bench, then recaptured her fingers in his other hand. Gently, he rubbed his thumb over them. "What was with Beth tonight? She acted stranger than normal." He laughed.

"We'll talk of that another time. That's between us girls. She just has some...peculiar notions, besides being a notorious tease. I told her I wouldn't tell her anything ever again if she teased us."

He tilted his head to look her full in the face. "Like that's going to stop her? She's sweet, but irrepressible."

"Okay you two, break it up," Doc said, laughing as he came out the front door and descended the stairs. He turned as Pastor Parker stepped out followed by his wife. "Thanks for the wonderful meal, Sandy. My wife will want your recipe for that meatloaf. It was outstanding. Barb hasn't found a recipe she likes yet, but I'm sure this'll be the one."

"I'll write it out and give it to you tomorrow, David."

Doc glanced toward the swing. "Okay, kids. We have a busy day tomorrow, and I want you two bright-eyed, bushy-tailed, and in full possession of all faculties while you inspect the equipment. That means a good night's sleep, Jacob. You'll have plenty of time tomorrow to impress this young lady with whatever you haven't said tonight."

Kathryn's face glowed crimson.

Jacob stood and winked at her, then pulled her up from the swing. They went down the steps and strolled to the Mercedes.

"Good night, Eric," Doc called over his shoulder and then slid into the driver's seat.

Jacob slipped in on the passenger side and rolled down the window. He stuck his hand out and she placed hers in his. "Good night, milady." He pulled her close and kissed her fingers. Then he released her.

Just as he started to close the window, Beth ran down the stairs and toward the street. She stopped next to Kathryn and waved. "Goodnight, Doctors."

As his boss pulled the car away, he finished closing the window and chuckled. He hoped the curly crop wouldn't start teasing Kathryn again.

On the way to the hotel, her nightmares came into his thoughts. Those dreams of hers troubled him. She'd probably talk to her dad tonight.

*Nuts!* He forgot again to tell her about the man he'd seen at the bank the night of her birthday. Maybe he shouldn't tell her. Not now. Not while she was enjoying her family. Besides, they were hundreds of miles from Pensacola.

# Chapter Thirty-Two

$\mathcal{J}$acob ran up the porch stairs of the Parkers' Cape Cod home early the next day. As Kathryn stepped onto the porch, he smiled. "Good morning, milady."

"Good morning. I hope you slept well."

"Okay, I guess. About as good as I can in a hotel."

The couple headed down the stairs to join Dr. Hartley, who waited in the Mercedes.

Beth's singsong voice rang out behind them. "Take good care of my maid of honor."

With a grimace, Kathryn glanced over her shoulder.

Jacob called back, "Don't worry, she's in good hands." They hurried to the car. "Doesn't she ever give up?"

"Never. Never has. Never will." Kathryn laughed. "But she's the best friend I've ever had, even if we aren't truly sisters."

"And me?"

"Best ever." She blushed.

Jacob stopped at the curb and opened the rear door for her. She got in.

Dr. Hartley glanced back at her. "Good morning, young lady. Ready for a trip to town?"

"Ready, sir."

He checked the GPS and followed the directions to the interstate. After maneuvering through Chicago's rush-hour traffic, their boss parked in the showroom parking lot.

Inside the building, Kathryn headed to the area marked office equipment. Jacob kept his sight on her all the way, until she passed through the doorway. He turned to find his boss had moved to the next room. He'd better get his mind off his lady fair and onto what Doc brought him here to do.

When he caught up, Dr. Hartley called Jacob's attention to a piece of equipment. "Take a look at the specs for this. I'll check the model over there. Then we can compare notes during lunch."

"Sure thing, Doc."

His boss moved around a floor-to-ceiling display case and on to the other side of the room where he engaged in a conversation with a sales rep. Jacob lifted a brochure from the clear plastic holder in front of him and read.

When he finished, he turned to rejoin his boss and found himself almost nose to nose with a woman. She threw her arms around his neck and kissed him passionately on the mouth.

Jacob grabbed her arms and pushed her away. "Patricia!"

He surveyed the area. Kathryn was nowhere in sight. *Thank you, Lord.* Dr. Hartley still stood next to the other man, who pointed at something in the display in front of them. Good. No one else saw.

Jacob's blood boiled. "What are you doing? Where did you come from? What gives you the right—?" He stifled his outburst and glared.

"Oh Jacob, you're still so old-fashioned. I've always found that intriguing."

He backed away from her.

"I've missed you terribly, darling." She stepped closer. Her seductive voice made him cringe. She put her hands on his chest.

He pushed her arms down and stepped back again as he scowled. "Don't touch me. I'm not your darling, or anything else."

She pouted. "But, I've been so lonely without you. When you left, I fell apart. I realized you were the only man I'd ever loved." She fluttered her long black eyelashes. "When I finally discovered where you'd gone to work they told me you'd moved on to Florida, but no one would tell me where. And us almost engaged."

He'd escaped from this scheming femme fatale just in time, saved from making a huge mistake.

Patricia's arm rose to his chest again. "When I saw you standing here all alone, I knew I'd been given a second chance. Darling."

He pushed her arm away. "Stop calling me that. I said I'm not anything to you, nor are you to me."

"But we could be. I've moved to Chicago. Now here you are too. It's fate."

Jacob spotted a ring with a huge diamond flanked by smaller stones on Patricia's right hand. "Looks like you've received a proposal, *Pat*. Wearing the ring on the wrong hand, aren't you?"

Patricia's smug smile turned to a frown. She jutted her chin toward him. "Yes, I'm engaged. To someone who appreciates a real woman."

Jacob narrowed his eyes while she flashed the ring under his nose.

"I'm taking it for a test drive. But I'm not sure I like the idea of being tied to one man." The next words spat out of her mouth. "People don't think as narrow-mindedly as you anymore. You'll never change, will you? The same old-fashioned stick-in-the-mud you were when we were together. Too bad. Your loss."

"I don't intend to change, *Pat*. I wouldn't want your lack of morals for anything. And not everyone in the world thinks as you do."

She spun on her spiked heels, took two steps, and stopped. She rotated, glowering at him. "I suppose you've found yourself a sweet, innocent little thing that worships the ground you walk on."

Jacob smiled. "You're partly right. I have met someone both sweet and innocent. But if anyone should worship the ground someone walks on, it'll be me worshiping her. She's what I think a *real* woman should be, and I intend to marry her. Because of her, I know I've never been in love before, not *real* love."

Patricia rushed toward him and swung her hand upward toward his face. He caught her arm and grinned. She wrenched herself free.

As she stomped away, she moved the ring from her right hand to the left. When she reached the door, Patricia shot daggers over her shoulder and then bolted from the room.

After a deep breath of relief, an urgency to find Kathryn came over Jacob.

Tears surged down Kathryn's face as she raced toward the restroom sign. She burst into the ladies' room and stopped. A lady at the sink spun, a wet paper towel crumpled in her hands.

Kathryn's face flooded with heat. "I'm sorry."

The lady smiled. "It's okay. I thought I locked the door." Then her brows lowered. "Are you okay?"

Kathryn shook her head.

"Do you need help?"

Her head shook again.

"Okay." The woman left the room.

Kathryn flipped the lock and sat on a small chair in the corner. Who could that beautiful woman with Jacob have been? The picture of her lips on his wouldn't go away. Kathryn's temples began to pound.

She thought her heart had stopped for a second when she walked into the showroom after finishing her notes for Dr. Hartley. All she could think of was finding Jacob. But not like that.

Why? Why had he deceived her? They must be engaged. Or was she his wife, surprising him? Maybe he hadn't yet told Dr. Hartley he was married. Had her boss actually said Jacob was single, or did she assume it?

Kathryn moaned and wrung her hands. "What kind of game has he been playing?" She massaged her forehead. She knew it was too good to be true. Why did she have to fall in love with him?

Her hand went to her throat. The necklace. Why had he given it to her? What had he expected in return? Yet, he'd always been a gentleman with her. None of this made sense.

Half-blinded by tears, she removed the necklace and tossed it into her purse. "Why?" She slammed her hand down on the seat.

Several minutes later, Kathryn rose from the chair and washed her face with cold water. After a series of deep breaths, she left the restroom and hurried out of the building.

Jacob strode through each room looking for Kathryn. Where could she have gone? She'd be too embarrassed if he kissed her here, but he had to hold her, just for a minute.

After checking the office equipment showroom again, he entered the foyer to check another room. As he passed the plate glass entrance doors, he glanced outside. Kathryn? Where was she going? He barreled past the entry.

Halfway across the parking lot, within a few feet of her, he called, "Where's the fire?"

She kept walking. "I finished and decided to wait at the car. Where's Doctor Hartley?"

"Still inside. Are you okay?"

She stopped at the Mercedes. "Fine. Just fine."

"You don't sound fine. What happened?" Could she have run into Pat? She couldn't have. That devious female had no idea who Kathryn was.

When she didn't turn to him, Jacob placed his hand on her shoulder. She shrugged it off.

"Jacob." Their boss rushed up behind them. "What's going on? I turned around and you were gone." He stepped around them and cupped Kathryn's chin in his hand. "Are you all right? You've been crying."

Jacob's jaw tightened. She'd seen Pat kiss him.

Kathryn pulled a tissue from her purse and wiped her face. "It's allergies. There must be something in the air. I'm not feeling well." She rubbed the side of her neck.

Her boss unlocked the car. "Let's get you back to your parents' house."

She got into the back of the car.

As Jacob sat in the front passenger seat, his mind whirled. He had to explain. But if he tried to talk to her right now, it might upset her more. She wouldn't want to discuss this in front of Doc. Better to wait until they were alone.

While their boss started the engine, Jacob shifted in his seat so he could gaze at Kathryn in the rearview mirror. She dabbed at her eyes.

After pulling away, Dr. Hartley looked in the mirror. "Kathy? Should we find an urgent care room? You don't look well at all."

"It's just an upset stomach. This happens sometimes when my allergies act up."

"Okay. I thought for a minute you two had a disagreement. Again." He laughed.

She didn't smile.

Jacob clamped his teeth together until his jaw hurt.

Kathryn glanced at their boss. "Doctor Hartley, could you stop at that gas station on the corner? I need to use the restroom."

Doc pulled the car into a parking space at the side of the convenient store. When he turned off the engine, she flung the door open and ran into the building.

With wrinkled brows, Doc glanced at Jacob. "It's not allergies, is it?"

"No. I'm afraid I'm the one making her sick."

His boss shook his head. "But you two are together now. I was teasing a minute ago about the argument. What happened?"

"It wasn't me. Remember the woman in Minnesota? The one I almost proposed to?" He refreshed his friend's memory of the story.

"She showed up here and kissed me before I could stop her. I'm sure Kathryn saw it."

Doc let his head fall back against the headrest and closed his eyes. "Well, you'd better explain things to her fast."

"I want to, but I don't think she'd like me to say something in front of you."

After a minute of silence, Doc hit the steering wheel with his open hand and shifted to face Jacob. "I've got an idea. I'll take a detour onto Lake Shore Drive, which runs alongside Lake Michigan. Once we're next to one of the harbors, I'll stop to use the bathroom. That'll leave you two alone in the car."

Jacob sighed. "Thanks, Doc. Hopefully she'll listen to me."

"I'm sure she will. Kathy's always been levelheaded and forgiving. She forgave you once." He chuckled.

Jacob stared at the glass windows of the store. "She's been in there a long time."

"You're right. I'll go check on her." Dr. Hartley went inside.

A minute later, he ran out. "She's gone. I had the clerk check the bathroom."

# Chapter Thirty-Three

athryn glanced over her shoulder as she ran. Jacob bolted out of the car and headed in the other direction. She ducked into a storefront and waited. Dr. Hartley scanned the streets at the intersection and returned to the black Mercedes. A minute later, Jacob got in.

When the car pulled away from the gas station and rounded the corner, she made her escape.

Blocks later, she entered a greasy-spoon-type diner and sat in a rear booth. She gulped air as she pulled her phone from her purse. Her hands trembled. She pressed the number for the Parkers' home.

"Parker residence."

"Beth." Kathryn opened her mouth to speak again, but nothing came out but a sob. Tears filled her eyes. She swiped at them with a tissue from her purse.

The waitress, with a mix of mousy brown and gray hair standing at the counter, stared.

Beth's voice came through the receiver again. "Kath? Is that you?"

"Beth."

"What's wrong?"

Kathryn took a deep breath and let it out. "Can you come get me?"

"What happened? Where's Jacob and Doctor Hartley? Why are you crying?"

"We—we were separated. Please, come get me."

"Sure. Where are you?"

"Hold on." Kathryn put the phone down, blotted her tears, and slipped out of the booth. She approached the plump waitress. "What's the address here?"

The woman held out a menu and pointed to the bottom with the orange nail of her forefinger. "Right here, honey. Are you okay?"

"I will be. Thank you." She hurried to the booth.

Kathryn slid in and picked up the cell. "I'm at a diner called Jake's on Kimbark Street." She gave Beth the address. "How long will it be?" She lowered her voice. "I feel uncomfortable here. I've never been in this part of the city before."

"Let me check the app on my phone to see where you are."

Rapid clicks from Beth's footsteps followed. "Okay. Got it. You're on the south side, so it'll take about an hour to get there. The traffic shouldn't be too bad right now. Just sit tight. I'll get there as soon as I can."

"Thank you. I'm sorry. I didn't know what else to do."

"It's okay. But what happened?"

"Please, Beth. Can it wait?"

"Okay. Bye."

After she wiped her tears again, Kathryn scooted herself into the corner of the booth. The waitress strolled over. "What'll it be, honey? Coffee or something?"

"Yes. Coffee. Please."

"You all right, honey? Did someone bother you out there?" The rosy-cheeked waitress nodded her head toward the street. "Did you call the police?"

Kathryn gazed up into blood-shot brown eyes. "No. It's nothing. I'm okay. I called for a ride. Is it okay if I stay here until she gets here?"

"Sure. But you're crying."

"Allergies."

"Right." The woman quirked her lips. "Do you want anything with the coffee?"

"No. I'm not hungry."

As the waitress sauntered to the counter, Kathryn peered past her. Through the large front window with dingy café curtains that covered its bottom third, she kept watch as cars passed by.

Beth had to get there before they found her. Kathryn bit her lip.

Searching through the open window of the Mercedes for any sign of Kathryn, while Dr. Hartley cruised up and down the streets, Jacob's pulse raced. Where had she gone? Why would she run away like that?

"Doc, something could happen to her wandering alone in the city. I'd like to wring Pat's neck."

"Relax, Jacob. Remember, Kathy spent her teenage years in Des Plaines. I'm sure she and her brother travelled all over Chicago before they moved to Pensacola. She's no doubt still familiar with the area. Let me pull over and call the Parkers. We need to tell them what's happened."

Jacob took in a deep breath to calm his nerves. It was such a big city.

After Dr. Hartley pulled the car into a parking space on Kimbark Street where they'd been cruising, he scanned his contacts. "Great! I never put it in here. I left his card on the dresser at the hotel, and I don't even remember the street. Do you?" He glanced at Jacob with furrowed brows.

Jacob shook his head. "What about the GPS? Isn't it in there?"

"No, only the hotel, the showroom, and the airport." Doc put the car in gear. "I'm sure I can get us from the hotel to the Parkers' home though. We've searched long enough here. I'll bet she's headed that way on public transportation."

"I'll never forgive myself if anything happens to her." Jacob sighed. His eyes stung.

After the Mercedes pulled into traffic, he clenched his teeth so hard his jaw ached. Scruffy young men leaned against the bricks of a diner. "God, please keep her safe."

"Stop imagining the worst, my boy. Try to figure out what you'll say to her when you get the chance."

What would he say? This was his fault for getting involved with that redhead in the first place. He'd told Kathryn he loved her. She had to listen to him.

Kathryn moved to a table closer to the entrance of the diner. The waitress brought her a mug of coffee and left.

As she propped her elbows on the table, Kathryn took a sip and gazed out to the street. A large black car slowly rolled by, only the top quarter visible above the curtains. Her heart jumped to her throat. A man with dark wavy hair looked through the vehicle's open window. "Jacob," she whispered. Keep calm. He couldn't see in here. Not with the sun's reflection on the glass. The car passed.

Two young men wearing torn jeans came through the door of the diner. After they ogled her, they took stools at the counter. The waitress shouted out their lunch order to the cook, while Kathryn stepped to the back end of the counter.

The woman strolled over. "Can I get'cha anything else?"

"Nothing else." She paid for her coffee. "Where's the restroom?"

The woman pointed to a dark hall at the rear of the long narrow diner. The two men at the counter grinned. She moved back to the corner booth. If she saw Jacob coming, she could duck into the ladies' room. Surely, he'd just peek through the window and move on.

An hour later, her uncle's minivan pulled up in front of the restaurant. She left the half-full mug of cold coffee, grabbed her purse, and dashed past the young men and out the door.

Beth opened the rear door for her, and Kathryn jumped in. "Mom and Dad wanted to come." Aunt Sandy sat in the front passenger seat.

Tears threatened again as the mini-van moved away from the curb.

Beth laid a hand on Kathryn's arm. "What happened?"

"Not now." She sniffed. "Later." The waterworks spilled onto her cheeks.

Aunt Sandy handed her a handkerchief. "It's okay, dear. We can talk at home." She patted Kathryn's knee and gave her daughter a shake of the head.

Turning to the side window, Kathryn focused on the blurred figures of people walking along the sidewalks.

Several minutes later, Uncle Eric asked, "David and Jacob are all right, aren't they?"

Her Irish temper burned inside. "They're fine. I guess." Jacob's lips on that woman would never leave her mind. She fumed while her heart ached. "We got separated." Not exactly a lie, but not as bad as Jacob's.

Before his boss turned off the engine, Jacob jumped from the car and ran up the Parkers' porch steps. He rang the bell and knocked at the door. He knocked again before Dr. Hartley reached him. Jacob knocked and rang once more.

"Jacob, there's no van in the driveway. I don't think they're home. We'll wait on the porch until they get back."

"How can I sit here and wait?" He rubbed his neck and faced Doc. "I don't know what's happened to her."

"Getting sick about it won't help. Now sit down and try to keep calm."

Jacob strode to the swing at the corner of the porch and stared at it. Last night they'd sat there. He'd held her hand as they talked, and she smiled. Such a soft hand. He closed his eyes for a second, and then paced the length of the porch. "Where do you suppose they've gone? I don't know what to do. Maybe we should call the police."

"And tell them what? That you and Kathy had an argument?" He cocked his head to the side.

Jacob tromped down the steps and paced the sidewalk to the end of the yard and back. He returned to the porch and retraced his footsteps there. *God, please bring them home. Please watch over Kathryn.*

After what felt like hours of trips up and down the steps, the Parkers' minivan came into view. He leaped over the stairs and sprinted to the street.

When the rear door opened, he held out his hand to Kathryn. "Where did you go?"

She wouldn't look at him.

Doc rushed up. "You had us scared to death, young lady."

Without Jacob's help, Kathryn stepped out of the van. "I'm sorry." She darted to the house, up the stairs, and stopped at the locked door.

Beth whizzed past the doctors and let her sister into the house.

Jacob stood with his mouth agape. What should he do? He had to talk to her. She had no idea what really happened.

Pastor Parker hurried around the vehicle and opened the passenger door for his wife. She rose from the seat, and they turned to Jacob with wrinkled brows. The pastor asked, "What happened?"

"Sir, are you busy right now? I can explain." Jacob stared at the ground.

"Let's go to my office."

As Jacob entered the study, Pastor Parker pointed to an armchair next to an old mahogany desk. Jacob plopped into the seat.

From behind the desk, the pastor riveted Jacob with his gaze. "Now. Tell me what's going on."

After dropping his head forward, Jacob closed his eyes. "I've made a mess of things, sir. It's all my fault. If only I hadn't —"

"Hadn't what?"

Jacob's eyes sprang open and met the man's angry stare. *He thinks I did something to Kathryn.* "Hadn't ever dated the woman in Minnesota who showed up here today. That's what I was going to say."

The pastor leaned back and laced his fingers together, his elbows on the armrests. "Go ahead."

After Jacob explained the circumstances surrounding his move to Pensacola and how he'd fallen in love with Kathryn, Pastor Parker breathed out a sigh.

Jacob rubbed his forehead. "I would never have hurt Kathryn on purpose. I had no idea she saw Pat kiss me, or I'd have explained right away. After that woman left, I went in search of Kathryn. All I could think of was being with her."

The pastor sat up straight and folded his hands on the desk. "So how did Kathy wind up alone in that part of the city?"

A vision of the loiterers on the street filled Jacob's mind. He wrung his hands. "She said she was sick. From allergies. We got in the car to come back here. She asked Doc to stop at a convenience store, and she went inside. When he checked on her, she wasn't there. We drove around the area but couldn't find her. Doc was going to call you but he'd forgotten to enter your number in his phone. This has been a nightmare."

For a moment, Pastor Parker said nothing. Then he stood, walked to the window behind his desk, and looked out. "What a mess."

"I'll say. But now what do I do? How can I explain when she won't even look at me?"

Pastor Parker came around the desk and laid his hand on Jacob's shoulder. "Right now, we need to pray. Then you should go to the hotel and let me talk to Kathy. I'll tell her what you told me. I'm sure this can be straightened out and everything will be normal again by tomorrow."

The door to the bedroom opened and clicked shut again. Kathryn recognized the footsteps that sounded on the hardwood floor. She pushed herself to a seated position. Beth sat on the edge of the bed and reached her arm around Kathryn's shoulders.

When the sobs quieted, Kathryn wiped her face with the wad of tissues she'd collected. "Beth, I've made a fool of myself."

"You mean with Jacob? You love him, don't you? And, he loves you."

"No. He doesn't. It was a game to him." Her tears streamed over her cheeks.

"What do you mean?"

Kathryn told her sister what she'd seen. "They were kissing. Right there."

Beth's jaw lowered. "Why don't I make some herbal tea and bring it up to you. It'll help you calm down." She rose and headed for the door.

Kathryn laid her head on the pillow. "Beth," she murmured.

"Yes?" She turned.

"The necklace. It's in my purse. Take it. If he's downstairs, give it to him. Tell him to give it to her."

Jacob stepped from the pastor's study just as Beth reached the bottom of the staircase. The Claddagh necklace dangled from her hand. His heart ached.

She held it out to him. "Kathy doesn't want it. She said to give it to her." Beth's eyes narrowed. "Why did you do that to my sister?"

The words cut into him. He stared at the Claddagh as a lump rose in his throat, and he shook his head.

"How could you hurt her that way?" Beth pushed the necklace toward him. "Take it."

Jacob took Beth by the arm and led her out to the front porch, sat her on the swing, and stood in front of her. "I love your sister. I'd never hurt her. That woman kissed me. Not the other way around." He squatted and told Beth how Pat came up to him. Then he explained how he knew her.

"But...why didn't you tell Kath about her?"

"Eventually, I would have. How was I to know she'd show up in Chicago, or that she'd—? I told Pat I'm in love with Kathryn."

Beth's eyes glistened. She rested her hand on his arm.

"After I'd realized she'd seen the disgusting kiss, I wanted to explain. But I didn't think she'd like it if I said anything in front of Doctor Hartley. I should have anyway. Your dad said to go back to the hotel, and he'll talk to her." His head dropped forward. "This has been one of the worst days of my life."

Doc came out of the house and stepped to Jacob's side.

When he looked back up at her, Beth nodded. "Let Dad talk to her. She's always listened to him."

"I hope so. Guess we'll go to the hotel and wait." He sighed and stood.

Doc patted him on the back. "Hang in there, son. It'll be okay."

When they reached the stairs, Beth held the necklace out to Jacob and grimaced. "Just for now." She dropped the Claddagh into his outstretched hand.

A knife stabbed his heart. Kathryn had been so happy yesterday.

# Chapter Thirty-Four

*J*acob trudged to the hotel elevator, pressed the button, and turned to watch Dr. Hartley at the front desk. The girl behind the counter handed him several pieces of paper.

While Doc spoke with her, the elevator doors opened, and Jacob stepped in. His mind drifted to Pastor Parker. Would Kathryn listen to him? The elevator doors closed. He pressed the floor button.

As he entered his room, he plodded to the dresser, tossed the keycard on top, and threw himself onto the bed. The memory of her tear-stained face wrenched his heart. "Lord, give her the grace to listen."

A knock jolted him upright. He rushed to the door and yanked it open. Dr. Hartley stepped into the room.

"Sorry I left you down there, Doc." Jacob slumped into a small armchair at a circular table in front of the windows.

As he walked to the table and sat down, Doc's brows knit. He held out his hand. "These notes are from the office. They've been trying to reach us all afternoon. Something's happened—"

"To Kathryn?" Jacob bolted from the chair.

"No. Not Kathy."

Jacob exhaled and dropped his head forward. "Thank God."

"Your father's had a heart attack."

"What?" His gaze shot to his friend.

Doc handed him the notes.

Jacob flipped through them. "This one says my stepmother's been trying to reach me. Why didn't they call my phone?"

"They tried. We shut them off before we left for the lakefront with Kathy to avoid interruptions. I forgot until I saw that note. They finally tried her phone this afternoon but only got voicemail."

Jacob nodded and sat. "She probably turned it off to avoid me." His head fell back.

"Your father must have asked for you."

"Why would he want me now? Or his wife want me. She made it clear from the start that she hates me." He leaned forward, propped his elbows on his knees, and dropped his forehead into his hands. First, he could lose Kathryn because of Pat. Now his estranged father had a heart attack. *What are you doing to me, Lord?* "What should I do?" he mumbled.

"He's still your father. He might be dying. I know he's hurt you in the past, but if he's asking for you..."

Jacob raised his head. "Doc, how can I leave her now?" He grabbed both sides of his head and ran his fingers through his hair. "But I'll have to."

"You may regret it for the rest of your life if you don't. It's the right thing. No matter what."

Jacob stood and paced, then stopped and gazed into his friend's sympathetic blue eyes. He was right. "Thank you for always being there to guide me, Doc."

Dr. Hartley rose and planted his arm around Jacob's shoulder. "Everything will be okay, son. Another hurdle for you to get over, that's all. If you need me, call. If you say the word, I'll fly to Minnesota myself and tell that old man a thing or two."

Jacob smiled at him. Then his brows rumpled. "Pastor Parker said he'd phone after he spoke to Kathryn. I feel like a heel leaving."

"Don't worry. Right now, see when you can find a flight. I'll drive you to the airport and then stop at the Parkers' on the way back. I'll explain everything. She'll be okay."

"Thanks." Jacob picked up his phone, turned it on, and contacted the airline.

Several minutes later, they loaded his bags into the Mercedes and left. It had to be God's will for him to leave. He'd found a seat right away. After he picked up a rental car at the airport, he'd drive to the house in Edina—no—to the hospital. Get your head together, man. He should be there within four hours.

He hadn't been back to that house since he graduated from high school. Never wanted to go back. Yet here he was, summoned.

Jacob shook his head and refocused on Kathryn. "Doc, everything will work out, right?"

"You mean with Kathy? I'm sure. She's a sensible girl. She'll listen to Eric. He's been her father since she was fourteen, when her own dad died. He loves her, and she loves him."

Jacob sighed. So unlike his own real father. He watched the cars go by as they turned onto the airport road. His world was crumbling, and he couldn't do anything to stop it.

At the concourse entrance, he turned to Dr. Hartley. "If you talk to her—"

"I know. I'll tell her, son."

"And you'll call when you've talked to her?"

"Yes. But I'm sure you'll speak to her yourself before long." Doc put his hand on Jacob's shoulder and squeezed. "Now get going before you miss that flight."

Jacob wrapped his arms around his friend. "What would I have done without you all these years? It's as if I'm leaving my real dad here and going to see a stranger."

Kathryn awoke with the late afternoon sun on her face. Rays filtered through the leaves of the tree she and Beth used to climb right outside the bedroom window. The birds sang, while her head and heart throbbed. The image of Jacob and the beautiful woman asserted itself in her mind yet again. Tears stung her eyes.

She swung her legs over the edge of the bed and rolled off to stand. In the dresser mirror, her reflection stared at her. Not the happy girl from that morning, was she? "Grow up and get over it." Not the first to have Dr. McLeod play games with her heart, no doubt. Nor the last.

Where was the tea Beth said she'd bring up? Guess she forgot. How long had she been asleep? A quick glimpse at the alarm clock on the nightstand gave her the answer. Almost dinnertime.

After a shower, Kathryn slipped on her favorite white dress. She stepped back and viewed herself in a full-length mirror. Her mind numbed as she stared at the hem with a row of little pink flowers dancing around it.

A minute later, she combed her hair, then left the room and descended the staircase. They'd ask a million questions. She could imagine what lies Jacob had told her family to cover for himself.

When she reached the bottom stair, the house was still. She listened for male voices. None. Good. No Dr. McLeod. He and Dr.

Hartley must have left. She slipped into the kitchen and fixed herself a cup of tea.

Cup in hand, with an aching heart, she stepped into the family room. Uncle Eric sat in the rear corner next to the brick fireplace. He peered over his glasses as she drew near.

Seated at a game table to her left, Aunt Sandy and Beth looked up from their Monopoly board. Beth pulled out the chair beside her. "Kath, come help me decide what I should do. Mom's winning."

Kathryn shook her head. She lowered herself into the chair opposite her uncle at the fireplace. The air grew heavy with silence.

Her gaze fell on the large multi-colored arrangement of roses in the firebox. Aunt Sandy always replaced the logs with those artificial roses for the summer. There'd be no more roses from Jacob. She squeezed her eyes shut. How could she work in the same building with him? She held her eyes closed until the tears retreated. When she opened them, she turned away from the fireplace and swallowed the lump in her throat.

Her uncle laid his paper on the table next to him. He stood and walked over to Aunt Sandy and Beth. "I'd like to talk to Kathy alone."

"I think it's time to prepare dinner, Beth." Aunt Sandy rose.

Beth followed her mother out of the room. "Let's try that new chicken recipe."

Kathryn watched them leave the room. She dropped her head into her hands and sighed. "Uncle Eric, this isn't necessary. I'm fine. I've had a rough day."

"Yes. You have." He caught her arm as she sprang from the chair and tried to hurry past him. He led her back to the chair and pulled the other armchair in front of her. As he sat, he leaned forward with his forearms on his legs. "Jacob told me what you saw today. But there's more to it."

"I don't care to know any more." Heat rose in her neck. Her breathing quickened.

"Kathryn!"

His voice was gentle, yet firm. He never called her Kathryn. She gazed at him. He'd taken her and her brother into his home without question, and never expected her to call him Dad, or Father, even though he'd always been one to her. But she couldn't talk to him about Dr. McLeod. Not now. Not ever.

She tried to stand again, but her uncle circled her wrist with his large, strong hand. "Kathy, you have to listen. Jac—"

"I don't care what he said to you."

"You can keep interrupting me, but I am going to say this, and we'll stay here as long as it takes."

She slouched back in the chair.

"There's been a misunderstanding." Uncle Eric gave her Jacob's version of why he'd moved to Florida and how the woman showed up that afternoon and accosted him in the showroom. "He told me how much he loves you. He said he also told her."

Sure. He made up a good story. How could what Jacob told Uncle Eric be true? Jacob was like all men who used their good looks to get as many women as they wanted. Wasn't he just a liar? He had to be. He'd hidden it so well—from everyone. She wouldn't be fooled into playing his game.

"Kathy, will you talk to him?"

The grandfather clock in the corner ticked by the seconds.

"Are you finished, Uncle Eric?"

"Yes. But will you talk to Jacob?"

"I'll think about it." She stood and marched toward the hallway. Halfway there, she turned. "I know you want what's best for me, and I love you for it. But this is something I have to work out myself."

She spun and headed for the door.

"With the help of the Lord...Kathryn?"

She stopped, and then kept walking.

# Chapter Thirty-Five

y the time Jacob drove to the hospital in Edina, Minnesota, it was after seven in the evening. He checked on his father's condition at the floor desk and then went to the room. When he opened the door, he found the man sleeping comfortably as the nurse had told him.

Jacob backed out of the room. He should call Doc to see if Pastor Parker talked to Kathryn. He strode to the cafeteria and dialed Doc's number.

"Jacob. Glad you called. How's your father?"

"Asleep when I arrived. Have you talked to Pastor Parker? Kathryn?"

"Kathy was asleep when I got to their house. Eric called a while ago and said he told Kathy what happened, but she's still upset. She needs time. Try not to worry."

Jacob propped an elbow on the table and dropped his forehead into his hand. "I'm trying, Doc. It's hard. All they've told me so far about my father is that he's stable and resting comfortably. I should go back to his room. I'll call you tomorrow after I find out more. Maybe you'll have better news for me then."

After they hung up, Jacob stared at the phone. He dialed Kathryn's number, but the call went to voicemail. No point leaving a message before he knew where he stood. He disconnected the call.

Jacob pulled the card Pastor Parker had given him from his wallet and dialed the number.

"Hello?"

"Beth? Why do you have your dad's phone?"

"He forgot it on the desk when he and Mom ran out for a few minutes. I heard it ring. Doctor Hartley told us about your dad. How is he?"

"I'm at the hospital. He's resting. Don't know any more right now."

"Are you okay?"

"I'm fine, except for this mess with Kathryn." Jacob's pulse quickened. "Doctor Hartley said your dad told her what happened, but she's upset."

"She wasn't very receptive. I tried later when we were alone, but she buried her head in the pillow."

His heart sank. Fatigue hit him full force. If only he'd wake up and find this was nothing but a nightmare.

"Are you still there, Jacob?"

"Yes."

"Don't give up hope, okay? I'll keep trying. Mom is praying, and Dad said he'll try to talk to her again in the morning."

"Thank you, Beth. Thank everyone. Tell Kathryn I love her."

He hung up and trudged into the hall. Was it only this morning they were so happy? It felt more like a week had passed.

When he turned into the last corridor, his stepmother stood at the nurse's desk.

She turned. "Jacob. Someone finally reached you."

Her ashen face had no hint of makeup. She looked as though she'd collapse any moment. "Are you okay? Is he worse?" He took her by the arm and led her to a bench near the elevators. When she sat, he took the seat next to her.

Abigail's slate-gray eyes filled with tears. "They keep telling me he's going to be all right now. But I was so scared he'd die."

Her disheveled, curly carrot-colored hair looked as if she'd brushed it with her fingers. "I'm so sorry, Jacob. He had the attack right in the middle of a terrible argument." She took out a handkerchief and wiped the tears from her eyes.

Jacob narrowed his eyes. What happened to the haughty woman he'd known? How could he be sympathetic to her after the way she'd treated him? Just like his father. A prick of guilt stabbed him.

A sob escaped Abigail. "William and I argued about the way we've cut you out of our lives. I said we were unfair and needed to make things up to you. His face turned red...almost purple. Then, he yelled. And collapsed."

She buried her head in the shawl she'd been twisting, and wept.

Jacob laid his hand on her arm. "Let's not talk about this right now." The resentment he'd held toward her for so long faded. He stretched his arm around her shoulders. "It'll be okay. I've done fine on my own. I'm in need of nothing."

Abigail lifted her head from the shawl and gazed at him. "Except your father."

His heart squeezed. Except Kathryn.

Early Tuesday afternoon, Kathryn waited in the Parker's foyer for Dr. Hartley to pick her up for their flight back to Pensacola. She glanced at Beth, who leaned on the banister. "I'm so glad we finished everything for your wedding while I was here. Now you can have peace of mind." Unlike she'd have at work with everyone badgering her about Dr. McLeod.

"Thanks, sis. I only wish we could have settled things between you and Jacob before you leave."

A homesick sensation went through Kathryn at the mention of Jacob's name. She closed her eyes. "Please. Not now. Not when I'm leaving."

"But he was so sad when he phoned this morning, and you refused to talk to him. Will you at least consider talking to him when you get back to Pensacola?"

Never thought she'd be happy to leave her old home. But she wasn't sure she'd be happy to get back to Florida either. Not back to work, anyway.

The doorbell chimed. Kathryn opened the door, and Dr. Hartley stepped into the foyer.

"Good morning, sir."

"Good morning, Kathy. All set?"

"Yes, sir." She lifted her carryon, and Beth handed Kathryn's bags to the doctor.

Aunt Sandy descended the staircase. "David, be sure to visit anytime you'd like. Even if it's only to flee from the muggy south."

"I'll take you up on that next time the heat becomes unbearable. I'll bring Barb with me."

Uncle Eric hurried down the hall and took Dr. Hartley's hand. "I'll call you soon to finish our spiritual discussion."

"Please do, Eric. I have questions we didn't have time for. But I'm not ready to make such a serious religious decision right now."

"David." Her aunt shook her head. "It's not religion. It's salvation."

"Okay, dear lady. I understand." He glanced at Kathryn.

She smiled. At least something good might come out of this trip besides Beth's inner peace.

"Time to leave, Kathy." Her boss breezed through the door Uncle Eric held open for them.

When they reached the curb, Kathryn kissed her aunt and uncle, gave Beth a tight squeeze, and got in the Mercedes. Her heart pinched as she recalled Jacob peering from the vehicle toward the window of the snack shop last Thursday.

Dr. Hartley turned the key and pulled away from the curb as all three Parkers waved.

Moments later, her boss glanced at her. "Did you talk to Jacob?"

"No." How could she when the pain he'd caused went so deep? She loved him. Now she had to get over him.

Silence reigned for the remainder of the trip. Kathryn stared out the side window.

After dropping off the rental car and checking their luggage, they waited outside the boarding gate. Dr. Hartley touched her arm. "Kathy."

She looked into sad blue eyes.

"Don't you think Jacob has enough on his mind right now without wondering if you'll ever forgive him for something that wasn't his fault?"

Tears filled her eyes. "I'm sorry this happened to him. It's a hard thing to lose a parent." Or brother, or anyone you loved.

"He hasn't lost his father. Mr. McLeod is recovering. But Jacob's hurting. I spoke to him early this morning, and he said you refused to talk to him last night."

She clenched and unclenched her fingers. With the certainty that she'd have to face Jacob at work each day with the deep feelings she had for him, she had to leave the clinic. His close friendship with Dr. Hartley made it even worse. She needed a new job.

"Kathy? Please let him explain."

"Sir. With all due respect—"

"Good afternoon, passengers. This is the pre-boarding announcement for flight thirty-eight, fifteen to Pensacola, Florida. We invite those passengers with small children, and any passengers requiring special assistance, to begin boarding at this time. Please have your boarding pass ready. Regular boarding will follow. Thank you."

Kathryn popped out of the seat and stood next to the line. At least on the plane she'd have peace. She fought back tears.

In flight, she opened her personal planner to write down everything she needed to do tomorrow. Item one. Update résumé.

With the heavy atmosphere inside the vehicle, the ride from the Pensacola airport seemed never-ending. Kathryn unfastened her seatbelt before Dr. Hartley brought the car to a complete stop.

He turned off the engine. "Kathy, may I ask a favor?"

Might have known she wouldn't escape without revisiting the subject. "What's that, sir?"

"Please consider what I said about listening to Jacob. He'd never have hurt you intentionally. The blame for what happened isn't his."

"I'll consider it. Don't worry. Everything will work out as it should." She slipped out of the car.

He got out and lifted her bags from the trunk.

"I can handle these. You're as tired as I am. You need to get home to Mrs. Hartley. She's missed you."

Her boss sighed. "Okay. I'll see you tomorrow."

Kathryn bit her lip as she stretched out the handle of her suitcase. With her overnight bag perched on top and her carryon slung over her shoulder, she headed toward the house. "Goodbye, Doctor."

On the porch, she fished her keys out of her purse and unlocked the front door. The minute she set foot in the foyer, Sheila bounded off the couch and ran to her. Kathryn plunked her carryon onto the floor. "Missed you, girl. It's so good to be home."

Mrs. Weaver left the couch and embraced her. "Welcome home, dear."

"I hope Sheila's been a good girl for you."

"She's been a sweetheart, as always. For some reason, she's barked more than usual, but that's fine. Probably just squirrels. It lets us know she's on guard." The silver-haired woman chuckled.

Mr. Weaver laid his newspaper and glasses on the end table and left his armchair. He picked up Kathryn's suitcase and overnight bag. "I'll take these upstairs. I think Carol set aside a plate of dinner for you in the fridge."

"No thank you. I'm really not hungry. But I am tired. I think I'll go to my apartment and rest."

He nodded. "Traveling does tend to sap a person's energy."

She smiled at him and grabbed her carryon. Mr. Weaver followed her up the stairs with the other bags. Sheila raced to beat her to the top step.

After opening the door, Kathryn threw her purse and carryon onto the couch. Mr. Weaver set her luggage in the corner of the living room.

He turned to go downstairs, and then stopped. "We're glad you're back, Kathy."

"Thank you. I'm happy to be home."

He nodded and closed the door behind him.

The silence of the empty apartment hit her. She gazed into the bedroom. After the dog's standard circle routine, she plopped herself in her favorite spot on the end of the bed.

She hadn't thought about staying alone in the apartment tonight with memories of Jacob to haunt her. But if she spent the evening downstairs, the Weavers would no doubt ask questions she didn't want to answer.

Her eyes rested on the now-wilted rose on her nightstand. She strode to it and clutched the plain glass vase. In the bathroom, she poured the water out, and then dropped the rose and vase in the trash can. The one in her office would meet a similar fate. For now, she'd unpack, take care of Sheila, and turn in early.

Kathryn trod into the bedroom and fell backward onto the mattress next to Sheila. "What am I going to do, girl? What will I say to everyone?" She wouldn't. Tomorrow, she'd call in sick. Jetlag. Good excuse. She had tons of unused sick days.

She rolled to her side. "You and I will spend the day together."

Sheila whined and cocked her head.

Kathryn pulled the little dog close to her. "You know something's wrong, don't you? It'll be okay, girl. As soon as I get over this slump in my life."

# Chapter Thirty-Six

*E*arly the next morning, Kathryn dialed the office. She'd leave a message with the answering service.

The phone rang several times before Haley's voice answered. "Scenic Bluffs Family Practice Clinic, Haley Smith speaking. May I help you?"

"Oh. Hi, Haley. It's Kathryn. You're there very early this morning."

"Yeah. I came in to finish some work that wasn't done yesterday. Are you back in Pensacola?"

"Yes, but I won't be in today. My head's splitting. Jetlag, no doubt." Guilt hit Kathryn between the eyes. She'd turned into a liar. Only this one time. "Please let Doctor Hartley know?" Good it was so early. She wouldn't ask about Dr. McLeod.

"Sure. Sorry you're not feeling well. That's unusual for you. And here I planned to drill you and Dr. McLeod about the new equipment.

I'll catch him when he gets in though. Get some rest and we'll talk tomorrow."

"Thanks." Kathryn hung up. Bet that wouldn't have been the only drilling she would have endured.

Late in the afternoon, she closed her laptop in disgust and lowered her forehead to her crossed arms. Tears stung her eyes. She'd spent much of the day in futile search for a new job. Nobody needed anyone with her skillset. The job market was as bad as when she'd searched more than a year ago. She had to find something. She couldn't work with Jacob every day.

Kathryn napped, surfed more job sites, played with Sheila, and took her for walks for the rest of the afternoon. "The Weavers picked a perfect time for a day trip, girl. They don't even know I stayed home today."

Dinnertime came and went with the peanut butter sandwich she tried to eat discarded in the garbage. An hour later, she rode to church with Mr. and Mrs. Weaver for the midweek service.

As Kathryn slipped into the pew behind the couple, she spotted Nick heading her way. She'd avoided questions from her landlords on the way by a monologue about Beth's wedding plans. But Nick was sure to ask about Dr. McLeod.

Nick slipped in next to her. "Welcome back to sunny Florida. We missed you Sunday. Hope you had a great time." He turned and glanced around the sanctuary. "Where's Jacob?"

Her heart sank. "Oh...didn't he contact your uncle?"

"What are you talking about?"

"Doctor McLeod has been called away to Minnesota." Not good. Her tone was too cold. "His father had a heart attack."

Nick frowned as he gazed at her. "I'm sorry to hear that. Tell Jacob I'll have the youth group pray for his father. Him too."

"I will. He could use the prayer." In so many ways. But she didn't intend to speak to him, if she could avoid it.

Nick's brows pinched. "Doctor McLeod? You said Doctor McLeod. Not Jacob."

"Yes. It is his title. Aren't you going to ask how everything went with Beth's wedding plans? That is part of the reason I was there." She smiled at him.

He chuckled. "Okay, Kathy. But you know men aren't much on that kind of conversation. I'm sure you and Beth had a ball though." He glanced at the seat. "May I sit with you? Jacob won't mind, will he?"

"I won't."

He cocked his head with a curious look at her but didn't say more.

During the singing, Kathryn peeked at him several times. Each time he responded with a grin.

After the service, Nick stood. "Kathy, do you want to go for coffee? You can attempt to pique my interest in what you and Beth did during your trip."

Perfect. He didn't mention Jacob. "I'd love to. Let me tell the Weavers I won't be leaving with them."

The older couple spoke with the pastor at the rear of the church. She and Nick stepped up to them. "Nick and I are going for coffee."

Mrs. Weaver's brows puckered as she gave her husband a quick glance. "Okay, dear."

Jacob had been at the house so much lately. No telling what was going through their minds now that prayer had been asked for Jacob's father in the hospital. Well, she'd explain everything to them later. They'd understand.

Maybe they'd think the relationship hadn't worked out after being together so much in Chicago. If so, she'd not have to say anything.

Nick and Kathryn zigzagged through the lot to his truck. He held out his hand to her, and she placed hers in it as she seated herself in the passenger seat. She gazed at him and smiled.

When the alarm chimed on Thursday morning, Kathryn awoke with a start. She still couldn't face everyone. No way. At least, not yet. She dialed the clinic number, and the answering service came on the line.

"This is Miss Kendall. Please tell Doctor Hartley I still don't feel well and won't be in. Ask him not to call because I'm going back to bed. I'll check in later." *After he went to do his rounds at the hospital.* She hung up.

Today, she'd send résumés out to appropriate offices, even if they weren't looking for help. Maybe something would come of it. She turned over and drifted off to sleep.

A terrifying voice filled her restless mind. *"Thought you'd get away from me, didn't you?"*

Her eyelids flew open and she panted. Sheila rushed to her. The nightmares were back. She'd never talked to her uncle about them.

Kathryn tossed back the covers and sat up on the edge of the bed. Would she never free herself from these horrible dreams?

With a sigh, she trudged to the closet and turned on the light. Moments later, she stepped out fully clothed. Sheila sat nearby, tongue hanging from one side of her mouth. She followed Kathryn with her eyes.

"Want to go out, girl?"

The dog jumped up and raced to the door.

As Kathryn sat on the rear porch stairs, Mrs. Weaver lowered herself next to her. "Kathy, are you okay? I'm surprised to find you home. You look pale."

"I haven't felt good for days." Kathryn sighed. "But I'll be okay. Tired. I'm taking today off to rest." *No sense dumping her problems on her sweet landlady.*

"Last night, we were sorry to hear Jacob's father was in the hospital."

"I'm sorry I forgot to tell you when I got back from the trip. Jacob went straight to Minneapolis before we left Chicago." Kathryn hoped she wouldn't ask more.

"It's okay. I wondered why you had asked to ride with us last night. And I meant to talk to you about what happened to his father, but you were busy with Nick." She continued to stare.

Kathryn kept her eyes on the dog. Mrs. Weaver wanted more information, but she'd be too polite to ask. "Come here, Sheila. Time to go upstairs."

Her landlady rose, and Kathryn followed her inside. Thank goodness the Weavers weren't pushy or nosey. Unlike the staff she'd encounter at work.

"Let me know if you need anything, dear. I'll be here."

"I will." She gave the woman a hug. "I'm going to bed." What she needed was for this entire mess to be just another nightmare. What she needed was Jacob. But he— Tears fell as she trudged up the staircase behind Sheila.

A few hours later, Kathryn's cell rang. She checked the number before answering and sighed in relief. It was only Nick. "Hello."

"Hi, pretty lady. I called you at the office to see if I could take you to lunch, but they said you weren't there. Is everything okay?"

"Everything's fine." Liar. "I took a couple days off."

"Good. You deserve time off. May I interest you in going out to dinner with me tonight instead of a late lunch?"

She laughed to herself. He hadn't asked her out since before her birthday party. "I think I'd like that." In her mind, she could see his lips pulling into a grin. She had always loved his smile.

Nick's friendship was exactly what she needed right now.

Jacob sat at his father's bedside Thursday evening. The old man's breathing seemed relaxed and even. Wish he could say the same about his own. Kathryn still refused to answer her phone when he called.

He left the room and headed to the doctors' lounge. When he entered, he slouched onto the couch and punched in Dr. Hartley's number on the cell.

Doc answered on the second ring. "Jacob, I was hoping you'd call with an update on your father."

"He's recovering. The doctor should release him soon. My father's always been tough. The worst part will be getting him to follow doctor's orders at home. Abigail hired a nurse, and I'll stick around to make sure he gets settled, but I should be able to leave here then."

The McLeod family physician walked into the lounge.

"Doc, let me call you later." They hung up and Jacob approached the other doctor. "How's my father today?"

"Haven't checked him yet. I just arrived to make rounds and will see Mr. McLeod in a few minutes."

Jacob strode back to the hospital room. Abigail sat in a chair next to his father, who appeared frail lying there in the bed. *So different from years past.* Jacob approached the bedside. The man glanced up at his son.

Tears hovered in William McLeod's eyes. He took a deep breath and let the air out slowly. "It's time for me to say this, son. I've been wrong. So wrong." His brows pinched together. "A heart attack will cause a man to see things differently."

The first apologetic words Jacob had ever heard from the man. The first words the man had spoken to his own son in the past week, for that matter. What had happened to his father?

"I've heard you've become a fine doctor." His father pinched his lips together. "Will you forgive me, son?"

"I already have...Father."

Abigail got up and kissed her husband. He returned her kiss. Had his father ever loved Mother? A twinge of pain surged through Jacob.

His father's doctor came through the door. "Well, Mr. McLeod. You might be able to go home tomorrow. Let me check you over tonight and again tomorrow. If all is well, then I'll discharge you." He turned to Abigail. "Would you step out for a few minutes?"

Abigail withdrew to the hall. Jacob followed, and they strolled to the atrium. They sat gazing out the windows for a minute.

He looked at her. "Abigail. You and my father have changed. What happened?"

She smiled and lowered her head. "It started with an argument a month ago. I stormed out of the house and found the old church you and your mother had attended. As I stumbled through the cemetery, crying, I came across your mother's grave."

His heart squeezed. He hadn't been there in years.

"The tombstone read, 'Laura Beckett McLeod, Faithful Wife, Beloved Mother.' I knelt and talked to her as if she were right in front of me. I felt every pain she'd suffered. But I deserved his rough treatment. She hadn't."

She laid her hand on his arm. "I'm sorry for what she went through." Her eyes misted.

"The pastor found me and brought me inside. That's when I found The Watcher Who heals broken hearts. The pastor called Jesus that."

Jacob nodded. "I remember him referring to the Lord as 'The Watcher.' I'm so happy for you, but that doesn't explain Father's change of heart."

Abigail's smile grew. "The day before you arrived, the pastor talked to him. By the time he left the hospital, the Lord had taken up residence in William's heart. Like he said, his attack made him see things in a different way."

"I wish Mother—" Jacob bowed his head. "I'm happy for both of you. Why hasn't he told me about this?"

"I'm not sure he knows how after all he's done. Give him time, Jacob."

His father's physician hustled into the atrium. "Things still look good for your husband. He's still weak, but I'm sure he can go home tomorrow with restrictions. I'll check him again in the morning. Have you arranged for a nurse?"

"I did."

"That's good. He needs to have someone run roughshod over him for a few more days. That Scotsman is a handful." He chuckled. "And I understand you'll be around too, Doctor McLeod. That will help."

Jacob sighed. He wanted to go home. Home to Pensacola. But his father needed him. "Yes. As long as I'm needed."

# Chapter Thirty-Seven

"N o! No!"

Kathryn awoke Monday morning with a start. "Sheila, I'm so sorry. I almost knocked you off the bed again, didn't I, girl?"

The little dog whined, licked her cheek, and bounced onto the floor.

"Okay, let me get dressed, then the backyard." She had to go back to work today. Where had the weekend gone? But after dinner last night with Nick, she could face anything. Even that horrible nightmare that awoke her.

Nick had been so sweet. Even worried about how little she ate. At least with the leftover lasagna she'd brought home, she wouldn't have to cook for a couple of days. She laughed. There'd be even more leftovers after her date with him tonight.

His actions showed he still cared for her. He'd even almost kissed her. Close...but he hadn't. Her heart pinched as Jacob's kisses at her birthday party came to mind.

After she dressed and took Sheila out, Kathryn hopped on the bus and alighted a few doors from the practice. She took in a breath of fresh air and exhaled. It would be a long day.

By the end of the workday, she leaned back in her chair and massaged her neck. If Dr. Hartley or anyone else asked about Dr. McLeod once more today, she'd scream. She glanced at the office clock. Almost quitting time. She'd get to relax tonight with Nick at dinner. At least his affection for her was real.

Her cell rang, and she glanced at the screen. Good, it was Nick. She'd run out of excuses why she couldn't talk to Jacob each time he'd called the office. At least she could ignore his calls that came through on her cell.

Kathryn pressed to answer. "Good evening, Nick. Afraid I've forgotten our date?"

"No." He laughed. "Just wanted to see if you'd like a lift home."

She loved the timbre to his voice. A ride home would be wonderful, but the Weavers would see her with him again. They hadn't said anything, but still. "That would be nice, but...I need time alone to unwind after my first day back. The bus ride provides that. I do appreciate the offer though."

"Okay. I'll see you tonight at six then."

She heard the breakroom door click shut. Dr. Hartley stepped into her office.

"I'll be waiting, Nick." Kathryn hung up.

Her boss's brows drew together. "So how is that youth pastor I met at your birthday party?"

"He's fine. Nick is taking me to dinner again tonight." *Why did you tell him?*

The muscle in Dr. Hartley's jaw twitched. "I know you've been under quite a strain—"

Please don't bring Doctor McLeod up again. "Excuse me. Be right back."

She rushed out of the office, through the breakroom, and into the restroom, fighting tears all the way. Why had she told him she was going out with Nick?

A few minutes later, she returned to her office. Dr. Hartley was gone. Kathryn slipped in and shut the door behind her.

She lowered herself into the chair and leaned back. Her walk with Nick in the moonlight after dinner the night before had been magical. She'd skipped on the white sugary beach and kicked up sparks of phosphorous in the sand with her bare feet. He'd captured her hands, and they'd twirled around as if they were kids. What fun. She needed fun right now.

The skirt to her white gauze dress with the purple sash and her lace shawl's shimmering fringe flared out as she spun. She had whirled right into his arms. His lips moved closer and almost touched hers. But she'd pulled away.

Kathryn's pulse raced. Her cheeks blazed with heat. More tears rose as green eyes took the place of the gray in Nick's now, and then. The memory of Jacob's warm lips on hers reasserted itself, and arrows shot into her heart. She had to forget him. Why had he hurt her?

Why couldn't she love Nick that way? She could learn to love him. Nick had guessed that Jacob did something to hurt her. Although, she wouldn't tell him what it was, and he didn't press the issue. Nick understood it would take time for her to get over it. He'd wait. She *would* learn to love him that way.

From the seclusion of the bank doorway, Mathew watched as Kate left work and walked to the corner. He mounted his bike and flipped on the helmet. Now he'd find the perfect opportunity to nab her. He'd follow her until she ventured into a place where no one would notice.

A bus pulled to the curb, and Kate climbed on board behind a couple of other passengers. The door closed and the bus pulled away. Mathew started the engine and followed until she got off on the corner of her street. Quiet enough street. Too many people outside to do anything right now.

As she headed to the house, his narrowed eyes followed. She passed an old abandoned home two houses from the corner.

Another victim of Hurricane Ivan. Boards on the windows. *Hmmm.* Padlock on the front door. That might be just what he was looking for. She'd walk right by it again in the morning when she left for work. A sneer spread across his face.

He snickered as she climbed the steps to the front porch where she lived. "See you tomorrow morning, Katy-bird," he whispered. "It'll be a morning *you'll* never forget."

Mathew put the bike in gear and rode off. From a rearview mirror, he caught another glimpse of the black Crown Vic pull from a parking place. About a block from Kate's street, Mathew stopped next to a curb. The vehicle passed him.

Had to be coincidence. Couldn't see the driver this time. Not with those tinted windows.

# Chapter Thirty-Eight

acob sat in the library at the mansion where he was born in Minnesota with his cell to his ear and listened to the phone ring. "Come on, Doc."

"Good evening, Jacob."

"It is. I have good news. I hope to be back next week sometime. My father's doing well. The in-home nurse Abigail hired is doing a wonderful job and will stay here until he's fully recovered."

"That's great. Glad to hear it."

Jacob smiled. "Thanks for encouraging me to do the right thing."

His boss chuckled. "T'weren't nothing, boy. You'd have gone anyway. But..I'll be glad when you're back."

Dr. Hartley sounded solemn with his last remark. "Is something wrong, sir? Kathryn's okay, isn't she?"

336

"She's okay...but—"

"What?"

"She still hasn't talked to you, has she?"

Jacob's heart sank. "No. I've tried to call her on her cell. She doesn't answer. I tried at the office. She makes excuses for not coming to the phone. But when I get back, I'll find a way to get her to listen."

"I hope it's soon, son. You remember Nick, the youth pastor?"

"Yes."

"He's taking her to dinner tonight. And apparently this isn't the first time. Don't think she meant to tell me that, but she let it slip before she left work tonight."

Jacob's stomach knotted. He clenched his teeth. Nick.

"Sorry for the bad news."

"It's okay. Nothing I can do from here. But Lord willing, I'll be home soon."

They hung up and Jacob trudged back to his father's room. From the doorway, he watched as Abigail helped her husband get into an armchair next to the bed. They had both changed so much.

Jacob's mind wandered back to a fight between his parents when he was thirteen. He'd never forget that day. He could still hear his mother's pleas.

*"You can't send him away, William. Please, he's too young."*

*"I'm sick of you babying him, Laura. Now, shut up and pack his things. Military school will make a man out of my weakling son."*

He'd been sent away, and his mother no longer had anyone to comfort her after the abuse she'd receive from his father.

When Jacob tried to stand up to him, he wasn't strong enough. Not then. As a preteen, he'd yelled at his father. *"I'm not going!"*

*"I didn't ask your opinion. Who do you think you are, eavesdropping on my conversation with your mother?"*

Jacob had always been intimidated by the man's six-foot-two-inch, muscular frame. It wasn't the first time the man had swung an arm like a battering ram and struck Jacob with the back of his hand. He wound up on the floor and could only watch as his enraged father grabbed his mother by the hair and shoved her to the floor too.

*"Get out of here and get his things together before I give you what you really deserve."*

Blood had oozed from his mother's knees and tears rolled from her emerald eyes as Jacob helped her to her feet. He'd held back his own tears.

He hated that memory. His jaw clenched. But he forced a smile and stepped into the room. "Need any help?"

Abigail shook her head as her fingers touched her husband's arm. "I'll be back with your tea, dear. You two talk for a while."

As she passed Jacob to leave the room, she patted his arm.

His father motioned him forward. "There are things I need to tell you. Things I don't want to put off another minute. Sit down."

Jacob's neck muscles tensed as he pulled a chair closer and sank into it.

After a deep breath, his father finger-combed his thick, dark brown hair. He leaned forward and gazed into his son's eyes. "Last night, before I fell asleep, I realized that the memories you have of me are all bad. How I treated you and your mother. I need to try and counter those. Tell you something good to hang onto."

How could his father change the images that he burned into his son's boyhood memory?

"When I met your mother, she was the most beautiful woman I'd ever seen. I was amazed she agreed to marry me, being twelve years my junior. But she did." He slowly shook his head.

"You look so much like her. Except for your physique and that mop of hair you inherited from me, of course." He chuckled.

The man had never laughed before. Not with joy, anyway.

"I thought I'd married an angel. Nevertheless, I made demands on her I never should have. The sweeter she was, the angrier I became. Guilt, no doubt. But she never argued or got mad at me. I blamed her for things that weren't her fault."

Jacob shifted in the seat.

"There were times when I'd feel overwhelming tenderness toward her. Just never told her. That's what she really deserved. If I could make it up to her now, I would."

Jacob's heart ached. "She's in a place where there is no more sorrow or pain."

Tears welled in his father's eyes. "So many things to ask forgiveness for. You already said you forgave me, but I'm asking again." The tears spilled over onto the man's rugged face. "I wish I could ask for her forgiveness."

He dropped his gaze to his hands. "I've asked God to forgive me."

Jacob placed his hand on his father's shoulder. "Mother already forgave you, Dad. And so have I."

"You're a far better man than me, son. You'll treat your wife right."

*If Kathryn will ever forgive me.*

Jacob sat at the bedside and watched as his dad's eyes closed. The old toughie had argued, but finally resigned himself to the fact that he'd be a semi-invalid for at least the next few days.

Soft snores filled the room. Jacob smiled.

Never thought he'd be sitting next to this man as he told stories about Mother, much less laughing with him. Every memory he had of his parents' life together up to now had been a painful one.

Joy flooded Jacob's heart. Now he knew she'd had happy years before her marriage turned sour. Those were what he'd remember.

He rose from the armchair and retired to his old room where he knelt beside the bed.

"Heavenly Father, I have so much to be grateful for. Thank You for helping my father with his recovery, and for bringing both Abigail and him to Your Throne of Grace. Still hard to believe it happened. Thank You for the testimony my mother had which brought them there, and for reconciliation between me and my father."

After spending a few more minutes thanking the Lord, Jacob pushed himself onto his feet. He closed his eyes and dropped to his knees once more.

"God, whatever happens between Kathryn and me will be what You decide is best. But like the woman in Luke eighteen, who petitioned the king for justice, and because of her persistence, he granted it, I'm asking. Please make things right between Kathryn and me."

He lowered his forehead to the bedspread. "And this deal with Nick. I have no idea what to pray, Lord. It's tearing me apart, me here, and him in Pensacola with her." Jacob took in a sharp breath.

"Oh, Lord! I forgot. That blond guy. He's there too. Lord, please protect her. In Jesus' Name, Amen."

Jacob shot to his feet and grabbed his cell. He punched in Dr. Hartley's number and paced as he listened to the ringing.

"Hey, Jacob. Is your father still okay?"

"Yes, he is, but there's something I've forgotten. Kathryn might be in danger."

A knock came on the door. "Come in." Abigail stepped into the room. Jacob held up a finger as he continued to talk on the phone.

He explained to Doc about seeing the man outside the office before they left for Chicago. "Doc, can you get in touch with Kathryn? Tell her to be careful. She still won't answer my calls, and I've got an uncomfortable—no, I'm downright frightened for her safety."

"I'll try, but she's avoiding me too. Have you thought to phone her friend Nick? Since she's seeing him tonight, maybe he can prove useful in watching over her until you get home."

Jacob ran his fingers through his hair. "I will. Wait! I don't have his number. Do you?"

"No. Sorry. Call the church and ask his uncle for it. I'm sure if you explain everything to the pastor, he'll be happy to give it to you."

"Good thinking, Doc. Thanks, again."

Jacob hung up and glanced at his stepmother. "One more." She smiled and headed for a chair. He flipped open his wallet and dug out the church card. Then he dialed the number.

"Oh great! Voice mail."

Before the beep sounded for the signal to start a message, Pastor Marshall came on the line. "Roman's Road Baptist Church, Pastor John Marshall speaking."

A sigh of relief escaped Jacob. "Pastor, I'm so glad you answered. This is Jacob McLeod. I may be in trouble for saying any of this to you, but I don't care." He gave the pastor a quick explanation of his fear that the man who once attacked Kathryn might be still stalking her. "She's not answering her cell because she's mad at me. I thought...I wanted to tell Nick so he can keep an eye out for her, but I don't have his number."

"She told us about the PA when it happened. This is cause for concern. I'm sorry about your father. Nick asked us to pray."

"Thank you, Pastor. My dad is recovering, and I'll be home soon, but I need Nick's number. My boss told me Nick...is taking Kathryn to dinner tonight."

"Why don't you let me call Nick and tell him everything? You sound stressed. Take care of things there, and let me handle everything here. Okay?"

Jacob's brows furrowed. He dropped into an armchair beside his bed. "Okay. If you think it's best."

After hanging up, he let his head fall back on the chair. His stepmother cleared her throat from across the room. Jacob's head shot up. "Oh. Abigail. I'm sorry. I forgot you came in."

She rose and walked toward him. "I'm not surprised. Are you all right?"

"Not really."

She sat on the edge of the bed. "Talk to me. It might help. I heard most of what's troubling you. Is there more to it than what you told the pastor?"

Jacob sat forward and told her about Kathryn's dreams. "I'm worried that what happened to her, her dreams, and this blond guy somehow is all tied together." He went on to explain the misunderstanding Kathryn had in Chicago and how he was in love for the first time in his life. "Now I could lose her."

Abigail shook her head. Her eyes misted. "I'm so sorry. I feel terrible. Calling you away before you straightened out the situation."

"It's not your fault. You did what you should have. And it's in God's hands."

She patted his arm. "It *is* in His hands, but why didn't you tell us sooner?" She pulled her mouth to the side. "Never mind, I know why you didn't. But you need to get to Florida."

Abigail stood and rushed to the door. She reached for the handle and turned. "May I tell your father? We can at least pray about it."

"Yes." Jacob shut his eyes and nodded. "Fine."

"Good. Pack your things to leave."

His eyes popped open. "My place is here right now." Even if his heart wasn't. "God will see to everything else."

"I know, but get your things ready. I'll be back in a few minutes."

"But what—" Before he could finish his sentence, she was out the door. He moved to the bed and lay back.

As Jacob prayed silently for Kathryn, Abigail reappeared at his door. "Your father needs you."

He jumped up and sped to the room. When he entered, he found his father in the armchair. "Abigail said you needed me. Are you okay?"

"I'm fine. Fool of a business, that nurse ordering me to stay in bed." He smiled at his son.

The smile disappeared from this father's face. "Abigail told me the girl you love might be in danger, son. And there's another man seeing her while you're here. She said you and your Kathryn had a misunderstanding. You need to go to her and fix this problem."

Jacob was speechless.

"But first, I want you to bring me something from the big safe in my study."

His dad picked up a sticky pad from the nightstand and wrote down the combination. He tore off the top sheet and handed it to Jacob.

"Inside you'll find a large antique box. There's something important in it. Hurry."

Jacob took the note and studied his father's face. "But you're okay, right?"

"I'm better than I've been in a long time, son. Now go."

Jacob left the room and strode through the halls of the mansion to the study. When he returned, he set the box on the bed next to his dad and stood beside him.

When his father opened the box, Jacob gaped at the fortune in jewelry rivaling a pirate treasure.

"Each piece is a family heirloom handed down from father to eldest son in the McLeod family. I always hoped to give it to you one day." He laid each piece out on the cover of the bed.

Jacob ran his fingers over the sparkling dark blue diamond engagement ring his mother had worn. Why had this been taken from her when she died? He glanced at his father's moist eyes.

"You're wondering about the ring." His dad smiled. "It's the oldest piece in the collection. Your mother was buried with the gold band engraved with our initials as per family tradition. This ring has been passed on from the day it was first crafted generations ago. These are the rarest of diamonds."

Mother had told him the story behind the ring when he was a boy. Of the ancestor who had searched for the rarest and most beautiful diamonds for the girl he loved. He'd chosen blue, her favorite color, and had the largest mounted in purest gold with smaller white diamonds running down the sides of the band.

His dad placed the ring in Jacob's hand. "It's believed that a true McLeod bride's finger will be just the right size for this ring. So far it's held true." He smiled. "But I guess that's more myth than anything."

He lifted a smaller old box from the bottom of the chest. "These are from your mother's family. Before she died, she made me promise to save them for you." Tears glistened in the old man's eyes as he moved the first set of jewels aside and lined up the Beckett family heirlooms. "They belong to you too. To your bride. Both sets."

Jacob stared open-mouthed at the massive collection of jewels. "But wouldn't Abigail be upset about the McLeod jewelry?" His eyes shot to his father's.

"She's never seen them. Her family has their own wealth, and she has the jewels I've bought for her. She'd want you to have these now anyway." He gently placed everything back in the two boxes and handed the chest to his son.

"Go to your Kathryn. She needs you more than I do. And you need her."

"Are you sure you're well enough for me to leave?" He wanted to return to Pensacola, to Kathryn, but what if his dad still needed him?

"I am, son. I don't really need all this attention. Between Abigail and the nurse, I have enough people worrying over me and telling me what I can't do. Get on the phone. Find a ticket. Work things out with your girl, and keep her safe. I'll not be responsible for any more pain in your life.

# Chapter Thirty-Nine

*E*arly Tuesday morning, Mathew waited in the doorway of the abandoned house on Kate's street. Hidden by an overgrown azalea bush he kept watch for Kate to appear and walk to the corner where she'd catch the bus to work.

In the tree next to the sidewalk, A Mockingbird sang to an overcast sky. He glanced up at the bird. "Shut up." Stupid bird. He snaked his way down the steps, picked up a stone from the yard, and threw it at the tree, missing the bird by an inch.

As the bird flew off, Mathew backed up the steps, crouched next to the porch railing, and refocused his attention on the house where Kate lived. What a great vantage point. He had a clear line of sight all the way to Kate's house.

The front door to her place opened, and she stepped out. "Come to papa, baby." He smirked.

Seconds later, as she strolled toward the bus stop, Mathew checked the street. No one in sight. He squatted on the steps, licking his lips. As he waited for her to reach the front of the house, he pulled a knife from his pants and a cloth-wrapped vial from his shirt pocket.

He snickered, uncapped the bottle, and flipped the cloth over the bottleneck, shaking the vial a couple of times.

Kate strolled closer to the house. Good outfit, Katy-bird. Loose red skirt. My favorite color. I'll have to thank her for wearing it for me. Interesting blouse, too. Dozens of buttons down the front. What fun.

She drew level with the bush and glanced toward the door. Her eyes rounded and her jaw dropped as Mathew lunged for her.

Kate turned to flee, but he snagged her wrist and yanked her into his arms. She managed half a yelp before he covered her mouth with his. After taking pleasure in the deep kiss while she fought him, he put the chloroform-laced cloth over her face and dragged her onto the porch.

As she quieted, he flashed the knife in front of her eyes. Her legs gave way for a moment, but she pushed herself upright.

He swore and struggled to keep her from escaping as he inched her closer to the door. *Didn't put enough on the cloth. This'll be better anyway.* "Just enough fight to make things exciting, huh, Katy-bird."

Mathew regained a good hold on her waist. "I'm not going to hurt you. You and I are going to have a private party inside this little hide-a-way."

He pressed his mouth against hers once more, smashing her slender frame to himself with her arms pinioned to her sides. A muffled scream escaped her.

Mathew dragged her across the porch and kicked the door open. Even in her weakened condition, Kate thrashed about. He had to fight for a better hold. "Bet you didn't give your new boyfriend this much trouble. You're nothing but a tease, aren't you? Quit squirming and relax. You'll enjoy this. I'm an expert at giving pleasure to ladies."

Kate rammed her foot into his ankle, and then brought her knee up to his groin. He cursed and mouthed vulgarities to her. Then he slung her through the doorway, hitting her head on the frame's broken hasp.

Her body slumped in his arms.

After arriving in Pensacola Tuesday morning, and a harried trip home in a cab, Jacob had hopped into his Austen-Healey and sped toward Kathryn's apartment. A few houses down from the Weavers' home, he'd parked the car under a Spanish Oak tree and glanced at his watch. He'd made it in time.

She should walk out the door any minute. He'd wait until she left the porch, then he'd approach and try to reason with her.

If only he'd found an earlier flight. His body ached from fatigue thanks to the frantic trip.

His eyes began to close, but Jacob jerked awake. His gaze drifted upward to her bedroom window. Dark. As he looked back at the front porch, movement down the street caught his attention. A slender woman in a red flared skirt and white blouse strolled toward the bus stop. Red wasn't one of her usual colors, but it had to be Kathryn. He must have dozed off and missed her.

The engine revved, and the car lurched forward. He had to reach her before the bus came. A large van pulled out in front of him from the side street. Jacob slammed on the breaks.

When the van passed, Kathryn was gone. Where'd she go? No bus had gone by.

Her nightmare flashed through his mind as he pressed the gas pedal to the floor and propelled past the Weavers' home.

He reached the spot where he'd last seen her, parked the car, and jumped out. As he searched the area, a door slammed shut on a rundown house with boarded windows three houses away from him, closer to the corner.

When he ran to the front walk, sounds of a scuffle came from inside the house. He approached the stairs. A white shoe stuck out from under an azalea bush next to the sidewalk. He pushed the branches aside and picked up the sandal. Kathryn had worn one like this the day they'd met.

His heartbeat galloped into overtime. He dropped the shoe and rushed up the stairs. A small dark vial lay next to the door on the porch. He bent and raised the bottleneck to his nose. Sweet odor. *Chloroform!*

Jacob's heart pinched as if wedged in a vise. He sprang upright and saw a red smear on the door's broken hasp. Blood? Prickles, like dozens of tiny pinballs, careened up his arms into his neck. He reached for the knob. But, before his fingers touched it, someone yanked him down the steps to the side of the bush.

A stocky man clamped a hand on Jacob's shoulder and held him in an arm lock. "Shh. Who are you, and what are you doing here?"

Jacob jerked his arm to free himself, but the man wouldn't let go. Jacob rolled, and the man landed on top, pinning Jacob to the ground.

"Answer the question."

"Let go of me. Kathryn's in that house, and she's in danger. Who are you?"

"Oh. So...she's *your girl*."

"I'm going to marry her." He pushed on the man's chest, but despite Jacob's advantage in size and muscle, the stocky man slammed him back to the ground, grabbing his throat. A knee pushed into Jacob's abdomen.

The man glared at him. "I'm Detective Brewer. Now who are you?"

"McLeod...Jacob."

Brewer eased pressure on Jacob's throat but kept his knee where it was. "Is Pierce a friend of yours?"

"Who's Pierce? Let me go. I need to help Kathryn."

"Look. I've been after Pierce and his buddies for months. You're not going to blow it for me." He squeezed his brows into one hairy line on his forehead. "If I let you go—No. You'll try to get in there, won't you?" He removed his knee from Jacob's gut and let go of his neck. "I shouldn't do this, but follow me. And *stay behind me.* If you don't, I'll knock you out cold."

Jacob nodded and followed the detective to the door where Brewer drew his gun and turned the doorknob.

Once inside, the detective checked the first room. Jacob tapped him on the shoulder and pointed to blood on the floor leading in the direction of the hallway.

As they reached the entrance to the hall, Jacob peered around the stocky man. In the room at the end, a blond-haired man knelt over Kathryn on the wooden floor. She didn't move or make a sound. He smirked at her and unbuckled his belt while he slid a knife across the buttons of her blouse.

Jacob's blood boiled. With lightning speed, he pushed past the detective and stormed through the hall. He grabbed the degenerate and slung him into a corner of the room as if he were a rag doll. "You scum!"

From his crumpled position, the guy scrambled to his feet and swung at Jacob, who blocked the fist with his left hand and delivered a right cross to the attacker's jaw, knocking him back into the corner.

The detective dashed in and checked the unconscious man's pulse. "Well, at least he's alive." Brewer cuffed the assailant, and then whipped out his cell.

Jacob examined Kathryn's head, then placed his jacket over her to keep her warm as he tried not to imagine the worst. He tore off his shirt and used it as a bandage on the oozing gash in her head. Her wheat-colored hair was nothing but a mass of red on one side. Minor head injuries often bleed a lot, but this could be much more serious if it turned out to be a penetrating head injury. His knowledge only fueled his fears.

"Oh, Lord, please don't let her die. Help us."

When the unconscious man came to, Brewer stood him on his feet. "If you're smart, you won't move a muscle."

Jacob turned to Brewer, who had the cell to his ear. "That better be nine-one-one you're calling. She needs help. Now!"

In the distance, sirens wailed as Jacob did his best to stop the blood flow from the gash in the side of Kathryn's head. He had to keep positive. But it might be a hematoma in the brain that was causing her loss of consciousness. God had to help her. She couldn't die.

Brewer watched as Jacob checked her head again. "You a doctor?"

"Yes. Lot of good that does me now." Without the technology afforded him at the hospital, he was useless.

"Will she make it?"

Jacob shook his head. "I don't know." He focused on Kathryn without another word. She could wind up with permanent brain damage.

Pierce gave the detective a body-shove and bolted two steps away before Brewer seized his cuffed hands and yanked him to the floor with a thud. Obscenities flew from the miscreant's mouth. Brewer flipped the assailant to his stomach and placed his knee on the man's back. "Stuff it, buster."

Backup came hurtling through the hallway and dragged Pierce out of the house. Paramedics rushed in with a gurney. Jacob drew in a deep breath.

An eternity later, the paramedics had Kathryn secured and on the way to the hospital.

Jacob sprinted to his car, jumped in, and sped down the street to keep up with them. "She's so pale, Lord. Please—" The rest of the words would not pass the lump in his throat. *God help.*

# Chapter Forty

acob followed as the paramedics rushed Kathryn through the Emergency Room doors. He shouted orders.

A nurse named Lynne Temple, whom he knew from his rounds at the hospital, clutched his arm. "Doctor McLeod, they have this. Let them do their jobs. You should go to the desk and give them what information you can on the patient. Sorry, but you're not the doctor today."

"But I—"

"Not this time, Doctor."

He stared at her with blurred, burning eyes. She was right. He needed to trust Kathryn to them, and the Lord. He nodded.

Lynne accompanied him to the admission desk.

"Are you working in the ER today, Lynne?" She was a good nurse.

"No. I had to drop something off and walked right into all the commotion. I heard you telling them what happened to her. Are you okay? You're covered with blood."

"It's Kathryn's. I don't know." They stopped at admissions, and he took a seat.

A young man asked questions, and Jacob answered as best he could. When the man finished, Jacob rose from the desk and trudged to the waiting room.

She'd lost so much blood. What should he do? He couldn't just sit. He paced through the entrance and stood outside.

Pastor Parker. Pastor Marshall. He had to tell them what happened. The Kendalls. No. Not Kendalls, Parkers. Dr. Hartley. Jacob fumbled with his wallet to find the number to Pastor Marshall's cell. Maybe he'd call the Parkers. *I can't tell them.* He dialed the number.

Was the blow hard enough to fracture her skull and enter the brain? Was she hemorrhaging? Time had been of the essence to have a good outcome.

When the pastor answered, Jacob's hands shook. The cell slipped and fell into the grass. He snatched it. "Pastor!"

"Jacob? Is that you? You sound terrible."

"Yes. Me. I'm here at the hospital. Kathryn was attacked. She's...she's—"

"Is she okay?"

"No. They've taken her to—I'm not sure what they're doing. She was so white."

"Calm down. Which hospital?"

"Baptist."

"I'll be there as soon as I can."

"But. But her family. The Parkers." He almost dropped the cell again. "I don't think I can tell them. Can you?"

"Of course. Pastor Parker gave me his number when they visited. My wife can call on the way to the hospital. Pray. We will too."

"Thank you." Jacob hung up. He paced in front of the entrance a dozen times, running his hand over his hair, breathing in deep gulps. *God, why? Why not me? Why her?*

He needed to call Doc. Jacob lifted the cell he still grasped and pressed the number.

When he heard the connecting click, he blurted out, "Doc, Kathryn's in the ER. The guy attacked her."

"What? Jacob, I can't understand you. Slow down."

He took a breath. "I'm here at Baptist. They took Kathryn back. He attacked her. I have no idea what's happening in there. She was so pale."

"Okay. I'll be right there." Doc hung up.

Again, Jacob paced. He came back in the entrance and strode to the desk. "Can you tell me what's happening to Kathryn Kendall?"

The man glanced up at Jacob and shook his head. "Sorry, Doctor McLeod. All I can tell you is they're working on her."

Jacob strode through the hall again. As he headed toward the entrance, Pastor and Mrs. Marshall hurried through the doors, Nick in their wake. He'd forgotten about Nick. As they rushed toward him, Jacob pressed his lips together.

With his fists clenched, Nick reached Jacob first. "How did this happen to Kathy? Is she okay?"

Pastor Marshall laid his hand on Nick's shoulder. "Easy, Nick."

Jacob shook his head. "They're working on her. That's all they've told me."

Nick pinned Jacob with the anger in his eyes. "But how?"

Jacob blinked. *He really loves her. How could he tell Nick she might already be—?*

Mrs. Marshall took her nephew's arm. "Nick, let's sit and wait for more news. We can learn what happened later."

After he'd paced for almost an hour, Jacob finally exhausted himself enough to sit next to Pastor Marshall.

Detective Brewer walked into the waiting room. He approached the admissions desk, flashed his credentials, and spoke with the young man.

A few minutes later, Brewer took the seat next to Jacob. "The nurse told me your young lady is holding her own. Have they said any more to you?"

Jacob closed his eyes for a second and after a deep, shaky breath, he peered at the detective. "They hadn't told us that much. Thank you."

"Look, Doctor. I'm sorry for this, but I have to ask you some questions."

"Sure."

Lynne brought Jacob a cup of hot coffee. "Here, Doctor McLeod. Drink this. Thought I'd come down on my break and check on you."

He took the Styrofoam cup and gave her a shaky smile. She nodded and turned to the pastor and his wife. "Would you like something to drink?" She faced the detective. "You, sir?"

Brewer waved her off. "Thank you. Won't be here that long."

Both Mrs. Parker and the pastor shook their heads.

She strolled a few feet to the other side of the room where Nick wrung his hands and fidgeted in his seat. "May I get something for you? Coffee? Tea?"

Nick glanced up at her with furrowed brows and shook his head. "Thank you, no. I'm fine."

Jacob finished answering Brewer's questions. "You might contact Doctor Kenner, I believe was the name. Wait a minute. Here comes my boss. He'll know."

Dr. Hartley burst through the entrance and dashed across the room to Jacob. "How is she? Sorry, got caught by a stopped freight train."

"They told the detective she's holding her own, Doc. No one's come out yet to let me—" He glanced at Nick, "us know more. Was Kathryn's former boss Doctor Kenner?"

"Yes, why?"

Brewer rose from the chair. "Detective Brewer. I'm investigating what happened this morning, among other things. Doctor McLeod told me I could get more information about the assailant from Miss Kendall's former boss."

Doc and Brewer wandered from Jacob as they spoke.

When they returned, Brewer gazed at Jacob. "That jerk'll pay for what he did."

He turned to Dr. Hartley. "We've had this gang under surveillance for a long time. Weren't quite sure how the young lady fit into the picture, until Doctor McLeod showed up."

After he lowered himself into the seat next to Jacob, Brewer said, "Adding what that lowlife did today to other evidence, he'll be an old man before he's free. But even if not, I don't think he'll want to take *you* on again."

Jacob gave him half a smile.

Brewer stood. "I wish the best to you and your future bride, Doctor."

Nick's eyes opened wide. His lips stiffened into a straight line.

Detective Brewer handed Jacob a card. "Call me if you think of anything else. And don't worry, she'll be okay. She wouldn't have the heart to leave someone who loves her as much as you." He winked at Jacob.

Nick's eyes narrowed.

# Chapter Forty-One

Kathryn stirred, conscious of a painful bright light above her. Dizziness overwhelmed her. Where was she? Mathew's face loomed in her mind. His arms around her. His mouth on hers. Bile filled her throat. She couldn't breathe. Tears ran down the sides of her face.

*Jacob. I'm so sorry.*

Her head throbbed. Something held her arms. "Help!" Everything went black.

Her eyelids fluttered open as Kathryn thrashed about. Where had he taken her? She turned and pain surged through her head. Someone held her hand.

Tears flooded her eyes. "Why are you doing this?"

A shadow released her and moved away. Blackness surrounded her.

Kathryn awakened to a darkened room and voices murmuring in the distance. When she rolled her head to the side, pain shot through her. A light glowed and created a halo of colors. Her hands were still bound to something on each side of her.

She called out. The specter from her nightmare materialized. Tears spilled out as she moaned. Her pulse quickened. The room spun. She drifted into darkness.

Someone stood by her as Kathryn opened her eyes. A dark-haired man. "You're not Mathew," she whispered.

Her blurry vision cleared. "Jacob. What are you doing here?" Her pulse increased. "Run! Mathew's here!" Blackness overtook her again.

When she regained consciousness, a hand cradled hers. A muffled voice. Jacob's voice. *What did he say?* She focused on his face.

His eyes glistened. "You're safe now, Kathryn. Everything's okay."

Relief poured into her body and mind. A dark blanket descended over her consciousness as she fell asleep.

Kathryn awoke and found herself in a hospital room. Her head throbbed. She tried to move her hand but found her wrists tied to the bedrails on both sides.

She gazed across the room. Beth slept in a chair with her legs draped over the armrest.

"Beth." The word barely came out. Her throat, so hoarse.

Her sister jumped and bolted to the bedside. Dark circles showed under her eyes. "Kathy. You're awake. Praise God!"

"Oh, Beth. He grabbed me. He pulled me...into a house." Kathryn gasped as she sobbed. "I couldn't...get away. He kissed me...and then—"

"It's okay. You're okay now."

"My head hurts. What happened? Why am I tied up?"

"You're in the hospital. Everyone's been praying for you." Beth pressed the call button for the nurse. "Everything's going to be fine now."

A nurse with short chestnut brown hair, wearing a nametag that identified her as Lynne Temple, rushed into the room and up to the bed. "Well. Hello, Miss Kendall. It's nice to see your eyes open on their own. You gave us quite a scare." She checked Kathryn's vitals and removed her restraints.

Kathryn smiled at the nurse. Such cheerful hazel eyes. "Your voice...sounds familiar. Have we met?"

"Yes. Several times, but you weren't very communicative. Your eyes would open for a second and then close again. But I've seen you here at the hospital once or twice before you were brought in. Usually with Doctor Hartley. I understand you're his office manager."

"Yes." Kathryn almost didn't get the word out. "So tired."

"You rest now. I'll tell the doctor you're awake."

"Thank you." Kathryn closed her eyes, but they sprang open right away. "Beth."

Beth retook her position next to Kathryn but turned to the nurse as she started to leave. "Nurse, would you please have someone tell my parents, too? They went to the cafeteria."

"I'll page them. Don't tire out my patient. She's still not in good condition."

Beth nodded and faced Kathryn.

"Beth. How long...have I been here?"

"About a week. We were really worried. The doctor said you were stable, but you didn't want to stay awake. He said you might be trying to avoid something. When they brought you in from ICU—" She gulped a breath of air. "You fought with everyone who came near you. That's why they had to restrain you. The only one you'd let touch you was—oh, Kath. We thought we'd lost you."

Tears filled Beth's eyes as she held Kathryn's hand. "You've been in and out of consciousness for days."

Kathryn peered at the fatigued face of her adopted sister. Dark tracks of smeared mascara covered her cheeks. Tears welled in her own eyes. "How did I get here, Beth? The last thing I remember was Mathew's laugh. And a sharp pain on the side of my head. I tried to get away. But he was too strong. Held me so tight. His mouth—" She bit her lip. "Did he—?" How could she ask?

"No, Kath. The doctor said he hadn't...you know."

She closed her eyes and let out a sigh. "How did I get here?"

"Let's talk about everything later. I'll check on what's keeping Mom and Dad. Doctor Hartley and Doctor Griffin have been in every day since you were brought in, worried to death about you. Pastor Marshall, Mrs. Marshall, the Weavers, and of course, Nick. I think I hear Mom in the hall." Beth flew out the door.

A second later, she came back into the room, followed by her parents and a doctor. "Hello, young lady. We haven't formally met. I'm Doctor Smith." The doctor examined her bandaged head. "You are not to get out of bed. My anxiety level may not be able to take it." He grinned and left the room.

When the door closed, Kathryn fixed the remaining group with a pointed stare. "Would someone please tell me what happened after I passed out in that house?"

The Parkers looked at each other. Beth drew closer. "Probably best to tell you so you won't fret about it. Jacob rescued you. But he hasn't told us the details. He's been too busy worrying over you."

"Jacob?"

"Yes, Kath. He saved you from that fiend, and he's been here in the hospital ever since."

"Jacob saved me from Mathew? He's here?" She rubbed her temple. "I thought it was a dream. Where is he?"

Uncle Eric approached the bed and took her hand in his. "He's right outside. Like Beth said, we don't have the details from that morning, but he could tell you."

"Sis, he's been sitting here right next to you for days. He stayed until you came to and recognized him. Then he moved to the hallway. He was afraid he'd upset you." Beth touched her shoulder.

Kathryn took a deep breath. "May I talk to him?"

Her uncle smiled. "As long as you stay calm."

"I will." She squeezed her uncle's hand.

"Do you want me to stay?"

"No. Thank you. I'm ready to listen now. I've been such a fool."

He patted her hand, and everyone left.

As the door closed, Kathryn pictured the kiss between Jacob and the woman in Chicago. Then she recalled the pressure from Mathew's lips on hers before she could stop him.

Jacob paused in the doorway. When Kathryn smiled, he stepped into the room. "Beth said you wanted to see me."

"Yes. Thank you for helping me. Please tell me everything that happened." She lowered her eyes as he stepped closer and took the chair next to her.

He wanted to take her into his arms and never let go. He had to be careful not to upset her. "What do you want to know?" His pulse quickened.

Her eyes filled with tears as she gazed at him. "Jacob, I'm so ashamed of the way I acted. Of being so—" Her voice caught. "I should have let you explain. It wasn't until Mathew kissed me against *my* will that I realized what you had said was the truth. I should've known you were a better man than that. It just hurt. Can you forgive me?"

He touched her hand. "I don't blame you for thinking the worst. If I'd witnessed someone from your past kissing you that way, I may have jumped to the same conclusion. Let's put it in the past. You're okay now. That's all that matters."

Nick came through the doorway, but he stopped short. Jacob's eyes met his.

The worry and fear on Nick's face in the ER flashed into Jacob's mind. She needed Nick right now. Someone she knew she could count on. He turned back to Kathryn. "Nick's been worried about you. I'll leave you two alone."

Jacob rose and strode out of the room.

Jacob turned the corner at the end of the hall, stepped into the stairwell, and trudged down the steps. At least Kathryn wouldn't think the worst of him anymore. Maybe their relationship wasn't God's plan.

Halfway down to the first landing, a door opened above him and quick footsteps descended. "Jacob, where are you going?"

He had no desire to talk to Nick right now. Jacob's jaw tightened.

A few stairs behind him, Nick came to a stop. "Kathy's been through enough without your walking away and leaving her heartbroken."

Pierced with the words, Jacob's heart burned. He stopped on the landing and turned to face his rival. He couldn't take any more. "What are you talking about? You wanted me out of the picture. I could read it on your face that day in the ER. And she wants you."

"Yes. I wanted Kathy. I wished you had never come here, at first. But when I spent time with her while you were in Minnesota, I realized she loved you...not me. She's never loved me that way. She loves me like a brother. Can't you see that? All I want now is for Kathy to be happy."

Jacob stared at him. "But she turned to you. Not to me. She wouldn't even talk to me when she thought I'd betrayed her love."

"But Jacob, she *loves* you. When she came back from Des Plaines, she thought she wanted to be with me. I represented safety. What she didn't want was to hurt anymore. That's all."

Nick leaned against the wall. "I followed the detective out of the ER, and he told me what you did. Until then, I blamed you for what happened to her. You loved her enough to risk your life for her."

Jacob shook his head and peered up at the youth pastor. "I don't know what to think."

Nick moved to the landing. "When you walked out of that room just now, she cried. I didn't have to ask why."

"She's only grateful for my saving her life." Jacob continued down the stairs.

Nick followed. "Okay, so she was mad at you. So what? She's not anymore. And if you turn your back on her now, you're dumber than I thought any doctor could ever be."

He grabbed Jacob's shoulder and stopped him. "Look, I love her, too. Enough to give her up to you, beat the pulp out of you, and drag you back there unconscious if I have to. You're not going to break her heart. Not if I can stop you."

Jacob pulled away and kept going.

"Jacob, if you love her, you'll be sorry for the rest of your life if you don't go back now. That's all I'll say."

Rapid footsteps climbed the stairs behind him, as Jacob continued down the staircase.

# Chapter Forty-Two

Kathryn stared at the ceiling and let tears stream down the sides of her face. What had she done? She'd lost the one man she'd ever fallen in love with, all because of foolish pride, her stubbornness, her temper. And had she even once bothered to pray about it? No.

Jacob had said he understood. That he'd have thought the same thing if he'd seen someone kiss her. But he hadn't said he'd forgiven her. Only that they should put it in the past. Had he meant everything between them?

It served her right. *Father, please help. I love him.* She rolled to one side, curled her knees, and covered her face with the lightweight blanket on the bed.

Nick reentered Kathryn's room and sat next to her without a word.

She glanced at him. "I'm sorry for the way I've acted. I've been so wrong." More tears poured from her eyes.

"It's okay. You needed me. If Chris had been here, you'd have gone to him. I'll always be here for you, Kathy. The brother you need."

"Did Jacob leave?"

Nick blew out a long breath of air. "I'm not sure. Give him time. He's confused, and we need to pray."

Kathryn closed her eyes and bowed her head.

Nick scooted the chair closer. He slid his fingers under hers resting on the covers.

*Thank you for dear Nick, Lord. He needs someone to love him. But not like a sister.*

"Father, Kathy and I come to You asking for Your intervention in this situation. Neither of us know how to make things right again, but You do. Please tell Jacob how much she loves him, that it's not just gratitude. I'm not sure what else to pray...except, help Kathy not to hurt anymore. Help me be the brother she needs in her life. In Jesus' Name, Amen."

When she opened her eyes, Nick was smiling at something behind her. She rolled to her back. Jacob gazed down at her, a bouquet of white roses in his hand. Kathryn sniffed back her tears.

He held the flowers out to her. "The lady at the gift shop told me white roses were a sign of truce." He stuck his tongue into his cheek. One side of his lips curled up, and his brows pinched. "Maybe she said surrender. As in my heart." A grin spread over his face.

Nick rose from the chair and left the room without a word.

Kathryn bit her lip, and then laughed softly. "Does this mean you forgive me?"

"There's nothing to forgive, unless it's for you to forgive me for ever getting involved with Patricia. I regretted it long before she showed up in Chicago. But not nearly as much as I did the day she kissed me. And even more when you disappeared."

Jacob took out his handkerchief and dabbed at her tears. He lowered his face to meet hers. His breath reminded her of hot mint tea. He kissed her mouth.

Her heart thumped against her chest as her lashes fell. She reached up to his neck and held him close. Was she in another dream?

When he straightened, he rounded the bed and sat in the chair Nick had left. Jacob took her hand in his. "Kathryn, I love you. I've never been so scared in my life as when you lay there so still on the floor." He shook his head. "When everyone assured me you'd recover, but you didn't wake up, I was afraid I'd lost you."

She stroked the new growth of facial hair on his chin. It tickled. "When you walked out, I thought I'd lost you."

Jacob reclaimed her hand and kissed it. He took the bouquet from her and laid it at her feet. Then he clasped both her hands in his. "The nurses told me you'd wake up and call for me. They said I was the only one who could calm you, but I thought they were just trying to cheer me up."

"I wanted you. No one else."

His brows rose. "What about Nick?"

"Nick will always be an important part of my life. But, as the brother he says I need. He's right. He filled Chris's place for me." She wrinkled her brows. "But I feel terrible. He needs more than a sister. He deserves more."

Early the next morning, Jacob walked into Kathryn's room with a single white rosebud. "I spotted this little guy alone in the gift shop. Thought he should join the rest." It was all he could do to keep a cry of joy from bursting out. Now if she'd just say yes.

He handed her the rose wrapped in green florist paper and tied with a white ribbon. The smile on her face filled his heart to overflowing. "Untie the bow."

She tugged on the loose end of the simple bow. The ribbon drooped on one side, and a ring slipped downward. She gasped.

"Let me help." Jacob slid his mother's diamond engagement ring off the ribbon and held Kathryn's hand as he knelt beside the bed. "Kathryn Kendall, will you marry me?" A tingle ran through him from his hair roots to his toes. He slipped the golden circle on the third finger of her left hand.

Her jaw dropped as she fixed her eyes on the ring.

He lifted her chin with his finger. "That's your cue to say, 'Yes, I will.'" He kissed her fingertips and winked.

"Yes. I will. Oh, Jacob. Of course, I will."

He eased himself onto the edge of the bed, leaned over, and pressed his lips to hers in a deep kiss that made his heart throb. When he pulled away, she gasped again. Her cheeks held a rosy glow.

"Now that's a better color to your complexion, milady." He'd do his best to bring *that* glow out as often as possible.

Jacob examined the ring on her hand. "Perfect fit. You are definitely a McLeod bride. Tradition says so." He beamed at her.

The color in her cheeks deepened.

"I'll tell you the story behind that diamond and the tradition later, but right now, I believe this belongs to you." He pulled the Claddagh from his breast pocket.

Her eyes sparkled with tears. "Ooh. I was so afraid you'd gotten rid of it. You never gave up on me, did you?"

He fastened the emerald-jeweled necklace around her neck and kissed her forehead before sitting again. "I almost did, yesterday. And for that, I'm ashamed. But it was only because I thought Nick might be a better man for you."

She touched the side of his now closely trimmed beard. "Nick is a good man. But not my man. He needs someone who loves him the way I love you, milord."

Jacob chuckled. "You don't have to call me that."

"I know. But it fits." She let a tiny giggle escape. "By the way, I love your new look. The beard suits you. Very regal."

Jacob leaned in to kiss her again.

The door opened, and Lynne Temple backed into the room holding a breakfast tray. She turned. "Oh. I'm sorry."

Kathryn waved the nurse in. "No. It's okay." She grinned at Jacob.

He glanced over to Lynne. "Come in. I think Kathryn wants to show you something." He reclined in the chair.

Lynne drew closer. "What is it?"

"You can be the first to know."

"Correction," Jacob broke in. "She'll be about...let's see." He started counting off on his fingers. "Your aunt and uncle, Beth, my father and stepmother, Doctor and Mrs. Hartley, Doctor and Mrs. Griffin...I guess that's it so far. Oh, and Nick." His ten fingers wiggled in the air.

Kathryn started laughing. "Ooh...can't laugh so hard. Makes my head hurt." She held out her hand toward Lynne and wiggled her own fingers.

Lynne's mouth opened, and her smile grew like a ray of sunshine. "How beautiful." She looked up at Jacob. "Congratulations, Doctor."

Jacob smiled. "Thank you."

He'd seen Lynne often while doing hospital rounds. Always so cheerful. She had a way with patients and made sure she took time to say a few kind words to their families. Another sweet soul who needed someone special in her life. He thought about the last bit of gossip he'd overheard in the staff lounge. "*...somewhat of a loner, except for a few female nurse friends.*"

While Lynne talked to Kathryn and placed the single rose into the vase with the others on the nightstand, Jacob's mind went to Nick. *I wonder.*

Kathryn handed Lynne one of the white roses from the vase. "For your workstation."

A knock sounded at the door, and Nick's head peeked into the room. "Hey, what's going on here? A party with pretty ladies...without me?"

He strolled in, glanced at Jacob and Kathryn in turn, and then gazed at Lynne. She blushed.

As Nick took on a faraway expression, like a little boy who'd received his first Christmas present, Kathryn grinned at Jacob with wide eyes. She stifled a giggle. "Nick, you've met Lynne, haven't you?"

His mouth opened, but nothing came out.

Jacob leaned toward Kathryn. "Nick has met Lynne." He waved his hand up and down at Nick. "Haven't you? In the ER? She was kind enough to bring me coffee. Asked if she could do the same for you."

Nick's eyes remained glued to Lynne's. "Yes. I remember. I guess I wasn't very talkative then."

"Everyone was under a lot of stress." Lynne smiled.

Jacob squeezed Kathryn's hand. As she faced him, her brows rose. He nodded his head toward Nick. She did the same toward Lynne. She tugged him closer and whispered, "We may not have to worry about Nick after all."

Lynne's attention returned to Kathryn. "Guess I'd better get back to the patients who need me more than you do at the moment. You appear to be in good hands."

"The best, if you ask me." Kathryn smiled at her fiancé.

Nick also turned his attention to Kathryn. "She's right, if the ornament on your finger means anything." He laughed. "I'll leave you two alone. For now." He followed Lynne out.

Jacob resumed his place on the edge of Kathryn's bed and gently wrapped his arms around her. His lips found hers.

Another knock came and the door opened. He turned. "Can't a guy kiss his girl without all these interruptions?"

With Dr. Hartley, Mrs. Hartley, and the Griffins on her heels, Beth burst into the room. In the background, Uncle Eric held the door open. He and Aunt Sandy peered in. Everyone grinned.

Beth blurted out, "Congratulations. Double wedding on the horizon." She laughed.

Dr. Hartley rested his arm across his wife's shoulders. "Every cloud has a silver lining. I guess it's true, all's well that ends well."

Mrs. Hartley narrowed her eyes as she turned to him. "Enough happy ending clichés, dear." She shooed everyone out of the room.

Arms around each other, Kathryn and Jacob laughed.

# The End

# *Epilogue*

While Kathryn recovered from her injuries, Beth made plans for the double wedding of which the girls had always dreamed.

The wedding took place in Pensacola on a clear, crisp evening in February with a candlelight church ceremony. Pastor Marshall officiated, and Pastor Eric Parker walked both of his daughters down the aisle, one on each arm.

Jacob and Tom stood at the front of the church. Each gazed at the woman who, in a few moments, would be his wife, and thanked God.

Kathryn and Beth wore matching wedding gowns of white antique lace and satin. Their cathedral-length trains and veils stretched several feet behind them. They each carried three white rosebuds with dark ivy trailing from a simple white lace bow.

The blue diamond engagement ring sat on Kathryn's right hand until after the ceremony, and her cherished Claddagh necklace hung from her neck. She had vowed never to take it off again.

Bridesmaids wore floor-length flowing dresses the color of violet that gradually deepened down to the flared ankle-length hem. They carried nosegays of deep purple and white violets.

The wedding reception was held at the historic Barkley House, overlooking Pensacola Bay. When the brides were ready to throw their bouquets, they positioned themselves on the porch of the elevated first floor. The single ladies gathered in the grass below.

The brides winked at each other and threw their flowers at the same time. Lynne Temple was surprised to find both bouquets making a beeline straight for her. The other girls backed away. Kathryn and Beth giggled.

When questioned later about it, they both insisted they had not planned the outcome of the toss.

Nick grinned.

Jacob stole Kathryn away to Ireland.

"Now, will you let me forget my ethnic slur on your heritage, milady?" He gazed into her smiling violet blue eyes as he carried Kathryn over the threshold of the picturesque, thatched-roof cottage he'd rented in the lush, emerald-green countryside on the outskirts in the village of Glengarriff. It was the place where her mother had been born.

"Never, milord." She smiled into his sparkling green eyes and pushed back the persistent lock of hair from his left brow as he carried her into the bedroom. "But I will follow you anywhere, and never, ever, run away again."

They had both chosen the right path.

He restoreth my soul: he leadeth me in the paths of righteousness
for his name's sake.
Psalm 23:3

# About The Author

Sharon K. Connell was born in Wisconsin, but lived in Illinois from five days later, through college, and for most of her adult life. California, Ohio, and Missouri all became home at one time or another through the following years, until she moved to Florida to study the Bible. For over twenty years, Florida was her home, and during that time, she graduated from the Pensacola Bible Institute.

Now retired from the business world, she resides in Houston, Texas, where she spends her days writing Christian Romance Suspense, with a touch of mystery and a lot of laughter. She also writes short stories in a variety of genres.

Except for six, Sharon has visited every state in the United States. She has travelled to Canada and Mexico, as well. The stories in her novels reflect some of the experiences she has had during her travels.

Sharon writes stories mostly about people who discover that God will allow things in your life that will help you grow and/or increase your faith. To her, the most important reasons to write are to provide a good story for her readers and to please God with the gift He has given her.

# *Memberships & Places*

American Christian Fiction Writers (ACFW): https://www.acfw.com/
Houston Writers House: http://houstonwritershouse.net/
2 Elizabeths Literary Magazine: https://2elizabeths.com/
CyFair Writers Group: https://www.meetup.com/CyFairWriters/
Christian Womens Writers Club (CWW): http://cwwriters.com/


Website: http://sharonkconnell.com/
Amazon Author Page:
http://www.amazon.com/author/sharonkconnell
Facebook Book Page:
https://www.facebook.com/averypresenthelpbook1
Facebook Author Page:
https://www.facebook.com/ChristianRomanceSuspense/
Twitter: https://twitter.com/SharonKConnell
Goodreads: https://www.goodreads.com/SharonKConnell
LinkedIn:  https://www.linkedin.com/in/sharonkconnell
Pinterest: https://www.pinterest.com/rosecastle1/
WordPress: https://sharonkconnell.wordpress.com/

# Other Books by Sharon K. Connell

*A Very Present Help*
*There Abideth Hope*
*His Perfect Love*

Thank you for reading

www.ingramcontent.com/pod-product-compliance
Lightning Source LLC
Chambersburg PA
CBHW051524250626
47156CB00001B/216